Agents of Paradise

by Christopher A. Miller

Phase 5
Phase 5 Publishing, LLC
PO Box 1595
Asheville, NC 28802
www.phase5publishing.com
First Edition April 2016
Copyright 2016 Phase 5 Publishing, LLC
Story Copyright Christopher A. Miller 2010, Licensed to Phase 5 Publishing, LLC
Cover Art, Copyright 2016 by Phase 5 Publishing, LLC; Gun Bullets Copyright aerial6 at Crestock.
Editor: Rebecca Ledford

Classification: Science Fiction. Another world; cosmology; advanced science; advanced beings; shifting reality; anachronisms; forgotten worlds; fear; freedom.

Appropriate for Teens and Adults: Moderately Explicit Violence and Death, including wartime battle; Brief non-explicit sexual situations; Mild profanity; Death of animals

Phase 5 Elements: Another World 125; Fabricated Reality 241; Ideas 42

ISBN 978-1-942342-94-6
More: www.phase5publishing.com

Printed and Distributed by Lightning Source, a member of the Ingram Content Group.

Table of Contents

For Katy and Colette.

How does newness come into the world? How is it born?

Of what fusions, translations, conjoinings, is it made?

How does it survive, extreme and dangerous as it is? What compromises, what betrayals of its secret nature must it make to stave off the wrecking crew, the exterminating angel, the guillotine?

Is birth always a fall?

Do angels have wings? Can men fly?

\--Salman Rushdie
The Satanic Verses

1. A More Precise Location

"Please step out of your vehicle," ordered the Comanche soldier at the gate.

V was driving, a virgin for the second time that week. She was no younger than seventeen or eighteen but no older than twenty-two or three. Her hair was long and brown, her eyes were quick, her skin was flawless. On the wheel her hands were painless again and she had been staring at them in appreciation. The blue-uniformed soldier with the white claw patch on his shoulder waved them forward, took their papers through the window. V was chewing a bit of sarsaparilla bark and she spat it out.

The climate, this close to the burning city, was fickle. Yesterday, coming over the plains from Duran Town, V and Kholos were among forests filled with ferns. Brooks trickled by and the sun was warm in a blue sky. Today the world was parched. The landscape around the gate was pebbles and sand and scrub, a lonely patch of dying pines here and there around a muddy pool. The mountains, the Asinwati, seemed to change color, gain lighter shades of red and brown as the rocks and grass and gravel that comprised them shifted in the distance moment to moment.

The sun beat down hot and heavy. Yesterday there had been sleet, and ice topped the water jugs when V, much older then, unscrewed the caps with arthritic hands to heat some water for their breakfast. Today she felt smart and tough. She felt nineteen years old.

V put the truck, her truck, into park and stepped out, little puffs of dust coming up from the heels of her boots. Kholos, on the other side, opened his door and stepped out as well. This was all new to him, though he understood everything, from the protocols of the Comanche military to the name of the mountain range before them.

As he stepped out the truck lifted a little. Kholos was tall, taller than any of the Comanche troopers manning the gate and even taller than the little hut where the controls were housed. Probably he was taller than any man any of the Comanche had ever seen. Soldiers gathered in a tight group around him.

"Your papers, please," said a soldier to V.

V reached into her envelope-sized wallet and fumbled around for her Columbium identification and the Universitat travel permit. Columbium travelers always received extra scrutiny. Oran County, the paper said, resident of Duran Town, married. The paper listed her age as twenty-nine years old. It was signed by Dr. Nathan Voss, Universitat representative for Duran Town. The soldier noted most of her first name had been crossed out by a black marker, leaving only the single first letter, V.

The soldier looked at her. "This isn't you," he informed her. "This is for someone older."

"It's me," V said. "I'm Fractured."

The soldier stepped back. Twice. Like he might catch something.

On the other side of the truck, three soldiers had come up around Kholos. They were studying him, speaking about him in the Ute language.

"This is a nice truck," said the soldier before V.

"There's a Universitat note in there," V said. "We should be clear to travel."

The soldier unfolded the papers fully and the hand-written but officially stamped note from Dr. Voss fell out. The soldier picked it up and read it, looking back and forth from the paper to V. The note was legitimate. Dr. Voss had inscribed the numerical codes unique to the Universitat, in the special script that could not be forged.

V looked back down the dirt road, not a real Universitat road but just a straight strip of dust heading back west, towards Duran Town and Oran, Columbium country, and wished they had arrived at the gate when there was more traffic to get through. Or perhaps on a day when there was snow instead of sun. The Comanche might have hurried things along, then. As it was they were the only travelers. And she was the only Columbium, as well, a white-skinned descendant of refugees from the Republicant wars.

All of the vehicles were military vehicles, Comanche vehicles or at least they were Comanche vehicles now. There were attack cars with thick, high tires and rocket launchers mounted in their rears, massive armored half-tracks parked in a row, and small tracked tanks with twin cannons. All of them were painted blue and had a single white claw stenciled on their hoods or their doors.

A couple of attack cars were whizzing about the edges of the base, stirring up trails of dirt and pebbles among the scores of single-story, whitewashed buildings. Cyclone fencing was set up in a giant square around the base, with towers on stilts at the corners where soldiers stood watch to the west, lazily leaning over gun barrels. A dull buzz of the electricity flowing from some local generator reverberated everywhere. Televia wires ran over the base like a net.

The yellow flag of the Incorporated Nation of the Third Comanche flew over the biggest building, the only building on the base higher than a single story. Cables ran from this building out into the empty countryside and up and into the mountain pass the base guarded, heading east. V thought about the messages those cables might carry. She wanted to get through the gate and over the pass. Out beyond the burning city where Kholos could start looking for what he believed would set him, set them both, free. Absolutely free. What did that even mean, nineteen-year-old, V thought as she stood in the sun. Absolutely free?

She missed Michael. Then she looked at Kholos, taller than the top of her truck, and missed Michael a little less.

"We're taking the truck," the soldier said, folding the papers back up and returning them to her. "Get your gear out, and you can go on."

"What?" V demanded. "You're what with my truck?"

After shifting his rifle over his shoulder the Comanche took a pad of papers from a pouch at his hip and a pen from the pocket of his shirt. Ignoring V, he stepped around the pick-up, writing down details about a couple of little dents and dings, the condition of the tires.

"You can't take my truck!" She waved the crunched up Universitat note from Dr. Voss. "We've got permission to travel! Universitat permission!"

The soldier did not look up at her. "We have a Universitat representative here," he said. "Would you like to tell him why you are not in a center for the Fractured?"

Kholos stepped around and his trio of onlookers followed like a wake.

"We have a little money," he said.

The soldier stiffened, then turned to V. "There's a war coming, young lady ... Miss," he continued. "We have the right to commandeer any materiel we need in support of that war. This right," he added, "was recognized by the Universitat as well. You should thank us. We're defending you Columbiums too."

He touched a dent along the driver's side door panel. Dust came up on his fingertip. "Besides, you'll be fully compensated. Probably more than the vehicle is even worth. Just take this to any Comanche bank. They'll honor it. With interest, if you hold onto it long enough."

V's face flushed. The other soldiers watched her. Kholos could deal with them, she knew. Deal with them all in a blink. She had seen it happen. Or rather, she had seen it not happen.

"Don't you tell me there's a war on," she said. She'd had the truck since she was fifteen. Properly fifteen, not Fractured fifteen. She and Michael had put in long miles in this truck. "My husband died in that war."

"Your husband?" said the soldier, standing up from behind the rear bumper where he still scratched at his pad of paper. "He's dead?"

"That's right." V said .

"If that's so, then who is this?" The soldier pointed with his pen at Kholos, who, according to Dr. Voss's note, was the husband of V. This was not a lie. V had lost a husband, more than a husband, in the war against the Stalinistas. This man was not Kholos, however, and she was not married to Kholos in the way the Comanche meant.

For a moment the entire party stood staring at one another. V furious. The soldiers nervous. The Comanche with the pad of paper half-grinning, his pen in mid-air.

Kholos took a deep breath, put a hand on V's trembling shoulder.

"How far to the highway?" he asked all of them, asking with the thunder.

He spoke barely above a whisper, but his voice rumbled and it carried up through the soles of the boots of the soldier with his clipboard. One of the soldiers gasped but none of them answered, just stared.

Kholos repeated, "How far to the Universitat highway?"

"Through the pass," said the Comanche in charge. "Just over the mountains."

Kholos nodded. "And how long to cross the pass?"

"Couple of hours in a car. Less in clear weather."

"On foot?"

"Two days."

Kholos looked back at V, who was nearly shaking with rage. Then at the soldier. Kholos thought: *is this man part of me*? The soldier swallowed.

"Let us take out our equipment and supplies," Kholos said, without the thunder this time. "Then we'll be on our way."

All of the Comanche exhaled.

"No!" shouted V. "No! That's my truck!"

"We packed too much anyway," said Kholos. "Let it go. There'll be transport on the highway of some kind."

They unloaded.

Kholos said, "You'd fight them for the truck, risk yourself, knowing we can go on without it?"

"No," she admitted. "But you could have stopped them. Couldn't you?"

"You're nineteen today," said Kholos. "No more than that."

"What does that matter? You know I'm right."

"You want me to destroy this place, kill all these men, make this a hole where nothing will ever live again? I can do that. But then we would get nowhere, and I would be caught, and you would be alone. Alone again. This is what it is worth to you to keep your truck, because you are nineteen today. This is what you want?"

V sighed but kept her arms crossed. "No," she admitted. "That's not what I want."

Kholos looked down at the bags and cans and bedrolls. "Only what I can carry."

Kholos could carry a lot. The big backpack they had brought from Duran Town he packed with three days of food and water, a length of climbing rope, matches and torches with batteries, a handheld mirror, a compass (useless this close to the burning city), a tarpaulin, and four thick blankets, made from sheepskin. Also packed were an assortment of clothes for V: little jumpers and bootie socks, a training bra, five different sizes of underwear, a tiny pair of children's canvas shoes and a pair of slippers with rubber soles stitched to the bottoms, a second pair of jeans, and a brown shift that she had sewn herself, which when combined with the red sash of velvet would fit her body in all of its older stages, from mid-forties to crone. For Kholos there were only some extra socks and underthings, a lined leather coat, and a wool cap. Everything else he already wore, or else was hidden in the closely tied brown canvas bags.

What was hidden was his armor and weapons. Rust-colored in its current state, it was stacked into itself inside the bags. The helm with its flat visor. The breastplate and backplate with the hinges at the shoulders and along the obliques. The wrist and shin greaves. The gauntlets and the boots. And, mostly importantly, the twin canisters, which when Kholos activated them would allow him to fly on wings of solid light and move faster than time.

What was also hidden was the list. The list of saints. The list of Adonai. The miracle list, that Dr. Voss had given him. Would give him, Kholos corrected, much later.

His weapons were more conspicuous, but still concealed. The sword was wrapped in canvas in its scabbard, but it was long and wide and the grip was visible: a metal guard over a hilt shaped to Kholos's own hand and his hand only. The sword cut through the spaces between molecules. The rifle was even more obvious, long-barreled and with a stock of almost golden wood, a sharpshooter's weapon. The canvas wrapped and tied around the barrel did nothing to conceal what was inside. At least, Kholos thought as he strapped the sword and the rifle across the bulging pack in an X, the strange ammunition for the gun was not visible. Nor the scope that could see forwards in time.

With ease Kholos hefted the sword, the gun, and the pack up onto his back. Then he adjusted the pistol he carried, a big

Columbium gun he had bought in Duran and now wondered why he had bothered. The frosted peaks of the mighty Asinwati Mountains rose before them, the gravel and dirt road that led through the fort and up into the pass winding between two sharp slopes just past the blue-and-white striped gate of the base.

The soldiers were watching them, gaping a little at the size of the pack Kholos carried, the long gun and sword criss-crossed there. They had never actually raised the gate for them, and clearly were not going to even as Kholos and V walked briskly towards the low white barrier. It was made of metal, activated by an electric motor, and weighed about four hundred kilos.

As they approached the soldiers stopped talking to watch as Kholos and V approached, Kholos in the lead. Despite his height he was thin, lean, with a completely bald pate and a gaunt face, very, very pale. Paler even than most Columbiums.

Without breaking stride Kholos put his hand on the gate and snapped it in two, using just his thumb and forefinger. One piece fell onto the ground. The other side, still attached to the little guardhouse and the arm apparatus, swung straight up into the air and vibrated there.

"Hey!" shouted one of the soldiers as they moved on up the slope, not looking back once. "Hey!"

V smiled the smile of the just.

Later that afternoon Colonel Ute Redroot, Commander of the Fighting First Claws regiment and current Commandant of Fort Tamu, as the Comanche called the base at the foot of the pass, stepped out of the two-story building where the flags flew and the wires terminated their east-west runs. He was a young man, handsome, with high cheekbones and red skin he insisted he had not had chemically tinted. He stared up at the winding road leading into the pass, even though there appeared to be nothing to see there except the mountains and the dirt.

With him were two other officers and the soldier who had commandeered V's truck. In Redroot's hand was a flimsy piece of paper, printed from the Televia machine, sent direct from the capital in New Taabe. The paper was stamped with a level of priority Redroot had heard about but never seen before. When the orders had arrived the adjunct had called him into the communications office, and Redroot assumed, hoped, that the Incorporated Nation was at last joining the fighting up in the northwest against the Stalinistas, that the orders were for his Fighting First Claws to mobilize to the front.

Instead, the orders had instructed him, and all other Comanche commanders anywhere within the Incorporated Nation, to pursue a single man. A description of this man followed. The orders were signed by both the Comanche War Chief and Peace Chief from New Taabe, which was unheard of.

They were strange orders.

Redroot read the description of the man to the soldier, again. "You're certain?"

"Yes Colonel. Tall, pale. Looked Columbium, but then they all look the same to me. There was a woman with him. Said she was Fractured." He was following Redroot's eyes into the mountains. "They had Universitat papers," he added, apologetically. "Sir."

Redroot re-read the orders. There was nothing in them about a woman. Just the man. And just pursue. Not capture. Not kill. Just follow him, and report in.

"This makes no sense," said one of the officers. His name was Stands-Tall-Under-Cedars and he was Redroot's blood brother. They had sworn the official oaths and signed the legal papers, and now shared all things. Houses. Wealth. Wives. Stands-Tall was also the Fighting First Claws' Tank Commander, a Major in the Incorporated Nation's mighty mobilized military. "The whole army on alert? For one man? With the Stalinistas already landed?"

"He must know something," said the other officer.

They stood on the steps and watched Colonel Redroot. The mountains. Redroot. The mountains again. Only the colonel kept staring up at the road through the pass, ignoring them.

"All I know is what this says," said Redroot, at last, holding up the paper. "And what this says is, opportunity for the First Claws."

"For Colonel Redroot, you mean," said Stands-Tall, with a laugh.

"Yes," said Redroot, with a smile. "For Colonel Redroot, and for the Fighting First Claws, as well." He had not taken his eyes off the road. "This is from New Taabe. Not HQ. Not even Tacoma.

Whatever it is, it matters. Matters enough the whole nation is about it." He added, "They're on foot. They can't get far."

"Just report you've spotted him," said Stands-Tall. "That's what the orders say. Explicitly."

"Yes, but we do this correctly, we assume he's dangerous. Get Lieutenant Galai, have him take a sniper team in an attack car. Observe, but be alert. Take out his legs, if they have to."

"The woman?" asked the second officer. "What about her?"

But Redroot was already turning out of the heat back into the command building, reading and re-reading the orders from New Taabe. Without looking he waved his hand up in the air, dismissively.

"The orders say report his location, Colonel," Stands-Tall was repeating. "Report. Not shoot."

"We'll be able to give a more precise location," said Ute, "if he can't walk."

2. The City Burning Forever

The shale in the Asinwatis, being so close to the burning city and its weird effects, was treacherous. Kholos with his heightened hearing could make out distinct rumbles, echoes from kilometers away. These rumbles signaled a sinkhole that could be hundreds of meters deep and hundreds of meters wide or a pocket eruption.

The Universitat highways, somehow, were safe even in this unsettled region. But the local paths and roads, the ground everywhere, could be riddled with craters or soon-to-be craters. There was no predictable pattern to the cave-ins. Suddenly, a bed of shale would turn to dust. Poof.

Or, a stream could dry up in an instant. Or a flash flood could tear down the slope. The weather, the terrain, the air, could all change in a blink around the burning city. This was one of the mysteries Dr. Voss was investigating in his basement laboratory, back in Duran Town.

In the evening sky the stars began to trace their arcs. By midnight, when V would change, they would cut long silver trails, criss-crossing one another in a lattice that would outshine the half-moon. The night was clear, for the moment. The stars had only made little lines.

After finding a place set away from the road, Kholos and V made camp. The little tarp they used as a roof was tied slant-wise between to sapling poles Kholos had cut. Under the tarp sat the big pack, the weapons, and the rest of their gear. So long as the sky held they would sleep in the open. A small fire burned between them. They had not bothered with making a fire circle of stones, and the dust under the hot sticks had flattened out under the heat. A tin pot with a fold-away handle was set to the side. The remnants of some baked cornmeal mixed with beans and a little bacon sat inside the coals, two spoons nestled together along the lip. A water jug was open next to Kholos. They were close to the peak of the pass, having made good time with young V in the lead. Even with the compass useless V could time their pace and note their direction. After all, she had made her living back in Duran as a guide, before Kholos, before she was Fractured, before Michael died.

Now they sat, full and tired, on opposite sides of the fire. Being tired, physically tired, was still new to Kholos and he looked at his long legs and stared at them. V pulled her knees up to her chin. She had unrolled her sleeping mat and her bag, patched in so many places with denim and canvas it was hard to discern the original color of the cloth. Kholos stood, staring at the sky, at the slopes. V had seen him do this many times before, looking up, looking out.

She had seen Michael Staffa do this, too. The only difference was that Michael had wondered, but Kholos seemed to know. She shivered a little even though the night was warm.

"When we find them," V said, unlacing her boots, "I don't want you to kill them."

"I might have to. If it helps us to be free."

"I don't want to go around murdering the saints. That can't be wise."

"Maybe we'll get lucky," said Kholos. "Maybe the first Adonai we find will know how to reach the Celestial City, and we'll just have to ask them nicely to show us the way."

"Free," said V.

"Free of the Aetherian, or whatever name you wish to use. They have plenty of names."

"Can I be enslaved by something I never heard of?" she asked.

"Oh yes," said Kholos. "Easily."

"I'm not a slave to the Adonai, though," she said.

At nineteen she felt confused about their mission. Did she want this? Want him? Yes. But it all made more sense when she was a child. When she was old she did not care as much, either way. And when she was young, stubborn, strong, she wanted it all to fit together.

"The Adonai?" said Kholos. "They don't rule me. Nor you. The Adonai are probably more slaves than either of us. Except for maybe Pang. I don't know. Yet."

V was not religious, especially. But like every woman in Duran Town, like every Columbium woman whose home she had been inside of, she had her little shrine to Theresa, with the ribbon and the scented herbs, a sprinkle of flour, and, for those in rich homes, some cinnamon. Perhaps, for some women, a pair of lacy panties.

And like every town everywhere she had ever heard of, Columbium, Comanche, Republicant, Duran had a church to Pang. There were others, great lists of them the Universitat priests and professors expounded upon as examples, ideals to follow, ways to think. The Adonai.

The idea of hunting down, say, Pang, seemed crazy. Certainly the Adonai lived in the world, everyone knew that. They were real, like the stars were real. But to go after them was crazy as going after the stars.

But it was crazy the way Michael was crazy. It was crazy the way being Fractured was crazy.

"Tell me again," she said. "About Michael and you."

Kholos, still standing, looked down at her. His eyes were big, dark, golden in the firelight. His beauty was still somewhat frightening to her, unreal, like a picture of beauty. This crazy man who said he could fly. Nothing could fly. Everybody knew that.

Kholos began his lie, again.

"At the front," he said, "against the Stalinistas, I met a man. A young man named Michael Staffa. They thought he was a soldier, but he really was a poet. He was my friend. My closest, dearest friend."

This was what V liked to hear.

"And what did Michael Staffa tell you?"

"A lot of things," said Kholos. "Tales of a town with good sandwiches."

"Go on," said V, almost laughing now. Almost crying now.

"A town named Duran, in the middle of nowhere, in a nowhere little county, with a very curious Universitat Administratum man."

"And?" V said. "And?"

Kholos squinted and furrowed his brow, like he had to think hard. "And a taste for elk steak?"

V threw a rock, a small rock, at Kholos. It hit his bald head and he laughed. "Good aim," he said. Then the laughter vanished and his face flattened, and the golden eyes turned on her full force. "Michael Staffa showed me how to look at the world in new ways. Ways only he could explain. Could write. Beautiful ways. He gave me everything. He gave me you."

Kholos paused. The lie was mostly truth.

"He gave me the love of a girl. A girl named V-"

"Don't say it!" V squealed. "Don't!"

Sometimes when Kholos told her the story, especially when she was old, it could make her weep. But it seemed the younger she was, the more it made her laugh. So silly, it seemed when she was six, seven, even ten years old. It was hard to believe.

Kholos did not say the next part: Michael Staffa died. At the front, in a trench, fighting against the Stalinistas.

"And the love, the love of that girl, was mine, just like it was Michael's," said Kholos. "And I knew before I could be free, before I could escape this false place, I had to find her, and bring her with me, if she would come." Kholos paused. "Will you, still come? Even if it means we kill some gods?"

V started to say something smart but stopped. Kholos could see into people, see things, patterns, he knew she was wondering. She nodded. Yes.

"I can give you nothing but freedom," said Kholos, softly.

They spoke a little while longer, about their supplies, about how far it would be to reach the highway on the other side of the pass. V asked if they would see the city, the burning city, and Kholos said yes, the little glow in the east was the flames. He said this sadly, but not regretfully.

Then V lay back and closed her eyes, and fell asleep. Kholos watched her a while, thinking of how the god Golgothan, the renegade Adonai, could be anywhere in the mountains around them. Kholos wondered if he would feel it, the presence of another one made not born. But he felt nothing except trapped in a cage where the trace lines of the stars were the bars. He watched V sleep. How he loved her. Loved her like Michael loved her.

Later V rose from her bedding. The air was still warm, tangy but dry. Her body was still young, firm. She felt it, warm and alive. It could stay this way for days, she knew, or be gone for weeks. She undid the buttons on her jeans and roughly jerked the sweater off of her head, stood there a moment in her socks and panties looking at her shadow with its tiny waist in the embers of the fire. Deftly she tied up her hair with two twists of her fingers. *These little powers,* she thought, *are mine again.*

Kholos was snoring on top of his sheepskin blanket, his hands neatly laid out at his sides. V lowered herself astride his body and rubbed herself against the muscles of his chest. Her hair fell out of place as she kissed the column of his neck, the bar of his chin, the planes of his cheeks. Her body was electric and she paused to feel it, how it jumped and sparked where her skin touched his. Her toes inside the wool socks curled. She tried to remember Michael's body: short, a little shorter than she was, even. This was not Michael, she reminded herself. This was Kholos. Kholos who wanted to be free. Kholos the Deserter, from the war, Kholos from nowhere, Kholos who let her feel a little less pain.

Kholos was awake. His hands were on her back, her shoulders, her bottom. He started to rise but she kissed him, pushed at the muscles for him to lie down.

She whispered. "Let me free you for a little while."

Snow, suddenly but softly, began to fall, hissing where the flakes hit the hot coals of the fire and melting with little cold kisses where they landed along V's back.

In the morning she was a crone. They had slept cuddled together wrapped in Kholos's blanket, moving under the tarp as the snow came down. Kholos woke to feel old bones against his skin and heard V's soft groans. He recognized the sound: the pain of her arthritis. Her hands were nutty claws, swollen at the knuckles and spotted brown. All of her muscle from the day before was gone, her limbs thin as sticks and the skin loose. Her hair, what was left of it, was white.

A little spittle rolled out from the corner of her mouth, her eyes darted about in confusion as her mind tried to adjust to her body. She was old, old. The wrinkles of her face were thin and shallow and ran in maplines down from her cheekbones.

Kholos knelt alongside her. She smiled and there were maybe four teeth left.

The world, high summer the day before and then with snow overnight, had turned to spring. Fog hovered over the ground. Aspen and alder and poplar had sprung up. With a glance over his shoulders Kholos noted that their tarpaulin shelter had risen to twice the height of where he had tied it off, as the saplings had thickened and shot up while they slept. The sky was cloudy and low. A little wind, promising growth, blew over the ashes of the fire. Buds of tiny flowers poked through soil that had been sand when Kholos slept. The road, pebbles and dust when they had walked it, sprouted with weeds and there were patches of mud along the edges. It felt like a little warm rain might fall.

Kholos had set some wood under the tarp the night before for their fire but this had changed as well. The old wood now was mostly green, a couple branches with little leaves on the twigs. Still there was some wood that had stayed seasoned, somehow, and Kholos snapped it into kindling and brushed away the wet ash with the edge of his hand and blew on the coals underneath until the little twigs caught. He rinsed out the pot from their supper and poured a little oat and raisin mixture from a pouch, added water, and set this among the coals to cook.

How strange, he thought, that the old fire was still an old fire, while the trees were all different?

He turned to V. She had curled into the blanket and stopped shivering, and was watching him. There were times Kholos remembered when she had woken up old and not known who he was at all. Kholos cupped a little water in his hand and lifted her up against him, let the liquid trickle into her mouth. After she had swallowed he set her back down and washed her with a small soft cloth, wiping away the dust where it still stuck to her from the previous day. After rummaging in the pack for a moment or two he found the brown dress she had made after she learned she was Fractured, just before they decided to leave Duran to try and be free.

It was a practical garment, sewn in such a way with button holes strategically placed so that it could be worn as a sack or a shawl or, even, a proper dress with a pretty red sash to tie around the waist. Kholos helped her, holding her head like baby's and then fitting her arms through the sleeves. Then he buttoned the little brass buttons in the places he thought would best keep her warm.

"Kholos," she said, reaching up and touching his ear with the back of her hand. "Kholos, I dreamed I was young and strong forever. Like you are."

"Was it nice?"

"No," said V. "Not really." She looked down at herself. "You buttoned me all wrong."

V at eighty, ninety, a hundred years, complained a great deal. She needed help for everything. She could carry nothing. She confused names and places, called him Michael, Dr. Voss, her father, her brother, the butcher, and meant them all.

After eating a little breakfast and spooning some mouthfuls of the oatmeal into V, Kholos cleaned up their campsite and packed. Before hefting up the pack, with his weapons again lashed across the back, he took his sleeping blanket and folded it twice over, then used a little cord to tie off the ends narrowly. He then tied this off over a shoulder, so that he had a little pouch across his chest and belly, stretched from shoulder to hip. Before testing out this reverse-papoose he checked to make sure he could reach his pistol. He could.

V watched him from where he had left her, seated before the fire. She was rubbing one of her feet through her socks. "That won't ever work," she said.

"We'll see." He hefted her up like she was nothing and she cooed a little on the way up. She had to pull her knees in, which was uncomfortable and she said so, but it was also warm. She lay back, and smiled up at him. They moved out, back onto the road. Soft now from the new climate, the new ecology of the Asinwati Mountains. The fog lifted, slowly. The sun came up.

"Kholos?"

"Yes?"

"I'm sorry I'm so old today."

They were across the peak and descending quickly when the Comanche sniper shot Kholos. The bullet should have blown out his knee and sent him toppling forward, crushing V. Instead Kholos cried out and his leg buckled halfway, but he did not go down. Pain shocked him.

V gasped, and he saw the terror on her face. Carefully Kholos knelt, touched the place where the bullet had hit him and looked at the blood on his palm. An unknown, having never bled before in his short existence, although of course he had in a sense bled a thousand times over. The pain was hot, like a burn and he found this curious. Looking behind them, in the direction of the shot, he spotted the hidden Comanche. They were concealed within a stand of poplars up the slope some four or five hundred meters distant, with the shooter working madly to reload. Kholos concentrated, and could hear them whisper.

"You were not ordered to fire!"

"I didn't! I don't know what happened!"

"You missed, at least."

"I did not miss. I don't know how he's standing. I shot him right through the knee."

Clack of the bullet in the chamber. Click of the bolt.

"Shoot him again. To wound."

"What? Why?"

"We'll bring him back. Alive. It will be alright."

"He's already shot."

"I'm in command here. Shoot through the pack. Incapacitate him. We're almost out of Incorporated Nation territory, we can't let him get any farther. The Colonel will be furious as it is. We'll take him back. Do it."

Then, a rustle of green leaves shuffled as the shooter aimed.

Kholos braced himself. Huddled over V. There was a strange half-instant when Kholos thought he felt the impact of the shot but heard it afterwards. It did not hurt at all, this shot, just a tap against his neck from the pack. He sweated. His knee hurt. He concentrated. Could he even die? No, the Aetherian would remake him, all those bits and cells, those skills and lessons, washed out, recycled, reused, into a new pattern. And then another. And another.

V's mouth was open but her eyes were closed and she was moaning a bit. The big pack was covering everything but the soles of his boots and the points of his elbows and the back of his head.

"Fly us away," said V.

"It's alright," said Kholos. "I'm alright. The armor in the pack, they can't get through it."

Another shot. Impact, a thud. The little rock V had thrown the night before had hurt more. Kholos reached for his pistol.

"Oh, no," said V. Her hands clutched at his shirt.

Kholos listened, then waited for another shot. This one was higher up the pack, but still it impacted his armor and did not pass through. There would be a click and a clack, a few long seconds for him to fire. With the gun in his right hand he spun, cradling V close to him to protect her with his left arm. She hid her face against his chest.

He saw them. Four of them, two prone, two kneeling. One with a long rifle, almost as long as Kholos's own, another with just a scope. The two standing held up binoculars, stared down at him from behind the tree trunks. There were fresh branches tucked into the webbing of their helmets and their faces were smudged with dirt and mud.

"What's he doing? Is he surrendering?"

"He can't hit us from down there with that!"

Bang. Kholos shot the sharpshooter. Bang. Then he shot the soldier with the scope in the forehead. Bang. Then he shot the one who had commanded them to shoot. One two three. The fourth leapt up and was running, back up the slope, crouched, unarmed. Kholos drew a bead on the back of his head, then put his gun down.

He looked at the bodies. He looked at what he had done. He had killed hundreds of men. He had never killed anyone before.

The sniper bled out through his eye socket into the dirt, the spotter lay face down with his arms out like was trying to swim. The officer's eyes were still open. The Aetherian might well come to this moment, this place to harvest them, Kholos thought. He holstered his gun.

"It's over," he said to V. "They're gone."

"You killed them." It was a statement, as if she had said it was raining or she was hungry. "You killed Third Comanche soldiers."

"I killed some of them," said Kholos, standing back up on his wounded knee. "Three of them."

V lay back in the sling. Her eyes seemed to dim a bit.

"They'll come after us now," she said. "Now we have to run."

"It's not the Third Comanche I'm running from."

Kholos had slipped off the pack and was taking out the first aid kit from its little metal box and she swayed some as he worked.

She began to say she could make a brace for him, but then felt the icy ache in her fingers. Perhaps tomorrow she could.

His knee throbbed, but he believed he could walk on it once it was bandaged and cleaned. It was late in the day. Kholos could make out the glow of the city burning, not so far away now, to the east.

"We're murderers, now," V said as Kholos grimaced from the alcohol he poured over his leg.

"I always was," said Kholos, staring at the glow.

Kholos's knee slowed them, and they did not top the last ridge until the day was almost gone. This made the light from the burning city, the city everyone knew but no one could remember, all the brighter when they finally came to the last length of the road down through the pass and looked across the plains and saw it there, aflame.

The fires flickered and danced but consumed nothing. Kholos watched with his telescopic vision. The beautiful tall buildings built from steel and glass, so high they seemed to soar. Parks. Schools. Trolley tracks. Store windows. Shopping plazas. Cathedrals, both for learning and for worship. Homes and tenements. Mansions. Boulevards lined with trees. Museums. Gardens with sculptures from the Republicant, from the Incorporated Nation, from Mayans and Incas, from the Inuit and Iroquois, from Ebon Empires, from everywhere in the Columbium counties.

There were people everywhere, Kholos could make them out, could remember their stunned faces as he descended to eradicate them. Now, he knew, they stood as if frozen, bathed in the same white and red flames as their streets and their buildings and parks, immobile, locked in the instant he fired the red bullet, fired down upon the sinning city from his wings of light. They did not scream. They did not move. They did not even blink. He was moving out of time, deliberately firing the wrong bullet, to make good his escape.

They burned. It burned, all of it burned. A little rend in space and time, left open.

Kholos took a deep breath. Here he had started running. Running to get his girl. Running to get away, to be free, free, free.

He had no idea, then, what consequences his decisions would bring. He did not particularly care, so long as it meant a chance for freedom. But standing on the ridge the enormity of what he had done that day above Anvir—that was the name he had taken out of existence, Anvir—the widening ripples of unreality, the Fractured, the declaration of war against the gods—was not lost on him. In the flames he saw his rebellion.

"I did this," he confessed.

V reached up from her cradle and touched his cheek with her crone's hand.

"Silly man," she said. "You were in bed with me with this happened. Don't you remember?"

3. Gyr Zax Trucking Co.

The Borac caravan was arranged in a wide semi-circle. The ends met at the slopes of the Asinwati Mountains, while the arc of the circle just barely skirted the tarmac of the north-south Universitat highway. The highway, after the infinite incineration of the city, had been diverted westward away from the flames, so that now it belled out towards the mountains before returning to a pure northerly course. It was a sin against reason to approach the burning city, as the effects closest to the flames were wild and unpredictable. The Universitat reported horrible consequences for even looking into the flames for too long.

The sun was setting over the peaks to the west, so the Borac encampment was already entirely in shadow. However, the glow from the burning city, even many kilometers away, added a strange light to the many small fires and naked electric lights from the caravan.

There was music, both the crackly, tinny-sounding music recorded for play on Televias, and live music: Borac women and children singing, playing handmade instruments. There was also the lowing of the saurs and the caws of the dactyls, ebbing out from somewhere deeper within the encampment. The louder gasoline roar of the diesel engines of the big trucks, which formed the perimeter of the semi-circle, echoed off the rocks.

A tiny part of Kholos was Borac, the skills and experiences of the person transferred whole. Kholos, searching his mind, found that he knew how to speak a handful of Borac words, and, interestingly, how to handle and care for a dactyl.

"What is all that racket?" V asked. She had fallen half asleep during the last daylight hours of their walk down through the pass. She shifted in her sling to peer out at the lights of the camp. Kholos had slowed his pace, sure that there would be pickets out. He needed to rest, needed to clean and dress his injured knee, needed to top off their water, needed to wait until midnight for V to change, hopefully, into a shape more suited for travel.

"Boracs," said Kholos. He limped fitfully on. "Traders. A big caravan."

"Boracs," said V. "I never."

Kholos closed his eyes and paused, tried to organize memories that were not his but were now.

A small race of big people, the Boracs hailed from the swamps and forests and low hills of the Southeastern reaches of the Northern Columbium Continent.

Before the coming of the Columbium, even before the Universitat, the Boracs had farmed and hunted, lived in small clusters, fought amongst themselves or against their neighbors, the Slythe. They had a language more complex than most of the Iroquois, Shoshone, Cree, and Cherokee tongues, and were well-known for their metalwork and their control of anima, the binding force of the world. This despite Universitat insistence that laboratory tests proved anima did not exist, and that Pang had explicitly stated there was no such thing.

When the Columbium came to the Borac lands, the Boracs had little trouble pushing away the disease-ridden and hungry white people. But, as the flow of refugees increased, the Boracs' lack of numbers, as well as their insistence on being a decentralized, ungoverned people, began to tell.

Unlike the violent history of human contact with the Slythe, human battles against Boracs were rare, usually accidental. And the Borac nation, such as it was, still stood unthreatened. But over the centuries, the Columbium from the east and the Comanche from the west and all the other peoples crowding the continent pressed the Boracs. Like the Slythe, the Boracs were dying out.

Now the Boracs were a race of traders and shippers, hauling immense cargos across the continent, from the great eastern port cities to the Inuit marches to the north, west across all the little Columbium Counties to the great metropolises of the Incorporated Nation of the Third Comanche, and down south to what remained of the Aztec Empire as it struggled against the Stalinista invasion.

The Boracs also carried news. The advent of the Televia technology had eliminated the need for mail, but there was other news that could be shared, sold, hauled. Little news, the Boracs called it. Visions of the changing saints, rumors of the Stalinistas, gossip about Universitat Bishops and Deans. Boracs moved this as well as their goods across the continent.

Whether news or cargo, the Boracs moved their goods using saurs and dactyls. These ancient beasts were all albino, ghostly white with red eyes. The Boracs bred them in the swamps of their homelands, keeping the lines alive for hundreds of millennia after the animals should have been extinct. The saurs did the carrying. Bigger than houses, they could carry twice their own massive body weight. Long-tailed, long-necked, and small-brained, the saurs lumbered down the continental highways, loaded up along their flanks, and with three or four handlers guiding them by ropes and chains attached to elaborate harnesses.

Traditionally, Borac traders lived atop their beasts, building tiny one-room huts with rope ladders attached. They climbed up in the evenings and cooked, ate, talked, sang, loved, and slept all on wooden decking laid across the spines of their saurs. Then in the mornings they would climb down, burn their garbage and see to the feeding and grooming (checking the feet of the saurs was very important, and very dangerous) then move on.

The dactyls were more intelligent than the saurs. With wingspans that stretched out to their full size and a full third again, the dactyls were flying beasts with long beaks and leathery skin. Dactyls were bred as scouts, trained to relay information back to their handlers as to where, exactly, the caravan was and what was ahead. A tug or a swing one way could signal to a handler bandits or a forest fire or a flood. A caw could signal right of way to another caravan, or a location. Their eyesight was exceptional.

They could also fly. This was impossible, of course. Because, as proven morally and logically by the Universitat's greatest thinkers, to attempt to fly is a sin against both one's creator and one's fellow men. A sin against faith and a sin against reason. Objects might glide, they might be thrown for a certain distance, or they could float, but nothing could actually fly under its own power. Pang had decreed this, and Universitat research proved it empirically.

Kholos paused and looked up. Circling slowly, pale in the shadows of the mountains, was a single dactyl, cawing out to its handler below the arrival of Kholos and V.

Kholos pointed up at the thing. "Look, V, a dactyl."

V squinted with her old eyes. Kholos watched as she registered what the sliding shape up in the sky meant, and her eyes grew wide.

"Impossible," she said. "They told us in school that was impossible. It's just some smoke or something. They told us dactyls just glide, like things thrown. It's not really flying."

Kholos smiled. V stared on. Two Boracs were walking slowly towards them from the trucks.

The most distinguishing feature of a Borac was not their great height—a full head taller than Kholos—nor their greenish-gray skin (their blood was a dark green), but their tusks. Every Borac, men and women, or *glan* and *glin* in their language, from adolescence until death, decorated and maintained their tusks as an expression of themselves, of who they were. They etched them. They carved them. They gilded them. They sharpened them, dyed them, affixed enamel to them. Jutting out from the lower jaw, the tusks came out a thumb's length over the lower lip, then shot up for a roughly equal length at a right angle. The tusks came to a point, but some Boracs capped their tusks, while others sharpened them.

The Boracs coming towards Kholos and V had both kept the tips of their tusks pointed. One had honed his with a lattice work of steel, like a little net, barbed and edged so that they caught little flakes of the firelight and the beams of the headlights from the encampment. Kholos imagined they might even spark. Under the latticework the tusks were coated or dyed with some substance that gave them a blue patina.

The second Borac's tusks were tipped with red tassels that swung as he walked. Screws were drilled into the tusks below the tassels, each screw head showing a different metallic shade, some rusted, some bronzed, some silver, some gold. The screws had made little cracks in the enamel of the tusks but the tusks were coated with some lacquer that sealed the cracks. The effect was of metal screwed into fine marble.

Both Boracs carried rifles, old rifles that clearly dated back before the Comanche Manifest, some Republican relics passed down through generations of Boracs, probably traded for from the earliest of the washed-up Columbium refugees. The furniture on the guns seemed to almost glow, it was so worn. At their hips they carried their *kops*--the long knife/short sword every Borac warrior, or *cumbel*, carried.

In his catalog of memories Kholos could find all this culture. Knew it as if it was his own.

"*Cumbel*," whispered Kholos.

"What?" said V. "What are you whispering about? I can't see anything."

The dactyl up above the encampment was swooping low, watching them closely with its red eyes. The engines of the trucks forming the perimeter of the caravan rumbled low. A few tentative stars had appeared and edged just a bit across the sky. The damp woods of the morning already seemed to be shifting here, becoming dry and cool, like grassland.

"Evening," said the Borac with the distressed tusks. The voice was deep and rough, gravelly and low. Neither raised their guns. The dactyl cawed.

"We've just come through the pass," Kholos said. "We could use some water. And, as you can see, I'm injured." Kholos looked at the trucks, lined up tailpipe to cab. "Could we rest here for the night?"

The Borac with the screws in his tusks brushed aside this question, instead asked, "Did you see any Comanche in the mountains?"

Kholos answered, "You mean, at the base?"

"No," the Borac explained. "In the mountains. In the pass. Second Comanche."

Kholos understood now why the trucks were circled, why there were armed guards on the backs of the trucks. The Second Comanche were raiders, Comanche rebels who refused to acknowledge the government of New Taabe. It was the Second Comanche who had, after the surrenders of the other Shoshone peoples, continued to hunt down and kill Kiowa, Apache, or Sioux survivors. Especially Kiowa survivors. The only Kiowa left alive now across the Columbium continents were kept in camps, far to the south from their homelands.

The Incorporated Nation of the Third Comanche tolerated the Second Comanche, provided they exercised their violence on non-Comanche targets. The Second Comanche for their part considered the Third Comanche, with their cities and laws, anathema. They had no reservations killing a Third Comanche patrol, kidnapping Third Comanche tourists for ransom, or burning outlying Third Comanche businesses and homes. They called this work "bleeding the beast."

The Third Comanche considered the Second Comanche as they might wolves or snakes: dangerous but rarely lethal. But to Columbium settlements, or a Borac caravan, they were killers. Kholos had encountered the Second Comanche once already, back in Duran Town. Or rather, he would soon.

"No," said Kholos, carefully. "We didn't see any Second Comanche."

"How did you hurt your leg?" said the Borac with the screws in his tusks. Kholos did not answer. The Boracs looked at one another, then back at Kholos. "Is that a child you're carrying?"

"No, a woman. She is old at the moment. Very old."

"What do you mean, at the moment?"

"She's Fractured. She changes her body every day."

Unlike the guards at the Third Comanche base who had flinched when V explained her condition, the Boracs only nodded. Kholos had never heard of a Fractured Borac. Maybe they had been spared, or maybe they simply ignored the Universitat edicts about the Rehabilitation Centers.

"Follow us," said blue tusks. "No point in standing out here. You can rest here and get some water and food, at least. Our leader would like to speak with you, as well."

"He knows we're here? Already?"

"Oh yes," said Blue Tusks. "We've been waiting for you. Stopped here just for you, actually. But we thought you'd be alone."

The dactyl cawed again and circled up a little higher.

They walked under the flat beds of the trucks through an opening in a wall of wooden crates just wide enough for a Borac to pass through. The truck tires were taller than even the Boracs and as wide as Kholos's shoulders. All of the beds were open, with crates and barrels strapped on the back. The cargo had been shifted and stacked to form walls both under the beds and on top.

Every flat bed, Kholos saw, was manned by a Borac lookout. Sitting around small butane fires they ate from skewers of meat, drank beer out of glass jars, and listened and watched to different Televia sets.

As they walked, Kholos saw laundry lines hung from a door handle to an antenna. Many truck cabs had been painted on their doors and hoods, showing young topless green-skinned Borac women smiling lasciviously, or with dactyls glaring, red eyes.

Within the perimeter Borac children without pants or without shirts or without both ran and played everywhere, climbing up on bales and boxes, tripping on guy lines for tents and tarps. Dozens of cooking fires burned greasy chunks of various meats while Borac women sang in a chanting-hymn about a *cumbel* who went to a city and lost his anima. Kholos recognized the words. Babies were washed in old oil drums cut in half, *kops* were sharpened on whetstones.

Kholos smelled the saurs and dactyls before he saw them. Damp, like a freshwater pond. Then came the shadows of the saurs, so big for a moment he thought that they were part of the slopes of the Asinwatis. The saurs were, Kholos saw, being fed. In a pen made from tent poles and old rope, Borac handlers forked piles of straw down on the ground and cracked the tops of drums of water and tipped them over. One handler, using a rope and harness, was climbing up the backs of the saurs and checking them for any injuries, rinsing away the dust and debris of the road with a hose.

The dactyls came next. Except for the one still circling above to keep watch, they were all perched on a metal pole as long as one of the trucks. They were also being cleaned and fed, their tethers and cables carefully wound and piled nearby. The leather cuffs around the dactyls' ankles were never removed, but were oiled nightly. A young *glin* in a dirty calico dress was rubbing oils on each creature with her bare hands as they passed. A handler wearing thick leather mittens that came up to his elbows was, carefully, almost delicately, holding out chunks of raw meat from a wooden bucket out before each dactyl. The long teethy beaks snapped as he passed, click clack. The sound brought up memories for Kholos, the smooth feel of the dactyl's wings, the tug of their flight against his shoulder.

The food, Kholos recalled from someone else's memories. There was an ingredient in the food that kept the saurs and dactyls alive. An enzyme they required. He winced again, not from the knee but at the sight of the dactyls all tied to their pole. He was the Liberator Pattern, after all.

They were deep within the encampment. Things were a bit quieter, the tents darker. Music still played but it seemed to come from fewer places. Kholos saw that the perimeter was not entirely made up of trucks, but in places was just crates and barrels stacked up, mostly facing the burning city to the east.

The Boracs, he realized, were deliberately not looking at them. The vertical pupils of their circular eyes snatched sidelong glances. The *cumbel*, the *shama*, all of them. Kholos tried to read their expressions, saw anger, perhaps, a bit of fear. He did not understand. V touched his chin from her papoose.

"Are you sure this was a good idea?" she whispered, hoarsely.

Kholos only said. "I didn't know Boracs drove trucks like this."

"This is Gyr Zax's caravan," said Screw Tusks. "He's very modern."

The trailer stood like a tiny house among the tents, back against the mountains. It was powered by a little generator and the lights inside made it glow now that the sun was gone. A small cooking fire, mostly burned down to ash, was set a few paces from the steps leading to the door. The door to the trailer opened, and in it appeared a huge Borac.

"I am Gyr Zax," he said. "And I believe you've come to kill me, correct?"

In the dark it was hard to see much except the blocky shape of the Borac's head and broad shoulders.

"Perhaps," said Kholos, cautiously.

The Borac smiled, his tusks lifting like doors to his face. "Well. Let's have something to eat, first."

Inside the trailer there was Borac food in ceramic bowls and plates: rabbit meat on skewers, beef cubes raw and seared and seasoned with pepper and salt and cumin, chicken cut into strips.

Boracs could only eat meat, and it was only with the coming of the Columbium and the Republicants that they had started to cook their food at all. Inside a blue kettle tea seeped and there were matching cups around it in a circle. The dishes were set around a round wooden table which, along with four simple chairs, occupied one entire end of the trailer. At the other end was a cot that could have comfortably held two human beings but looked narrow for Gyr Zax. Around the cot were various chests and sets of drawers, all of the same wood as the table and chairs. A wooden door led to what Kholos assumed was the toilet, and a smaller door that hummed slightly, Kholos guessed, was the icebox.

A glaive with an ornately etched blade hung on the wall, across from it a submachine gun made of gold and chased with strange runes. Kholos studied the gun: recognized it as a powerful weapon, probably powerful enough to kill even him. Maybe, and with the right ammunition. A fan, placed on the floor in a corner, circulated the air pleasantly and spread the spicy smells of the meats and the tea.

Gyr pulled out a chair for Kholos, then noticed V. He seemed surprised, but instantly pulled out another chair. Kholos started to lift her out of the sling, but then noticed she was asleep.

"We've had a long day of travel," Kholos explained.

Gyr Zax grunted, noticed Kholos's bloody bandage. "You'll find some supplies for your leg in the cabinet next to the sink."

Kholos set V down on the cot, where she seemed tiny as a child, and arranged her old bones as comfortably as he could. She slept on.

From the cabinet Kholos took bandages, a needle in a plastic sterile sleeve and some surgical thread. He brought these things to the table, where Gyr was sipping some tea and eating a piece of chicken.

"You're going to do that at the table?" Gyr asked. "While you eat?"

Kholos finally looked at the Borac in the full light. Gyr's eyes were yellow, a common color for Boracs, his hair was black with stripes of gray. He also, Kholos saw, had covered his tusks with two black squares of cloth, tied at the bases.

"Your tusks?" Kholos said. To cover one's tusks was like covering your face.

"Yes, my tusks," Gyr said. "That is why you're here, after all. To take my tusks. I'm surprised it's taken you this long to mention them. We were never sure this would work to begin with, but clearly the ruse has held. If it even matters any longer." He seemed annoyed, almost. He sipped his tea leisurely.

"Why would I take your tusks?"

"Ha. Let me ask you, what was the purpose of coming here like you did, on foot? Carrying a Fractured woman? Shot in the knee? I expected you to fall down upon me like a star, or creep through my camp at midnight and cut my throat. Isn't that how it's been done? We've kept a dactyl aloft for two days, to keep a watch."

"How do you know that?"

Gyr did not answer. He put down his tea, and stared at Kholos with his yellow eyes.

At last, Kholos took a deep breath. "All I ask of you is a place to rest, and some water, and, possibly, some better attention to this," he pointed at his shot knee. "That's all. I'm not here for anything else. I didn't come here planning to kill anyone."

Gyr Zax watched him.

"You are an agent of them," Gyr said, pointing up at the ceiling.

"How do you know about... ?" Kholos paused. He was worried V might hear them. "How do you know I could be an agent of someone?"

"Of someone." said Gyr. "What should we call them? Our lords and masters? Our puppeteers? The Aetherian? Yes. I know the Adonai are not the last powers of the world."

Kholos said. "I am an agent of no one. I am only trying to escape."

Gyr Zax stared at him without speaking. For a long while. This was disconcerting. The vertical pupils dilated and the lids, which were horizontal, did not blink. The black squares of cloth over Gyr's tusks wavered a bit as the big Borac sighed.

Kholos said to Gyr. "What do you see?"

"Broken lines," said Gyr. "Like sticks, snapped off at the end. In many colors."

"I am not here for your tusks. Believe me."

At last, Gyr blinked. He sipped his tea and ate another cube of beef. The black cloths moved up and down as he chewed. When he swallowed Kholos noticed the Borac's entire posture change. The shoulders came down, and Gyr put his elbows up on the table.

"You're a renegade," he said, after swallowing. "I've heard of your kind."

"My kind?"

"There is a company of you, I've heard," Gyr explained. "Far to the south. Farther south than my own swamps. But they are all broken. Broken, not Fractured. Physically maimed, some unbelievably so, from the stories I was told. They don't want to be re-made again," Gyr said. "They want to die as themselves. Does that make sense to you? It did not to me."

Kholos thought a moment. If he failed, if he had been injured, when he had been sent to destroy the city, he knew he would be undone, piece by piece, and re-made into a new version of himself. A new Kholopatiron. With whatever individuality he had mastered, created, and earned, melted away. He might choose to live injured, in pain.

And apparently he had chosen.

How could the city have hurt him, he thought. *Was that what the Aetherian feared?*

"It makes sense to me," Kholos said. "But I am not hiding. I am running."

Gyr said. "A woman leads them. They called her a Witch-General, in the story I was told. Little news, you understand."

"A Borac woman? An animist?"

"No, not Borac. Not human either."

Kholos reached out and took a piece of meat. Gyr was nodding at something.

"What do you want here?" Gyr asked. "Since you are not here to kill me."

"I told you. Water, dinner. A clean bandage for my leg. Some talk from the road, little news."

"No," corrected Gyr Zax. "I meant here, in this world. You are like the Boracs, I can tell that much. You don't belong here any more than we do. So what do you want? Where are you going?"

Kholos thought of his list. "North," he said. Vaguely.

"I thought you would fly, burning the sky to come for me. Here you are limping. Going north, you say. Indeed." Gyr laughed again. His square head rolled back. "What do you want, here, of this world? If you've abandoned your post for the puppeteers, what are you after?"

"Freedom," said Kholos. Said it simply. "Freedom from everything."

"And you will achieve this ultimate freedom how? By going north?"

"I have a plan. It need not concern you."

"But how? I am a Borac, I can see the anima, I know what you mean when you say, freedom, real freedom. But how? Tell me you want to fly, fine. Tell me you want to live forever, indeed. But freedom? True freedom? From life? From death? From creation? From Pang's zero? How?"

Kholos looked back at V. She was asleep. He told Gyr what he had told her. "There are machines."

"You understand how to work them? They are simple to use? You can build one?"

"All I have to do is reach them." Kholos added, "I will be free. Free of everything. Death. Time. Bodies. I will make my own universe."

Gyr blinked. "I am dining with an insane person."

Kholos grinned.

Then he added, "I know the Aetherian care about their Adonai, care about this world, or they would not have sent me here. And so I believe the Aetherian have a way to travel to and from their city outside of time, into the world. I know it, because it was the way they sent me here: through a tube of light. If I can find that way, I can find the city. If I can find the city, I can find the machines I need. They stitch together the universe. And they can unstitch it a little. Enough for us," he looked again at V. "To leave."

"And you will learn how to run it, then and there, with the makers of reality all about you?"

"I have some plans for that."

"Golgothan?" said Gyr Zax, hopefully, trying to understand. "You are perhaps an avatar of Golgothan? He is a renegade as well, of course."

"The Universitat have gone to great lengths to eliminate that name," said Kholos. "But no. I am Kholopatiron. And I will be Kholopatiron, completely. You understand what that means?"

"I can see your lines. I understand what they mean even if I don't grasp your name. But," Gyr countered, "from the little I gather of your masters, this could all be part of their plan. Your mission might be to remind the Adonai of their masters' reach. Or to make way for new Adonai, new ideas. Or something else entirely."

"No," said Kholos, thinking of the city. "The Aetherian were afraid of something here. Something in the burning city, something that threatened their plans, their saints, their ideas. I don't know what it was, but I know I didn't destroy it, as I was tasked. I used it to hide my escape. But I am not free, yet. I know they will pursue me."

He thought of the dreams and visions, and poems, of Michael Staffa. His love for V. How it drove him.

Kholos licked the grease from his fingers. The food was good, and Kholos said so. He drank down a cup of tea, poured himself another. After wiping his hands clean he set to work on his knee again. As he looked at his tattered pants he saw it was mostly healed, the skin closed. He looked up at Gyr.

"It's *shama* anima, female work," Gyr said. "The healing lines. But I am old enough to have a speck of it. You should stay off of it for a few days, or it will get worse. We are heading north from here, as it happens, you can travel with us. There is an Adonai's domain that way, I have heard on the road, some more little news for you. Of course it may have shifted already. The Lipstick Country, hidden in the woods somewhere."

"You want something from me," Kholos said.

They stared at each other across the table.

Gyr put his hands up towards his face, each grasping one tusk through the black cloths. "I thought you were a Thought Assassin, come to kill the Borac ideas. And I was prepared to die here, in the hope of sending those ideas on, beyond your reach. But now

I wonder if you might take something with you. A gift, even, for your new home, wherever it might be."

Gyr removed the cloths over his tusks. There, carved into the tusks so finely, so perfectly, were the remaining Borac gods. There was Shirusu, the fat old mother, holding her bucket of buttermilk with both hands, her hair in braids. There was Hindel Koosh, the iconic *cumbel*, *kop* raised, bow on his back, eyes narrowed towards Kholos. There was Trimea Mea, the goddess of flowers, of spring. Slender like a vine, buxom like a peach, she was, in bas relief, and beautiful as a garden. Last was Jotund, fat and frivolous, the god of plenty and eating, accumulation, munching on a sheep leg.

Four ideas. The world felt suddenly better. Something new could happen.

"The others are dead," Gyr said.

"I thought they were all dead," Kholos said. "I thought all the vestiges of the ideas outside the Universitat pantheon were dead."

"There might be a few left, most so battered and ignored their existence no longer matters. Thssiss, the Slythe god, I believe he is captured, though, not killed."

"You thought I'd come to kill your gods," Kholos realized.

Gyr Zax replaced the cloth. The ideas vanished.

"There are many of us with our tusks prepared to take them and hide them. We use anima triggers to send them on. I can send them away to another carrier, someone else to tote the ideas of our race. I do not know to whom. In fact, I do not know with certainty that there are any carriers left. Other carriers have been found, you see. Found and killed, but not before they sent on the gods. It is not a matter of time, you understand, to send them on."

"I understand," said Kholos.

"Then take them," Gyr Zax said. "Cut them from my face, and take them with you. There will never be another, better chance for us. The Stalinistas are on the Columbium Continent now. The ideas of the Universitat are supreme. We will vanish. But if you take them? Somewhere beyond the Aetherian's reach? Who knows? They might re-create the Borac people entirely. Look at them," he said, lifting the cloth away again. "Tell me these are ideas of this world. You can't. These are new. Who knows how they might help you?"

Kholos crossed his arms across his chest. "They are very interesting."

"They could give you worlds, Kholos," Gyr added. "They could give you thoughts and chronologies."

Kholos said, "This is why you travel, isn't it? To keep them moving, always on the roads. Never in one place. Your entire race?"

"Yes," Gyr admitted. He pointed at his face. "I bought the trucks, hoping they might help us keep just a little ahead, when I saw my death in the anima. I assumed it was for the tusks, but, perhaps not. Perhaps it does not have to be. The anima can be wrong, after all.

"Listen. We can see, we Boracs, we can see the tiny strings moving through everything, how they shiver. We can pluck one or two. Shape a speck, an instant. But I look at your lines, Kholos, they end at you, they are all cut. You exist impossibly. You could do impossible things. You could escape. I don't understand who, what, you are, but you could escape."

Kholos said nothing. He was afraid V might hear.

"I don't want them," said Kholos. "This is your burden. I will make my own worlds where I go."

"But they could help you," Gyr pleaded. "They could be allies, weapons. Think, Kholos, the Aetherian fear these ancient gods enough to destroy them, like the burning city. Think how they could help you."

Kholos leaned forward. Trimea Mea seemed to beckon under the cloth. Shinusu appeared to laugh.

"I might bargain with them," Kholos whispered, looking up at Gyr. "I might trade them, for my freedom."

Gyr leaned back. They stared at one another across the table, across the meats Gyr had prepared for his death meal.

"I have made a mistake," Gyr Zax said.

At that moment the first salvo of rockets from Colonel Ute Redroot's Fighting First Claws regiment slammed into the encampment with a hiss and a roar.

4. Fighting First Claws

"Don't stop for prisoners," ordered Colonel Redroot. "These are Boracs. They are not real people."

With the receiver of the short-range Televia in his left hand and a pair of binoculars in his right, Redroot stood in the back of an attack car, bracing himself with his elbows on the roll bar. The cars were four-wheeled, with wide rubber tires, and were open-roofed to accommodate the weaponry they carried. Redroot's command car was equipped with a six-tube rocket launcher.

He was leading the southern prong of the regiment's attack against the Borac encampment. The plan called for Stands-Tall to wait for Redroot's order, then come from out of the glow of the burning city with the tanks. Anyone and everything within the encampment would either be destroyed with their backs against the slopes of the Asinwatis, or else funneled north where a deployment of Comanche foot soldiers were dug in, waiting for anyone attempting to flee. His deserter would either be killed or captured.

Ute Redroot was the youngest Comanche in the history of the Incorporated Nation to reach the rank of Colonel. He believed in speed and firepower, and disdained the fixed positions the old Comanche War Chiefs advocated. Now that the Stalinistas had crossed the Pacificum and landed in their endless hordes on the Columbium continent, Redroot was sure Colonel was only the beginning.

He would be the one who turned them back. The man who stopped the Stalinistas.

He touched the button on the Televia again, "I want those trucks destroyed," he said, calmly. "Aim for the cabs, not the beds. We can pirate the cargo."

A salvo of rockets, prepared with Universitat prayers to arc properly, raced through the night sky. They landed about, over, and on top of the Boracs firing out feebly from behind their barrels and crates and bales. The engine of a truck exploded, sending the hood and the doors high into the air. Black smoke piled up. The saurs and the dactyls screamed. Some Boracs had huddled together in the center of the encampment, while others ran about randomly with drawn *kops*.

The crack-crack-crack of the machine guns on the regiment's attack cars sounded up ahead. They had engaged close-in to the Boracs, perhaps even within the encampment itself. Peering through his glasses once again, Ute saw in the flicker of the gasoline fires that his cars were whizzing up close, making arcs in front of the Boracs on and under the beds of the trucks and opening up their cargo barricades with storms of bullets.

"Knife cars on point," he barked into the mouthpiece. "One of you braves see if you can slip under the beds of those trucks. Rip them up a little from the inside. Keep an eye out for our deserter."

An old Shoshone battle-cry responded to the Colonel's command. Ute watched as a car aimed straight for the Borac trucks and accelerated, its gun clattering out its arrival. It crashed through a pair of crates that appeared to hold some kind of fruit or rubber balls.

Splat. The car was into the encampment.

Shaking his head, Colonel Redroot smiled. Brilliant, he was brilliant.

Privately, when he and Stands-Tall-Under-Cedars drank alone back on the Redroot family estates down in the Red River country, Ute would admit he was glad of the Stalinistas. Glad because they gave him the chance at greatness. He would lead the Third Comanche Incorporated Nation to its rightful place as the rulers of the world. He had drawn up battle plans to throw the Stalinistas back into the sea, as well as written his acceptance speech for his election as War Chief. The speech was, Stands-Tall admitted, quite moving.

"Hammer cars," he said. "Pull into a crescent formation and lob our shots to a range of nine-nine-zero. Knife cars copy that command, don't push into our fire."

The knife cars copied. The hammer cars, fitted with the six-tube mortar launchers, pulled into a wedge with the apex towards, rather than away from, the edge of the caravan. This was another innovation of the Colonel's. It allowed for no safe rallying point for the enemy. It also spared Fighting First Claws. Despite driving at high speeds over the dirt and stone next to the Universitat highway, the hammer cars formed up quickly. For a moment Ute let the cars idle.

"Remember, he killed our own," he half-whispered over the Televia. "Fire."

The rounds whumped and whistled their way into the encampment. They landed as one, and raised a curtain of flame.

Ute Redroot was a descendant, obliquely, of Quannah Parker (ironically a half-breed), the Comanche War Chief who had initiated what he called the Manifest Destiny of the Comanche race. Ute believed in Quannah Parker, believed in the Comanche, and believed in himself most of all. His family was established Comanche aristocracy, a long line of ranchers and leaders and, in later generations, railroad barons. His wife, who stayed always back at the Redroot ranches when the Colonel was deployed, was a very pretty girl from a neighboring family of status. Ute saw little of her but dutifully wrote her letters every day in which he outlined his plans for the estates, for their family, and for their people. She sewed him decorative, traditional vests of precious beads and platinum, which he wore under his uniform always. Her name was Yahto, and she was a cousin of Stands-Tall-Under-Cedars.

Stands-Tall and Redroot, as blood brothers, were under specific legal responsibilities to one another. These included support of each another's families, obligation to invest in any business ventures his brother might undertake, and to share a certain percentage of any wealth with the other brother. The pact also required, whenever possible, for the brothers to be present at one another's death. Somewhat archaically, being a Comanche blood brother also meant that if one brother was unjustly killed, the other had to seek justice.

"Two, this is one," Redroot said clearly and loudly into the mouthpiece. "Respond, two."

"Two, acknowledged," answered Stands-Tall. His voice mixed in with the rumble of the tank engines.

"You had better hurry, major," said Colonel Redroot. "There won't be much left for you."

A laugh and the slam of a hatch answered Redroot. "Two, engaging," said Stands-Tall.

Ute swung his binoculars to the east. He wondered if this deserter, whose description was now pasted on the dash of every attack car and inside the cabin of every tank, was allied with the Boracs or had simply paused to trade for supplies. It did not matter much, he decided.

The tanks, like the attack cars, were painted a dark blue that matched the uniforms of the troopers themselves. Each was stenciled with a number and the claw insignia, and each featured a single, low-caliber cannon on a mounted turret that could swivel 360 degrees. Ute Redroot loved his tanks, even more than his cars. He saw them as the means by which to defeat the Stalinistas.

The one flaw in the tanks was their ammunition. Their shells were self-propelled, so they essentially flew: a sin against reason and faith, sure to bring disaster sooner or later. Redroot did not much care for the Universitat warnings, especially as their engineers and laypersons were now strictly rationing his shells. For the attack on the encampment, Redroot had ordered Stands-Tall to carry only two shots per tank. He wanted stockpiles to deal with the Stalinistas.

"Ai ai ai!" shouted Stands-Tall, with joy, over the Televia. So loud Redroot had to move his ear away from the receiver.

"What's happening?" said V. "What's going on?"

"We're leaving," said Kholos.

"Take the tusks," begged Gyr Zax, blocking the door to the trailer. Already fire was spreading through the encampment. The rough-skinned, four-fingered hand clutched at Kholos's wrist. "Please. Take them! Let them be free!"

"What is he talking about?" asked V.

"Nothing that concerns us," said Kholos.

Kholos pushed the big Borac out of the way.

He was cradling V, still old and bony, in one arm. Their equipment and weapons he had slung over a shoulder, hoping he was not leaving anything behind. They stepped out of the trailer into screams and fire. Coming on from the distant glow of the burning city was a cloud of dust from Stands-Tall's approaching tanks. Kholos considered joining the Boracs trying to flee, running with the crowd out of the encampment, to the north, but decided not to.

The cars of the Fighting First Claws were deep in the encampment. Each car carried three soldiers: a driver, a gunner, and a trooper with an automatic assault rifle who could deploy on foot. Those foot soldiers were leaping out of the cars, covering each other and establishing fields of fire. The trucks of Gyr Zax, his modern trucks, were broken and burning. The cargo of the caravan lay scattered everywhere: ropes, melons, bolts of cloth, screws, planks, sheaves of wheat.

Surveying the wreckage Kholos froze.

He had seen this before. He had been here before. Impossibly, he believed he could hear the microscopic machines of the Aetherian come to harvest the specific, individual cells of the fallen for the construction of new agents, new patterns. His skin felt cold. For an instant, the night seemed coated with amber. A wire of pain shooting up from his knee made him blink.

"Kholos?" V croaked.

"I was here?" Kholos said. "Of course."

A blue dome of soft light permeated over the scene. Sound stopped. Kholos could feel the air stop. Could feel the world stop under the soles of his boots. Clutching V closer he braced for the fire of ignited time he was sure was about to fall about them.

He could never be free. He would never be free. They had caught him already.

He looked at V, her old face. Her terrified eyes. "I love you."

"I can't hear you," she said. "What is it?"

But the hammer of time never came, and Kholos realized the blue light was something else. He ran for the pens.

The flood of Boracs was streaming by, pushed north by the attacks. One knocked Kholos down to the ground and V with him. For a moment, Borac feet, shoeless and four-toed, stomped about his head as Kholos looked up in the sky. The stars had vanished and clouds were moving in, along with the smoke. The temperature, Kholos realized, had dropped. And, under the back of his head, he felt a short, scratchy grass growing. The cataract of disturbed conditions around the burning city was changing the climate again. The saurs and dactyls were screaming, the fires had reached their pens.

He sorted through the experiences he held in his brain. Anima. Tethers. A sense of unbelonging. Words and gestures. A taste for raw meat. Fear. A leather cuff on a thick wrist. Peeking down at V he wondered how much she weighed.

Along the edge of fleeing Boracs, he began to work south, towards the fires and the cars.

The bodies of *cumbel* with their *kops* drawn or with their old rifles still clutched in their square hands lay everywhere. Kholos recognized their escorts from the afternoon, Screw Tusks and Blue Tusks, both dead. From the burning cabs of the blasted trucks a stinky heat rose against the sudden cold. Engines popped apart in fireballs and sent doors, hoods, screaming.

A few flakes of snow fell. Kholos kept to the shadows. The dust cloud from the approaching tanks was larger, the sound of their engines quite clear even over the crackle of the fires. The knife cars were pushing the Boracs forward, not pausing to check for stragglers.

At the pens for the saurs and dactyls Kholos slipped in a pond of blood, twisting his shot knee again. A few of the Fighting Claws' rockets had landed among the animals, and wounded the saurs terribly. The enormous white hulk of one of the beasts lay on its side, its long neck craned pitifully towards the water barrels just out of its reach. A gaping hole big enough for an attack car to pass through bled out from its belly. Kholos could hear orders being shouted behind him. The Comanche who had left the cars were moving in patrols throughout the encampment, looking for him.

Kholos found the dactyls up against the mountains, tethered with a cable as thick as his leg. The reptile-birds were terrified, flapping their white wings and fanning flames, snapping their long beaks at the dark. Somewhere, Kholos understood, their handlers were either dead or fleeing. The snow was falling harder.

By the light of the fires Kholos fumbled through one of the metal boxes nearby where he knew, just knew, the tack for the dactyl handlers was kept. With a kick he opened the lid and, setting the whimpering V down on top of another lid, grabbed the first gauntlet he saw. It was huge, but he took some of the rope the handlers used and wrapped it tight around his wrist, and then under his shoulders and around his waist as well. He looked at V, thought of their equipment, and did some quick math in his head.

Finally, ducking all the while against the snapping beaks and whooshing wings, Kholos approached one of the dactyls closely enough to slip the cord through the ring on its ankle band, and tied off the knot all dactyl handlers learned as children. Returning for V he picked her up and held her tight. Looking at her wrinkled, sunken face, he kissed her on her forehead.

Finally, drawing his sword Kholos gripped the hilt in one hand and slashed down at the cable. His blow cut through not only the cable but the bar underneath, and well into the ground below it the bar.

"*Tapatu!*" he shouted, in Borac. His voice rang clear above the gunfire.

The dactyls, now that their tethering chain was gone, as a flock, began to ascend. The cable coiled on the ground next to Kholos and V unwound itself in lightning-fast loops, rising up up up into the falling snow. When it reached its end, knotted onto Kholos's wrist, one dactyl jerked down from the rest, then rose again, this time significantly more slowly than the others.

Dactyls could not fly with any heavy load, including a Borac. But Kholos and V were not equal in weight to a Borac. And this dactyl was panicked enough to try. Around his shoulder Kholos felt the jerk of the cord and grunted.

They rose. Straight up.

Kholos tried to keep his back to the rock so that if they smacked against the slopes he would take the blow, and not V. Below he saw the attack play itself out. The encampment was destroyed. Borac bodies lay at odd angles. The Comanche were fanning out, shooting up tents and knocking over crates and boxes. A few soldiers pointed up at the departing dactyls and fired, but weakly. His shoulder burned where the cord had yanked him up.

Kholos watched a knife car park itself in front of Gyr Zax's trailer and bisect the trailer with bullets. Then, apparently unwounded, Gyr himself burst through the door with his gold machine pistol blazing. He shot two of the Comanches before he was hit across the belly, but he fought on. His tusks, Kholos saw, were wrapped tightly with the black cloths. The Boracs who had fled from the Comanche were spreading out into the steadily falling snow, the tanks closing in on them now, pushing them back into the cauldron of destruction that was the encampment.

Looking down Kholos took in V's face. Her old eyes were wide. It was almost time for her to change. But something made Kholos look away, this time farther to the east, where a second cloud of dust, only now it was not dust but snow, was rising from just behind the oncoming tanks. Blue flashes, the blue Kholos had thought was his pursuit through time, sparked in the cloud. Kholos thought he saw horses.

The weight of V changed. He looked down, and saw a 12-year old girl clinging to his waist, she was still terrified, but now there was wonder as well. Her mouth was agape.

"This is crazy!" she cried out. "We're flying!"

"Hang on to me," he told her.

Half-laughing, half scowling he tried to speak to her through the increasing howl of the snowstorm coming down about them now in earnest. Up above them the dactyl, flapping furiously against their weight, cawed and shrieked.

Gyr Zax fought like a Borac. He emptied half a magazine into the first Comanches to reach his trailer, and then drew his *kop* to decapitate whatever soldier was closest, this even after Gyr had been shot. But then a spit of bullets from the heavy machine gun on the attack car blew out his body at the thighs up to his heart, and he slumped to the ground, bleeding and messy, sitting in his own green blood.

The Comanche, believing him quite dead, moved north through what remained of the caravan. Painfully, slowly, unable to move, Gyr twitched at the anima of the world, listened to the tiny fraction of the music of the universe he could still hear. The tone sounded. He would die, here, it sang, there was no song to stitch his guts back together.

Around him Gyr watched the surviving *cumbel* take up positions where they could behind random crates and overturned barrels. Boracs always fought alone, there was no order, no tactics. He saw one warrior, a woman *cumbel,* take cover from behind the bulk of a dying saur. She picked off, one, two Comanche soldiers with single-shots, then a rocket cut through the air and crashed directly behind her. Gyr closed his eyes. There was a smell of burning meat.

The moans of his saurs tore into his heart. He groaned, tried to raise his gun to end their misery, but his arm would not work.

With pain and fury Gyr Zax watched as the little cars bolted under the beds of his burning trucks. Gyr expected them to pause and loot the trailers, where the Boracs kept their jade chits, but instead they simply moved on to the next tent, the next truck. The deserter, Gyr Zax understood, they were looking for the deserter. The destruction of the encampment, of Gyr Zax's life's work, was incidental. The soldiers wanted Kholos, whatever he was.

Behind him a volley of tank shells thudded throughout the encampment. The range was long and the attack shattered against the slopes of the mountains, sending down a mist of powdered and chipped rock. The saurs' chorus of fear reached a new pitch. Gyr cringed. He had raised many of them himself.

He wondered why the Third Comanche wanted Kholos so desperately. The attack had been so perfectly planned, he realized, only a handful of moments had passed. Then he noticed the tanks had stopped, outside the perimeter. Blue sparkles appeared among the snowflakes, along with the clattering of hooves.

"Two, what are you doing?"
Static replied to Redroot's question.
With a few gestures Redroot ordered his hammer cars forward. They came up close to the burning perimeter, stopped, and unloaded their foot soldiers. The dismounted Third Comanche rushed into the encampment, picking off the few Boracs either still daring to fight or trying to flee. They kicked over crates and rolled over bodies with the barrels of their rifles, searching for Kholos. Hopefully, Stands-Tall-Under-Cedars had surrounded the other side just as easily.

"Two, respond!"

Again, static.

"This is not a time to be flippant, Stands-Tall," he rasped. "Secure the Pang-damn encampment."

The driver of Redroot's attack car turned and passed up the binoculars back to the Colonel. "Sir, there's movement on the western edge of the theater."

Redroot lifted the glasses. He saw Kholos, swinging and swaying jerkily at the end of the line attached to the lurching and dipping dactyl.

"Can we shoot that down?"

"Not from here, sir. Easier shot for the tankers, sir."

Redroot flushed. He shouted into the vox-piece. "Two! Two!"

No response. Redroot scanned the caravan encampment through the glasses, again. He could see where the tank attack had done its first work, blasting the living quarters and tearing up the ugly saurs, but when he swept the glasses to the east all he saw was the cloud of dust and snow brought on by the charge, with strange little flashes of electricity he assumed were due to the strange weather in the area. Then he realized the tanks were firing their final shells, at close range.

At what?

"Was there any significant resistance to the east of the theatre?" he asked.

"None, sir. Even less fight than here."

"So where is our Major, then?" Redroot lifted the glasses. He did not like the dactyl making its way out of the encampment. "Relay to the rocketeers to take their chances. I'll give an eagle feather to whoever hits that thing."

Redroot looked through the glasses again, and saw them: Second Comanche, on horseback.

The backward cousins who hunted buffalo, painted their faces, all that nonsense. Redroot found them embarrassing.

"Two, do you copy? Savages seem to be in your vicinity. Anything I need to worry about?"

There was more static. Redroot cursed. Killing the Seconds would be impolite at best, a political risk.

"Colonel?" said Stands-Tall-Under-Cedars over the vox-piece. "Colonel. Two here."

"One here," Ute shouted. Over the receiver came the sound of small arms fire and men screaming. "Report, Two."

"Encountering stiff resistance, One. Second Comanche braves, en force. Request relief. Immediately. Hurry, Ute. Please."

Ute scoffed. "Push them aside, Stands-Tall. Try not to kill any of them, if possible."

"Negative, One," came the response. "Resistance is... exceptional. They've got new weapons, brother. I've lost eight tanks. My gunner and my driver are both dead. My tank's stuck, both tracks broken. They're all over us. Came out of nowhere. Please, help us."

"What kind of weapons? Came out of where? Explain."

"Their spears are charged up with something. They explode when they touch a tank, or a soldier. It's like lightning. Blue lightning. Ute, get over here. I'm stuck in here, I think my feet are gone," there was a bang loud enough that Ute heard it from his position, without the aid of the earpiece. "They got another. They got Blue Eyed Buck. His tank's all melted. Pang! Ute, brother, come help us. Please!"

Ute looked through the glasses. The white dactyl flying up with its man-sized load rose up, up.

"Stands-Tall, my deserter is getting away."

"Ute! We are all dying! Forget the deserter!"

Redroot looked at the receiver as if he had never seen it before.

"They've found me," said Stands Tall. "They know I'm still alive in here."

"Stands-Tall, they're Second Comanche." Redroot said, as if this explained everything.

There was a pause before Stands-Tall responded. "Yes, sir."

"I'll send over some knife cars," Ute said, at last.

"Avenge me, Ute. Treat my wife well."

A crackle, a Comanche war-scream, then static.

"Driver!" Ute called, about to lead the cars to move to Stands-Tall's position. But then he thought of the dactyl, flying away. "Gunner!" he changed his mind.

"Sir!"

"Fire," Ute looked east. He could see the light from the burning tanks now, hazy through the snow. Distant war whoops were echoing through the night. "Fire at that thing flying up there."

"Yes, sir!"

As the gunner launched high, arcing, random shots, Redroot looked at the dust cloud through the binoculars. He saw bright flashes, like ball lightning, within, as well as the shapes of horsemen drawing up in a circle, like they were assembling at the edge. His mouth went dry as he could just make out the shapes of two men with blue-tipped spears standing astride a tank, shadowy in the weird light of the fires from the caravan. The two stabbed the tank, leapt clear, and then howled as the metal shell of the vehicle fizzed and cracked in a shower of sparks. Fires burned white hot within the husk. Redroot, his eyes dry against the eyepieces of the glasses, thought of his wife.

He put the glasses down. He nodded to his radio-man in front of the car.

"Medic," he whispered. The thump of the mortar drowned him out. "Get a medic over to the tanks."

"Sir?"

The horsemen were coming. They were charging.

"Oh, no," Redroot said. He yanked up his Televia. "Knife cars! Reload your troops and engage east! Repeat, engage east! Second element under heavy attack! Engage east!"

Redroot lifted the glasses again. They were coming, the Second Comanche, coming out of the dust, straight for him.

"Corporal," he shouted. "Form us up! Hammer cars, form up!" Redroot lifted the glasses again. Then he realized there was no reassuring "Sir!" from the comm-man. "Corporal?" he asked, leaning forward.

He saw the arrow through the man's throat. The point appeared to be made from pure blue light, and had passed clean through the engine block of the truck. Redroot put his hand on the driver's shoulder.

"Impossible," he said. "They're too far away."

A second arrow thunked into the eye of his gunner. The man slumped back in his seat, blood pouring down his face. Redroot looked through the glasses again. They were coming on, firing bows with strings that glowed like the tracks the stars left.

Another arrow landed next to him and he crouched down just as one of the electric spears struck against the front tire. The car jumped up into the air, a full two meters, and flipped over, sending Redroot flying free. He landed hard on the wet, cold ground, felt something give way in his leg with a snap.

He could hear them, coming on. The gallop of their horses, the hiss of their arrows. The explosions of their spears. Blue light flashed everywhere. They wore their warpaint, but they were not whooping and ai ai-ing, as he had imagined. They were shouting, shouting a single name, over and over.

Golgothan.

Kholos woke on his back. V, twelve-year-old V, was kneeling next to him. She had, he saw, made a little shelter with the tarpaulin from the pack over him to keep the snow off, and unrolled their blankets over top of him. It was morning but the weather from the evening had held and it was cold, with a light snow still falling. Looking about at the little ridge they had reached Kholos saw the dactyl tripping about. It was sick, quite sick, without its special food, and Kholos understood it would die soon. V was stroking his head.

"You took care of everything," Kholos said.

"I'm an Orado girl," she said. "I can cook a stew, shoot a gun, drive, sew, sing, dance, and clean a cut and set a bone all in a day. You just never let me."

"When you're nine or ninety, no, I don't let you. But thank you."

Gingerly, Kholos rose, using the butt of his rifle, again, as a crutch. V walked with him. At the edge of the cliff they looked down at the smoldering rubble of what had been the immense encampment of Gyr Zax's caravan. V gripped Kholos's hand in her own. The air was clear enough they could see the blackened husks of the trucks and n the split-open tanks and the huge bodies of the bled-out saurs, whiter than white against the snow.

"We did that," said V. "We made that happen."

"I did," said Kholos. "Not you."

"Is it going to be like this? Are we going to kill people?"

"I didn't kill any of those people down there," said Kholos.

"But you didn't stop it, either."

"No, I did not." Kholos paused.

V shuffled her boots in the snow. "Kholos, I love you. But it's not right," she said. "To bring pain like this to people. They didn't know."

"What happens in this world," said Kholos. "It doesn't matter to us. We're leaving."

"It matters to me," said V.

Kholos did not answer. He thought of the dactyl, dying behind them in the snow. The beast had given up on flying and lay with its wings folded over itself. He looked at it blending slowly with the falling snow.

"Wait here a little while," he said. "I have to go back for something."

"What for?"

He moved to the pack and undid a few ties and clasps until he found his magazines of colored bullets. He took out a white one. He had used a red one at the city, and left another red one with Dr. Voss, in the future. He had only two white bullets, but they were much better than canisters, left a trail much harder to track. You had to be in the physical area to see the traces. You had to see the moment. Carefully he broke one of the cartridges apart and poured out just a pinch of white powder, perhaps two or three hours worth, no more. It was much less powerful than the red, to say nothing of the black. He looked at V.

He said. "I'll get a car ready for us."

"You can't go back down there. They could still be looking for you. And how are you going to get down?"

Kholos rubbed his thumb and finger together. The granules of the powder reacted, locally, and he was gone. Then he was back, in less time it took V to cry out. In his hands he carried, carefully, a small bundle of black silk, tied into a pouch.

"There's a car for us," he said. "Down to the north."

V crossed her arms. "We could have just kept my truck, you know."

Nonchalantly Kholos tossed aside a few handfuls of white barley from his pockets, the white barely with the enzyme, in the direction of the dactyl.

5. Tuskless

Redroot cried out. The sound of his own voice shocked him enough that he lay in the snow for a moment and did not move, did not make another sound. Pain came up from his leg. He blinked, and by blinking realized he could see. The pain was stronger, and he focused on it. *I am still alive*, he thought.

He sat up with a lurch, was amazingly dizzy, and fell back down. His head throbbed. Slowly, again, he sat up. The snow fell off of him, from his face and his out of his mouth and ears and nose, and he shivered from the cold. He glanced down and saw the spot of blood seeping out from around his shin, where his left leg was broken.

"Help," he coughed. His voice was weak as a child's. "Someone, help me."

No answer.

Redroot tried to rise, nearly made it up on his wobbly feet, but his leg buckled and he fell back down. The pain came on in a surge but he focused through it.

"Hello!" he called out. "Fighting First Claws!"

No answer. There was fog and the snow was thick, but there was no wind. He could hear the echo of his own voice off the mountains.

Redroot collected himself.

Slowly, after the dizziness and nausea were under control, Redroot began to move. He did not try to stand again, but instead dragged himself through the snow with his hands, letting his injured leg extend out behind him. The cold helped. After a short stretch he was panting, but he was aware enough to make out his surroundings: overturned cars, the bodies of horses, the bodies of his men, scalped.

Every so often he called out. No answer. Although there was no wind to freeze him, he was not wearing winter gear and his uniform was cold and wet, and he was badly injured. He needed shelter, a fire and some food, and he needed to tend to his leg. He reached a hammer car and pulled himself up and leaned against the metal panels along its flank. The car he had found had been hit, like his command car, with a blast to its nose, and its hood was smacked open and its frame melted into a metal soup. The heat was still in it and Redroot crept close. Snow steamed on top of the engine and ran down as water. He drank.

The windscreen, made of shatterproof plastic, was collapsed back in on where the driver and Televia operator sat. Splotches of their blood were visible against the inside of the windows. Redroot reached up to try the door, bent inwards from the force of an explosion and with its paint peeled and flaked away. It came off in his hand and banged to the ground with a slap. After it came the torso of the comm operator, the body broken and the face flattened. The soldier could not fall completely out of the truck, however, as his legs were mashed under the dashboard, pinned between the seat and the engine.

Redroot yanked at the soldier's body, cursing Pang, Zome, and any other saints he could think of, until it came free with a rip. The soldier lay like a broken doll on the snow, one leg still caught in the truck and the other splayed out on the snow. Redroot knew him, a lieutenant, a Brave who had served with him for years. Redroot grabbed the corpse's earpiece and listened. There was only static.

"This is one," he said raspily. "Any units, respond."

Static.

"Say again, this is one. Any units, respond."

Nothing. Redroot looked out at the world. What did he see?

A mess. Tragedy, failure. He looked down at his broken leg.

Plans, Ute reminded himself. I have plans for myself and for my people.

The pain in his leg making him see spots, Redroot hopped himself up onto the running board of the car. Wireless Televia signals only worked at short ranges, though, so he heard nothing. He cranked the handle, thinking perhaps he might get a signal over the pass, to the nearly-empty base at the pass the Fighting First Claws were supposed to be guarding.

"This is Colonel Ute Redroot, Fighting First Claws," he said, measuredly. "Resistance encountered, requesting relief at following coordinates." He enunciated the numbers of the map grid that corresponded to the location of the Borac camp.

Static. Redroot tried again. "Colonel Ute Redroot here," he sucked in a big breath, then again mentioned the map coordinates, "seem to be having some trouble raising Fort Poncha. Any First Claw units in the region please respond."

He waited. Nothing. Ute dropped the receiver.

He slid himself back out of the car and into the snow, winced when his ankle touched the ground.

This is only an obstacle, he said to himself. He said it out loud, "This is not my fault. I had nothing to do with this. I was daring and I was bold, and I went after this deserter the Chiefs were so afraid of. The rest of this, this was incidental, something to overcome."

He thought of his blood brother's wife. Whom he had married for love.

"This is not my fault," he repeated. "No no no. This is incidental. I did not do this." He tried each on, twice, three times. He shouted it at the sky.

He wept, and then he shouted it again. For a while he stood against the car, staring up into the snowflakes falling into his eyes, like ashes.

You are Colonel Ute Redroot, he told himself. You will be War Chief. You are a leader of your people.

After a moment Redroot limped and leaned his way around to the back of the car. Inside a small lockbox there was a first-aid kit, along with an extra rifle clipped to the lid of the box in two pieces and several clips of ammunition. Ute opened the medkit and took two of the pinkish analgesic pills, then added the stronger stuff in the syringe on top of that. In another compartment there was a set of fatigues, an emergency blanket, and a few days' worth of dried rations.

The drugs wafted through his body. *Not my fault. Only an obstacle.* He wriggled out of his officer's uniform, cutting away the pants to spare his ankle, and put on the dry fatigues. Although he could put no weight on his leg, the pain was not so blinding with the drugs in his system.

When he was dressed he took out the wraps and metal splints from the first aid kit. The leg was impossible for him to set himself but he struggled with it anyway, trying to pound the bones into place, pushing on the swollen parts until he saw spots again and the nausea roiled up in his guts and had to stop. Eventually he simply tightened the splint around the shin, knowing it was not set properly.

Ute looked at the ruins of the Borac encampment. A few of the headlights of the trucks burned dimly on. Limping slowly, keeping his mind clear, he limped forward on his assault-rifle cane.

He found Gyr Zax still alive, moaning softly. The Borac's guts spilled green and yellow and orange out of his belly. His blood was spread out like an evergreen wreath in the snow.

"Where is the deserter?" demanded Redroot.

Gyr Zax looked up at Redroot, the vertical pupils dilated. "He fled," he croaked.

"Which way?" said Redroot.

Gyr Zax did not answer.

Gyr's golden submachine gun was on the ground not far away, within a step of Redroot. The Colonel reached it, huge in his human hands and poked the barrel at Gyr's bursted belly. Green blood trickled out and Gyr Zax cried out.

"That's a god-killing gun," panted Gyr. "You can't just shoot it."

"Which way did he go?"

Gyr Zax looked at him. "I might have handed him over. If you asked."

"No," said Redroot. "You would not have."

Gyr admitted to himself this was probably true. "You attacked. He fled."

"No, no," he said. "You defied the Comanche, and all this is your punishment."

Gyr Zax chuckled, just a bit. The rise in his lipless mouth made Redroot realize there something odd about Gyr Zax's face: the tusks were gone. Only two stumps remained.

Redroot could not stand to be laughed at. "What? Tell me."

"You assume we all think like you," Gyr explained, weakly. "You assume I control my caravan like you control your soldiers. You know one way, and one way only. I could say, with truth, that your own impatience did this. And yet here I am, dying a bad death, all I have done in ruins around me. I was quite prepared to die, just not like this. Not like this at all."

Ute Redroot said nothing.

"Perhaps," Gyr said. "I would ask you to do something, for me. A small thing. A favor from my better."

Redroot aimed his gun at Gyr Zax's head.

"Why should I?"

"Because if you do this, I will tell you where the deserter went."

"What is this thing you want me to do?"

"Feed my saurs, the ones left alive. They must eat the white barely, in the barrels in the red tent. Just spill it all out. There is enough there to last them weeks, probably more as you have killed most of them. Another caravan might pass this way. The dactyls will return. They might all still live. They don't have to all die here."

"And you know where the deserter went?"

"I do. I think."

"So you were protecting him?"

Gyr Zax was close to death. "What I told him, I told him for the Boracs," he tried to explain. "Not for him."

Redroot looked around. The red tent was to the north, where several huge lumps of snow stood that, Redroot assumed, were the bodies of the saurs his rockets had killed.

"Tell me, and I will spill out those barrels."

Gyr Zax had gone blind. He could feel nothing. The Colonel's voice was a whisper. He had a strange memory of his tusks. The thought of their removal was new, somehow, although the memory of the work was old. *This is death, then*, Gyr thought, distantly, *everything of an instant.*

"All right, then," said Gyr. "The deserter fled north, northeast, looking for the Lipstick Country there, where the women's saint can be found. I have heard she has settled on a bay of ice, where no one lives, and she grows peaches that turn to gold. I heard it all on the road."

"St. Theresa? The women's Adonai?"

"Yes. The human's Whoracle."

Ute Redroot looked north. The deserter was his prey. He would not falter.

"Borac," Ute said, suddenly curious. "What happened to your tusks?"

"My tusks?" The anima strings played softly now, but also sweetly.

"They are gone. They looked like they were sawed off."

"I thought you took them. One of your men."

"No," said Redroot. "Not us. We do not loot."

Gyr grinned, a huge toothy smile. And then Gyr Zax the Tuskless, died.

Redroot limped his way through the encampment. His splint held, and he shouldered the assault rifle after replacing it with a broken spear. This served as a much better crutch. He found an attack car still mostly intact, a knife car with a machine gun, and loaded with the standard supplies. Foraging for a little while, he added some provisions from both his own troops and the dead Boracs. He also hoarded several first-aid kits, with their analgesics. Every so often he tried to raise other Fighting First Claws on the Televia, but there was still static, nothing.

By late afternoon Redroot was loaded and the car was warm, its tarp keeping the seats dry. Gingerly he lifted his leg into the car and set his crutch close by. He took another pill.

It did not occur to Redroot to feed the saurs. If he had, he would have seen the white barely already laid out in the troughs before the saurs and stuffed in the feed bags for the dactyls. It was expertly portioned, stirred with just the right amount of water to allow the animals to last a week, perhaps longer, as if a Borac handler had done the work.

6. The Size of the Pin

In the middle of Duran Town's Emergency Services station were three desks, a wood stove where a tin pot of coffee percolated, hurricane lamps in the event the power went off, which was often, and the big box of the Televia machine that allowed the four-strong force of Duran's emergency workers to maintain communication with one another, within limits.

In addition to this industrial-strength Televia there was also a normal, entertainment and information model Televia in the station, which sat on Deputy Byron Bonson's desk. The screen was off. There was a gun rack locked with an old padlock, but with the key in the lock already, where a half-dozen Third Comanche surplus rifles stood. There were maps pinned to the walls between the windows, mostly of early Columbium surveys in the time of General Zebulon Pike, but also a few modern, detailed maps from Third Comanche Geoengineers who worked north and west of Duran at the gas plants. These showed the town and its tiny grid of streets, its attendant farms and ranches, and the purple blotches spreading out like floods—these marked the natural gas deposits that, for the time being, kept Duran Town relevant in any way at all.

In a dusty corner stood a little shrine on an overturned plastic crate. A red figure, also plastic and posed for combat, stood atop the crate. On the figure's face was a grimace and his eyes were narrowed. He was grotesquely muscular, and wore huge metal boots that looked, Kholos thought, a bit like clown's feet except for the nasty spikes on the toes. The figure wielded machine guns in both hands, pointed at some unseen enemy, or perhaps Kholos who stared down at the little plastic man. A pair of truncheons hung from the figure's belt, which was made of interlinked handcuffs. The detail was impressive. A pair of candles stood on either side of the figure, striped candles. They had never been lit. In a paper cup behind the figure in what could have been juice a dead fly floated. A chariot, rested behind the figure on an oaktag stand. One of the wheels was missing and it was propped up with a pencap.

"Who is this?" Kholos asked. Pointing at the little man.

Sherriff Barney Turl looked at the little shrine. "That's Zome," he said. "Saint of soldiers, policemen, jailers. You never went to school? Never learned your saints and such?"

Kholos shrugged his shoulders non-committally. He was thinking he should know who Zome was, should know the name. So many soldiers' skills and memories were in his body.

Turl poured himself another cup of coffee from the pot on the stove. Kholos sat alongside. Turl did not know what to make of this tall, thin, pale, bald man who came walking down the road with a funny gun and seemed to know everyone in town.

A moan from the one occupied cell wafted out along with a stink of sweat and frustration, followed by another curse from Deputy Effa. Kholos looked back at the cell where the female Deputy was attending to someone, clearly ill, on the cot by wiping their face with a wet cloth, holding their hair up in a bunch when the cell's occupant rolled onto their side to puke into the bucket. Turl was surprised when he saw the hurt on Kholos's face as he watched this scene.

Turl was an observant man. "You know Effa Staffa?"

Kholos swallowed. Did not answer. Because how could he?

"Not a drinker?" Turl asked.

"No," said Kholos.

"Those weapons," Turl said, seating himself in this chair. Turl was older, gray hair, a weathered face, but he was fit and trim and knew several ways to break a man's nose from a seated position. His slowness in taking his seat was an act to lure Kholos into thinking he was in charge. "I'm guessing you're a soldier, even if you don't know Zome and his golden machine guns."

"I was. I left."

"I see. A deserter, then."

"That's right."

"May I ask which army?"

"What are my choices?" It seemed such an honest question Turl could not take it as smart talk. Kholos smiled again. It reminded Turl of someone but he could not say who.

"Around here," Turl said, counting off the options with his fingers. "There's Third Comanche, Columbium Militia, Second

Comanche, which I know you ain't already, and I guess these days I would have to include Stalinista, too.

"If you tell me Third Comanche you will have truly ruined my day. If you tell me Columbium Militia I will lock you up and report you for punishment. If you tell me Stalinista then I don't know what I'll do. Because if you're Stalinista? Well. I don't know. I guess I'll go home and shoot my dog or something."

"You think I'm a Stalinista?"

"I don't know what you are." Turl truly didn't. Kholos was white-skinned, like Columbium people. But his face looked like some kind of Republicant statue. His build was thin, muscular. It could be a Comanche body, but so tall Turl might even say he was part Borac. Not really, but still. Humans and Boracs couldn't have children, it was a sin against reason as well as a sin against faith. Pang made that clear.

"Listen, Sheriff Turl," Kholos said. Turl realized that despite being nothing but polite since Deputy Bonson brought him in, the stranger had never called him sir. In fact, he had up to this point called Barney by his first name, like they were old friends. "I believe in a situation like this, you should report me to the local Universitat representative, yes?"

Turl's mind raced. As assassination of Dr. Voss? Crazy Nate Voss? The idea was beyond stupid. Like Stalinista forces walking into a tiny town in the middle of nowhere. Besides, hadn't he been told on the Televia you couldn't ever, in no way at all, encounter a Stalinista alone? King Close himself had reported that.

"I'm not a Stalinista," Kholos said. His face was very serious. "Nor Columbium, or Comanche, or even Republicant or Ebon. The army I've left is not one you've heard of. But I was fighting the Stalinistas, you could say. I fought alongside someone you knew."

Turl licked his teeth. "Go on."

"Michael Staffa," said Kholos. "I knew Michael Staffa. Well."

Turl winced at looked at the cell where Deputy Effa Staffa was still attending to V. To V, who was Michael Staffa's beloved, who drank and drank to try and ease the fact of Michael's death.

"I apologize for my entrance. I've come a long time, I mean a long way, to be here. I'm just very happy to be here, in Duran. Happy to see you, too, Barney Turl. I've heard so much about you, about everything here." Kholos smiled, sincerely, seriously. Turl was sure he recognized the sentiment, just not the face. It was, he admitted, just like Michael to say something like that.

"Michael told me," Kholos lied, in a way, "that when I came here, I should talk to Dr. Nathan Voss. That he could help me. As the Universitat representative, I believe he is in charge here?"

From the outside, the house of Dr. Nathan Voss was different from its neighbors only in that it flew the Universitat flag over the door: an eight-point compass whose points were fishes on a red field. Kholos remembered the flag, noticed it was even more tattered at its edges than he recalled. The house was directly on the Duran square, across from the shops: grocer, guns and supplies, and general dry goods. Both Sheriff Turl and Deputy Effa walked Kholos over. Effa insisted he be cuffed. Turl insisted he wear a coat over his armor and remove his goofy, rusty helmet.

And so they walked Kholos, grinning again at the sidewalk, the sky, the shop signs, around the square. They passed under the old and weathered statue of General Pike, who stood leaning on a glaive and peering westward with one hand raised over his eyes. An explorer, Zebulon Pike had paused at, or at least near, the site of Duran Town long enough to find some fresh water and hire a translator to talk to the established native civilizations in the area. He was, most agreed, the greatest Columbium person ever to walk on the continent, an echo of the high days of the Republicant, before the endless civil wars sent the great nations into decline, and the steady stream of white refugees heading across the ocean.

The temple to Pang, made from white stone and the best-built structure on the square, was next to Dr. Voss' house. This was the church to Pang, the Zero, the always was, the always will be, the Con-cat of Reason and Faith, the central Adonai of the Universitat Pantheon. Pang, the Creator. Kholos wondered why he recognized Pang, but not Zome or St. Theresa or Powder or any other of the Adonai. The doors to the temple were painted the same red as the Universitat flag over Dr. Voss's door, with the fish-point compass in bas relief on the panels.

They brought Kholos inside the house.

Immediately inside, stacked up everywhere, was a strange collection of optometry equipment, loose leaf papers and tattered books, Televia tapes, geological samples from the Asinwatis, a Comanche arrowhead set on a piece of foil next to a fish skeleton, a naval sextant, and an ancient map of the early Republicant. On the walls were pinned a periodic table showing all 88 Universitat-recognized elements, local survey maps, handwritten timelines of Columbium settlement demarcated with different colors of yarn, and various religious and scientific verses which Dr. Voss had appended with notes and observations.

There were also many, many pieces of paper. They were folded into strange shapes and patterns. They rested on top of books on the shelves, on the thick carpet, on seat cushions, on windowsills, atop the boxy, Universitat-use-only Televia. Some papers seemed to take entire sheets, others were just scraps that looked like they had been crumpled, at first, until one looked closely and saw they had been folded dozens of times.

"Morning, Barney, you forget how to knock?" said Dr. Voss as he appeared around the corner, from the kitchen. He was stuffing his shirt into a pair of pants, zipped but as yet unbuttoned. "Effa," with a nod. Then, taking in Kholos from his boots to his cuffs to his beaming, happy smile, "And who are you?"

Dr. Voss's accent was eastern and educated. He was young, especially for a solo Universitat representative, and had black, unkempt hair and curious brown eyes.

Turl spoke before Effa could. "Says he's a deserter, Dr. Voss. But won't say from where."

Dr. Voss was thin. Hairy-knuckled, mostly knees and elbows in his mis-buttoned white shirt and dusty black pants. The only sign of his office was a gold-plated medallion around his neck of the fish-compass. Knowledge and faith, faith and knowledge, feeding on one another, pointing the way. The medallion was tarnished, Kholos noted. On the doctor's face was a bristle of black stubble. His fingernails were stained.

Deliberately, Dr. Voss stared at Kholos. He worked his way up from his boots, to the cuffs around his hands, to the beaming smile, the look of familiar glint in the eyes he had seen where?

Then he went back down again, this time scratching at the stubble on his chin. Finished, at last, Dr. Voss sighed.

"Why is he cuffed? Has he tried to hurt anybody? Did he resist you?"

"No," said Effa. "But he was armed. He had a rifle. And a sword."

"A sword?" Dr. Voss studied Kholos a moment. Thinking, thinking.

Sheriff Turl stared at the toes of his workboots.

"Take them off of him," said Dr. Voss.

Sherriff Turl undid the cuffs with a little key from his pocket. Effa Staffa scowled.

"Do you want me to call him in, Barney?" asked Dr. Voss. "Is that why you brought him here?"

"Actually," said the sheriff. "He asked to come over here. We were just kind of an escort. Up to you whether you call him in or not. I got three cells empty, as of this afternoon. You tell me."

Dr. Voss stared at Kholos a little while.

"Michael Staffa told me to talk to you about a list," said Kholos.

Dr. Voss blinked. Then swallowed. "Barney, Effa, would you mind leaving us alone for a bit?"

"I'm escaping," Kholos said. "Deserting from this existence, if that makes any sense to you. I came here to see if V would come with me. And also because I need your help. Michael believed," Kholos lied directly this time, "that you would assist me."

"Escape this existence. With our V." Dr. Voss listened to Kholos. He seemed to weigh the words carefully. He did not appear shocked. He appeared interested.

"Correct. I'd like your list of Adonai. You know the one I speak of. Also, I have to warn you that my being here puts you in danger. Perhaps I've covered my tracks very well, and I can pass through here completely unnoticed. Or, perhaps I haven't and Duran Town was doomed the minute I walked out of the mountains."

"That sounds dire," observed Dr. Voss.

"It is. You may choose to get on your Televia and contact your Universitat superiors in Caego and tell them about me, although, knowing you, I don't think you will. But if you do contact them, I promise it means the end of Duran Town, one way or another. I also think I should tell you, if you tell Sheriff Turl to put me in a cell, I will not consent. I will also tell you, not as a threat, but just as a fact, Sheriff Turl can't contain me if I don't wish it."

"Not a threat," Dr. Voss repeated.

"No," explained Kholos. "But I won't be locked up. Ever."

Dr. Voss puffed on his pipe. Then he leaned forward and put his hands between his knees. The gesture, Kholos realized, was familiar: Dr. Voss was thinking, thinking hard.

"Michael told you about me? About our talks? About the list of Adonai? Their places of power?"

"He did," Kholos lied again. "We were very close. At the front. He told me everything about you, the town, V. He told me you were his best friend, his teacher. I promised him I would come here, to meet you myself. And he said you would give me the list if I explained it to you."

"I see."

Kholos continued. "Honestly, what happens to Duran Town neither helps nor hinders my plans. But I don't want to see any harm come to you, this place, these people. I'm just here for V, if she'll come. And also to see you, as I said. I consider you a friend," Kholos hastily added, "already."

"You want my list."

"Yes. But I did want to speak with you, regardless," Kholos repeated his lie. "I promised Michael." Meaning, I promised myself.

Kholos sat in one of the chairs, Dr. Voss sat on the couch, the sun from the square coming into the room and showing the dust. A pair of split logs cracked in the stove. The room was warm. Dr. Voss cooked eggs with a kind of gummy, sharp cheese, and then they smoked a pipe and now they sat, and talked. Dr. Voss, all the while, fiddled with pieces of paper. Different sizes of paper, different colors, different shapes. He was constantly folding, creasing, unfolding, and trying again.

Kholos kept looking at the shale samples from the mountains. The destruction of the city was rippling out, still, through time. That morning, the event was unarrived. Kholos wondered when it would come, when the city on fire would lose its name. This man is a scientist, Kholos reminded himself.

Dr. Voss leaned back into the couch. His eyes blinked rapidly and he was almost grinning. "You seem to know me so well. So let's begin there."

"I do know you. Michael told me everything about you."

"Tell me what you know, then."

"I know you were born in Neo Cumae, to a wealthy merchant Columbium family."

"Yes, fine."

"I know that you got into trouble, though, at the Universitat Institute at Caego, for being a little too inquisitive. A little too observant."

"So they sent me here," Dr. Voss completed Kholos's sentence, waving out the window at the square. "For my sins."

Kholos said, "I know you believe it is possible to fly, despite all Universitat teachings and findings to the contrary. I know you watch the stars and try to measure their arcs, which is also against Universitat law. I know you have samples of all different kinds of rocks kept in little vials downstairs in the basement. I know you believe you can calculate the age of the universe if you only knew its size. I know you ascertained Pang would not have given you such a brain if he did not intend for you to use it. I know you also discovered a paradox in Pang's edict about causing no more harm than one would stand to receive. I know, because Michael knew, that you probably would have been a Dean or a Bishop, if you hadn't asked so many funny questions at the Caego Institute."

Dr. Voss laughed. "Yes, perhaps that's true. But only perhaps."

"I know in your first Institute catechism on faith and logic you were presented with the question of how many angels can fit on the head of a pin. You told Michael you did not see any paradox. You asked 'how big is the pin'? And this is where your duality principle stemmed from. Which you believe in to this day, regardless of what they told you at the Institute."

Dr. Voss chuckled again. "Michael told you that story, too? Please, enough."

"He did," Kholos paused. "Dr. Voss, how many of me do you think would fit on the head of a pin?"

Dr. Voss stopped laughing. A silence hung in the room, as several different expressions passed over the face of Nathan Voss. Disbelief. Fear. Wonder.

"You're telling me … what, exactly?"

Kholos nodded. "Michael said you would understand."

"I would understand?"

"I am Kholopatiron, the Liberator pattern. I am beyond your Adonai."

Dr. Voss stopped, and for a long time stared out the window, at the town. He thought about time. About flight. About distance. About walking through the hills and the mountains. There was something wrong with the shale, for example, around Duran. It crumbled for no reason.

He missed Michael Staffa terribly, their talks, Michael's poems. For some reason that pain was eased in the presence of Kholos. Perhaps that was why he trusted him.

"You said you spoke with him," said Dr. Voss. "You said you fought with him against the Stalinistas."

During his student days in the renown halls of the Caego Institute, Dr. Voss had calculated the speed of light using two pencils, a piece of string, and a paper folded six times. Only he did not know this was what he had calculated. For this and other sins against reason he was denied a Professorship and sent to oversee the minds and souls of Duran Town, population about 5,000 and falling. Michael Staffa was his student, his best student, and, later, his best friend.

"I did," said Kholos.

Dr. Voss, still staring out the window, said, "The Universitat teaches that, although faith demands, reason dictates. And so the crux of our education and our calling is to balance these two dual but absolute forces. Faith immovable, reason unstoppable. Do you understand?"

Kholos understood.

"An early part of our training was that we are faced, constantly, with the faith in Pang the Creator and our connection to the Creator's will. This is, says faith, a direct connection: the Creator made *us*, the Creator cares about *us*. The Adonai are here for *us*. This is faith.

"But our knowledge, our logic, it finds this explanation of a direct connection lacking. The universe was not cut from whole cloth: reason proves this. The Universitat then, is the link. The connection is a straight, direct, connection, yes, but it passes through the pure knowledge, the ideal faith, embodied not in us, but in the Universitat. The Universitat is our connection.

"Now you suggest to me, perhaps even prove to me by your presence here, possibly, that there could be entire levels of reality between us and Pang the creator."

Kholos waited. Dr. Voss was still thinking.

Finally, he said, "Honestly, I do not have a problem accepting that you are from one of those higher levels. Why should I? The Universitat, in my experience, is hardly the connection it claims to be. The mystery to me is why would you come here, among us? Why would we even perceive you? It seems more likely you would do work beyond us entirely. We would be ants to you, beneath notice."

"Dr. Voss," said Kholos. "I am, in some ways, greater than your Pang. There are forces and entities above Adonai. And above me. A god above god above god. Shapes beyond your comprehension."

"That's heresy."

"That's a fact."

"The two are often inseparable, I've found. Now you say you want to leave all of it," Dr. Voss paced the room. "So go on."

"If I dance among these stars," Kholos pointed at a chart. "I dance among their stars. I have escaped, Dr. Voss, but I am not free. Truly free." Kholos paused a moment. "Michael made me see this," which was not a lie.

"And you can accomplish this in Duran Town? Here?"

Kholos laughed. "Dr. Voss, I came here to talk to you, to see you. I have the ideas that Michael gave to me. But I need your list. Would any other representative of the Universitat even consider such a request? Would any other admit the list exists?"

"And yet Michael told you. I'm surprised he shared that secret. He must have truly trusted you."

"He did," lied Kholos, again. Then, "It was his idea I seek you out."

"An idea from Michael. He was a dreamer, yes," agreed Dr. Voss. "A poet. He might well react that way to this story."

Kholos continued, "I know you as his friend. I wanted to explain to you what is happening. What it might mean to you."

"What it might mean to me," said Dr. Voss. "An angel, of a sort, sitting in my living room. What might that mean to me? Are you here to perform a miracle of faith? A divine leap of invention? No. You are here for the secret, ever-changing Universitat list and a certain wonderful girl. Michael's girl."

Calmly, Kholos picked up a piece of paper. After taking a deep breath, he folded and creased the paper a few times. Then, staring Dr. Voss straight in the eye, he gently sent the paper through the air. It flew across the room and landed at Dr. Voss's feet without a sound. Dr. Voss' mouth hung open, he swallowed, he gasped, he shook his head.

"Listen to me," Kholos said. "I tell you this as a friend. I was dispatched to destroy the city of Anvir. I did this, but not in the manner ordered. You will notice you have received no news regarding Anvir for some days. You have not thought of this until I just mentioned it, but now the idea is in a shape you can hold. No news from Anvir."

Dr. Voss caught his breath. There had been no news. How could he have not noticed? Hadn't he just read some interesting papers from Anvir? Where had they gone?

"I am hiding in time, Dr. Voss. I may have hours. I may have weeks, or perhaps a month or two, even many years. But then the city you know will be gone, only not in the manner prescribed. Instead of removing it from this vector entirely, I used the city's destruction as an escape hatch, a secret door to get loose among the days. I am in this light, now, and I am hidden here because my entry was disguised by what I did to Anvir. I can be in two places at once, Dr. Voss, I can do two things at once.

"The moment of Anvir's destruction will repeat itself, infinitely and in one place. What external effects this might have on the time in this reality I cannot say. Time does not move in the directions you believe it does. It is not a river. Nor a series of points on a line. It does not move at all. It is like a force, like electricity or gravity.

"But, at last, when the city appears, finally, trapped in its flux state, it will bring the agents of my masters, others like me, down upon this existence. I do not know what they will do. I only know that my actions are echoing even now. Your rocks and powders. I did that."

"Those are hundreds of millennia old. You arrived this morning."

"Exactly," said Kholos. "Listen. There was something my masters were afraid of in Anvir. I don't know what, but I had a mission planted in my mind, and I acted upon it. And now I am running, because I want to be free. And I came here to share all this with you, because Michael wanted that, and to invite V to come with me. Because I want her, desperately. As much, I think, as Michael did."

"And?" said Dr. Voss. "And?"

"And I need your list, your help, to make my attempt."

"You know what the list is? Exactly?"

"The list is the names and locations of the Adonai on this earth. The saints and their domains."

"You know it changes, but that you cannot perceive the change? It can fluctuate at any moment, names and places, they shift, according to the will of Pang. It is my compass, as the representative here, to know what Pang wants of us, to know what he offers us. It is not a document to be shown, let alone lent. Let alone given away."

"I know. I do not ask this lightly."

"But how will it help you? From day to day the names and places may change. Only Pang is the constant, and he is not on the list!"

"Dr. Voss," said Kholos. "There is a way, on earth, to reach heaven. I have to find that way to escape. There are," Kholos paused, trying to think how to explain. "There are machines, engines, that stitch together realities. I need to reach one, just for a moment. To cut a hole into reality beyond their control."

Dr. Voss thought. Time as a wave function. There were advanced classes at Caego, lectures you had to attend in secret. Rumors about how matter was a wave. Electromagnetism was a particle. Sin could be split, went one story, to release to power of the stars. But first you had to refine the sin.

Could time be cut and spliced, like threads in a tapestry?

"What would it mean for this world," Dr. Voss asked, his mouth dry, "if you succeeded."

"Knowledge," said Kholos, he pointed at the paper on the floor he had tossed.

"Why here?" Dr. Voss demanded. "Why now? Is this time and this world so crucial to the plans of the gods? I am, by most measures, a failure. And yet you visit me? In Duran Town?"

"Blame Michael," said Kholos. "He believed you were special."

Dr. Voss stared at the paper that flew across the room.

"Don't decide now," said Kholos. "I can come back and collect the list from you years from now."

7. Am I Terrible?

Most Columbium women, whether in the wealthy cities of the Northeast or the impoverished towns of the west, kept a small shrine to St. Theresa in their homes. St. Theresa represented many things. There was need, desire, passion, drama, love. Also, warmth, the hearth, the home, the table. She also, somewhat, embodied the martyr and the matron. Sculptors and painters showed her as a dark-skinned woman, curvy and beautiful, with long, strong legs and long hair. Most showed her wearing a long skirt and a sheer blouse over full breasts. Traditionally she received oranges, chocolate, knives, and lengths of ribbon at her altars.

At the tabletop shrine in her house on the north edge of town, V left the woman's saint overturned shot glasses and apple peels. Once in a while, she lit a scented candle as well, but not often. Mostly she drank and stared at the ceramic figurine, and cried while she waited to feel nothing.

Kholos came to V's house his first night in Duran.

It was a cheap, thin-walled trailer with a flat roof, white-washed, set up on blocks with steps leading to a front door. The divisional flag of the Orang Militia, Michael's unit, flew from a pole set in concrete inside an old tire. Outside the front door V's truck was parked. Kholos noted the gun rack, and the antlers stuck on the hood. From inside behind the plastic over the windows the house was dark.

Kholos walked up the steps and opened the door. He knew the place intimately, felt as though he practically lived there, as in a way he had. The door was open, and by the twirling starlight outside Kholos could see her in the little parlor. She was sitting next to her shrine to St. Theresa, a bottle of Black Bison bourbon in one hand drunk down through the neck.

"V," he began.

In her other hand she had a pistol. She fired. The doorframe splintered behind Kholos's right ear.

"Get the hell out of my house!" V fired again. She missed wildly.

"Stop it!" Kholos said. "You'll hurt someone!"

"Oh yeah," shouted V. "I guess you're right." As she fired again Kholos ducked and rolled nimbly through the door into the kitchen, which was separated from the parlor and the shrine, and V, by a small half-wall. He noticed there were dirty dishes piled in the sink, a moose steak thawed out on the counter but uncooked that, he sniffed, might have been out a day or two too long. Breathing in the smell of the house, the light on the pine panels of the walls, the buzz of the old Comanche-made icebox, Kholos felt a sudden surge of nostalgia. He had walked naked through these rooms, shouting poetry. He had cut squash and baked a cake at this counter. He had sat and talked and talked and talked to his V in this house.

She was coming around the corner. He heard her put the bottle down on the counter with a clink. When she came into the kitchen Kholos rose, slowly, as V aimed the gun at his face. With no effort at all Kholos grabbed it by the barrel and tugged it away from her, yanked her to him, and embraced her.

Just held her, smelled her hair.

At first V kicked and slapped and scratched but Kholos held on, and, soon, she went limp against him. He made no other move, just held onto her. Then, softly at first, she began to cry. Kholos held on. Her tears were hot against his chest, and Kholos was glad Sheriff Turl and Deputy Effa had insisted he leave his armor and weapons at the station, or he would not have been able to feel this. When she had settled somewhat she looked up at him.

Kholos called her by her full name. It was like a key. Her face opened.

"Who are you?" she breathed. "What are you doing here? Why do I feel this way?"

"I am Kholopatiron," Kholos said. "The liberator. I'm escaping this reality. I love you. Desperately. Come with me."

V, neither accepting nor struggling against Kholos's arms, reached behind her for her bottle.

They sat on the floor in the kitchen. The night grew cold but neither moved to close the shot-up door or feed the fire in the wood stove. Kholos sat in the lotus position. V held her knees to her chest. Light from the night sky came in through the window over the sink.

"I'm not Michael," Kholos said. "I'm Kholos."

"No," said V. "You're not Michael. Michael died in a trench fighting the Stalinistas. They sent Dr. Voss a card."

She was fit, strong, lean. A little streak of early gray ran through her dark hair, and her face was long, narrow, finely featured but weathered around the eyes from all of the time spent outdoors. She had long strong legs and hands with delicate but calloused fingers. V made her living as a guide for Comanche engineers and geologists, Comanche tourists out to hunt big game, Comanche students out to experience rural, impoverished life for a week or two. She could knit and sew, she could butcher her own meat, she could shoot the tail off of chipmunk at 100 paces. She could not, would not accept the death of Michael Staffa, her lover, her fiancée, her poet.

In a wooden box Michael had carved from a single piece of ash--the hardest wood--V kept the poems Michael had written her, rolled them up and tied them each off with string. V told herself this man sitting like some kind of foreign Universitat mentor in her kitchen was not the man who wrote her those poems. But this man could recite them all.

"He told you all that?"

"He did," said Kholos.

"Just in case?"

"Something like that."

She sighed.

"I'm not coming with you," she said at last. "It's crazy."

"Alright," said Kholos. He rose and without a look back stepped towards the door.

"Wait," said V. "Wait. You tell me you come across time to find me, you risk everything, and then you walk out? Just like that?"

Kholos looked back at her. "I will force no one to do anything, unless they hinder me in some way. I came here to bring you with me. But if you do not want to come with me, I respect your decision. Every moment I wait here could bring pursuit."

"Just," V said, "just wait a moment. Sit back down. Like a regular person."

"What for?"

"Because I like the way you smell, ok? Sit down. Because I miss him, alright? And you knew him so well, I guess. As well as I did, almost, it seems. Pang, maybe more."

Kholos sat back down. V, however, stood up, turned on a little lamp, and closed the front door, as best as she was able. After looking at the damage she had done she sighed again.

Then, without a glance at Kholos, she began to clean up the kitchen. First the moose steak went into the trash, then she turned on the water in the sink and started to scrub the dishes. She wondered why exactly the hell she was doing any of this. But it felt right.

"Now tell me," she said. "You would be escaping where, exactly?"

"Out of this reality. This existence. There is a way. I know it."

"But if I like this reality?"

"You like this reality?" Kholos asked, honestly.

"Sure," said V. "I like to hunt. I like to sew. I like to work on my truck. I like to get my hair done, when I can afford it. I like to make nice clothes for myself. I like the mountains. I like it fine here." She started to say, as long as Michael was here, but stopped. She surprised herself by not reaching for her bottle of Black Bison. After the dishes were clean she heard her stomach grumble and realized she had not eaten since the day before.

"It's fine here," she mumbled. To herself she added, so long as Michael was here.

"Michael's not coming back," Kholos said.

Rummaging around in a near-bare cabinet for some corn meal V turned on Kholos. "Stop that! You're not allowed to know me that well." She poured some of the cornmeal into a bowl and began to add a pinch of salt, a dash of sugar, bacon for fat. With Kholos still on the floor she stepped around him and stirred the fire inside her stove, added a log. The house began to warm.

"I know he's not," V said. Her voice cracked. "I know he's not. I just don't know why. Why? Why Michael? He wasn't a soldier. I could have gone. I would have survived. I would have come home to him. It makes no sense. No sense at all, that this had to happen." The tears streamed down her face. She looked at the bottle and took a deep breath. "Why am I telling you this? I'm not coming with you. You're crazy. You can't kill the Adonai. You can't fight the Universitat. And you sure can't bring Michael back. Go away already."

Again, Kholos rose and stepped for the door. V looked at the bottle. She looked at Kholos's back.

"Kholos!" V shouted.

He stopped. He turned.

"I don't know you," she said, weakly. "But I feel like I should. I feel like I want to. Help me get there?"

"You'll have to hurry," Kholos said. "I don't know how much time I have. This may have already happened another way."

They ate the cornbread with beans on trays in the living room. Kholos remembered the taste but had not actually eaten this dish, and his eyes rolled back into his head in ecstasy and he groaned as the buttery flavor cascaded along his tongue. V laughed, proud, even a little, just a little, happy.

They did not leave the house for three days. Deputy Effa, who made twice-daily visits, was furious, then curious, then finally relieved when she saw the color in V's face, smelled the cooking smells, noticed the rugs had all been cleaned, and saw the elk hide tanning on its rack in the gravel of the backyard.

"I don't know what to make of him, myself," Effa said to V as she left on the third day. "But he's good for you."

"I know," said V. "Am I terrible?"

"No," said Effa. "You couldn't be. It's not in you. And like I said, it feels, it feels alright, somehow. I know this is crazy, but he reminds me of Michael, sometimes. The way he looks at you. The way he talks to me. Is that terrible?"

V did not answer. They stood outside in the gathering cold and dark.

"He wants me to leave with him," said V. She did not mention the saints. She didn't see the point. Leaving was leaving.

"I heard," said Effa. Then she hugged V and walked down the steps.

8. Who Decides This Crap?

The fifth day after Kholos arrived in Duran Town the Second Comanche attacked.

It was again a cold morning, so when Byron Bonson did not report back in over the Televia Sheriff Turl did not think too much of it. Instead once Deputy Larmar came in from his rounds up through the north side of town, Turl sent him out again to make sure Bonson was alright and not stuck in a ditch somewhere. These patrols took the deputies in a roughly 10 kilometer radius around the town, and mostly involved looking in on those Duran Town residents who had small farms or cabins up in the foothills of the Asinwatis or provided various services to the Third Comanche engineers and miners to the north. Rare was the patrol that encountered anything at all.

So when Deputy Larmar called in to report that he had found Bonson's truck abandoned and riddled with arrows in the tires, blood in the cab, and a smashed windshield, Sheriff Turl immediately went to Dr. Voss and his direct-link Televia.

"Call for help, Nathan, we got Second Comanche to the south," Barney Turl was carrying a shotgun, fully loaded.

Dr. Voss put the earpiece to his head and held the mouthpiece in his hand. The Televia fuzzed and hissed. Dr. Voss turned a tuning dial, but could locate no response.

Dr. Voss put the mouthpiece down. He looked at Barney Turl and shook his head.

"Pang damn!" said Turl.

"They might pass us by," said Dr. Voss. "They might not even know we're here."

"Yeah," said Turl. "Except they already got Byron Bonson and probably Luth Larmar."

"Oh, no," said Dr. Voss. "Not Byron and Luth."

"And they might also be a thousand strong and just waiting for night to fall. Who's left in town that can fight?"

Dr. Voss knew his town. Stumbling over his furniture he reached a dusty file cabinet and began to rifle through his records. As he thumbed through each page he mouthed "militia" over and over. Sheriff Turl began to pace.

Dr. Voss said, "Farmers, mostly. A couple guides. V, Effa, of course. Everybody else went to fight the Stalinistas."

Turl nodded. "I'm sending Effa down south, tell her to get everybody she can into town. We'll barricade a few streets, make a stand here in the square."

"I'll go see the Comanche at their mines, maybe they can help us."

"I was going to do that myself, but you're right, they might listen more to you, being you're the representative and all. Pray to King Close they've got a working Televia line up there, even. Not that troops at the fort could help us in time. I'll set up a hospital at the station. Then we either beg Pang they pass us entirely by or we pay off Zome so we kill enough of them they think twice."

V was the best shot in town so she took the center of the line, on the edge of the barricaded square, facing to the south of the town. It was not much of a barricade: a few cars and trucks and boxes, stretched end to end, manned by hunters and guides and the few able-bodied young men not taken to fight the Stalinistas. All told, they were perhaps 100 strong, all under General Pike's stone gaze. Dr. Voss, despite his pleading, cajoling, and shaming, had succeeded only in a thank you for the warning from the Third Comanche engineers, who then promptly shut down the gas lines into town, so all the street lamps went dark. Their own Televia lines were dead as well, Voss noted. And that was to the north of town. Up in the mountains.

Before the sun set the smoke from the fires of the farms and homes the Second Comanche had already attacked formed thin dark lines on the horizon. Effa Staffa, perhaps the bravest person in Duran Town, was still out there, trying to reach as many of the scattered citizens as she could. A trickle of scared farmers and their families had come into town all day, telling of stampedes through their fields and the slaughter of their livestock. They also reported the Second Comanche had rifles, not just bows and spears, but real rifles that shot some kind of blue electricity. Sheriff Turl looked south through a pair of Third Comanche binoculars. Dr. Voss, already in surgical scrubs, stood next to him. The sun set, suddenly, and the southern horizon was a soft glow of burning fields.

"Come on, come on," said Sheriff Turl. "Get home, Effa girl."

Dr. Voss put his hand on the Sheriff's shoulder.

"Oh, Pang," said the Sheriff. "Oh Pang damn it. V? You see this?"

"I see them," said V, looking through the ancient brass scope on her big-bore hunting rifle. "I see her."

Sheriff Turl raised the glasses to his face again. Effa Staffa, an arrow in her shoulder and one hand on the wheel of her dented and dinged white emergency truck, was racing on three tires for the town. The fourth tire had been shot out and her truck limped and jerked its way forward. Behind her, stretching from lens to lens of the binoculars in a single, whooping line, came a horde of Second Comanche raiders. A thousand, fifteen hundred maybe, strong. They were gaining on Effa.

With the glasses back to his eyes Turl could see sparks on the truck where Comanche shots struck it. Second Comanche weren't supposed to use rifles. This was all wrong. Who would give Second Comanche rifles?

The windshield of the truck had been shot out entirely and hung in a flap over the hood, allowing Turl to see the blood spattered there. Effa was fighting the busted tire, hard, with her good arm.

V aimed, fired. A brave went tumbling down under hoof as she reloaded. Hers was the only gun on the line with a scope, the others could see the dust cloud, the fire glow, and the single truck, but nothing else.

Kholos, calmly, stepped in beside Dr. Voss.

"And what do you want?" Dr. Voss snapped. "Did you bring this on us? Get your silly gun, do something."

"Dr. Voss," Kholos asked, very seriously. "Do you want me to end this? I can. I make this never happen."

"Of course I do."

"Wait, understand me," Kholos continued. "If I fight, I can promise you none of your townspeople will be hurt. Byron Bonson. Luth Larmar. Effa. All of the farms untouched. But there will be consequences. To fight will be to reveal myself, immediately. I do not know what might happen. You could all vanish in a blink. But I don't want this to happen, either. I don't want Effa to die. I don't want any of you to be hurt."

Dr. Voss paused and thought. He did not take long.

"Kholos, we are all dead anyway if you don't do something." Dr. Voss was pointing at the temple to Pang and the school, waving people inside. "They'll burn the town to the ground. You say you were so close to Michael, well they've just about killed his sister. And they've already killed some of his friends. So go on and save us."

Kholos nodded. Then he closed the visor on his helmet.

On the line V ordered everyone to fire. She was killing Second Comanche as quickly as she could, picking off the ones closest to Effa as they rushed forward on their foaming horses. The raiders were a wave, coming on all at once, ten, twelve deep, hollering and whooping the Shoshone war cries. The rifles popped and sparked. Firing his heavy pistol Sheriff Turl stood atop a pile of cornmeal sacks pocked with arrows and aimed at distant shadows, hitting nothing but feeling better for the trying. Between shots he lifted the binoculars to his face. Effa Staffa was slumped over the wheel, probably already dead, the truck chugging along without guidance towards the town like an announcement for the proper destruction to begin. Sheriff Turl saw headdresses, white war paint on angular faces, handprints on the necks of palomino ponies, and rifles tied round their furniture with beads and silver chasing. He fired again. A bullet struck him and knocked him onto his back with a thud and a yelp. Dr. Voss was with him in an instant, stuffing gauze onto the wound.

"Pang damn," Sheriff Turl shouted. "Why did all this crazy shit have to happen? Who decides this crap?"

"Shut up, Barney," said Dr. Voss. "Just hang on."

Barney Turl bled out through a hole in the back of his neck. The last thing he saw was a star.

Then the star closed the visor on his helmet.

The star began to fall. It was pure white, so bright it lit the plains and the town and even the slopes of the Asinwatis many kilometers distant. The men and women along the barricade shaded their eyes. The Second Comanche's whoops grew suddenly softer, then silent. The star grew larger, brighter, faster. The star was happening, before it fell. The star was always there. Had always been there. A roar of thunder cracked.

"Oh, little town of Duran," said Kholos.

Down the barrel of his rifle Kholos sited the plain. The scope of his gun traversed not only distance but time: it saw where a target would be and where they had been. A blue bullet fitted in the chamber, his armor no longer rusty but shining pure light. His canisters were open, a touch. He was flying, flying parallel to then, on an updraft of particles, against time.

Kholos fired. The bullet whispered its trajectory backwards through the hours, struck the weave of reality the Second Comanche occupied, and froze it all, every particle, every second, under a fine crystalline lattice extending infinitely through the seven unseen dimensions. Kholos spread his white hot wings wide across the sky. They seemed to stretch, impossibly, from the mountain peaks to the far oceans. They made shapes of impossibility.

Kholos slung his rifle over his shoulder and drew the sword.

He attacked.

Every last Comanche was not killed. They were removed from existence. Every horse was dispatched to a primal state of being, particles separated and that particular possibility amputated from all realities. Every bow and rifle and spear broken, reverted. On his wings Kholos flashed from point to point, slashing once, twice, finished. It was a shower of gold. It was a singularity.

And so Kholos murdered the day, completely.

As Kholos descended, and his light and his glory exuded through the cosmos for all eternity, the galaxy-clock machines of the Celestial City of the Atherian detected the faint beat of a heart out of time. A dot, a blip, on the pure intelligence of the Aetherian observers, registered plainly. Location and speed, measured simultaneously. This instant. This iota.

Listen, said a Borac, somewhere long, long ago: here is a string that plays out of tune.

Gears construed of nebulae ticked.

Patterns brought to bear, experiences harvested like grain. Matter/anti-matter cauldrons.

Scalpels of quivering quarks performing surgery on the laws of physics.

A measured cost of time and space. Stitch, stitch, stitch, snip.

Then, almost with a sigh, the stars turned.

Kholos landed. His wings vanished, but his armor held a pure whiteness in each plate that was hard to look at directly. Duran Town was fast asleep, midnight of the eve before. Kholos saw the shapes of mad things at work in the sky, the frayed ends of existence dangling from the carvings of stars.

The next morning, no the same morning, V awoke. She felt wonderful. She wanted to run, she wanted to make love, she wanted to cook and clean, she wanted to hunt and cook. In the darkness she clawed at Kholos next to her in bed, and they rolled and kissed and tussled up all the sheets. V felt electric. Her muscles were fast and strong. Her skin so tight when Kholos touched it she could sense the vibrations of his fingers. And then they did it all again, backwards forwards and upside down. She felt she knew everything. She felt everything was new.

"What a beautiful day," she whispered to her window.

As the sun rose V went into the washroom to brush her teeth. Pulling her hair back from her face she noticed the wrinkles were gone from the corners of her eyes. Then she noticed the gray was gone from her hair.

"Kholos?" she said. "Look what's happened to me! It's crazy!"

Kholos studied her a moment, weighed her breasts. Looked into her eyes. Stroked her hair.

"V," he said. "What is the name of the city on the other side of the mountains?"

"That place has been burning for ages," V answered, with the certainty of teenager. "Nobody ever knew its name."

Already they were working to track him.

"I have to leave," said Kholos. "Will you come with me, or not?"

9. Lipstick Country

They stayed on the Universitat highway, away from the burning city, heading north. V remained twelve or so years old for three straight days. Kholos ground his teeth.

"Let me drive a while," she said.

"Tomorrow," answered Kholos. "If you're older."

"I can drive, you know," she said. "I'm probably a better driver than you. I haven't forgotten how to drive."

As if in support the attack car bucked as Kholos upshifted. He had broken down the machine gun and left it behind them in the wreck of the Borac caravan and stretched a white tarpaulin over the crossbar for a roof. In the back of the car, where the machine gun had been placed, were the backpack and his rifle and sword. From the Boracs Kholos had taken only water and food, but from the Third Comanches he had taken a sidearm for V, winter fatigues, and a better-stocked first-aid kit. As they headed north the weather normalized and they wore the hooded wool greatcoats of Comanche officers as the cold came on.

"What will we do when we run out of gas?"

"Walk."

"Meh." V answered. "Can I carry my gun, at least?"

"When you are older."

"You *know* I'm a better shot than you are. You *know* it. I've taken down goats from almost a kilometer away. Ask Effa Staffa."

"Were you twelve when you did this?"

"Meh."

The Universitat highways criss-crossed the Columbium continent in long paved slashes that divided the land into nine segments. Three of the highways ran east-west, with enormous iron truss bridges and deep diving tunnels spanning whatever lakes or rivers or mountains stood in their way. Three other routes ran north-south. Each cut across the continent equidistant from one another. They were, somehow, perfectly maintained and always safe, wide enough and sturdy enough for a saur to tromp on. They were considered a miracle, an instance where faith and reason came together in harmony, which was the ultimate stated goal of the Universitat.

This was also how the Universitat justified their approval of the Stalinistas slow, inevitable conquest of the world.

Beyond the pavement were local roads: Comanche and Columbium across the midwest and west, Iroquois in the northeast, Cherokee to the southeast, and, far to the northwest, Inuit.

"Do we know where we're going?" asked V.

"Northeast. There is a bay of ice, the list says the Adonai is there. Gyr Zax confirmed as much."

"The list," said V. "I thought you said you didn't have the list when we left?"

"That's right. I will go back and collect it, later. At least, potentially. I have it now."

"Right. So we just drive for a while, turn northeast sometime, and we'll run right into her."

"Something like that. We'll probably run out of gas first."

"Meh."

"Please stop saying that. It doesn't mean anything. Curse Pang, if you want to. Probably he deserves it."

They went on for a while longer in silence. Kholos thought how when V was ancient and demented, he loved her the same as if she was one of her many younger selfs. But as an adolescent, he had to remind himself he loved her.

The Universitat taught all children across the world. Comanche, Stalinista, Zu, Ebon, Republicant, all of them attended Universitat schools and were given their lessons in theology, literature, technology, history, ethics, logic, morality, and all the rest. The highways, which were also present on every other continent, were presented as one of the great gifts of the Universitat.

Along with steel, the combustion engine, the Televia in all of its forms, and penicillin, and also along with the spiritual gifts of the saints and their domains, the highways were evidence of the Universitat's love of knowledge and progress for all. Dr. Voss, V remembered, had personally given the lecture to their classes back in Duran. Trade goods, news, ideas, he had said, could all flow quickly and safely along the highways. Michael Staffa had asked, V also recalled, how the highways worked, when they were built, why they went straight through instead of around. Dr. Voss had smiled and nodded at the questions, but had not answered. V remembered all this. She remembered everything about Michael.

Kholos looked at her. Her eyes were wide, a child's eyes no matter how much she might wish otherwise.

"What?"

V looked away. "Forget it."

At night they camped alongside the highway. They built a small fire from sticks they collected, V cooked with their meager rations, and they slept cuddled together under the tarpaulin, still wearing their coats against the cold. In the morning V would chip the ice from the top of the water jug for coffee, they would wash, eat some of the nuts and dried fruits they carried, and then be off.

There were little roads off the highway that led to small Columbium towns for the first couple of days north and V argued that they should go and get more supplies, more fuel. Kholos insisted they not. He knew the agents of the Aetherian were after him.

He had, to save Effa, Dr. Voss, all of Duran Town, announced his place in space and time. His velocity and his position, simultaneously. His decision to retrieve the tusks of Gyr Zax offered another clear sign, although that was not so blatant. Constantly as they drove Kholos swept the sky, narrowing his eyes whenever a cloud of a particular shape floated by overhead. The hours unspooled like the asphalt. Distance spun away.

On the morning of their third day of travel they exited Columbium territory and entered an unclaimed zone. A wooden sign written in Inuit and Columbium lettering stated that the next nearest settlement was some 2,000 kilometers away to the northwest. A dirt road cut out left into a pine forest next to the sign. The highway, unheeding, stretched on north before them. The land was cold, dry, spotted with trees and tundra in all directions. Patches of snow and brownish grass, white rabbits. Kholos paused and turned off the engine, stepped out and stretched his legs. The body was familiar in ways he did not expect but the requirements of his muscles and joints were all knew to him. His knee still ached where he had been shot.

They had passed nothing but two trucks for all of their last day, heading south.

"It's time to turn off," Kholos said.

"How do you know that? You may notice there is no road to the northeast."

"I could be wrong. But we are turning off."

"We're going to run out of gas. Soon."

"I know."

"Meh!"

Built for combat, the car did well on the broken terrain, crossing streams and small rivers, skirting the banks of big lakes. They clunked and jostled their way over half-blazed trails, pausing often for Kholos to clear the way or widen the path with his sword, slicing through tree stumps and even boulders. There was much mud despite the increasing cold, many fast little rivers to ford. Sometimes they found a bridge, left behind from some timber trail. Sometimes they had to drive for hours to find shallows. They were carefully traversing a stream of silvery cold water with bits of ice flowing along its surface when V pointed out they had only a quarter tank of gas left.

"Are we close, at least?"

Kholos did not answer. He was upshifting and rocking back in forth on the far bank of the stream, trying to gain traction. They were in another patch of pine trees and the air smelled of the sap. Snow had fallen the night before and it melted in crystal drops and made the forest look like a kaleidoscope. The tires spat up arcs of clay. The white claws on the doors of the car were completely obscured with dust and grit and mud.

Maps of the known world were incomplete. The Universitat was responsible for geography and cartography, of course, and taught both subjects at their many Institutes of Highest Learning. Local knowledge of the surrounding landscape was always available, and there were good maps of the Columbium territories and the Incorporated Nation, the Eastern regions as well. There were also empty places on the maps. The peak of the world, for instance, was simply a white circle on most globes.

Kholos was sifting through his memories, trying to see if he had any knowledge of this area. Some glance at a Universitat-only globe. He did not.

The premise, Dr. Voss had explained, was that the needs of a community, a city, a nation, humanity itself, could and did shift. Therefore, the foci of worship would change with them. It was a gift from Pang, the Universitat taught, this shifting collection of deities, each with their specific domains. The local Deans were educated in the miracle but even they would not perceive the changes. The lists themselves were linked, through a miracle of faith and reason, to some impossible place. It was all the same list, they were taught, somehow. The Deans and Bishops would remember the list as it appeared before them. There had to be some constants, though, as pilgrimages were allowed, even encouraged in some cases.

Kholos and V lurched free of the mud and moved on.

V was rambling on, complaining about something new.

"Kholos, are you listening to me?"

"No."

"Well, I asked if I could die. Not that you seem to care."

"Nothing dies." Kholos did not tell her how the Aetherian might harvest her, might trap the light of her existence in their folds and creases for their own uses. As they had done to Michael Staffa. As they would do to him, if they caught him. "Everything is happening all at once, forever, all together. Only your mind cannot perceive the shape of it. Mine cannot either, honestly."

"I mean because I'm Fractured," V continued. "What if tomorrow I was so old that I just died? Could that happen?"

Kholos had not thought of this.

"I mean," V said. "Could I wake up really sick one day? Or wake up pregnant? Or blind? We really don't know, do we? We didn't go to any of the Universitat camps, of course. They might have told me."

"It won't matter, when we leave this existence. You'll be yourself, truly yourself. You'll see."

"But what if it happens before then?"

Kholos looked at her. His gaze was as strong as his voice. "Then I would find you, and I would bring you back."

V swallowed. "Kholos," she muttered.

"It's alright," he reassured her. He studied the shape of her face, so young and bright.

"Kholos!"

As they were not going very fast, the impact of the car into the tree did little more than jar them in their seatbelts. It did buckle in the hood of the car, however. A pile of snow fell from the branches down onto them and steamed where it hit the heat of the engine. The block was cracked. Kholos sighed.

"You should have let me drive," said V.

V was a baby the next morning, perhaps one-year-old. Kholos, after making a diaper for her out of one of the emergency blankets, swaddled her in the brown dress and carried her across his chest. She cried most of the morning, but then slept through the afternoon. Through the snow, Kholos tromped on, heading northeast. He could control the temperature of his body to a degree, and the cold did not affect him terribly. He worried for V, however. He took off his breastplate and carried it on his back to keep her close against his chest.

Snow began to fall heavily in the evening. A thin skim of ice had formed on the stream where Kholos went for water, and he could see his breath. V, ruddy-cheeked and grinning and drooling, coughed up on his chest. Kholos kissed the top of her fuzzy head.

"Not so tough now, are you?" he teased.

"Coo," said V.

That night Kholos consulted the list. It told him St. Theresa, the saint of hearth, home, and bed, was located on the edge of the Vandermeer Bay, which was a huge body of water to the northeast that had never been properly mapped.

The next day V was perhaps twenty or twenty-five, with her body perfect and responsive. They paused, twice, to make love on beds of soft fallen pine needles, their parkas open and their bodies warm underneath. The smell of the sap stayed with them all through the day and V would smell it on her fingers and in her hair with a smile. She was slightly older the next day, then a little older still the day after that, maybe forty or forty-five. Kholos cut their rations by a third, then by half. On the seventh day after they left the highway, twelve days since they left the ruins of Gyr Zax's caravan, they were down to handfuls of nuts and a little jerky. They rested. The air was cold, cold, and snow, more snow, was falling.

"What will we do tomorrow?" V asked. She was teenaged, perhaps seventeen or eighteen. She had a great deal of energy and her thoughts were inquisitive, eager. She also wanted a great deal of food, more than they had left. "Or the day after that?"

"We might find the place we're looking for before tomorrow," Kholos reminded her.

"And if we don't?" V asked. It was intellectual, not accusatory.

"Don't think that way."

They had been resting on the banks of a stream, seated on some rocks to catch the warming rays of the sun. Kholos was cleaning his rifle, counting out his many colored bullets. Next to him on the rock was his sword.

"I'm serious," V insisted. "I don't want to starve to death."

"You won't," said Kholos. "I promise. I'd feed you the muscle off my bones if I had to."

"Ew."

The next day they ate the last of their supplies. V was old but could still walk on her own, although she stepped very slowly because of pain in her hips. They climbed a little ridge before sunset, the snow piling up now almost to their knees. Soon, they understood, the weather would turn so cold no Comanche winter gear could protect them. The first blizzard of true winter could arrive at any moment.

At night there were no silver slashes across the sky, clouds covered everything, but it was, thankfully, still.

"I'm hungry," said V.

Kholos did not answer. He was trying to watch the clouds.

"I want a sandwich. A pork sandwich, fresh, from Mrs. Mosha's bakery, on the square."

Kholos looked northeast. Even with the lack of starlight, he could make out a single high hill there. They were close to water, he thought. Perhaps the great bay. And when they hit the shores of that bay? Go north or south? There was no way to know.

V could almost taste the bread, still warm, in her mouth. She could smell the ovens, the way the warmth spilled out into the square. She could taste it, the sliced roll with the folded pork and the horseradish spread, perhaps a little crisp lettuce too. She closed her eyes. She wanted food, warmth, safety. She wanted a pork sandwich on fresh bread and her bed at home, with the old quilt with its worn patches. A proper pillow. She was hungry. She was tired. She desired. She closed her eyes. The fire was warm and crackling.

Kholos said, "V, look."

V opened her eyes. In her hand was a pork sandwich, the bread steaming hot. A little horseradish sauce spilled out onto her lap. Around her shoulders, wrapped snugly, was the quilt from her bed. Behind her, settled neatly under the tarpaulin, was her bed itself, the pillows fluffed and the blankets pulled back, except for the quilt obviously.

"A miracle," said V.

"I think we're close," said Kholos.

V ate her sandwich.

A biting wind blew into Kholos's face and, even through the good winter boots V had packed for him, his feet were cold. There was nothing else for miles, just the woods and cold marshes behind them, now covered thick with fresh snow, and the bay before them, stretching out forever. Shipless.

V was perhaps forty-five or fifty, mature in her face and her body and her mind, with a streak of gray in her long hair Kholos found rather attractive. There were little wrinkles at the corner of her mouth and her eyes and she seemed, Kholos thought, shorter somehow.

Then there was the hill. There was no way over that Kholos could see. The hill rose almost straight up from the dark sands along the shore of the ice-covered bay. It climbed up fairly high, perhaps twenty or thirty meters, and extended out into the bay by about a third of its circumference. The thing made no sense, but then he had not expected it to.

As Kholos tromped around the hill, pawing it and pushing at it looking for a purchase, V stood back and watched. Her hands, in the heavy wool mittens she had knitted, were folded before her and her face was low against the wind. She looked almost as if she was praying to Pang, or another of the Adonai, maybe even St. Theresa herself.

The walls were impossibly lush and blooming: green ivy and bright blossoms streamed down from its top. The smell of peaches and perfume was everywhere. But, even after they had spent all of the morning walking around to the place where the water met the southern edge of the hill, there was no way in, out, or up. Kholos tried to grab ahold with a fistful of vines and climb to the top, but the vines came down on top of his head followed by a rain of flowers and he fell onto the pebbles. When he looked where he had yanked the vines down, Kholos saw only more vines and more flowers, not the hard rock he knew had to be underneath there somewhere. Kholos put his bare hand against the side of the hill. It was warm.

A few fat snowflakes fell. Kholos looked up into the clouds, back at the hill, and sighed. "We should make camp," he said. "Perhaps you can wish us more food."

V smiled at him. It was indulgent and wise, like she was smiling at a child.

"In the morning I'll try and throw our rope up, perhaps I can scale it that way," he was looking up the side. "There must be a ridge or a lip up there somewhere." He looked at V. "What? Do you want to try?"

"Not to climb it, no," said V. "But I would like to go inside. I imagine it's warm in there, at least. I imagine there is plenty to eat."

Kholos pointed at the summit of the hill. "And you will what? Fly? The walls are slick and smooth. There is no crevice or gate that I can find. We have to find a way up there."

"No," said V. "We don't have to find a way up there."

"Did you see a way in?"

"No," she explained. "But I think there is another option."

"Which is?"

"Go under? Right there?" She pointed at a place on the beach.

Kholos blinked at her. "What do you mean, go under? It's a hill of stone? How could we?" Kholos trailed off as he realized she was right. The walls of the hill made no sense above ground, why should they below ground? "Would you pass me the shovel, please?"

V fetched the folding entrenching tool they had taken from the Comanche car. Kholos kicked away several inches of snow and stabbed the head of the shovel down into the sand. When he lifted the shovel a small sliver of golden light emerged from below. Three more stabs and the sliver was a circle. Soon enough he had cleared away a small area of sand to reveal a set of stairs, going down and leading to a passage that headed east, under the hills. It was candle-lit and warm, built from polished stone. Warmth and the smell of jam and bread wafted up the stairs towards them.

"How did you know?" Kholos asked. "This particular spot?"

"Women's intuition," V said. "This is St. Theresa's place, after all."

Then she walked down the steps, and into the tunnel below. After fetching the pack and his weapons Kholos hurried after her. Underground the cavern was vaulted but not especially tall, and Kholos had to crouch. A brighter light and the sounds of children laughing came from up ahead.

They stepped out, but not up, into sunshine.

There was a blue sky overhead, with rolling orchards all around them, and vegetable gardens stretching in neat rows beyond the fruit trees. The land had soft curves and rises to it, and between the little dips ran trickling streams. A few featured millwheels, which formed the center of a handful of tiny villages. There were huts with thatched roofs, a couple of cabins, nothing taller than a single story. Copses and stands of oaks and maples stood here and there, but mostly the acreage was taken up by the orchards. Up the walls on the inside, Kholos saw, the same flowering vines ran. The hill was not a hill at all, he saw, but a cylinder.

There were children playing in the streams and in the dusty paths of the villages, running around in tangerine-colored, baggy pants and blouses, barefoot. They looked tan and healthy and there were quite a few of them. In the orchards men and women worked, harvesting peaches and apples and oranges and pears and cherries. They wore the same color clothing as the children, and it was just as gauzy. The men went without shirts as did a few of the women, but mostly the women wore loose, flowing dresses that fluttered around their bodies in the warm breezes. They were all young, bronze-skinned or darker, and beautiful, with dark hair and wide dark eyes. The women were curvy and firm with long hair, while the men were lean and glistened with perspiration as they worked in what seemed to be an afternoon, not a morning, sun. A few young girls carried baskets of peaches on their heads towards one of the villages. No one wore shoes.

Narrow paths crisscrossed everywhere, connecting every village and meadow and garden and orchard. In the center of the scene was the only building bigger than a single story: a mansion of white wood, with gables and windows where white curtains blew out in little puffs. Twin chimneys on either end of the mansion emanated white smoke, which was where the smell of the baking bread came from.

Kholos and V stared. They had come out into an orchard. A few of the people working there looked at them and smiled.

The warmth was enough that both of them had taken off their heavy coats, and V, scanning the area, saw a couple making love in the shade of a tree close by. As everyone was equally beautiful it was hard to discern their genders. V looked up and away, and gasped.

"Kholos!" she pointed. Following her finger, Kholos saw among the vines fluttering shapes, like bits of paper when they rose from a fire. But these objects floated and danced from flower to flower, and were present in bright and beautiful colors. "They're flying!"

"They are called butterflies," said a voice sweet as honey. "I make them here, myself. But sadly I cannot let them out into the world. Not yet, at least."

Walking towards them was a coffee-colored woman. She wore a shift of white gauze that hid nothing: full breasts, wide hips and narrow waist, long legs and small feet which were, predictably, bare. Her eyes were almond shaped and cat-like, her lips full and red. Her hair was tightly curled, and fell in black ringlets down her back. Her walk was slow and sultry, her palms were open towards them. Children, who had been playing among the peach trees, ran out to her and hugged her around her legs. Both Kholos and V filled with wants and desires: for comfort, for food, for sex.

"I am St. Theresa," the woman said in her simultaneously gentle and alluring voice. "The human's Whoracle."

V gaped. Kholos considered.

She turned and looked at V, up and down. The look was at welcoming and considerate. "You are a seamstress," she said. "And a cook?"

V stiffened, just slightly. "And a hunter."

The Adonai before them laughed in a voice that was all love and honey. "But I suspect you make your prey come to you? Yes?" Then, with a squad of men, women, and children all in tow, she approached V, brushed away a strand of hair, and embraced her, kissed her fully, on the lips. "I sensed your wants, last night," said St. Theresa. "Did you eat and rest well?"

"I did," V said, a little breathless, a little stunned, a little hungry, a little aroused. "Thank you."

St. Theresa moved to Kholos and put her hands inside his coat, ran her hands up his flanks and over the muscles of his chest and belly. Then she kissed him, as she had kissed V. After she stepped back she looked at the pack Kholos carried, with the sword and rifle tied to the back.

"Are you here to kill me, then?" she grinned.

Kholos looked her up and down. "Perhaps."

All of her followers gasped but the saint just laughed again. "I've never had worshippers come here to hurt me," she said. "I don't think you will either. This is a place of peace and love. Desires here are sated, not inflamed."

A few butterflies flittered their way down from the vines and played at the edges of her curls. "Alright. First, let us eat, and be warm, and be safe. Tonight, we will see about anything more than that." Her eyes were locked on Kholos as she spoke. The men in the little group around her, and many of the women as well, smiled along with her.

Tall tapered candles were lit all around: on the table, on windowsills, on side tables. The chairs at the long wooden table were fitted with stitched cushions and the cloth was white. Dishes of squash and beans, baskets of loaves and rolls, hot rice, steamed up and down the length of the board. There was no meat, but there was a centerpiece of flowers from the vines where a single butterfly with yellow and blue wings danced. A soft breeze blew in from the window carrying the sweet smell of spring. There were crocks of honey and butter, vials of vinegar and oil, and grinders for salt and pepper laid out, pitchers of milk and iced teas and bottles of wine as well.

Kholos, as they all sat down to eat, tried to count the number of people at the table but found it impossible. The table seemed to lengthen and shorten every time he blinked: there were twenty people in the room, all talking and laughing and embracing, children and men and women, all cleaned from their work but still dressed in the loose, billowy clothing. Then there were only eight, all adults, then a dozen, all children, and on and on. Kholos looked at V, who was seated across from him, at the foot of the table, but she did not seem to notice. Instead, she was touching her face and Kholos realized why: her wrinkles were gone. As was the gray streak in her hair. She was her true age again.

St. Theresa entered carrying a huge pot of vegetable stew. She set the dish down in the center of the table to light applause. Before taking her seat between them Theresa kissed V on top of her head affectionately and touched Kholos on top of his hand.

"Children," she said, "Eat, please, I made all this for you. You are safe here." Hands reached and grabbed across the table. "I promise."

Before coming down to supper, some of St. Theresa's attendants—strapping young men in orange pants—had led V and Kholos to their room on the second floor of the mansion. The room was clean and, like almost everything in the house, painted white. At a small vanity table were laid out cosmetics: lipsticks, eyeshadow, powders, which V had applied. The effect, Kholos admitted, was stunning.

On a four-poster bed complete with canopy were laid out clothes for both of them, orange pants for Kholos and a dress in the same color for V. They wore these garments as they ate, grateful after the days gnawing on dried fruits in the wilds, wearing their dirty heavy clothes. Children came and hopped up and down from Theresa's lap, who only nibbled on a roll and some lettuce leaves but encouraged everyone to take seconds, then thirds. She poured glasses of milk and tea and wine and passed them down, or leaned up to kiss someone who came into the room with fresh bread or more fruits and vegetable dishes. Kholos watched and listened. Along his shin he had tied V's knife with a piece of rope from the pack.

After the table had settled into a pattern of eating and talking, hugging and laughing, Theresa leaned back, a plump baby bouncing on her thigh, and turned to Kholos and V.

"I am so proud of you both," she said. "To find us here, so far away. I'm sure your journey was hard. I hope I am worth it," she gave a smile that could mean a dozen different things, all warm, all welcoming.

Kholos spooned up the last of his soup, his second bowl. "Do they come to you, to give you your orders?"

"Whatever do you mean, child?"

"Your masters," Kholos said. "Do they visit you here? Inspect your domain?"

Kholos realized that the others at the table were deliberately ignoring the conversation. V was staring at him, scoldingly.

"Kholos," she said. "Don't be rude. We would have frozen to death if she hadn't allowed us in here."

The Whoracle patted V on her shoulder. "No, no," she said. "You're so resourceful. You would have found a way, my little hunter. I know you would. All my children make me so proud." She kissed the baby on her lap.

"These are all your children?" asked Kholos.

"Everyone in the world is my child," she answered. "My child, my lover, my charge, my darlings. I only want the best for all of you. I want you to feel safe, and well-fed, and loved. Everyone has a home here."

"They just have to find it," said Kholos.

"Or defend it," said Theresa, not looking up.

At that moment, through the doorway to the kitchens, there was a crash of plates followed by some upset whispers. The table went silent, all eyes suddenly on the saint. Then, in the doorway, appeared a man. He was not fit and tan and muscled, but sickly thin, with a dirty beard and a sunken chest sprinkled with salt and pepper hair. His tangerine pants were tattered and stained and he smelled bad. On his face and hands Kholos saw the black marks of frostbite.

"Mother," he said. His red-rimmed eyes welled up with tears. "Please. I'm sorry."

The dining room seemed impossibly large, perhaps 50 seats at the long table now. But no one spoke. Theresa, from the other end of the room, continued to play with the baby. "Do you hear something, little one," she said. "Do you hear some bad sound?"

"Theresa," said the man, his voice shredded by guilt. "I love you. Please. It's so cold outside. I didn't know how hard it was, out there. Alone."

Two men came in behind the intruder. They grabbed the scrawny man by his arms. "Forgive us, mother," one of them said. "He came in through the tunnel. He must have been waiting outside, hiding."

Theresa looked at the guards. "It's alright," she said. "I know you did your best."

"Mother!" the man screamed. "I'm sorry. Punish me! Anything! Don't send me away! Please!"

St. Theresa gave the baby to V, and stood up.

"You broke my heart," she said, touching her breast. "All I gave you, all my love. And you could not do the one little thing I asked of you. To stay with me, and be safe and loved here, always."

Kholos winced.

"I'm sorry! Let me come home, please!"

Without answering, Theresa slowly sat back down in her chair. Calmly she took the baby back from V. The guards shuffled the man weeping and moaning out. Kholos watched through one of the windows as they dragged him, one on each arm, out across the dark fields.

"What did he do?" asked V.

"He left me," said Theresa. "Probably he wondered what was outside. Well," she glanced out the window. "Now he knows."

That night V lay on the bed. She was herself, beautiful in her lipstick and powder. Kholos turned down the flame on the lamp and stood by the window. The bed was so soft and warm it was hard for V to stay awake.

"I know this place makes no sense," said V, softly, "But I feel so safe here. So wanted. It's the perfect home."

"I think that's the point," said Kholos. He was watching the lawns leading up to the mansion. There did not seem to be any guards on the grounds. In the distance the lights in the windows of the huts of the villages went out, one by one. "Each of the Adonai must have a purpose on this world, some part in the Aetherian's plans. St. Theresa's might be to present people with concepts worth desiring, worth protecting. Home. Love. Safety. The hearth and the bed, the table, the cradle."

"There are plenty of all those things here," V yawned. "And I feel so good. You know, I wonder. Am I even Fractured here? I don't feel Fractured. And I do love her. I can't help it. I want to please her, whatever she wants. I just want to please her. It seems so important."

"It's a trap," said Kholos. "A trap for the entire world."

"What does that mean?"

"Nothing. Sleep, V."

"Aren't you coming to bed?"

"Soon, I'm not tired."

"Alright." V closed her eyes.

Kholos stepped over to the bed and stroked her hair. Then he kissed her, on her pretty lips. "I love you," he said softly. "So, so much. I will free you, as best as I can."

After he stroked her hair a few more moments, she was sound asleep.

He rose and opened the door into the hall. He carried nothing except his sword, kept in its scabbard. Shirtless he padded, still with a little limp, down the quiet halls. The corridors were filled with closed doors, and turned at strange angles, always leading to an open window. One door seemed larger than the others, and he touched the knob and found it ice cold, locked tight.

He stared at it a moment. It was different, somehow. It frightened him.

Then he moved on.

For a long while he walked, feeling the weight of the sword, feeling the desire and easy sense of security in the place. He did not know which room the Adonai occupied, but he let his lust for her, for the place, guide him to a certain door, just open a crack. The light from a single candle glowed within. Kholos pushed it open. A spicy perfume hung heavy in the air.

"I know you desire me," said the saint. "I know you need me. This entire world needs me."

The gauzy shift was gone. Naked, oiled, she lay on a round bed with the sheets draped over her feet. The room was electric with desire, and with blue and purple butterflies flitting along the ceiling. Her lips, her breasts, her calves, her shoulders, glistened. In the candlelight Kholos stared into her eyes. He stepped to the bed, said nothing.

She rolled over onto her stomach, facing him. She grinned, "Anything you want. I am any woman, every woman."

Kholos looked around the room. A huge closet full of dresses, shoes, and sashes, a vanity table like one in the room where V lay sleeping only with even more lipsticks, more powders. There was a needlepoint piece half-finished on a rocking chair in one corner, a porcelain bathtub with clawfeet where the water steamed. In several places, hung on the wall, perched on swiveled stands, were gilt-edged mirrors. Butterflies landed on the frames.

She touched him.

"You can't resist me," she whispered. "Not at my table, not in my gardens, not in my bed. I am all desires here. All loves. Your safety, your home. You want to be desired, yes. You want to be loved. Truly loved, for what you are, your raw self, by that young woman with you. I see it. I will do that for you. Give you all that, and more. All you need do is please me."

"She already loves me," said Kholos.

She whispered. "Yes but you keep some part of yourself hidden. Your desire is bright as stars to me. All desires. Show me, tell me, what that part is. I will keep your secret. You can trust me."

Kholos breathed through his mouth. His grip on the sword eased.

"Tell me what you are," she commanded. "And I will love you as you have always wished you would be loved. Everything wonderful forever. Safe. Still."

Kholos stepped back, out of her touch. Theresa sat up, stunned. Every inch of his skin burning to take her, Kholos took a breath and held it. A trap, he told himself. This is all a trap.

"Impossible," said the saint. "I am a god here. You cannot refuse me."

Kholos drew the first few inches of the blade of his sword, so she could see it.

"I can and did," he said. "Now tell me, do your masters come to you here?"

"You can't kill me," she complained. "Stop this. Or I will crush you with guilt. Make you choke on your own shame for disobeying me."

"Actually, I probably could kill you," said Kholos. "How do you contact the Aetherian? Is it an object? A device? Some way of thinking? Is the machine inside you?"

"What are you?"

Kholos thought of what V said, after the attack on the Borac caravan. "Just answer. I have no need to hurt you."

"I can give you anything," the Whoracle said. "Everyone wants something."

"What you offer disgusts me," said Kholos, bluntly. "I want freedom."

"No one wants freedom. True freedom. Everyone chooses a balance."

"Not I," he said with the thunder.

She leaned back. "No one has spoken to me like that, since, since-"

"Since what? You were somewhere else? The burning city?"

Theresa sat up, her breasts swinging. "I," she hesitated. "Before I built the Lipstick Country. Before all my children."

"You are just a tool," Kholos brought her face close to his. "Like me."

"I can banish you from peace and comfort forever! You will never feel safe again!"

"You assume I ever have," said Kholos.

Theresa looked at him, so beautiful. "They came through a tunnel," she said.

"What tunnel? Who came?" Kholos said.

"There are two of them. One is red, the other is blue. Everything stopped when they arrived. Only I could see them. They wore white masks. Are they-" she choked on her words. "Are they the ones that brought me here? Are they the ones who made me this way?"

"How do you call them here?"

She shook her head. "I don't. They simply came, once. They watched. As if they were waiting. I know that makes no sense. They appeared, and then they watched for a while."

 Kholos said. "Go on."

"They watched me, they walked, they floated, around my country, they said nothing. They were like ghosts, moving through everything as if it wasn't here. My orchards. My lovers. My babies. Then they left."

"They came through this tunnel? They didn't fly here?"

Theresa looked up at him, her eyes still teary. "Nothing can fly. Except for my butterflies. That was my allotted miracle."

"Show me this tunnel. Is it close by?"

"I told you what I knew." She pouted at him, ignored the question. "Now you tell me. How do you resist me? I would have made you so happy. Why don't you want me? Isn't that why I'm here? My purpose, to love and be loved? Don't reject me."

Kholos did not answer.

Theresa continued, "I've broken other men and women who thought they wanted someone else," she countered. "You saw my old lover, my lost son. He has to beg to return, and I will never let him. Forever. Everyone wants to be safe. Everyone wants to be loved. Men, women, children. You can't be so different."

"I didn't say I didn't want you, only that I want my freedom more."

"And what about her? Does she want your freedom just as much?"

The tunnel was in the cellar.

A circle, swirling different shades of blue and red, it hung on the wall like a mirror, the bottom lip of its curve hidden below the dirt floor. Around them were roots and bottles and casks, shelves where preserves and jams were stacked in glass jars, big bins of potatoes and carrots and sacks of dried beans, bags of flour and meal, unlocked chests where fancy plates were packed in straw. Bolts of cloth were lain against the walls in a thousand varieties.

There was no sunlight but there were lamps hung from the ceiling beams overhead. In the shadows the space seemed much, much larger than the mansion above, with enough preserved foods to feed armies. The tunnel was against the left wall, down the stairs up to the kitchen.

"Here," said Theresa. "This is where they went."

Kholos set the pack and the sword and rifle down on the ground and approached the circle in the wall. The colors moved like smoke. Carefully he put a finger against the membrane, then pushed through. He felt nothing, pulled his finger back and looked at it. It was still his finger.

"You've never stepped through yourself?" Kholos said. "No one has?"

Theresa half-smiled. "Curiosity is not a common quality here."

Kholos picked up a potato from a nearby bin. It was dirt covered and hard, fresh and still a little damp from the garden. Kholos, gripping it tight, pushed his hand through the circle and held it there a little while. When he pulled his hand back the potato had grown eyes and the dirt had fallen away. He did it again, and this time the potato came back peeled and ready for cooking.

"Oh, no," said V. "We can't go in there."

"It's alright," said Kholos as he shouldered the pack. "I think I know what it is. I don't know where it goes, though."

"You saw what it did to the potato," V pointed out. "Will it do that to us?"

Kholos said, "I think it's a tunnel through time."

"We'll come out into a different time?"

"No, not exactly," said Kholos. He collected his thoughts, or rather, Michael Staffa's memories of Nathan Voss' thoughts combined with his own understanding of the shapes of reality. "Another place, probably a place far away, but we'll do it very quickly. Time and distance are the same thing. If you could stand in one place long enough, stand without moving at all, you would eventually pass through everywhere. Because existence expands and contracts. I think this tunnel is a specific point like that. It is standing still while somewhere passes close by, probably somewhere specific.

"It's underneath time, a passage that connects two points using a time when these points were very close to each other. It only appears to be a tunnel to us. It's more like a piece of paper, folded into itself. When it unfolds, we will be far from the point where we started even though we only took a few short steps.

"I wonder if this is how the Universitat highways work." Kholos dropped the potato on the ground, wondering also if back in Duran Town in the sky where he spread his wings if there was a sign like this of his passing.

"But is it safe?" persisted V.

Kholos turned to V. "Don't you already age in an instant? Every day?"

"True," sighed V. "Alright. Let's go."

And then they were gone.

"Oh, Kholos," said V. "It's so bright."

Inside there was a pure light, a solid light, so strong they could not look forward but had to shield their eyes with their hands. They clung to each other, stepped forward once, twice. Up ahead, no more than a dozen steps away, was another circle, this one swirling red and blue as well. The light was nearly solid, like ice. It moved around their toes in chunks. V touched it along the wall and she shifted, immediately, from her age in Duran Town to perhaps another fifty years older, with her wrinkles deep and a sudden stab of arthritis through her hands and an ache in her hip. She groaned against Kholos. He put his arm around her and held her close.

"Touch it again," he said.

She did. She was a seven-year-old.

"Again."

Perhaps fifteen. Then fifty. Then ninety. Then three. Finally she was thirty, or so.

“Good,” said Kholos. The light was pounding at him. “It's not far now.”

“Where will we come out?” she asked.

10. Fire the Abstract Artillery!

Colonel Redroot, splinted leg protruding from the car, raced along. He passed the Columbium territories one after the other. Every so often, he tried to raise a Comanche channel on the Televia in the car, but there was only static. Eventually he stopped trying.

He had taken a rocket car, and made sure to carry surplus ammunition as well as plenty of cold weather gear, rations, fuel, and weapons. Also he had removed the painkillers from every first aid kit he could find, and took them liberally as he drove along. They deadened the pain in his leg, and kept his mind empty of everything save his hunt for the Deserter. Such as how he buried Stands-Tall-Under-Cedars in the crazy ground within sight of the burning city, the body shifting to bones even as he dug. Then dust. Then bloated.

The cold had come but without snow so he kept up his pace. Once, twice a day he would pass a truck going south and flag them down, ask if they had seen a Comanche attack car, heading north. The drivers, Columbium and Inuit men and women used to solitude, stared at Colonel Redroot as he stood by their cabs on the highway, leaning on his assault-rifle crutch with his dusty, bloody overcoat and his mud-splattered car, the rocket launcher hidden under a tarp. The drivers answered him honestly but obliquely, as if some of the things he said made no sense at all. Yes, they had seen a car like his, up the highway. No, they didn't know anything else about it. They never stepped out of their trucks, never opened their doors. When he said Comanche they all seemed to flinch.

Redroot wondered, watching them drive on, why they did not treat his uniform with the respect he was accustomed to. Perhaps, he wondered, it was the gun he had taken from Gyr Zax. He carried it over his shoulder, with a black strap he had fashioned from a utility belt. The gun was chased with strange Borac glyphs, plus it was made of gold. Decidedly non-standard-Comanche issue. It felt too light and too heavy, both at once.

After he had traveled north for several days he encountered a Borac caravan. Much smaller than Gyr Zax's entourage, they had no trucks at all, just a dozen saurs loaded heavily across their backs with timber, little tent houses erected on top of the raw logs. Probably the last run south before the snows came and closed the Inuit lumberyards. A pair of dactyls circled overhead. Redroot could make out the thin black lines tethering them to their handlers. One of the dactyls spotted him and cawed out, twice long, once short.

A pair of Boracs, walking slowly and carrying nothing more than their *kops*, approached. They wore long coats made from white fur.

"Do you need help?" one of them asked. His tusks were etched with scarlet and green and chips of turquoise and jade. The other, Redroot saw, was female. Her tusks were gilded with bronze that had reached a fine patina, and her hair was pulled back tight into a severe bun. The two big square heads atop the white fur coats peered down at him.

"I am Colonel Ute Redroot," he said. "An officer of the Incorporated Nation of the Third Comanche. I am in pursuit of a man wanted both by the Universitat and the Incorporated Nation for serious crimes. You are obligated to assist me in any way I might request."

The two Boracs looked at each other. "Alright," said the first. "What can we do for you?"

"Did a Comanche attack car pass this way? With a tall man driving? Perhaps a woman with him?"

"No," said the Borac with the bronzed tusks. "But there is news on the road of a car like yours, with a man and a woman. They were going in search of the Flowering Walls." She pointed northeast. "This was a day or two ago, we heard."

"The Flowering Walls?" asked Redroot.

"The country of the human Whoracle," said the Borac. "The little news says she keeps her domain along a great bay, past the woods."

"St. Theresa?"

"The same."

The Borac with the etched tusks was studying Redroot's car. The Fighting First Claws sigil was spattered with mud, as were the

Comanche markings. "Did you say you were Comanche?" he asked.

"I am. What of it?"

"Comanche, not Kiowa?"

Redroot flushed with anger.

"I am a descendant of Quannah Parker," Redroot nearly spit. "I am a full-blooded Comanche brave. An officer of the Incorporated Nation."

The Borac stepped back, his four-fingered hands up before him. "Alright. Only, there is no Incorporated Nation of the Third Comanche, so far as we have heard. Only the Kiowa Collective," he paused. "I think they keep the Comanche people in camps."

Redroot chuckled. "You're insane."

Confusedly the Boracs looked at each other. The ground began to shake, softly, as the saurs paraded down the pavement towards them.

Suddenly, Ute Redroot thought strange thoughts, remembered strange memories.

A childhood behind barbed wire. His defeated people. A father he never knew. A sister dead by typhoid. Hunger. He never rode a horse. He never led men. He liked the taste of corn whiskey. His mother whored herself to a Kiowa warden to keep him fed. A black tide, the memories came, covering everything. And as they receded they left a different Redroot.

There was no Incorporated Nation. There was the Collective.

He had escaped from his camp. He had hurt his leg climbing over the cyclone fence to get into the car lot. His best friend, Stands-Tall, had been shot as they raced out of the camp. Only he had escaped. Was that what made him insane? Was it the pills? What made him think he was a great man of a great people: the Comanche, masters of the Columbium Continent? *Ha*, he thought. *Ha ha.*

Redroot remembered. He had stolen the car, the clothes, from the soldiers at the camp, the camp at the pass, south of the Burning City. All of it—the War Chief, the Golden Towers of New Taabe, the Fighting First Claws—it was only his imagination. Now the guards would beat his mother because he had stolen their car.

"Colonel?" asked one of the Boracs.

"Don't call me that!" Redroot shouted.

He saw the submachine gun, Gyr Zax's gun. He gripped the trigger.

"No," he whispered. "I am right. It is the world that is wrong."

The woman noticed the glyphs on the gun. "Where did you get that weapon?"

Redroot shot her, through the chest, a quick burst.

Green blood soaked up into the white fur of her tattered coat where she lay on the pavement. The other Borac reached for his *kop* and had the blade drawn, but Redroot was faster, bringing the gun up under the *cumbel's* chin, and firing. For a moment the big Borac stood, then collapsed onto the road. From the approaching caravan came shouts and cries. The dactyls screamed out warnings.

Redroot shouted at the corpses. "I am Colonel Ute Redroot, Commander of the Fighting First Claws! I am a Comanche Brave, of the Incorporated Nation!"

A few rifle shots cracked at his feet, over his head. *Cumbel* were rushing forward from the caravan. Redroot, as fast as his injured leg would allow him, hurried back into the car, and drove over the meadow and into the woods, heading northeast. "Comanche," he shouted back at the looming shapes of the saurs. "I am Comanche!"

After a day of pushing the car randomly through the woods and across the little streams, Redroot found the car Kholos and V had abandoned.

Kholos and V emerged underwater. They had stepped forward through the circle, but somehow come out in dark, cold, and deep moving water. Instinctively Kholos, with V doing the same alongside him, kicked up for the dim light far above them. The pack, with the gun and the sword, was heavy and pulled at him, and, with no real choice, Kholos kicked and pushed it free. Finally, he came up gasping. V, relatively unburdened, had already broken the surface and was treading water easily. Kholos gulped air, blinked the water out of his eyes. Fog swirled around them.

Kholos kicked to keep his head above water and spat, gasped. Little waves broke into his face. The water was cold, and moving swiftly.

Kholos thought of the canisters of compressed light, the colored bullets, the rifle, and the sword, with Gyr Zax's god-tusks, their supplies, with all the rest. He was glad he had not put his armor back on when they left the Lipstick Country.

"Where are we?" asked V. She was circling in the water, trying to look around. Kholos realized she was the stronger swimmer, at least at this age. "This is fresh water, with a current. But I can't see through the fog."

Kholos squinted with his remarkable eyes. Through the mist he could make out shapes, tall shapes and small shapes, squat shapes and long shapes. And as he trained his ears he could hear the little waves lap at something, some kind of shore or breakwater. He peered, bobbing and tossing in the water while V held his wrist.

"It's a river," said Kholos.

"Can you see the shore?"

Kholos studied the shapes through the mist. Some were tall as hills, taller, some were low and stubby. They were familiar but they were also fuzzy, changing with every bob and twist of the water. "I can't tell," he shouted. "I think I see buildings. But they keep changing."

"What do you mean, changing?" V shouted. Her wet hair hung down the sides of her face, washing her makeup away. "Can we swim for it?"

"I don't know."

"If we're headed out to sea we're going to drown," V explained. "Is the shore that way or not?"

"I can't tell," he spat. "It keeps changing."

A slicing sound came from behind them, from the direction where the tunnel had popped them out at the bottom of the river. Splish splash, the sound came towards them, a steady beat on the water. Kholos and V looked at one another. Kholos nodded. They had no choice.

"Hey!" called V, spitting out more water. "Help! Hey!"

"Hang on," said a rough, masculine voice. "I'm coming."

The splashing stopped. Then, taking shape as it came out of the fog, emerged a white rowboat, narrow at the waist but long. A lantern hung from its prow and cut through the fog like a plow. The oars splashed faster, until at last the boat was alongside Kholos and V. A calloused hand with a ruffled cuff reached down and took V by the wrist, and helped her up with a little grunt while Kholos gripped the gunwale, and then V and the hand both helped Kholos up into the boat. For a moment Kholos and V lay in the bottom of the boat, catching their breaths. They only looked up at their rescuer after he had taken up the oars again and started the rhythmic splish splash. They were headed, Kholos realized, away from the shapes he had seen.

"Who are you?" asked Kholos.

"Today," said the man. "I'm Sergeant Dugan, Master of Arms at the Museum Fortress. Other days I might be Corporal Jigsaw, whichever the Baron, or Brian, wishes me to be."

The Sergeant was a stocky man, with a brushed mustache more gray than red. He wore a peacoat with a missing button and with paint splatters up the lapels. Patches of all sorts were sewn up the sleeves: pubs, Columbium militia regiments, sports teams, fire companies. His fingernails were stained with nicotine and ink. On his feet he wore workman's boots. They were untied and the tongues lolled over the laces. Like the coat they were also paint splattered and gummed up along their rubber soles.

Kholos thought of his list. Unlike the rifle, the canisters, and the sword, the list at least was in his pants pocket, tightly rolled. He had studied it often enough, even though he knew it changed. "I've never heard of you," he said.

"Me either," said V, running through the saints of her catechism.

"Yes," said Sergeant Dugan. "And you're not quite who I was expecting either. Brought the boat out because of the siege. Thought perhaps ... well, that doesn't matter as you're not them." He seemed more relieved than disappointed.

"Where are we?" asked V. "Is this the Mississippi River?"

The oars splayed the water. Sergeant Dugan chuckled. The boat was perfectly white, like an idea of a boat, a painting of a boat. Touching the gunwales Kholos felt no wood grain or shellac, just a smoothness he could not quite identify. *Bone?*

"Caego indeed," said the Sergeant, nodding with his chin behind him, at the shifting shapes Kholos had seen. "That's Neo Cumae, capital of the world!"

As Dugan rowed, the mist began to lift and sunshine broke out upon the water.

Skyscrapers, glass-coated and shooting high into the sky, appeared. The sun glistened on their facades. From the river, they saw glorious cathedrals to Pang, manicured gardens and parks, amphitheaters set precariously out over the river. There were docks that seemed as big as all of Duran Town where huge ships sat at anchor as an army of workers unloaded cargoes from the cities of the Republicant and the nations of Ebonia. A steady buzz of shouting and traffic and bells and doors and music oozed from the city.

V gasped. Dugan laughed.

"And you're here early," he chided. "But wait. A few more pulls here and you'll see something just as special. Just let me take us in."

Yanking on the oars, Dugan pulled them farther away. The city began to change. The skyscrapers shot up, transformed into crazy, jutting, impossible shapes. The ships became larger, longer, sleeker. The buzz grew louder. The crowds thickened and moved even faster along the promenades and through the parks. The cathedrals to Pang changed as well, the steeples gone and their roofs flattened, with strange machines perched atop them. All of the people seemed to be dressed alike, moved alike. This seemed to please Dugan, who nodded approvingly.

Kholos squinted and with his sniper's eyes saw that, despite the different races and genders and heights, they all looked alike somehow as well. And everything was the same color, the same shape.

"What's that?" asked Kholos.

"Oh, I wouldn't know," said Dugan, not looking back. "I'm just the help here. I'd guess you're probably looking at the future of Neo Cumae."

Kholos blinked. The city changed again.

The skyscrapers dipped, shrank, vanished altogether. The north end of the city turned to forest. The big diesel ships became vessels with sails. The parks were fields, planted with corn. Cattle grazed where traffic had raced. Republicant legionnaires with flintlock pistols and short swords on their hips patrolled docks where raw logs were lashed together, ready for loading. There was a simple temple to Pang, the Creator, no bigger and no more grand than the temple on the square in Duran Town. A few Iroquois men in beautiful robes were bargaining with some Republicant merchants on one of the docks.

"Then this is its past," Kholos guessed.

"That's right," said Dugan. "From the island where the Museum Fortress sits the city blinks it's way up and down through the ages. It can be quite beautiful." Dugan sighed. "I think Brian should paint it. But he's not interested."

"What is the Museum Fortress?" V asked, cautiously.

"The home of the Baron Storenko!" said Dugan, proudly. "Adonai of all art and artists!"

V returned his announcement with a blank stare. There was not much painting in Duran Town.

"Oh well," Dugan gave a last long pull. "Look behind you."

The Museum Fortress was bone white, ghostly white. A huge mass of a building, standing atop a small, rocky island in the middle of the river. A fringe of mist shrouded the banks but the museum itself seemed to shine.

A schizophrenic structure, the Museum Fortress was two buildings at once. One was a building with high fluted columns in the Republicant style and banks of long tall windows. Marble steps, pristinely swept, rose from a piazza where a fountain of water nymphs played, leading up to a wide and welcoming entrance. A frieze of artists at work—sculptors, painters, musicians—adorned the gable overtop the building. A more modern domed cupola rose from behind the gable, made of latticed glass where a glow rose. Abstract shapes in a variety of colors danced on the glass and even from the little skiff they could see pieces of enormous metal mobiles hung from the steel frame, spinning slowly. It was powerful, beautiful.

But jutting out from the wings of the museum were jagged shards of patchwork metal, rusty and peeling. There seemed to be holes in the roof, and wires crawled along the seams, some of them sparking blue arcs. There was broken glass on the ground around the wings, bits of plywood scraps and empty cans in piles, and bursts of weak color that seemed to have dripped and faded in the rain. All of it as chaotic as the central building was ordered.

Around the entire structure, ringing the entire island, was a wall. It was low, so low in fact Kholos was sure he could have traversed it with a running jump. But it was solid, thick enough that men could walk along its parapet, and it was rung all around with barbed wire in shiny tinsel colors. Behind the wall were arrayed canons, long-barreled but low-caliber, and these were assembled and decorated from random parts: peach crates, loose gears, old nails, empty picture frames, opened envelopes, newsprint papier-mâché, bottlecaps, car grills, light bulbs, desk tops, cereal boxes, book covers. Despite the array of materials, there was a similarity to the canons, a sameness. As if they were all made at the same time, according to the same plan.

All of them pointed out, at the water, in all directions. Soldiers, decked in strange uniforms consisting of pantaloons, goggles, and frogged jackets, walked the grounds, watching the waves warily. Kholos saw a couple of them speaking into hand-held Televias that were colored in day-glo pinks and greens.

"You're under siege here?" Kholos asked Dugan.

"Oh, yes," said Dugan. "Every day, we have to repel massive attacks. It's only the genius of the Baron that keeps us going. His creativity is limitless."

"Massive attacks from who?" Kholos asked.

"Oh," sighed Dugan. "Philistines. The uneducated masses. The reactionary horde. We are lucky they never seem to coordinate their attacks, or even Brian's powers might not be enough."

The skiff pulled into a narrow dock. One of ridiculous soldiers stood there, armed with a blunderbuss musket etched with what Kholos thought were translations of Pang's mantras, along with some stickers of bananas and oranges from Toltec shipping companies.

"Why is half the museum falling down?" asked V.

Dugan sputtered. "Falling down? Falling down? That's the future of the museum! That's the truth, right there. If you think that's falling down, you think the future is falling down. You have to really see it. You have to allow it to be seen, by you. You have to grasp the concept behind the work."

"What?"

"Does the Baron receive visitors here?" asked Kholos "Often?"

"Well. Yes. They usually appear right here at the dock. I thought you might be them, in fact. Except of course they never come out in the middle of the river. Usually they appear on the steps. They've been coming here often lately. They watch the Baron. They make me quite nervous, honestly. I don't know who they are exactly."

Kholos looked at V. "How long we take in the tunnel affects where we emerge," he said. "Pausing just for a second probably adds a dozen meters. If we'd stopped for too long, we might have come out in the middle of the ocean. Or even on the moon."

"Listen, Sergeant," said Kholos. "We arrived with some baggage, which I lost in the river. Is there a way I might be able to get that back?"

"We'll see," said Dugan. "It's certainly still there. And will be for as long as the city is there, in some form. First let us go inside. It has been some time since we've had patrons at the museum. Brian will be most pleased. For a long while only the best people came. From all ages of the city, they would hire boats to take them across, and I would give them personal tours. They were most approving. Most appreciative. But lately that has changed. I wonder if we couldn't bring more of them back, more of the best people, if not for Brian's problems in completing his masterpiece." Dugan shook his head, sadly.

They walked up the steps, past the found-art canons and the soldiers in their goggles. Banners fluttered from the tops of the museum proclaiming exhibits on everything from "Late High Outsider Republicant" landscape paintings to "Conceptual Photographs of the Un-Zone." Kholos noticed that, from the island of the museum grounds, the skyline of Neo Cumae had stabilized. It looked, he supposed, like it would if they had come upon it without traveling through, or under, time: tall skyscrapers and steeples, a great deal of traffic running along train tracks and sidewalks and streets. From the top of the steps, between the immense columns of the original Museum Fortress, the view was impressive.

Dugan led them up the steps and inside.

A great vaulted hall greeted them. Sunlight burst down from the glass dome they had seen from the river, illuminating tapestries, statues, paintings, and a myriad of other amazing, beautiful objects. V gasped. Kholos dropped his jaw. There were sculptures of dead gods and goddesses in white marble and bronze. There were paintings big as houses and as small as the palm of a hand showing a thousand scenes, a thousand faces. Some were photographs and some were oils, some were made with beans and macaroni and some with precious jewels. There were representations of people and places so lifelike they seemed to breathe, to almost move, to twitch, to shift in time. There were sublime abstractions. From the central vault, these wonders stretched on down six endless halls, each packed with pictures and alcoves housing a seeming infinity of objects. The building itself, with its impossible dome and its simple walls, framed everything.

"It's so beautiful," V said. "I never imagined anything like this could exist."

"Yes, yes," said Dugan. "Come on. This isn't the important part. Follow me, please."

Dugan led them down one of the long halls off of the main cupola. They passed masterpiece after masterpiece, many of them coated with dust, some hung askew, a few statues where bits of soldiers' gear and equipment were hung from them. There were empty alcoves, places were trash had piled up.

"Where did you get all this art?" asked V. "Why aren't you taking better care of it?"

"It was here when the Baron and I arrived," Dugan explained. "Just as you see it, only then there were great crowds here."

"And what were you supposed to do with all this?" said Kholos, running his finger along a marble pedestal and coming up with a smudge of grimy dust. "Maintain it? Present it? Hide it? Destroy it?"

"Do with it? I don't know. The Baron never told me to do anything with it. Mostly we have worked on the new wings. The contemporary areas. Brian has always been primarily interested in those areas. The future is forward, you know. The past is an albatross."

"What?" said V.

"But he's an Adonai," Kholos insisted. "What's he do?"

Dugan turned to Kholos sharply. "What he is supposed to do, is be an artist."

"So he makes art, then?" said V. "He paints or sculpts or something?"

Dugan looked at her and laughed, as if this question was beyond ridiculous.

They reached, at last, the end of the hall. Without care, Dugan began to toss away various portraits and abstract paintings, some ancient tribal pieces. After moving a couple of crates out of the wall he revealed not a door, as Kholos and V had expected, a but a red rope between two brass posts. With great care Dugan unhooked one end of the rope and ushered Kholos and V through.

"This is where Brian does his major work," Dugan explained.

The space was huge, empty, filled with dust and trash. The roof and walls were jagged, crazy. The light coming in was random and slashed, as if pulled from different skies. There was no way to look out, as the windows were all placed high up in the overlapping planes of the walls and ceilings. Rusted pipes ran along the walls. The floor was cement, chipped and stained with solvents and detergents. Somewhere, perhaps from the kitchenette in the corner, came the stink of food left out. The air was still. It was cold, cold enough that Kholos could see his breath. Over the chemical smells there was also a rank tinge of wet tobacco and unwashed clothes. From somewhere unseen tinny music hissed out. A half-dozen industrial sized sinks were set against the wall closest to them, each dripping. Underfoot were jumbled spools of colored tape, carpentry tools, and squeezed out tubes of paint.

Someone from one of the dark corners coughed.

"Brian," said Dugan. "You have visitors." Dugan looked at Kholos and V and smiled. "Potential patrons, perhaps? They actually came through the tunnel." He looked at V and Kholos, still wet. "In a manner of speaking."

A skinny shambles emerged from the corner where the coughing had started. His nails were filthy and long, his clothes stained with sweat under the arms and his pants splattered not just with paints but with what appeared to be bits of egg. He wore no shoes, only a filthy pair of socks.

"I am the artist," he said in scratchy voice. Then he started to cry. "My name is Brian. Brian Storenko. I feel imbalanced. I can't see you today. Leave me alone. I may have an idea at some point."

"What do you do here?" said Kholos, confusedly. "Paint?"

Suddenly, the artist turned on Sergeant Dugan and pointed at him with a long finger. "This is your fault! You're supposed to tell them! You're supposed to make them understand that they can never understand! And I told you, you are Corporal Jigsaw now! You are my idea! I bet you've been talking about technique and beauty."

"No, no! I just thought they might prefer," stammered Dugan. "I mean, this was the original form I was to take. Part of your statement included influencing visitors on the nature of beauty."

Still pointing, still weeping, Brian Storenko waved his cracked and blackened fingernail wildly through the air, disturbing the dust.

At first nothing seemed to happen, but then Kholos and V looked to Dugan. The man was transforming, stroke by stroke, line by line: his face was pulled down and his chin narrowed, his hair flashed from red to black and shifted from its neat cut to a mess of short curls. His ears grew large and his eyes grew narrow and beady. His limbs elongated and his trunk thinned. His outfit became a rumpled suit and trousers, a black jacket, an untucked white shirt. Stubble in iron gray poked from his jaw. He gave off a scent of vodka.

As Brian worked, sweat broke out on his face and his lips began to twitch. He shuddered, he whimpered, he whispered about his mother and about old lovers. The odor coming off of his body was terrible. Finally, he finished. Sergeant Dugan was gone. Corporal Jigsaw stood in his place.

"He's right, you see," said Jigsaw. He lit a cigarette and moved a stray lock of hair from his eyes. "You really have to understand where Brian is coming from to get his work. It's an expression of an impression, each piece deeper than the next, really. He is breaking the dolls of perception, here. He is teaching us to visualize what cannot be visualized. The work is him, him is the work. I interpret. I explain."

"What work?" asked V.

Jigsaw gestured with his cigarette at the space around them. "This is it, baby," he said. "This is creativity, unbridled. All around you. This light. This time, inside here. Me. You'll worship it, if you're smart. It's pure genius. Can't you feel it?"

Kholos started to speak, but then thought better of it. Brian had gone back into his corner.

"We are tired," said Kholos. "And wet. We've lost all of our belongings. I think it might be best if we took a moment to rest."

"Whatever," said Jigsaw disdainfully. "We're making art here."

Kholos and V stepped back out into the long hall, away from the debris and stink of Storenko's dilapidated wing. After walking a while they found an unused pedestal, fairly low to the floor, and sat down upon it. They were alone, Jigsaw having remained in the contemporary wing, and V took off her damp dress and wrung it out, then hung it over the arm of a statue of an old Republicant goddess in one of the arched alcoves. It was dim but it was warm, and offered a little privacy. They held each other in their underwear and waited for their things to dry, listened to their stomachs growl. After a moment they heard footsteps, coming from the direction of the newer, decrepit wings. V peered out around the cloth.

"Dugan," she whispered. "Or Jigsaw, rather."

The steps moved on, without pause.

"This place is crazy," said V. She put her arms around her shoulders and drew her knees up.

"I wish we had our clothes," she added. "And our food."

Kholos had taken out Dr. Voss's list of the Adonai, unrolled the paper and studied it.

"Here he is," said Kholos. "The Baron Storenko. Saint of Artists. It says nothing about a Brian, there's no second names at all. Let alone a Dugan or a Jigsaw."

"I think Dr. Voss told us about him in class," V recalled.

"Every Adonai has a purpose in this world," said Kholos. "A hidden purpose. Some mission of the Aetherian. Theresa gave us love and a home. What is Baron Storenko doing here? Destroying beauty?"

"You mean Brian Storenko."

Kholos laughed.

They slept cuddled up in the alcove, under the watch of a statue of a Republicant goddess. Kholos, before he closed his eyes, ransacked through the catalog of memories and experiences which were not his, searching for someone who lived by water, someone who knew how to fish.

In the morning V was a young girl, perhaps eight or nine years old, probably younger. She wrapped the brown dress, now dry, around herself like a shawl. Her stomach roared. Kholos was surprised she had changed at all: in the Lipstick Country time seemed to be contained, separated from the damage at the burning city. He assumed here it would be the same: the flickering of Neo Cumae seemed to suggest that. But, he considered, perhaps it was the opposite. Perhaps Neo Cumae held steady and it was the Museum Fortress that was flashing through the centuries.

"I'm so hungry," V complained.

"I know," said Kholos. "Listen closely. I have to go back for our things. The rifle and the sword. But also our food, as I don't think we're going to get fed anytime soon. I need you to stay here. Right here, in this little spot we made. I'll be as fast as I can, but you can't leave here. We have no idea what these people might do to us, good or bad. We'll decide where to go after I get back."

"Why can't I come with you?"

"Because you're a little girl and I don't think you could swim as well as you might if you were older. Just stay in this little place we made."

V looked sad.

"Just stay here, hidden," Kholos ordered. "Don't go out until I get back. I'm sorry. Truly, I wouldn't tell you to do anything you didn't want to do, but this once I need to know you're safe. I'll bring back some food."

V sighed. "Fine."

Kholos walked out the way they had originally come, back towards the rotunda of the masterpieces and the brilliant sunlight. As he walked along the marble floors he paused now and then and took things: some loose planks from a packing crate, some twine, a few nails and staples. Once he had too much to carry in one arm he wrapped everything up in a drop cloth. The disordered part of the museum ended before he had enough material, and he doubled back for a little while until he had a coil of twine that stretched many times around the length of his arm, along with a few dozen staples and finishing nails. Pieces of picture frames he bundled lengthwise.

Finally, he came to the rotunda, walking along the wide hall and looking at the statuary and the vases and even the Televia images hung and stacked there.

"They are all separate realities, you know," said Jigsaw, stepping out from the center of the dome. His black shoes clacked on the tiles. "Each one, a little existence of its own. The artists' own thoughts shaped them, formed them. They are all as real as anywhere, anytime else." Jigsaw tapped his foot on the marble. "As real as right here."

"Are they free?" Kholos asked.

"They were," said Jigsaw. "Each artist, you see, once they painted or crafted or sculpted what it was, they put their thoughts on that existence. The reality reflected their thoughts, not the other way around, if you know what I mean."

"I do," said Kholos, thinking of his plans, his dreams. "Exactly."

"Genius is a terribly dangerous thing," said Jigsaw. "It can undo universes. By accident."

Kholos turned to look at him. "You're quite different from yesterday, Jigsaw."

"Not as different as you'd think," said Jigsaw. "Not as different as you, maybe?"

"What about the Baron? Is he supposed to be imprinting realities?"

"My master?" Jigsaw waved his cigarette back and forth, he smiled. "Oh, no, quite the opposite. I think that may be part of the problem here. Brian's, the Baron's, art is supposed to be hollow, you see. It's supposed to be so meaningful and symbolic it conveys nothing but the symbol. It's supposed to require an interpretation. A barrier. Then I'm supposed to tell the world why it matters, why they're wrong about whatever it was they thought they saw. Why they can't trust their own eyes. These canvases and bronzes of other wheres and other times, these all have to stop. All this in the rotunda here? It's all behind schedule. These should be crated up in the halls."

"Who's schedule? Do you have contact with them?"

Jigsaw ignored the question. "You see Brian's not doing his job here. He's had all the training, all the indoctrination, he's learned to resolve the contradictions in rebellion and authority, process and product. But he can't quite make things empty. Interesting color contrasts slip through. Shapes. He is creative, and wherever they plucked him from, they didn't quite teach that creativity out of him. He can't help himself."

"They," Kholos said. "They come here, you said."

"Lately, yes, they have." said Jigsaw. "I suspect they are disappointed in the work being undone. They give me no orders, which is strange. I used to receive orders, about what to do with Brian. From only one of them, though. A tall man."

"Interesting. And do you have a way to contact them? Directly? Or do they just come through the tunnel, the one I came out of?"

"Through the tunnel. Although usually they arrive in here, or at least at the dock. You know you say them, but it could be only one."

"And they go back out through the tunnel," Kholos sighed, thinking he knew where the other end of the tunnel emerged already, no closer to the Celestial City and the machines.

"Actually no," said Jigsaw. "They, he, go into the city. But I couldn't tell you when or where in the city. We kind of float out here alongside all the cities, you understand. The city in any given moment. We are linked to it."

Kholos nodded. In the city. Jigsaw dropped his cigarette and stubbed it out under his shoe.

"Some people," said Jigsaw. "They used to come here to see the art. I would tell them how to see it. It worked very well. Nonviolent, if you know what I mean. Part of my work here is to disabuse the viewers of their emotions, make sure they won't imprint any further realities themselves. That's our little army out there, those who I converted to the conceptual, explained how they could not trust their own thoughts."

"Trapped them here," said Kholos.

"Eh," said Jigsaw. "They came willingly."

"Why are you telling me all this?"

"You're not the first," Jigsaw smiled, "to wonder what all this means."

"I don't care what it means," said Kholos. "I only want the way out."

The two men stared at each other.

"We'll be leaving soon. There's nothing else for us here."

Kholos turned and walked out of the rotunda and out onto the landing. The strange troops of the Museum Fortress still manned the parapets around the island, protected by the candy-colored barbed wire and the day-glo cannons. One of them, goggles lowered, approached Kholos as he made his way past the gigantic fountain in the museum plaza and headed towards the little inlet where the skiff was tied.

"Headed back to the city, sir?" asked the soldier.

"Soon," said Kholos.

"I see. I had assumed you'd be joining us here on the wall."

Kholos stopped and turned to the man, remembering what Corporal Jigsaw had said to him about how the Museum Fortress' guards were recruited. "Are you actually attacked here?" he asked.

"Well," he said. "Not directly, no. But Sergeant Dugan feels we should always be ready, just in case. Or Corporal Jigsaw, today."

"What do you think?"

The soldier shrugged.

"I think," said Kholos, putting a hand on the banana yellow barrel of a canon and looking back at where Jigsaw stood at the top of the steps, smoking, watching. "That your artillery is in poor shape. Why don't you see if you can get a can of paint, and do something about it?"

Back at the little shelter in the long hall, V grew bored and hungrier. She had tried to nap but the marble floors were cool and uncomfortable. She remembered, clearly, the kitchenette in Brian Storenko's studio, back in the jagged additions where they had seen the Adonai the day before. V did not care that Brian Storenko was a Saint, she cared that he might have food.

V walked down the hall, towards the doors that led to concrete floors and the sickly light and, she hoped, some eggs and toast.

The dirty doors behind the red rope opened when she pushed with both hands. The chemical odor hit her immediately and made her squint. The atmosphere was close and dank, smoky. V stepped in and the doors closed behind her. She could hear a fan, some scuttling that could be rats. Quietly she started to walk in the direction of the kitchenette.

There were eggs there, in a carton on a tray next to the filthy stove. Also there was salt and pepper, and in the refrigerator V found a little cheese. From a cabinet she found a skillet and a spatula.

But, first, she thought, a little cleaning.

She found powdered soap and a rag, turned the water on in the sink and let it run until it turned clear. Then she scrubbed. Scrubbed the counter top, scrubbed the stove, all the burners even though she only planned to use one. After throwing out some seriously wilted lettuce and something that might have been a potato at some point, she wiped down the fridge, inside and out, all the while rinsing and re-soaping her rag. Finally, she washed the frying pan out, then dried it on the hem of her brown dress. The little space shone amid the rubble and the stink.

Then she cooked. Three eggs, a little butter in the pan, a dash of pepper a pinch of salt. A pleasant smell of food and spice began to rise up from her work. When the eggs were nearly done she crumbled up the cheese and let it melt into the fluff, her mouth watering. From a cabinet she found a plate, cracked, and from a drawer she found a fork with a missing tine. Lastly she poured herself a cautious glass of cold water from the tap.

Then she ate her work, her creation. It was delicious.

Within a minute she had finished the entire plate, pinching up the last little bits to her lips. V burped, softly. I just ate a god's breakfast, she thought to herself.

Brian Storenko appeared before the doors, as if he had been lounging in one of the smudges and stains on the floors and simply materialized there.

"What did you do?" he demanded, staring at the clean kitchenette, the ingredients. A pair of flies buzzed around his dirty hair. "You were here yesterday," he said.

"I'm sorry," said V. "I was hungry. I saw the eggs."

"You were older yesterday. Athletic. Attractive. A woman in her prime. Beautiful. Now you are what? Eight years old? Completely different. How?"

V blushed, staring at her plate. "I'm Fractured."

"Of course you are," said Storenko, nodding. "Of course you are!"

"Can I go? I'm sorry about your food. I could make you some, too, if you wanted."

But Brian was pacing, slapping his hands together.

"Because we are all Fractured!" he said, to no one. He was not looking at her but up into the waxy light. "We are all displaced in society. We are adrift, alone, confused, imbalanced. Knocking up against one another. It's obvious! It's empty! It's pointless! It's perfect!" He reached out and put his hands on V's shoulders. His dirty fingers were cold as stones, and as hard.

"You will be the anti-masterpiece," he said. "With you I will end art."

"Let me go."

At the dock Kholos unrolled his bundle and spread out the cloth. Then he took the long lengths of twine and began to weave them, over and under with little knots. He knew how to do this because a Seminole boy who lived in a house on stilts off the

Miami Coast knew how to do this, before the Aetherian harvested his light, his experiences at the moment of his death, by drowning, and distilled them into suitable building pieces for Kholos.

Kholos said to himself. "Thank you, little boy. Whoever you were."

Back up at the artillery emplacements around the fountain several of the artist/soldiers were assembled at the canons, Kholos saw. From somewhere they had gotten paint, not paints in tubes but cans of paint. New colors and images were being applied to the barrels of the big guns. Kholos noticed that the soldiers were not working together but that each was working on a little piece of a canon. Some had stripped off their shirts while others had lowered their goggles.

They had changed in less subtle ways, as well. Some had lost their uniform haircuts and now sported long hair or shaved heads. Some were now tall, others short. Several had become women. Kholopatiron, the Liberator pattern, nodded approvingly.

The net was not particularly large but it did not have to be. Along its edges were hooks made from the staples and nails. A long line of braided twine, a good thirty meters worth, Kholos tied off to the prow of the skiff. Then, with the city fading and fuzzing on the horizon as it flickered through all its incarnations, Kholos pushed off from the island of the Museum Fortress and out into the river. The fog and the mist enveloped him immediately, but then thinned somewhat. After he had gone well out into the open water he stowed the oars and tossed the net over the side. He dragged for a while, then pulled it up once he felt something catch.

It was a pile of wet weeds, and it tore his net and yanked out several hooks. With a sigh Kholos repaired his net, then tossed it over the side again. And then again.

Brian Storenko pointed at V. "I'm from Chicago," he said. "Chicago, not your stupid Caego. You don't have a Chicago here. You have all this other stuff. Columbium, Kiowa, Republicant, Universitat. Pang. We have Pang, but he's Pango. And the Universitat is the Byzantium. I remember things, sometimes. About where I was. If I was actually there. I don't know. I don't understand. I was always a god, I was never a god. I can't hold these thoughts. Something happened to me.

"Did you ever go for a walk, and suddenly you were not walking in the same place you started? The air had changed, the time had changed, the pace had changed. The pace, yes."

V could not move. Even her eyes were frozen, she could not blink and her eyes burned. Storenko was moving his hands, pulling at the air. The atmosphere, the shades and shapes of the space, responded to his touch.

"And you looked around and thought about who you were and what you were doing, and you knew all that. You were sure of all that, you were out for a walk. Or eating a hamburger. Do you even have hamburgers here, now? But the thought slipped in: how long have I been sure of what I am and what I am doing? Is it really forever that things worked this way, or did it happen right now, just a second ago, and I only remember it as being like this always? Is it my mind accepting this? Or was it truly like this forever? Did that ever happen to you?

"I think it happens all the time. I think we are fading and coming back, like paint on a brush when you run it across the canvas lightly then press it to finish. We are like the color of that stroke. But our minds, even my mind, the mind of a god, can't feel it. Can't register it. We think we are the same shade. The same intensity, all along."

He was walking around her. As he lifted and lowered his fingers, never touching her but something worse, V's limbs moved as well. He raised one of her feet, one of her arms, then turned her chin up and then down. After a few long minutes of this he had positioned her with her feet flat on the floor, her legs together, her back straight and her arms out from her sides. He tried a pose with her hands balled into fists but then changed his mind and put her fingers out, splayed. As final touch he raised her chin slightly.

"They say I am the god of beautiful things but I know better," Storenko said. "I am the god of anti-beauty. It was in my head. It has always been in my head, forever, because I am a god. I am to twist and break beauty. Irony, concept, these are my true tools. I am to stifle creativity. I am to make art the territory of a few, maybe less than a few, maybe no one. I am the god who will erect the walls between creation and experience. I can make beauty meaningless. I have to, or I will not be a god any longer. I don't know what I'll be. Maybe I will be back on my walk, out for a hamburger in Chicago."

Her heart had stopped. She was not breathing. But she could see and hear and smell. She tried to think but it was hard. Her thoughts were slowing down, making less sense.

"I used to love to draw," Brian said, sadly. "All I wanted was to draw. But they, or he, I suppose, made me a god. I didn't ask for this. Don't blame me."

Brian looked up at the random windows cut into the rusty and stained metal walls that made up his studio. Some were covered and others weren't. Moving his hands about he changed the light. With a cupped palm he brought a gray beam in a patch under V's feet, then moved it behind her. Snapping his fingers it disappeared and this time he tried a yellowy, sickly light. He put it above her, alongside her, and right behind her head. This went on for some time.

"I will be uncreative," said Brian. "I will make something so worthless it will suck at the life of all the masterpieces assembled here. You will be pointed, loaded with agendas and overlapping meanings. You will render beauty so subjective it will die."

V could no longer smell. Her eyes were locked straight forward. As a final touch Brian pointed at her feet and raised them up so she was standing on her tiptoes.

Storenko pulled up his sleeves. "Let's get to work," he said.

Out on the river Kholos pulled up the pack. But it was not the pack. The sword and the rifle were pristine. The gun held no water and the varnish on its furniture was still shining. The sword, which he checked after pulling it from its scabbard, was also clean and remained razor-edged. But the pack itself was decrepit, with the leather and canvas decayed and the rations turned to nothing. The rope had nearly disintegrated, and the clothing was washed out of all of its color. It was, Kholos thought, as if the pack had lay on the bottom of the river for years.

Kholos, holding the ruined pack and the worthless supplies in his lap, looked over at the Museum Fortress, then back at the city of Neo Cumae, flickering through all of its stages of growth. Kholos untied the rifle and the sword and lay them down in the boat. At least he had those necessities, along with his special ammunition. Then he had an idea.

He tied his line around the bag, tightly. Then, after waiting for the skyline of the city to change to something he thought was fairly modern, he tossed the bag back into the water. As he pulled it up the vision of Neo Cumae changed from skyscrapers and cars to domes and strange, gliding creatures. The bag in his hands was a pile of muck, unrecognizable. Only the metal came up as solid, but even then it was rusted through and crumbly. Kholos threw it back, and tried again, watching the city closely. On this attempt he brought up the backpack wet and water logged, but not falling apart.

Pleased with his work, Kholos smiled as he began to row back towards the island and the museum. Pulling the skiff into the dock he saw that the canons had been completely made over. Some of them re-worked with torches and chisels so they no longer resembled canons at all. They were, Kholos thought, each very interesting, very original. Some were even beautiful, and he stared at them and let the designs and colors and lines and shapes strike him, move him.

As he walked along the emplacements, the soldiers of the Museum Fortress began to follow him. They did not attempt to explain their work, or tell him what it was he was looking at, but they were obviously watching his reactions. Kholos, after spending a few minutes on each artillery piece, turned to them.

"Impressive," he said. "I like them all."

Kholos saw the uniforms were gone. There were women and men of all ages, even a few older children and few very old people. Some wore overalls and others wore fancy suits, a few wore dresses and one or two wore some paint-splotched pants. One wore a welding mask and one was naked except for the bits of plaster stuck to her skin. They held hammers, paint brushes, pieces of wire, and chisels, spatulas, saws, a hundred other implements. Some had bright pigments on their fingertips, others a box of crayons. The canons, from the dark, surreal expressionist sculpture to the one done up in powdery pastels of ponies and flowers, all presented themselves.

A woman in coveralls and no shoes holding a hammer stepped up to Kholos. "What do we do now?"

"I can't tell you that," said Kholos. "You've been freed, so you have to decide that on your own."

The artists murmured among themselves.

Brian pointed at V's left leg. It changed. Changed from the lanky limb of a young girl to the shriveled and spotted leg of an old woman. He pointed at her scalp, and stabbed his finger in the air. Patches formed, some downy and thin like a newborn's, some frazzled and gray, some long and shining. V's mind fragmented along with her body. She was tired. She was aroused. She was confused. She was excited. She was nervous. She was confident. But of herself she felt nothing. She was a concept, an object.

Stepping lightly around her Storenko twisted her spine. It began straight like an athlete's and then slumped at the shoulders under the weight of old age. He charged one breast with cancer and the other he flushed with adolescence. He made her pregnant and then reconsidered and made her barren. One eye he blinded and the other he filled with wonder, like a child's. He rotted out her lower teeth so they were brown stubs, made half of her upper teeth baby teeth, and the other upper half shining white enough for a Televia program.

Unsure about her nose, he tried it small as a button and long and hooked, then broke it with a snap of his fingers. He re-set the end straight and tried it with one half mottled and speckled, the other half pure. Considering his choice under a sequence of different lights he manipulated with his free hand, he instead put her nose back the way he had first seen her when she arrived in his studio the day before. The juxtaposition of the pretty, symmetrical nose against the one sunken cheek, the wrinkled forehead, the bony chin, the three kinds of teeth pleased him.

V slipped farther away from meaning. She meant nothing as herself. She was gone.

After a few final experiments with V's toes and fingers, Storenko stepped back, lowered his finger, and admired his work. The figure before him was horrible. Unbalanced. Untrue.

"Go ahead," said Brian. "Walk a bit, say something."

The un-V took an ugly step on her re-wrought legs. It was disjointed and affected. Laden with abstract meaning.

"Broken blue bass fishing," said V, her voice a different speed and timbre with every word.

Brian laughed and clapped his hands. "Genius!" he whispered. "Genius! Jigsaw, come here!" he shouted. "I've done it!"

"Cats wiggle in the saucy pencil," intoned V.

At the little shelter in the long and dusty hall where Kholos and V had spent the night Kholos dropped the bag, the rifle, and the sword. He looked up and down the hall with his eyes narrowing and focusing like a telescope. The door to the studio off the wing, he saw, was ajar and the red rope was down. Kholos reached into the bag for his belt, and its canisters of purified, compressed light.

Jigsaw, in a ruffled tuxedo shirt and a pair of sunglasses, stepped out of a shadow. He was smoking a pipe. On his feet were tap shoes and as he walked his feet clicked and clacked on the cement floor. He smelled of vodka and smoked salmon, and he had grown a mustache. Circling V he smoked his pipe and nodded sagely.

"The anti-masterpiece," said Brian, pleased with himself.

Jigsaw continued to nod.

"Regimental discharged pet food in the morning," said V.

"Brilliant," said Jigsaw. "Total concept. I suspect your audience could go mad, if I were not there to explain what they were looking at. It's perfect. Ideal for telling people how to think."

"She could take a stroll through the rotunda," suggested Brain. "Imagine."

Jigsaw cleared his throat, and said, "This clever re-working of the 'Fractured' concept represents the artist's belief that art can never be objective, that beauty is without standard, perhaps standardless, that craft and technique must kneel before the artist's intent."

"Go on," said Brian, grinning with pride.

"You'll have to kill her, of course," said Jigsaw. "Kill her, for real."

"Oh yes, I was thinking on the Televia."

"Pincers bookshelf flick," said V. Half of her face laughed and the other half cried.

Jigsaw looked up from his critique. "Wait," he said suddenly. "Something's wrong."

Wings of light spanning through seven of the additional dimensions proven but not perceived, the threads of existence shrouding him in an aura of will and imagination, Kholos blasted his way laterally through time as he flew down the hall. Flickers of reality blinked in and out as he passed. His helmet glowed. It was the world zooming past Kholos, while he stayed still: there was V the day before, and Sergeant Dugan. The air froze in mid-motion, then slid backwards as if yanked.

Kholos, though, did not appear in these bits. He knew he was ripping a seam of reality, leaving a track for those who would pursue him clear as a signpost. Kholos had never walked the hall, the sweep of his wings dictated as they sliced away existence. The gap would scream alarm to his pursuit. Soaring down the corridor, Kholos felt himself look at himself, from back in the rotunda, from a different point in time. A different Kholos, in two places at once.

Kholos descended down through the seconds. A knuckle on Storenko's finger twitched at V. She flashed through physical forms, Fractured at infinite speed, moving backwards. Everything had happened. Nothing had happened. Kholos separated the instant when Storenko had discovered her, entered it. V writhed on the floor, wracked with pain and confusion, re-made but still undone.

Storenko screamed as Kholos grabbed the artist's hands within his steely gauntlets and broke his fingers, all at once. There was a series of cracks followed by a slow, cold grinding, like stones in a mill. The fingers burst and bled. The bones powdered. They would never heal.

"Jigsaw! Jigsaw! Help me!"

Kholos stood over Storenko, holding his ruined hands in the grip of his glowing armor. The heat of him scorching through, the smell of cooked skin. The smoke rose before Storenko's face.

"You're finished," said Kholos. His voice was the Thunder. With each word the walls shook and the glass in the windows shattered and fell upon them as dust.

Jigsaw, in a full tuxedo and wearing sunglasses, stepped forward from a shadow.

"And you," said Kholos. "What are you, exactly?"

Jigsaw smiled. "Ever your servant, here to interpret."

"What's that supposed to mean?"

An explosion burst through the wall. Sunlight streamed in through the dust. The canons etched and painted and embossed were arrayed along the parapet, pointing inwards. The army of conscript artists was in mutiny, and had turned their weapons against the walls of the Museum Fortress.

"Fire the abstract artillery!" shouted a woman commanding the artists. "Remember, just the wings, just the wings! Don't damage the rotunda!"

Kholos scooped up a trembling V and held her close, twisting down the dials on his canisters. He ran for the doors, and reached them before the next volley hit. Behind them, Jigsaw removed his tuxedo jacket. Before him holding up his wrecked hands before his face, Brian Storenko screamed and screamed.

Jigsaw held out his pipe at the army of artists bombarding the wing.

"This is not a pipe," he said.

11. Six Swords, Two Cats, and the Infinite Fractured

The Twin Towers of New Taabe shone like pillars of gold rising from the sea. They reflected the soft white waves and the sandy beaches of the Summa Pacificum as if to mirror their own perfection, then stabbed at the sky. The capital city of the Incorporated Nation of the Third Comanche, New Taabe had replaced the metropolis of Red River as the seat of Comanche government. New Taabe's status as perhaps the most politically powerful city in the world, at least in the non-Stalinista world, confirmed the city's glory.

Located on the southwestern coast of the Tezkan State on the edge of the Incorporated Nation, New Taabe was the site where the manifest destiny of the Comanche people was symbolically completed. The Great Expansion had begun as a nomadic and conquering enterprise largely undertaken by the alliance of separate Kwahadah and Nokoni tribes, two major parts of what the Republican refugees would misname the "Comanche."

When the expansion reached Tezkan, the united tribes formed permanent settlements. The work of the early Peta Nocona government of the Incorporated Nation moved to a more central location, in the city of Numunuh, which also allowed the Comanche leadership to deal directly with the last of the Kiowa tribes. Once the last bits of Kiowa resistance had been dealt with, however, the capital relocated back to Red River, in the home country, where it remained for generations.

The government of the Incorporated Nation of the Third Comanche was separated into two distinct and balanced wings, with each wing occupying their own tower. The functions of these two wings were executed by a Peace Chief and a War Chief, which were evolutions of the roles the original Comanche tribes had developed. In recent times, the Peace Chiefs had mostly been elderly businessmen who had either amassed great fortunes in mining or railroading, or built large companies in Universitat-licensed technologies such as automobiles or light bulbs.

Previously, Peace Chiefs had been diplomats or explorers. All were men, and all were well into their sixties and the time of their appointment. The War Chief, which had been a temporary post until the Great Expansion required a permanent military presence, was elected by the Comanche people directly. But, in an ingenious way of balancing power, the Peace Chief would call for a new War Chief election every six years. And then the War Chief could, if desired, appoint a new Peace Chief.

Each Chief was responsible for the Incorporated Nation within separated spheres. The War Chief and the various departments he oversaw managed military matters, economic policy, statecraft, public safety, and law enforcement. The Peace Chief was responsible for spiritual matters, domestic legislation, and education policies, among others. For nearly 200 years, the government of the Third Comanche had functioned with relative smoothness and, at times, brilliance. After the juggernaut of the Stalinistas, the Incorporated Nation was the most powerful nation on the planet. In the non-Stalinista world only the Republicant rivaled the Third Comanche in terms of cultural influence, and the Comanche were vastly superior to the war-torn Republicant in terms of economic power.

The power of the Comanche, in particular their strong spirituality, was codified by the decision of the Universitat to permit the Third Comanche to keep parts of their own system of forces and spirits. While all other races and nations on earth had over the centuries surrendered their myths and their ideas to the Universitat ideal of faith balanced with reason and reason tempered by faith, the Third Comanche were allowed to teach their children about the concepts of medicine and animal spirit. Provided they acknowledged the supremacy of Pang and the Universitat-approved canon of Adonai. Meanwhile, the gods of the Boracs were murdered, the god of the Slythe imprisoned, and all the various other human gods and goddesses were retroactively destroyed by Universitat agents. Only the Comanche "puha" remained independent. At least until the Stalinistas arrived.

Unlike other powerful Native Columbium peoples, the Comanche had not formed tyrannical Kingdoms, like the Inuit, or fragile little democratic republics, like the Cherokee and the Iroquois, but an immense nation of shareholders with a mighty standing army and dozens of continental companies and banks that dominated finance and economics throughout the non-Stalinista world. There was even an assumption that the historical inevitability of the Stalinistas could be halted on the shores of the Incorporated Nation: a heresy, to the Universitat.

All this was about to change, as at the peak of the tower of the War Chief, Thirty-Seven Bears died slowly and painfully. The six beings before him stood in a semi-circle around his desk and burned him with their heat, blinded him with their light, and pummeled him with their voices. He could not recall their arrival, but all of the windows in his offices were shattered and white puffs of smoke floated up from the places where their steps scorched the hand-woven carpets that lined the floor.

"What do you want?" Thirty-Seven Bears asked.

This was difficult to say as some of his jaw and mouth had been badly burned when the six entered his offices on their wings of white fire. He could not remember that they flew, could not believe that they flew, but Thirty-Seven Bears was an intelligent man and understood they had to have flown to have crashed through the windows. Fragments of the thick, golden glass were peppered across his forehead, and he was bleeding from several small cuts and gashes. He was pleased, however, that he had the strength to stand and face his attackers, even after being blown back onto the floor and out of his chair.

"Are you Stalinistas?" he could think of no other enemies capable of making such an attack. The Kiowa certainly had the motivation, but all the Kiowa were in camps or watched on reservations. He wondered what Peace Chief Quannah Reynolds, in his own tower across the way, was thinking. Surely the old man must have seen the flash and heard the explosion. Surely he would muster some kind of response to whomever, whatever was before him in his office. And where were all his braves? The elite Red Ravens who patrolled the towers?

Thirty-Seven Bears focused through his pain. He stood a little straighter. He thought, squinting and shaking in the wind and the heat and the broken glass and the blasting light. He thought, and his thoughts made him shiver despite the furnace heat.

"Are you agents of the Universitat?" he asked, softly, fearfully. Thirty-Seven Bears was a powerful man, privy to secrets, rumors, tales of special forces the Universitat kept hidden away.

"No," said the one to his side, a female. "But you are an agent of the Universitat."

Thirty-Seven Bears protested. "I don't understand."

"You have failed," said the one before him.

"At what?"

"At tracking the deserter," said the one to his right, another male.

"The deserter?" he asked. Thirty-Seven Bears remembered an urgent memo from the Universitat about a deserter somewhere in the lesser-know Columbium Territories. The order had come through an hour ago, less than that. He had, as the Universitat requested, dutifully signed the edict and distributed it accordingly. "I can assure you, the Universitat's wishes are being fulfilled as we speak."

"Not so," said another. Her voice chimes like wind over bones, wind through bones. "The deserter is at large, whereabouts unknown, and well-warned that the powers of this world are against him. Because of your subordinate's failure to acknowledge the supremacy of our orders. Now we must emerge in a different way, in a different time. You will provide that way and time."

The six were all tall, without hair on their heads, all with thin faces and wide eyes, long cheekbones and pale coloring. They had no eyebrows. Each wore armor of greaves, breastplates, gauntlets, boots, wrist guards, and helmets, all of which glowed so brightly that Thirty-Seven Bears could not look directly at them, even as they raised the visors of their helmets to stare at him.

"You're," he gulped. "Adonai?"

"We are beyond Adonai," answered the first.

Each of the six carried a long, slightly curved sword and a long-barreled sniper's rifle, crossed in an *X* on their backs.

The continuing heat, so strong, from their armor, had burned away Thirty-Seven Bears' eyebrows and singed his hands. The carpets, the wood paneling, the hangings on the wall, all of it was burning. The pain of the burn up his jaw throbbed and made him dizzy.

"He is waiting for help," said another, the woman who, somehow, seemed older than the others even though she looked the same. "He does not understand the finality of our judgement."

"We can be in two times at once," said another who stepped forward and put his hands on Thirty-Seven Bears' desk. The man's armor, unlike the others, actually flamed rather than simply glowed. His voice was the crackle and gush of an inferno, instead of the thunder. Instinctively Thirty-Seven Bears leaned away from the heat. "No one is coming. We have always been here."

"Enough," said the first. He carried some authority with the others, Thirty-Seven Bears realized. "My message is this." He stared at Thirty-Seven Bears. His words shook the room. "This instant provides our hidden entrance, nothing more. Now. The Third Comanche never were. They never are. They never will be. The Comanche are and always were and from this instant to infinity a tiny, backward speck of a race of no consequence, no power, and no future. This is your punishment."

Time tore.

A collapsing light, so bright, so fast, burst within the thoughts of Thirty-Seven Bears. The seams of reality unfolded, then refolded along new axes. A flower of crystallized moments blossoming and unblossoming in a billion different blooms, light escaping from the folds of petals comprised of thought and will.

Then the light slowed, and the universe began to tick again.

Thirty-Seven Bears looked up from his bowl of dried corn. There was not enough to eat. He sighed. There was never enough to eat. He wanted a drink.

The camps of the Comanche stretched from the banks of the Red River, polluted now from upstream where the Kiowa manufactured their trucks and cars. Conditions had never been good in the camps, but ever since the Stalinistas had landed, finally, in the Northwest and begun their conquest of the Columbium continent the Kiowa had been taking more and more away from their Comanche prisoners. There was no more meat, at all, and the scraggly few head of horses the Comanche were allowed to keep had been rounded up and shipped off in support of the war effort, probably for food. The Comanche had never been allowed rifles or firearms of any sort since the Kiowa armies had conquered their ancestral lands, generations ago, but now even their bows and spears were taken, so that the metal could be melted down. Also gone were medicines from the clinic, coal for heat, textiles, even chalk for the schools.

Thirty-Seven Bears had heard rumors that in some camps there were outbreaks of typhus and cholera. He looked out through the fence that marked the edge of the reservation. A fair distance if traveled by foot, the river was merely a trickle behind him on the horizon. No one wanted to become a Stalinista, but Thirty-Seven Bears wondered, his fingers clawed through the wire, how much worse it would be than living under the Kiowa. An imaginative man, Thirty-Seven Bears closed his eyes and let himself dream of another world, where the Comanche might own a few head of healthy horse, and roam freely through their own territory.

For a long while Thirty-Seven Bears waited by the fence. After a while he picked up his bowl and began the long walk back. The long drafty buildings of his people were smudges on the eastern vista.

"Now," said the one called Gabriel, the one who had announced the will of the Aetherian. "We must see to Kholopatiron. Whenever he may have fled to, it cannot be far."

Each adjusted the canisters attached to their belts and, on wings of solid light, rose.

Their patterns were: Gabriel the Messenger, Nathaniel of Fire, Raguel the Chosen, who was the elder woman, Ramiel of Thunder, and Sandalphon of Power. The young female was called Sraosha. Her designation was of Obedience.

Golgothan sits on a silver chair in a cave of frozen light. The peak of his current mountain scrapes the stars. Golgothan running from mountain to mountain, the rebel saint. The Adonai of Quests, the Saint of Escapes, of Explorers, of Wishes and Daydreams, Golgothan cannot settle. The silver chair is a pilot's seat, the cave is his cockpit.

All those who leave a warm and safe place for the unknown say an unwilling prayer to Golgothan. All those who ponder, 'what lies on the other side of the mountain?' They give Golgothan thanks. Golgothan has made himself the Adonai of questions. This was not his original purpose, but he asked himself, *why not?* And broke away. Now he is hunted, disdained, and slandered.

He does what he can to protect himself. Cats patrol the ledges and crevices of his mountain. They can be panthers, cougars, tigers, jaguars, or any other breed that suits the clime and the mountain's mood.

Golgothan's greatest defense is not his cats, although the cats would differ, but the one million streams and rivulets that run from the hidden lakes of wishes and dreams within Golgothan's deepest chambers, tucked away under meters and meters of stone. Through his streams Golgothan touches all the water of the world, and they talk to one another, and his ponds and streams tell him things. Golgothan knows, for example, that angels are loose in the world, but not why. *Angels cannot act other than the will of their masters*, he thinks, *but one of them, at least, is acting very strangely.*

Golgothan also knows from his waters that he is the last free god, the last free power not murdered or imprisoned by the agents of the Universitat. He appears on no sanctioned list. This is fine with Golgothan.

And he knows there is a rip in the world.

The water explains to Golgothan this was not the first incidence of a breaking and re-making of days, years, decades, aeons. And that, in little minutes here and there, the rips have continued. Golgothan does not know why the world is put together this way, made and unmade. *Do the stitches in time occur naturally? Or are they somehow artificial? The will of something, someone?*

What would someone want with an entire world? What would one do with a world?

Why would they take it apart and put it back together, over and over, just so?

To make a hat?

He thinks, patiently, on what it means now that he is the last free Adonai. It means his power grows in correlation to the un-free saints. As magnificent as they are, so must he be. If they were feeble, then he would seem feeble. So he is mighty. These angels, all of them, could be coming for him.

Golgothan thinks, *Can an angel truly act beyond the instructions of its makers? Ever?*

With a blink Golgothan moves his mountain, his cave, his chair, moves himself. The jungles of a ruined continent steam up along his slopes. Toxic pink and green mists swirl about the ground. Something went terribly wrong in this place, but Golgothan cannot remember what it was. His guard-cats curl up on branches of newly formed trees, above the killing clouds. They are panthers now.

The thinking on a thing, the questioning, is Golgothan's strength. Deciding is not. Golgothan can fight, but his battles are won obliquely. Ideally, they are won without his opponents knowing they have fought. The avalanche is a last resort. He has built a new army, though. An army as lost as he feels.

Golgothan believes Pang, the Zero God, is the enemy he must defeat. But Pang is elusive. Pang made the world from nothing, then vanished. *Where is Pang? Who is Pang?* Golgothan wonders. *Is Pang truly in charge here?*

Gologothan rises. The light outside is brilliant. The stars illuminate everything: his loves, his hopes, his losses, his flaws. He considers their traces, *this star makes a shape like a sword, this one like a ruby big as a fist, this one like a dark and blinded eye. The light which composes them will travel on, beyond the world, forever. Dipping and curving and waiting, these things are eternal.*

The floor of the cave is intricate, a carpet sewn of mineral and metal threads: malachite, zinc, iron, copper. The cave had been gold and bronze and silver, encrusted with gems, before his revolt, but gold bores Golgothan. Alloys interest him, tungsten and titanium. Also igneous rocks hold some appeal. There are statues he has worked from flowing magma of his great cats, of women and men he has known as friends, lovers, enemies. There are also, lately, abstract shapes made from uranium and plutonium, secret names Golgothan has kept hidden in his cave. The Universitat, he understands, would erase these shapes and these names.

There is something new in these shapes: tessaracts, anti-spheres, curving sheets in five dimensions that stretch to the ceiling, mobiles that hang and dance from wires that spark with sea-lighting (because there are mountains under the sea). Some idea is hidden in these new stones. Golgothan only needs a man or a woman to start the climb to find it. He would bless their every step. The vault of the cave is lined with the bones of ancient fish and empty shells, all bleached. The music of winds and echos roll through, but tomorrow the sounds could be of the jungle, or of goats and sheep, or of cars and trucks.

In his cave on the shelves, the floor, in locked chests, Golgothan has saved what shreds of ideas he could. Shiva cycles through destruction and creation under a glass dome the size of an apple. Apollo tethers the sun to his chariot, but it is not the sun, just a coin. The concepts these gods represented are destroyed, though. If set free they would be toys in the Universitat world. No one would believe in them.

There was only one true miracle, says the Universitat: that the universe was created from nothing. Thus, faith in Pang, who began the universe from zero.

Not counting the Kiowa spirits and powers, only the Slythe god survived. Thssiss, was the name of this concept. Golgothan wondered, *why Thssiss? Why had the thick, black, oozing shape that was Thssiss been taken away in ghost chains? Why not just another Adonai? Why?*

And where were the Borac ideas? The Borac gods? There were no bodies.

The Universitat employed Copernican theory combined with a ghost dance to kill the idea of Raven. Raven's speed and location could not be observed, they added. Therefore, he was not part of Pang's perfect creation, only a myth.

The Pontifical Dean Isaac Newton gave a famous lecture soon after, noting that nothing could fly, only float or glide, and then only if thrown or launched correctly. In fact, Newton clarified, what goes up must indeed come down. He held up a ball to prove his point. He let it drop to the floor beside the lectern. It fell. Faith in Newtonian physics became a commandment of the Universitat teaching around the world. It was not to be questioned any more than the miracle of creation was to be questioned. Raven had never flown.

Does anyone still try to fly?

Above his cave and his pollution-proof panthers the stars wheeled, tracing mandalas against the darkness. Golgothan watched and listened to the hum and verve of the universe. He wore a long jacket with deep pockets over a sweater and dark pants. He appeared as a middle-aged man, unshaven but not unclean, with brown hair touched with gray. He wore black eyeglasses and tended to smell of woodsmoke, rain, and base metals. On his wide feet he wore sturdy boots, and carried a multi-purpose tool of his own design in a small leather holster at his hip. With this tool he could produce a thin single-edged sword, a long beam of blue light, a flame, a watch, a map, a coin, a cold drink, and several dozen other potentially useful items. When he was not staring at the sky or moving his mountain or walking through the deeper caves of himself, he tinkered with this tool. His latest addition had been a camera, with which he took pictures of the stars.

How could Golgothan reach the stars?

They had asked questions about the stars, he remembered, in the city by the Asinwati Mountains. *What was the name of that place?*

Golgothan was confused about this city. The city was still there, he knew, but it was hidden behind a veil of flames. Many questions were asked in the city, the city whose name no one could now remember. The city was always burning, and had always been burning. Pang had delivered it already formed and already aflame. To suggest otherwise was a sin against faith.

Golgothan did not understand what had happened at the city, or why he could not remember it happening only that it had always been that way, which made no sense. Golgothan was a saint of questions, however, and it did not disturb him that he did not understand something.

Golgothan stepped away from the mouth of the cave. The light shone around him. The cats howled and the streams gurgled to sound the warning of the coming departure, and then the peaks outside became other peaks.

In the pockets of his coat Golgothan carried two special cats, his talking cats, who kept him company and discussed things with him. One was a gray tabby with huge ears. The other was a brown calico. They both had white bellies and white paws and long whiskers. Golgothan considered them his advisors. Their names were Crick, the calico and more forgiving, and Busto, the tabby who felt that Golgothan was not especially intelligent.

"Busto, Crick, are you there?" Golgothan said. White paws and then the two whiskered faces of the cats peeked out over the pockets. Both had been sleeping when Golgothan called them and they blinked their eyes at the starlight.

"Yes, Golgothan?" said Crick. Crick was a female, and her voice was soft.

"What do you think happened at the city burning forever?"

"I think," said Busto in a husky, disdainful voice, "that they asked a question that set their city on fire."

Golgothan nodded at this answer. It seemed wise.

Golgothan thought on this. "Maybe," he said, "we can ask that question as well?"

"But what if the answer is the fire?" Busto demanded. "Duh."

"There are angels loose in the world," said Crick. "Again."

"But do you think he could be different, this time? Did I do the right thing, setting this angel in motion?"

Busto and Crick looked at each other. Busto's ears twitched.

When the city was destroyed, destroyed in perpetuity and painted with permanent fire, a ripple ran across the world.

There was no way to measure its passing. There was a city, at the foot of the mountains, and it was on fire because reason and faith required it burn, forever. The city was on fire because it was always on fire. But in the instant of annihilation reality had cracked, and spread like a stone hitting against glass.

Things changed.

Some people vanished, leaving not even memories behind. Tomas Tom, the baker's helper in Duran at Josie's, for example, ceased to exist. No one remembered him. Not his wife, nor his children. Not the other bakers. There was the empty locker with the apron and the white hat. Who had worn them? No one could say.

A few people, almost all within a certain radius of the city, suffered more dramatic and painful changes. Bodies split in two, either vertically or at the waist, carried on for an instant, and then died. Some were transformed. Children became trees, flowerbeds. Old men turned into meadows and clouds. Animals shifted in a variety of ways. Herds of cattle burst into shallow, clear pools. Dogs vaporized into clouds of fragrant steam. The weather and the ground around the city became entirely random, sunny one day then ice-covered the next. Shale, in particular, showed strange effects.

There were other, less visible changes. A man might have lost a decade from his memory, a decade amputated from his life. All knowledge and experience wiped away from the given months or years. A person's extremities might shift in size, so that a young boy could wield the hand of a giant, or a girl could have fingers long as knitting needles. According to rumor, however, the Stalinistas were as yet unaffected. But then, no one ever actually spoke to a Stalinista.

Most of those affected, though, were like V. Their bodies shifted day by day through seemingly random points. V could be a toddler one day, with her consciousness intact but hobbled by all the needs and wants of a three-year-old, and then the next day a woman of sixty-five, with a sharp mind but a bad back. It was as if their selves were disassociated with the normal pace of time.

The governments, Columbium, Kiowa, Inuit, and Republicant, struggled to address the problem from a political and economic point of view. But it was not until the Universitat announced that the condition, now called being 'Fractured,' was spiritual in nature that a coherent solution was presented.

Being Fractured was to suffer from a disease, the Universitat explained. Disease was a sin against reason, of course, the failure to acknowledge the power of hygiene, environment, medicine, mindset, and diet. But the Fractured manifestation was an epidemic of faith, a failure to acknowledge the power of belief, ritual, and progress. The Fractured, said the Universitat, were sinners against faith. It added credence to the Universitat's announcement that the most concentrated of the Fractured were in Columbium territories, as the Columbium peoples were known to be shiftless and untrustworthy in general.

The Universitat denied any connection between the City Burning Forever and the Fractured.

The Universitat--enlightened, humanist, and rational-- announced that it would face the crisis of the Fractured through quarantine and treatment. They established isolation centers, some of which were little more than camps in the wilderness, some of which were housed in buildings in cities and towns. The Fractured were required, by Universitat edict, to go for treatment at their nearest center. Ideally, the Universitat explained through its Bishops, Deans, Professors, Teachers, and Priests, the Fractured would be completely cured at the end of their stay.

Universitat representatives everywhere organized those Fractured, and sent them in the trucks and trains to the quarantine centers. After a few weeks, the Fractured were returned to their homes and families, fully cured.

Mostly.

There were differences, people said. Differences so small they were hardly noticeable. But they were there. Differences detected by spouses, children, friends. A word spoken. An expression. A touch. It was as if, said many wives of formerly Fractured husbands, he's not the same person, not quite.

Reports of the cure and its nuances spread. Still, the Universitat compelled all Fractured to come to the centers. Increasingly by force. They did not discount rumors that faithlessness could spread through everyday contact, everyday conversation. The Universitat began their program with the large cities, and then worked their way down the population centers in the following weeks and months.

Dr. Voss stood on the steps of V's house in Duran Town. He had a list in his hand, a list of the Fractured in Duran Town. He wore a thick parka against the cold night. The Universitat, after taking care of the Columbium cities, towns, and larger villages first, had finally come for the Fractured of Duran Town.

The door opened and light erupted from within. Kholos stood on the threshold, his wings and his armor blazing. Dr. Voss shielded his eyes with his arms.

"My apologies, Nathan," said Kholos, lowering his light.

"Kholos," said Dr. Voss, stunned. "What are you doing?"

"Please hurry, Dr. Voss," said Kholos. He held something small in his hand.

"Yes, of course. Listen. It's about V. I've got a list here of all the Fractured in town." He held up the list. There were seven names there, remarkably high for a town of Duran's size. V's name, her full name that she hated, was at the top of the list. "Is she in?"

"I know about the list," said Kholos. "I know V is on it. It doesn't matter. This has already happened, to you. I am loose in time as we speak. I am somewhen else, from your point of view."

Dr. Voss blinked. There was no way Kholos could know about the list. It had come on over the Televia just an hour before.

"Be that as it may," Dr. Voss started again, slowly. "I don't like the idea of forcing people to do anything when they're not hurting anybody. Being Fractured isn't contagious, obviously, and just as obviously there's something we're not being told about this treatment. So here's what I'm doing. I'm going around tonight and telling folks about the list. In the morning I'll come again, and those that want to come can, but if you don't want to come. Well, I would make sure you weren't at home in the morning. For a few mornings, perhaps many, many mornings. Am I clear? The truck arrives tomorrow at noon. There will be Coercionists, I'm told."

"I know, Dr. Voss," Kholos began again. "We've already left here. We left weeks ago, actually. After the Second Comanche attack. We stopped at your house before we drove away. You asked me to explain, again, how I made the paper fly. You came here to an empty house tonight."

"Comanche attack? I don't understand," said Dr. Voss. "You're talking to me right now. I don't remember you leaving."

"Yes, but only because I came back to tonight to give you these." Kholos held out his hand, and showed Dr. Voss the colored bullets: blue, red, white, and black. There was one of each. "V is in danger, and I have had to use my wings again. I decided since I was already moving through time, I would come here, and give these to you."

Dr. Voss stared at the cartridges.

"Doing this may even help hide my tracks," said Kholos. "I hope."

Dr. Voss stood on the steps and gawked. "I haven't given you the list of Adonai you said you needed."

"But you will, so it makes no difference. You will not remember what happened here," said Kholos. "Your mind is not built for the shape of time I am using. But those cartridges will still be in your possession. Keep them in your pocket. You'll stumble upon them eventually. You simply won't recall where they came from. But you'll recognize what they are. Do something with them."

"What," Dr. Voss stammered. "What should I do? Shoot them?"

Kholos laughed. It was like a star chuckling. "No, no. You couldn't in any case. Study them. Question them. Do to them what you do to the shale and the paper."

"But I won't remember this, you said. I won't remember what you tell me to do with them."

"I think you would do so anyway," said Kholos. "And then you will be better prepared for when I ask you about the machine."

"Kholos, why me?"

Kholos sighed. "Because you showed Michael Staffa it was alright to think. To imagine."

"Michael's dead, Kholos. I showed him nothing that helped him, in the end."

"Yes," said Kholos. "In your way of thinking, yes he is. But you helped him."

"What do you mean, my way of thinking?"

Kholos looked up, saw himself skimming along the curved edge of time that connected him, among infinite other potentials, to the Museum Fortress, where V had wandered into the studio of Brian Storenko, the Adonai of Beauty, looking for something to eat.

Kholos doubted Dr. Voss, even with his genius, would be able to make much of the white bullet, so he had emptied out the powder and instead place a note inside. The note was brief, written by Kholos in a script that carried the same truth and weight as his thunder voice. The note said: *The name of the burning city is ANVIR.*

Then, in a blink, a tiny sewing machine appeared in Kholos's hands. Dr. Voss gasped. "When you have a moment, would you look at this for me?"

12. The Whoracle

Through the mists Kholos rowed. V, afraid and confused and in pain, sat in the prow of the boat. Their equipment and weapons and rations were bundled up in the bottom of the skiff. As they worked through the thickest of the fog Kholos paused and listened, eyes closed.

V was alive but she was wrecked. Fractured all at once, her body had a hundred different shapes and thoughts. Kholos had wrapped her head to toe in the brown dress, trying to cover the worst of it. He had no idea how to heal her and was hoping come midnight she would shift into some coherent form. She lay and shook and sweat. The smell of her was awful. He could only imagine what her thoughts were like.

Kholos explained, even though he knew she could not understand, "We're on the edge of the zone the Museum Fortress resides in. Time moves at a normal, so to speak, speed once we make our way through the fog." He looked through the lenses of his visor at the shrouded skyline of the city. "I want us to come out at a point close to where we were when we left Duran Town. Just rest, V. I'll find you help."

"Grapes. Weather. Verbiage. I can't see my face."

Kholos stowed the oars. Through his visor he saw the shadows of tall, three-masted ships docking before brick warehouses. Too long ago.

"I'm trying to cover my tracks. Every time I use my light, my wings, I make a mark, I pull a thread loose. That mark is clear and bright to those who are after us."

"Hippopotamus," V said.

"We are tracing a parabola of probability points, not a line, and I'm not so much jumping back and forth as I am jumping clear of the curve altogether, and re-entering as close as I can to where I jumped the first time. Our pursuers will assume, I'm sure, that I would jump forward. Which is what we did when we went through the tunnel from Lipstick Country, and what I did when I stopped the Second Comanche attack on Duran. Doing it this way, manually, so to speak, might hide us better. Even if we are a few weeks or months off."

Kholos saw spires and rooflines rise through the fog. Electric lights hung from tall poles and Televia cables criss-crossed everywhere. A train puffed its way along the bank. He began to paddle madly through the mist. The fog rolled in thicker, then thicker still. Then it lifted.

V screamed: two huge cargo ships were suddenly passing by them, one on each side, and their waves sent the little skiff up and down on. Kholos, summoning again the skills of the boy who fished, cut the oars deftly and aligned the skiff so that its prow faced the waves. Then he let the oars rest, dipping them only to keep the boat sharply headed into the waves. One of the big boats sounded its horn. Kholos saw from its stern it was a Republicant ship, carrying wheat or steel or toys or ladies' gowns or something else before they would be hauled from the city on to the Algonquin, Cherokee, or Kiowan lands.

Calculating the carrying capacity of the enormous ship before them, puffing steam out from its funnels amidships and stacked high with crates tethered with ropes to the deck, Kholos realized he was utilizing the memories of a Republicant trader. He wondered, why would the Aetherian have included the memories and skills of a businessman in his making? Was he supposed to negotiate something on his attack mission?

The ships passed, one heading out to the bay, the other coasting towards the big docks where cranes three times as tall as the steeple of Pang's temple in Duran waited to unload them. Little tugs alongside each steered and pushed the big boats into place. Someone from a tug cursed at Kholos for his stupidity.

Once the ship heading upriver had passed the city appeared. Neo Cumae was alive and swarming with people, cars, trucks, trolleys, and trains. The skyscrapers of great trading houses rose up like candles. The headquarters of the Kiowan Collective, representing the largest consortium of traders and also the wealthiest, rose the tallest: granite-faced with a long spire at its peak, broadcasting powerful Televia signals of the local wireless variety: something unknown in Duran Town, where all Universitat information and entertainment was carried by cable across the mountains.

There were numerous cathedrals to Pang, stunning buildings that poked up at the arcs of the stars. There were stadia, modeled on old Republicant designs or the new stylings of outsider Columbium architects and the rigid forms of the Cherokee structuralists, where sports were played and dramas and comedies staged. There were shopping avenues where products from everywhere in the non-Stalinista world were available. There were silver trains that ran on single raised rails along the edges of the city.

And there were people, people everywhere. People in the windows of the tall buildings and the squat rows of townhomes. People on the sidewalks and in cafes and shops. People hanging over the rail above the embankment watching the traffic on the river go by. People drinking. People singing. People kissing. The entire city buzzed and glowed and moved. Somewhere close to the shore a Borac sang a song clear enough to carry out onto the river and reach the skiff. Kholos rowed for the sound.

Kholos thought, *Kiowan. Was it always Kiowan?*

"They changed it," he said aloud. He understood this probably had something to do with him.

Kholos with his big hand pulled the skiff against the stones along the shore of the city. There were stone steps leading up the embankment.

"Who changed it?" said V. There was a lucid look in her eye, one of her eyes, anyway, the elder one.

"The Aetherian unfolded and folded realities. They took a piece of another universe and stitched it in place of a piece of this one. I can tell when they do, but most people can't. They can just sense something, an idea that things have changed."

It was near midnight. Kholos watched V. Let her change, he wished. Let her shift. Into anything else but this.

"Who changed it?" she repeated. Then she groaned as the different pieces of her body rebelled against each other.

"V?" he said. "Do you understand me?"

"Foot-racing," said V. Then she started to laugh. "I'm trying."

Kholos brought the boat in and unloaded their equipment onto the wet stones. The night, down by the river, was chilly and V shivered in his arms. "V?"

"So shouldn't we try to stop them? Don't we have to? These people that play with my world?"

"We don't have to do anything, except escape," he had already started to climb up the steps towards the light and the noise above. He paused. "Get clear of this, reach the real freedom."

"Dr. Voss would try to stop them. Michael would have tried to stop them," V said, softly. She had her arms around her shoulders. Kholos held her tight. "Gladiola."

They walked up the steps and into the city. Kholos, before stepping out from the shadows of the docks, removed Dr. Voss's list from his pants pocket. Carefully he unfolded the paper and thumbed his way down the locations, instead of the names. He surveyed the city.

"King Close," he announced, reading the names. "King Close in Neo Cumae. Not a building or a street. Just Neo Cumae."

"Forged mornings," said V.

There were Columbiums, Kiowans, Inuit, Republicant, Algonquin, and Cherokee. There were Ebon people, with smooth brown or black skin. There was, also, the same Borac they had heard singing from the skiff. As they passed the Borac, a tall, young woman whose tusks were lacquered in soft red and blue swirls and with a fountain of oil-black hair sprouting from the top of her head, Kholos felt her eyes on his back.

"Let's find a place to rest," he said.

They passed a huge plaza lined with skyscrapers. They were, Kholos saw, on a wide boulevard called the Mer Via. It ran north-south on a plum line. Cross streets were numbered: I Street, II Street, III Street and so on.

Scents of strange meats roasting on skewers and dashed with foreign spices spilled out from narrow storefront stands. Placards and pamphlets were for sale on racks. Many were printed in strange languages, and some had no words at all, only pictures. Music poured out of a doorway, thumping sounds of drums and the rhythmic shouts of men and women in Cherokee. There were Republicant women in clinging short skirts and high-heeled shiny shoes, Columbium women in men's creased trousers. An Iroquois professional in a dark suit and briefcase sauntered by with a Mohawk dyed green.

V closed her eyes, images of Michael and Kholos and Duran and the Lipstick Country and the Museum Fortress combining with her confusion and pain. When she opened them again, it was as if everything had gone quiet. Just for an instant, V was all alone, clinging to Kholos's arm. She reached up and touched Kholos's angular smooth face with a jagged hand, the fingers all gone crazy. The crowd spilled around her and Kholos like water around a rock in a stream.

"Kholos," she half-said, half-wept. "Listen to the buildings."

Kholos saw many, many people, the city, the cars, and the stars of the late night starting to slow.

Then, Kholos saw.

Inside the right ears of all of the citizens of Neo Cumae was a small black dot, about the size of a pea. There was no wire attached to the dot, no antenna. It just rested right on the edge of the ear.

As they stood to the side of the curb and watched the multitude walk, dance, laugh, skip, and run by, there came a sudden, minute crackle through the air, as if a switch had been thrown and a charge was shot through the entire city, jumping from street to street and car to car and person to person. It took a fraction of a second.

The mood changed. Where before the citizens had been playful and rushing, now they were scowling and slow. On the street cars blared their horns and flashed their lights. People jostled on the sidewalks. The facades of the buildings seemed to glare disapprovingly down.

"What just happened?" asked V. "What just happened?"

They scanned the streetscape. Passers by frowned at them, mumbled things under their breath. The Kiowa men and women in their suits and severe skirts changed their posture, holding their arms in and their chins low. Republican grand dames with polar wraps and protected by handsome saber-armed escorts pulled away in disdain from dirty-faced Columbium delivery boys.

A breeze, chilled and slightly stinky, blew by.

On an alley off of IX Street, Kholos saw a bit of graffiti in Republican letters. The tag said "Pang is dead. Long live the King."

Kholos and V still had all of their money, although in Neo Cumae it was not much. After walking south for many blocks the crowds thinned some, and there were more row houses and apartment blocks and parks, fewer skyscrapers and stores and plazas. They passed taverns with names like the Appian and the Kroner, Branca's and the Karas. They passed bakeries and little crafts shops like a cobbler's and a cabinet maker's. Finally, they found a small hotel, and, using almost half of their funds, secured a room.

"Come from the Western Territories?" asked the man behind the counter. Kholos, with so many old-fashioned memories, had expected a question as to whether they were Universitat-married but the man did not ask that. In his ear was the black dot. V, thankfully silent for the moment, was wrapped up on a chair in the lobby.

"Yes. We're from Orang. How could you tell?"

"We get people from all over. Nobody's born in Neo Cumae. They just wind up here."

Kholos saw the man had an earpiece, and he pointed at it. "What do you hear on that?"

"What? The receiver? Forget I have it in, most of the time. I get the news. The real deal. All the buzz. You'll get your own, soon enough, you stay here in the city. Everybody gets one."

"Really?"

"That's right. What's wrong with your girl, there?"

"She has a bad cold. Where did you find the receiver? Does the Universitat distribute them?"

"Your receiver finds you," said the man, firmly. "I notice you don't have much of an accent yourself. You sure you're from Orang, buddy?"

Their room was a tiny box with a single window that opened onto an alley. The bed was thin and the sheets were scratchy, the pillows flat. Kholos dropped the bag on the floor with a thump.

Early in the morning, before the sun had risen, V awoke. There was a black dot on her pillow the size of a pea. V took the bud and put in into her ear. V listened. There was nothing. No, there was something.

It was a buzz, soft and steady. It was reassuring, it calmed her. The buzz spoke things, but she could not quite make them out, although she wanted to, badly. The buzz. The news. The truth. Underneath, behind, the buzz there was a voice, and it was calming and firm. V knew the voice agreed with her already, even though she could not quite make out the exact words the voice spoke. She turned her back to Kholos alongside her in the bed and let the voice speak to her. Then the buzz was gone. She shivered. Behind her Kholos sat, the receiver yanked from her ear in the palm of his hand. She could almost hate him.

"V?"

"Back. Give it. That one is mine."

Kholos gave it back. The voice was clearer now. It rose and ebbed, she could tell, something vanishing and leaving just the soothing buzz, other times roaring up. Her mind gelled according to the dictates of the voice. As she drifted off to sleep again the voice spoke clearly at last, clear as trumpets and thunder, a little like Kholos could speak, in fact.

Kholos suddenly shot up, staring at the door.

"This is King Close," said the voice in V's ear. "Speaking the truth. Distance is a lie. Reason and faith, my friends, reason and faith are all we have in the end. Pang provides. Stay tuned."

Someone was knocking. He yanked open the door. Standing there was the Borac woman who had been singing by the docks the night before.

"You're not safe here," she said, then looked at V. "She needs to take that out. Right now."

"Who are you? How did you find us?"

"You glow to me," said the Borac. She was very tall, even for a Borac. Tall and slender. Her hair was braided with metal bands. Her tusks were very beautiful.

"I glow?"

"What you carry, my gods. The tusks, from Gyr Zax. They glow to me. They will to every *exu*. I know who you are. I know Gyr Zax gave you his tusks."

Kholos recognized the Borac word, *exu*, for people or person.

The woman continued, "The Universitat will find you, if they are not already on their way. I will keep you safe a while," she looked at V and winced. "And I may be able to help her."

Kholos said, "Who are you?"

"Avalina," she said. "A whoracle of the *exu*." By which she meant, Kholos knew, a priestess of the Boracs, like St. Theresa. Lithe, with ropy arms, she had wide hips and long limbs. The black lines and blossoms and webs in the red and blue hues of her tusks, he saw, swirled and floated, changed with her movement. "Call me Val. Now, we need to get you away from here. Every minute we wait, you risk the ideas of my race, and the best chance I have to help a friend as well."

"What friend?"

"King Close, the Adonai of Neo Cumae."

At her waist she carried a narrow dirk. Thin-bladed, conical, it was a dull silver with a grip wrapped in black leather. Kholos recognized the metal as the same type that Gyr Zax's automatic pistol had been chased with. Not silver, something else that looked like silver. Kholos thought she might even be able to hurt him with that metal.

"How could I help you with King Close? This is his domain, no?"

"Help me free him," she said. "He is trapped here, a slave."

Kholos was the Liberator. The request was a command. "I came here to find King Close," Kholos said. "Get me to him and I will free him."

"Alright," said Avalina. "Let's go from here. The innkeeper may have already confessed to his pastor or his teacher about your arrival. We need to get out of this part of the city. Gramsea Meadow is no place for travelers in any case. You have brought a handful of wanted gods and a Fractured girl here. Likely there is a Thought Assassin on the way as we speak."

Kholos tossed their things back into the bag, then gently placed the black piece of cloth which held the tusks of Gyr Zax on top. His movements and gestures were identical to those Michael Staffa might have made, V realized.

"Who are you," V whispered. "Who are you really?"

Avalina watched the street from the window

The Zenoss Heights of Neo Cumae was a strip of land north of the campus of Zulun College, a prestigious Institute of the Universitat. The Heights were cheap, quiet, and unfashionable. The neighborhood was a constant churn of Republicant refugees from the endless wars and famines as they settled in the city briefly before moving on to the Western Territories where they could legally own their own homes and businesses. There were also many Boracs in the Heights, but like the Columbium few stayed more than a year or two before leaving to join a caravan.

Avalina was one of the few permanent Borac residents of Zenoss Heights. She led them up three flights of dimly lit stairs to her apartment. They could hear Borac children calling from outside, and cars braking and horses neighing as they crawled and clomped along.

Inside, her rooms were red. Red curtains, a soft red rug, red thin paper on the windows that made the gray light of the cool and rainy day outside seem warmer than it was. There was a radiator and also a kettle on an electric burner. Two low, white, wide sofas were arranged before the high windows. Scrolls in Borac were half-unrolled in a pile on a wooden table. On a hook near the door was a short bow, along with a quiver of small, nasty looking arrows. Kholos recognized the weapon was not for show.

As had happened the night before, at one point during their journey, from the pavement to the store windows to the engines of the backed-up cars, there had been a shift in the city. The mood had gone from surly and the weather from warm and sticky to an atmosphere of tiredness and the weather to a soft, cold rain.

Avalina apologized for having nothing for them to eat but put on water for tea. Kholos, after setting V down on one of the sofas, went to the window and looked up: Televia wires stretched everywhere. Avalina offered to take his cloak and hang it up over her bathtub--through a white door in the red wall into the second room--but Kholos declined.

"I'm going back out," he said. "To get us some food," he nodded at V. "You said you could help her?"

"I can try. It will take time."

Kholos kissed V's cheek.

"She'll be safer here," explained Avalina. "The anima of the *exu* is quite strong in this neighborhood. Even stronger here in my place. We can't keep the Universitat out, but we know when they are coming."

Kholos looked at all the red.

"What do you do here, Avalina?"

"I'll show you," and then Avalina walked to the white door that led to the second room.

The room inside was washed in red light, emanating from the hundreds of little bulbs strung across the ceiling. A single window, open just slightly, allowed in a slice of breeze. Gauzy red curtains puffed in and out. A tub rested against the wall, with a table next to the antique faucets where several slender bottles of colored glass held oils and lotions. In the center of the room was an enormous bed, rounded at its corners and with mahogany posters holding up a canopy fringed with white dangles. A wardrobe rested against one wall, with a divan nestled alongside. Behind a print screen but just visible from the doorway was a bidet, also a clothes rack where hung a sheer red robe and a puffy white terrycloth cover.

Also in the room was a second table. Standing on iron legs the table held a sewing machine that seemed as old as the tub. A stack of threads stood alongside the machine, along with swatches and patches of a dozen different shapes and colors. The table looked like it might have been lifted from a sidewalk cafe, which it was, as were the two chairs with filigreed backs that nestled underneath. A pack of cards and a pair of dice were neatly placed before one of the chairs atop the table. The sewing machine before the other. The room smelled of spice and bare skin.

"I'm a *glin shama*," said Avalina. "A whoracle."

Kholos's eyes were jumping around the room. To the sewing machine. To the oils and salves. To the huge bed.

Avalina explained, "I tell fortunes. I make love to men and women for favors and gifts. I teach wives tricks, or give husbands lessons of their own. I recommend names for babies. I dance, sometimes, in some of the lesser known clubs. I might weave little animas, some cosmetic things for some of my ladies. I sell a little of what I have, what I am."

"So you're a consort? You entertain, that is, clients?"

Avalina smiled. The tusks rose a bit. "You can call me a whore," she said. "It won't bother me."

Despite all his experiences, Kholos blushed. "And how do you know King Close?"

"He is a client, a lover. My favorite client." She pointed next to the bed, where there was a tiny little Televia set, with headphones and a microphone. The cable ran directly out the window, not into the wall. "I am the only one who can talk back to him. We can't converse, exactly. But I know he doesn't want to be here. I can feel it, almost. It's in his anmia. He's a prisoner here."

Kholos found himself fascinated by the sewing machine. There was something familiar about it.

Avalina continued. "This room is very safe," she shut the door behind her. A thick red candle, untouched, flickered to light. "I have anima alarms in here. Little deceptions, so a jealous lover wouldn't notice say, that their wife was nude in here. And you are definitely less likely to attract attention here than down in Gramsea Park. I don't know about the receiver, though. I think one will find you no matter what if you are in the city. Only Boracs seem immune."

"What are you going to do for V?"

"Her anima is knotted, snipped, tangled. She's no longer just Fractured. She's been shattered. But I will do what I can for her. She'll still be Fractured, but I can try and untangle her."

Kholos took a breath. "Don't hurt her."

And then he stepped back out the door, into the city.

"He loves you very much," said Avalina, knowing V could not respond. "When he looks at you his strings knot together tighter than any others I have seen. And I have seen many lovers."

Carefully Avalina lay V back on the sofa. With her squared off fingers Avalina touched V at her temples.

V's eyes flashed crazily. A bit of her thoughts organized themselves. With a shudder, she realized she did not miss Michael when Kholos was with her. She screamed.

"I'm sorry," said Avalina. "Let us start somewhere else."

13. Bad Bread

Out on the rainy street Kholos peered out from under the hood of the Comanche coat and watched the flow of the Televia wires as he walked. His eyes, attuned not only for the telescopic and microscopic, could also perceive patterns and flaws in the arrangement of things: matter, energy, time. There was, he saw, a pattern to the wires. He perceived shapes in the lines, in the door jambs and lintels, a structure of wires slung low and high and up and down buildings, like he was inside something even when he was outdoors.

He walked past the Zuluan Institute. Around him were crowds of students, the women generally red-shirted or in red rain-slicks, the color of the clergy of the Universitat, the men in brown, the color of the academics. One started to speak to him, a girl with yellow hair dripping wet. But then, immediately, everyone stiffened, glanced around, and began to hear the buzz and talk of King Close.

Kholos, still looking up, realized the signal was flowing along the wires, seeping out from the lines. Where did it originate?

The rain stopped. The students smiled. Sunshine fell on the neighborhood.

Moving quickly, he made his way out to another wide street, saw it bustle with smiling people, and kept going. Only when he had gone several blocks to the east did he find a street less crowded, and only did then did he slow his step and lower the hood of his Comanche coat. In this neighborhood the thrum and bustle was absent, just a few trucks and warehouses, elevated tracks turning towards the river. Down a lane of homes he saw the river, big ships looming into view, the mists that hid the Museum Fortress.

From a stand run by a swarthy Republicant immigrant in a purple Fez and a rose-shaded monocle Kholos purchased half a loaf of bread and a sweet drink in a red bottle. Michael Staffa had liked this drink, so Kholos did, too.

"That bread is old, and was out in the rain" said the man in the Fez. "It was made with grain shipped here from the mountains, and goes stale fast. I meant to throw it away. Pick another loaf."

"This one is fine," said Kholos. "I don't actually need to eat."

"Take it then," said the man. "And I guess I won't actually need to charge you."

As he gnawed on the bread Kholos recalled Gyr Zax, their conversation at the table before the piles of meats. He thought of Dr. Voss, and his theories, and the names Kholos had secreted away in the doctor's mind.

Kholos sat on a box before an empty warehouse, and watched the water of the river go by. He saw the tail of cat go around a corner.

How? Kholos thought. *Why?*

St. Theresa meant something.

Brian Storenko meant something.

King Close meant something.

St. Theresa and Sergeant Dugan both said one, or did they say two? How would Aetherian travel?

Fumbling at his baggy pants Kholos found Dr. Voss' list of the Adonai, and unrolled it hastily. All the names, their places of power. He read the names to himself over and over. Each had replaced old ideas. Each had a specific purpose in the world.

There was a pattern there. There was a plan to the Adonai of the Earth. For all their shifting, there was still a pattern. If he could discern it? If he could disrupt it?

At his feet a gray cat rubbed itself around the upper of his boot. The cat looked at him with intelligence. It had white paws and long whiskers.

"Ask the question," said the cat.

Kholos almost tripped over his box, but then collected himself. Words formed in his mouth: *who are you? how can you talk?* But he stopped and steadied his thoughts first.

"What is the purpose of the Adonai?" he said.

The cat sat back and cleaned its front paw. It was, Kholos observed, a very clean cat.

The cat grinned at him. "Good question. You should go find out. Be methodical. Don't rush around, just poking everything, destroying everything. That's been tried, you know. It hasn't worked."

And then it walked away, slowly, across the street and into an alley, where a second cat, this one brown and with a friendly face, watched it approach.

"We'll help you where we can," the brown cat mewed. "Go to the mountains, if they catch up with you. And they are coming. Watch out."

"What mountains?"

"Any mountains," said the brown cat. "Anywhere. And keep asking questions."

And then they were gone.

Kholos looked at the river. The alley. The man in the purple fez, who was now staring at him. Finally, the Televia wires.

The pattern was there: a tight, long spiral atop a star within a square circumscribed by an oval. Neo Cumae was a temple. Every edge of the island entered under the lintels of the wires, the points of the spinning star the wings of an altar blocks wide. The skyscrapers where nothing but pillars and posts from which to hang the cables. Neo Cumae was a single, throbbing church, each and every resident a worshipper to the buzz of King Close. A metropolis of acolytes, doing the work of their localized deity simply by living in the city.

Slowly, following the lines and flows of the wires emanating the steady hiss of King Close's instructions, Kholos's gaze moved south, south. Blocked by several buildings, Kholos understood where the terminus of the cables, the center of the star, the guiding throb of the voice, had to be.

He chuckled to himself at the appropriateness of King Close's throne. The Adonai of Neo Cumae resided in some way or another within the high black brick walls of the city's power generators. The Power Station. He turned and, walking fast now, headed back to find V and Avalina. He threw the last of his meal into a trash can.

"I told you that bread was bad," said the man in the Fez.

She started with V's mind. It was the most difficult part but also the most important. She stroked the off-set cheeks, the bridge of her nose. Put a fingertip on each eyelid and closed each eye. Fixing the face was an afterthought. The consciousness was the puzzle. It took hours to put together even a small section of V's personality back in place. But V was strong and all the pieces were still there, nothing lost. Whole.

By the early evening V's eyes were those of a woman in her late twenties. Both of them. She could look around the bedroom with comprehension. Avalina, exhausted, sweating, her hands trembling, had placed V on the big bed and given her an opiate to fight the pain. V's face was her own, again.

"You sew?" V asked, pointing, weakly, at the machine.

"Oh, yes," said Avalina. She moved over to the wardrobe, and swung open the doors with both arms. "All this, I made myself. Here. Look at this. Don't move too fast, though. Your face is all new."

V, groggy, gaped as Avalina took out a pair of red leather pants that tapered at the ankles. Matching the pants was a red leather vest, low cut. The set was stitched up with thick white thread in X-patterns. "I have a pair of boots I like to wear with these. And a set of gloves, but I didn't make those. The pants were tough enough, but the gloves are impossible."

The wardrobe was filled with beautiful clothes. Along the bottom, in neat rows, pair upon pair of boots and shoes were aligned.

"I like to sew," V managed. "I made the brown dress I was wearing, before."

Avalina took out two dresses. One was lime green, with a very short hem V did not believe could cover Avalina's backside. It had thin shoulder straps, a cinched waist, and appeared to made from a single piece of cloth. "I cheated on this," said Avalina. "I used a little anima to hide the seams."

The other dress was black, long, and elegant. Form fitted, it draped its hem along the floor. V stared at it. It was the most stunning dress she had ever seen. After another swallow her eyes began to burn with tears. Michael, she was thinking. Michael would have loved that dress. With a stubborn grimace she told herself she would not cry, and then her lip quivered, and then she did, in big gaping sobs. Avalina reached her and put her arms around her.

For a long time the Borac woman did nothing but give V a long and comforting embrace, careful not to jar her body. Slowly V began to feel better, her thoughts evened out some. Finally, she exhaled. She felt silly for crying.

"Don't," said Avalina. "It's alright."

"How did you know what I was thinking?"

"I can read the threads around you," said Avalina. "I could see it, even back in the inn. I thought perhaps it was only, well, not only, but because you are Fractured. Badly Fractured."

The colors of the Borac woman's tusks flowed, red and blue clouds wafting from base to tip. She did not say anything for a while.

"You've nothing to be afraid of here," she said, at last. "Why don't you tell me his name."

"Kholos?"

"No, no," said Avalina. "The one before Kholos. The one you are truly looking for."

V sighed. "His name was Michael," she said. "And he's dead. He was killed by the Stalnistas. Except when Kholos is with me, it feels like he might not be," V started to cry again. "I know that makes no sense."

Avalina asked, "V, do you know who Kholos is?"

"A soldier," said V. "He fought with Michael. But he deserted. To come get me, to take me away. Away from the world. I know that's crazy, but I believe him. Just like I believed in Michael."

Avalina was playing with a deck of cards at the side of the bed. V expected her to lay them out and read her fortune, but she just shuffled and reshuffled them. They looked thick and very old.

"And how did he know to come and take you away?" Avalina asked.

"Michael told him about me," explained V. "And I believe him. Because he does know everything about me. He knows my full name. My body. How I like my eggs. All of it. And," V hesitated. It seemed so impossible to explain. "Why am I telling you this?"

Avalina put the cards down, she stared at V a moment. She blinked, so that her eyelids were perpendicular to her vertical pupils.

"Your anima is unusual," Avalina said. "You're Fractured, not just this trauma but truly Fractured, at the source. I can see that plainly. The lines are bent at strange angles. We must not let the Universitat get you. You would never come back."

V nodded.

Avalina continued. "You left your home to find freedom with Kholos, or to be with Kholos, because of how you feel with him. After what, a few weeks? This doesn't seem like you, the you whose mind I arranged. As I said, the anima of a Fractured person is hard to read."

"What about Kholos? What is his anima," V said the three syllables each very slowly, "like?"

Avalina sighed. The black lines on her enameled tusks shifted into new designs. "We are talking about you, not Kholos." The Borac put her hand out and laid it on top of V's. The hand was huge, completely covering her own with the grayish, greenish skin, but touch was also soft, calming. "How long did you know Kholos, before he took you away?"

"He didn't take me away," said V. "I agreed to come with him."

"Fine, then how long before you agreed?"

"A few weeks. He and Dr. Voss talked and talked, Dr. Voss is our Universitat representative. He's, a little unusual, Dr. Voss. He could have been a famous Dean or a Bishop, but Michael said he was too smart." V paused. "You know, Michael used to do that too. Talk with Dr. Voss. For hours.

"I woke up one morning, and I was Fractured. And Kholos said if we were going to leave, we had to do it then and there."

She paused.

"I feel as though I've forgotten something. Something about what happened at Duran."

"It's alright. You said yes, to Kholos, you would like to come with him."

The cards went up and down in Avalina's free hand, where she worked them with her thumb and forefinger.

V's voice cracked. "It's more than that," she pleaded.

Avalina nodded.

"It's as if sometimes," she started to cry again. "Sometimes he is Michael. And I want him to be, which I know is not fair. But I do."

She continued, "There are times. There was one this morning. Maybe I am crazy. I am Fractured, after all. This is a sin against reason and faith, just being here and not going to the centers. But for little seconds, Michael is back with me. I want that."

Avalina leaned back, put the cards down. "You didn't agree to leave the world with Kholos," she said. "You agreed to leave with Michael."

V collected herself, wiped her nose with the back of her hand. "I guess I did," she admitted.

Avalina, her hand still atop V's, nodded and said nothing for a little while.

"V," she said. "I haven't been entirely honest. I do know some things about Kholos," she said, "I know that Kholos wants to be free, more free than you and I can probably imagine. He'll do anything to be free. He has to be free. He cannot be held, he cannot settle."

"Oh yes," said V. "That's all he talks about. Free free free. He's told me about the Aetherian who control the world. He says the Adonai are their pawns. He has a plan to find a way to the Aetherian, and then use their own machines to escape everything, go to a new universe. With me. We'll make a new world, with our ideas. It will be wonderful."

"With you," repeated Avalina. She glanced at her sewing machine. Thought she should cover it.

"That's right."

"V, let me ask you a question. Do you want to be free?"

V snapped, "What kind of question is that?"

Avalina took a deep breath. "I want King Close to have a chance to escape," she explained, slowly, and then, almost as an afterthought. "And I want the Borac ideas let loose. Which is why I waited for you at the river."

She continued, "Which is why I'm trying to hide you here. I want my gods, those crazy Borac ideas, to live again. Because I would call that freedom. Freedom to think like we want to. About what we want to, with whatever ideas we liked."

"I would say so," said V.

"Yes," Avalina offered. "But it's just a degree of freedom. Free to do a few more things, think a few more thoughts. Live and die in new ways. The Universitat and their ideas are constraining, I agree, more constraining all the time. There is no place for Boracs in the laws and facts of the cathedral or the academy. We cannot learn like you do. We cannot worship like you do. So we want to be free of the Universitat, yes. But total freedom? Freedom from everything?"

V replied. "Kholos wants that kind of freedom. Freedom from everything. No death. No Adonai. No Pang. A new universe, Kholos said. A blank place. Our own universe, just him and me. He said there could be mountains, for me to hunt in. A home for me. Children. Anything."

"Do you understand what anything means, the freedom to do anything, anything at all?" asked Avalina. "Your own time, your own light, your own reality, entire? That is a degree of risk and responsibility so great, so terrible. I know Kholos wants this. But this is what you want, as well?"

V drifted off, started to snore. Avalina leaned down and kissed the cheek she had just reconstructed. "I'm a deserter too, V. Just like Kholos. But I am not so sure you are."

The door to the outer room opened, and then Kholos entered.

He said, "There is something greater at work here. Some pattern to the Adonai. Also, a couple of cats spoke to me. We need to go the Power Station."

Kholos looked at V, then at Avalina. "You saved her."

14. The Fifty-First

Colonel Redroot, not caring at all for the hospitality of St. Theresa, came kicking to the surface of the river within an easy swim of the Museum Fortress. In the Lipstick Country he had eaten and had his clothes mended, then threatened to shoot everyone until St. Theresa showed him where the deserter had gone. Now he carried only his rifle crutch and the golden machine gun he had taken from Gyr Zax, his Comanche uniform, and a little hardtack.

As he lurched onto the dock of the Museum Fortress the mist weaved and huffed behind him, showing Neo Cumae as arboreal forest, then as golden spires, then as a polyglot city of temples and commerce, then back again. Redroot set his jaw and scanned his surroundings.

The battle of the arts raged on. Before him a plume of rainbow smoke rose over the museum. The sounds of art and war mingled and echoed across the grounds of the museum: an explosion, the chink of a chisel on stone, the scratch of paint on bare canvas, a scream. The jagged and mirrored roof of the wing to the left of the main building had been blasted open by what appeared to be shells fired from day-glo canons and wire-and-wood sculptures that launched globs of patina'd bronze.

Unshaven, in sunglasses and a rumpled black suit, Corporal Jigsaw repelled his attackers. Redroot watched as Jigsaw cut a trio of assailants in half merely by shaking his head no, back and forth.

Jigsaw was also wounded, Redroot saw. But wounded in unusual ways. There were bits of chipped marble stuck into his shoulder, and paintbrushes had fastened him to where he stood through his patent leather shoes. His face was bruised, as if he had been slapped about or punched in the jaw and the eyes, and yet his sunglasses remained settled on his lean nose. He needed a shave, thought Redroot.

As the Colonel pick-pocked the barrel of his crutch across the plaza, he checked his pistol, fully loaded. None of what he saw made any sense. He did not care.

"Everyone's gone mad," he whispered to himself. "Except me."

The Colonel walked through the art-battle as if it did not exist. His finger was on the trigger of his golden gun.

"I am looking for a deserter," he said. Then he quickly and accurately described Kholos.

Jigsaw studied this strange man, collected himself. "This area is currently part of an installation," he said. "It is not open to the public at the moment. You may enjoy the other exhibits of the Museum Fortress, however."

Redroot noticed Brian Storenko, on his knees, behind Jigsaw, weeping softly and cradling his destroyed hands. "Help me, Jigsaw," he said. "I can't see the art anymore."

"The Deserter," Redroot repeated. "Tall, thin, and traveling with a Fractured woman."

"I don't have time for this," Jigsaw said. "And your fashion sense pronounces you below my notice."

Redroot shot Brian Storenko through the head. The bullet was very real, without abstraction, and delivered an uninteresting and uninspiring death. Jigsaw looked at the body, which was not so much horrific as just ugly, and nodded his best critical nod.

"You just did what he couldn't," Jigsaw said. "You made something once of beauty utterly meaningless. What kind of gun is that? You shouldn't be able to just shoot an Adonai."

"The Deserter," said Redroot.

Behind him the liberated artists were preparing another assault on the contemporary wing. The abstract artillery let loose a salvo of primary colors, firing for effect. Jigsaw opened his mouth to speak and Redroot pushed his gun into Jigsaw's chest.

Click. Everything stopped. Light slowed to a perceptible speed. Time was spent.

Packets of energy, discrete, coasted by like ordered and sparkling dust. Time, shaved and raw, dotted and dashed its way around conceptual space, bounced off of the reflective surfaces of the hidden symmetry of the universe.

The duality approached.

The two figures who arrived through the miasma of light were shapeless, faceless. One appeared red, the other blue, each occupying a different edge of the spectrum. They moved like crystals forming in fast-motion. Soft triangles of color flowed down through the compacted dimensions around them, tricky rainbows undone and pouring themselves into liquidity on the white steps of the Museum Fortress.

Each of them wore a white, featureless mask. These masks spun around the red and blue shapes in three-hundred-and-sixty-degree arcs.

They were the Aetherian.

They had failed fifty times in their mission. But this was the first time, again.

They swirled into and apart from one another, their white masks the only thing distinguishing them from being a single entity. They flowed, folded, stitched.

"This Adonai is ended," experienced the blue. The red completed the message. "Its work gratefully incomplete."

The red congealed itself around Brian Storenko.

"This assembly of particles," it referred to Redroot. "Are anomalous. And, apparently, capable."

"Seven swords are dispatched. They are succeeded in most probabilities, but not all."

"This resource is no pattern of consequence. Still."

"Harvest and resurrect? Add to the Kholopatiron pattern, pending failure fifty-one?"

"No. Replacement Adonai: Focus. Single-mindedness? Will. Will, of course."

"Inflexibility."

"Unflexibility."

"Domain?"

"The deployment. Expensive, but an efficient use of this reality, yes. Easy to conceal from the local power. No second stitching. No removal. We are using too much light to deal with this problem."

Then the red and the blue floated away, having never arrived. Time regained speed.

Reality unfolded once more. Click.

Colonel Ute Redroot, suddenly, knew where the Deserter was, at that very moment. Ute swallowed, and looked around, careful to keep the gun up at Jigsaw.

"I'm after the deserter," he pronounced. "I'm a Comanche officer, on Universitat business." Even as he explained himself he felt it was redundant. That he had said this before, but now it felt heavier, as if he carried more conviction.

"Of course you are, Adonai," said Jigsaw. "And I am Jack Jigsaw. Wait. You're not one of ours ..."

Redroot shot Jigsaw in the chest, dead.

"I'm after the deserter," repeated Redroot. "Everything depends upon catching the deserter."

Redroot had always been after the deserter. He would always be after the deserter. His domain was the trail and his purpose was the pursuit. Will and determination, single-mindedness, pursue the deserter. His Fighting First Claws formed up behind him in ranks. They were all pale, translucent as if made of liquid silver. There was his blood brother, Stands-Tall-Under-Cedars.

At the docks, by the skiff, were a squadron of attack cars and light armor, floating like spirits.

"We're ready, Colonel," said Stands-Tall.

"Indeed," he turned back to the river. "Fighting First Claws!" he cried. "Mount up!"

And so Colonel Ute Redroot became The Colonel, the Adonai of Determination, whose domain was a squadron of attack cars, manned by the ghosts of soldiers from some nation long forgotten.

For seven days they hid. Avalina's anima helped V, but could not cure her completely. There were still wrinkles in her skin where otherwise her body was young. A toe that stubbornly stayed baby-sized. A place in her mind where thoughts of school angered her, another place where her memories of a day ago felt like they happened years ago. Her baby teeth came in and fell out, twice. Her hair grew in, then fell out in patches. But she could think again, talk again, after the first day. And by the fifth day she was one V again. Tired, sore, sad, Fractured, but V. A woman in her late twenties, perhaps early thirties. Who liked to sew and hunt, who missed her one true love.

She and Kholos made love in Avalina's big bed when the Whoracle went out to buy food they could eat. Kholos clutched her close throughout, like she might float away.

The entire sixth day, V and Avalina sewed, making two new dresses and a new swaddling cloth for V.

"All Borac women know how to sew," Avalina said to her. "We do not even have to be taught."

"But not all Borac women can fight with a magic dagger and a deadly black bow, can they?" Kholos asked, watching them from across the room.

It was easy to sleep, to eat, easy to talk. They laughed and ate and slept. V's body shifted at each midnight, but not as drastically: forties, teens.

On the morning of the eighth day Kholos checked the list. He saw a name he knew he had not seen before, The Colonel. He wondered how he could recognize it as new. Always the names seemed to emerge from his own mind, as if he had written the list himself and needed it only as a reminder.

"It will rain tomorrow," said Avalina. "I can see the lines." She was facing away from them, looking out at the dull lights of the city. "Unless King Close changes the weather." V was resting, her recovery had drained her and she slept often. Avalina said softly to him, "Kholos, she is still Fractured, you understand. She will always be Fractured."

"It won't matter where we're going. She'll be outside of such constraints. She'll have all of her potentials at once, laid out before her. She'll be able to pick and choose among them."

"Your escape. V told me about that, as well."

Kholos stared at her a long second. "You don't think we'll make it."

"I don't know," said Avalina, looking at V. "I hope you do. For the Boracs, I do. You could set our ideas loose in your new reality, perhaps. Give them a chance."

Kholos understood what she meant. "But not for V."

"She is that special to you?"

"She is."

Avalina studied him. His lines were clearer than before. "You're ready to leave. Right now."

"I am always ready to leave." Kholos said, "In any case, we're putting you in danger, being here. Just like we did with Gyr Zax. I cannot feel blame, or regret. I know that what most people think of as death is nothing but particles changing their direction and speed. But, I don't want you to be trapped here."

V awoke, and there was a new receiver on her pillow. As Avalina and Kholos spoke, she slipped it into her ear.

"Now," said Kholos. "We're going to leave, and go find King Close."

The buzz said to V, "Think of a place far, far away. Think of a place you have never seen, and never will. That place, now and forever, is the most important place in the world. You would die for that unseen place. You would kill for that unseen place. Your life will be for that place. Don't think too hard about the place. I'll take care of that for you, when you're just a little older," And then a lullaby began, a song about onions and a rabbit and a farmer with a trap, which he placed out in his garden before going to bed.

15. The Power Station

Out into the streets they went. The air was damp and still, cool, threatening rain. Thunder broke to the south. Collectively the citizens of Neo Cumae were looking for something, or someone. Lights shone everywhere, and the city seemed brighter than before. The windows of the tall buildings seemed to lean over, scanning the sidewalks.

Kholos had made V take out her receiver, and she was not pleased about it.

"The city knows we are coming," said Avalina. She was dressed in her red leather. At her hip was her little black bow, lashed to her thigh. At the other hip was a quiver of arrows. V was in her twenties, mostly.

Kholos could see the streetlamps swerve, not physically, but with a little flicker and play of shadow. They were scanning the streets. Kholos wondered if every bit of the city had its own receiver. *Did the stones hear the instructions of King Close? Did the wheels of the trucks? Would the street snatch his foot?*

It took long hours but late that night they reached the walls of the Power Station.

"This is his domain," Kholos said. "And you say you are his friend, lover. Can't he help us inside?"

"It's his domain, but not his orders," said Avalina.

"Why is it so quiet here?" Kholos asked. The streets were empty, only parked cars and identical shade trees.

"I don't know," said Avalina. "People say this is the safest part of the city."

"Let's go," said Kholos.

Graffiti contradicted itself on the bricks of the wall around the campus: *King Close is Pang, Pang is Dead. Long Live the King. Kill the King.* Sodium beams criss-crossed the sky, blotting the arcs of the stars. The streets seemed deserted, even though the Power Station was surrounded by block upon block of little brick row houses, and all were glowing with soft, white light.

Stepping from the mouth of an alley Kholos peered into one of the homes. The window was above street level, but he was tall enough he could look over the sill.

Inside were four shadows. A father, a mother, and two children: a family. The father sat on the couch staring at the black and white square of a Televia screen, the mother beside him. The children were sprawled on the floor. There was something off about them, and Kholos realized they flickered, like the black and white images on the Televia. On the screen a program Kholos could, sifting through his cache of memories, recognize: a popular story involving a dog and a castle and a Kiowa hero who went on several interesting adventures.

Kholos realized he had, through his composite parts, seen the program from its first episode, and part of him remembered it fondly. It was called *Plains Rider,* as the hero apparently traveled across the great heart of the Columbium Continent in a restored Republicant model sports car. Kholos, as Michael, remembered pretending to be the hero, Birch, remembered imagining his own adventures.

The people before him, the shades, were not imagining anything. They ebbed and flowed from two-dimensional shapes to three-dimensional ones.

Kholos stepped back into the alley. Avalina had drawn her bow.

"What did you see?" she asked.

"People listening to King Close," Kholos said.

Avalina nodded without a word.

"What are they doing?" Kholos asked her. "All these Adonai. St. Theresa was a mother and a lover, a place to rest and eat and feel safe and wanted. V had a little shrine to her in her house back in Duran, for good cooking and luck with her sewing. Brian Storenko was an artist who made things ugly. And here is King Close, sending out these instructions. What's the point?"

"I thought you didn't care so much about their missions?" V asked.

Kholos admitted. "A cat told me to."

They were whispering and walking. They moved quickly, circumscribing the wall, always looking for a way in. They saw no gates. Just the three tall smokestacks where steam floated up into the clouds, and the web of wires and cables shooting out into the city.

Avalina said, "All of the city services emanate from here. Televia broadcasts. Electricity. Piping. Everything. There are trucks and engineers out at work all the time. Whenever something breaks, they come. You must have seen them yourself, when you went out. White coats, with orange hats? There must be a place where they get inside."

"When something breaks," Kholos repeated. He drew his sword. Overhead the Televia cables ran down walls and into attics. Just barely he could reach one of the low-hanging lines.

"You can't cut a Televia cable," said V. "It's impossible. Like a pothole in a Universitat road."

Kholos cut the cable with a little slice. The ends of the cable sparked once, then fell, dangling down the street. "These engineers," said Kholos. "They come quickly to fix things?"

Avalina nodded.

"Let's find a good place to hide."

The truck arrived within minutes. They heard it before they saw it, a careening siren not especially loud but clear. The truck parked in front of the alley where they waited, tucked in behind a quartet of garbage cans. Idling at the mouth of the alley the truck itself was unmarked. A white truck with no letters, no numbers, nothing.

Emerging from the truck were three engineers. They were all dressed in white coats, black rubber boots and gloves, and orange safety hats. On their faces were respirator masks, their eyes hidden behind circular goggles. Three of them came out to address the wire. One carried a ladder, another a pair of splicers and a roll of black tape, the third some kind of lifting pole with pincers on the end. For a moment the three of them stared at the severed cable in the street, then one lifted up an end and studied it closely, taking a penlight from the pocket of his coat and shining it into the slice.

Kholos thought of St. Theresa's gauzy followers. The artists of Brian Storenko.

"This is quite a non-standard deviation," said the engineer, his voice raspy through the respirator. "This cable was not scheduled for replacement for several more broadcasts."

Kholos, leaping from behind the cans covered the distance to the engineers and thumped the one with the penlight on the back of his safety hat, hard. The engineer crumpled to the ground. Kholos faced the other two. The penlight plinked and plunked and shot its beam on the pavement.

"How do I get inside?" Kholos demanded. "I don't want to hurt you, but I will."

Behind their masks the engineers stared at him. "An impossibility of motion," said one. "The parabola of its arrival is likewise outside established norms."

"I concur," answered the other. "Perhaps this a trick of the light."

"Inside," said Kholos, in his thunder voice, the roll of timpani and brass. "How do I get inside?"

The engineers, blown back a step by Kholos's words, continued.

"Illusions although largely unstudied rarely have such clear physical manifestations," said one. "I suggest another hypothesis to test."

"Agreed," said the other. A trace, very slight, of emotion arrived in the engineer's voice. "But what if this event is in fact outside all established norms?"

"Impossible," said the other. "Don't you listen to your instructions, citizen? Do some science."

Kholos, with a sigh, hit the disbelieving engineer in the face. The plastic lenses of the goggles cracked, and the engineer dropped to the ground with a muffled groan.

"That happened," Kholos said. "And it can happen again. How do I get inside?"

The last engineer answered in a voice that sounded feminine. "I will take you. If you agree not to hurt me, or the other engineers, any further."

There were no windows in the back of the van, but they could see through the front windshield as the engineer drove them around the brick wall of the Power Station. All three of them had dressed in White Engineers uniforms.

The lights seemed to change. Brighter, then softer, they began to cross and merge, becoming a brilliant and gleaming band of white. The headlights of the van became part of the flash and glow. It felt as if the van began to float.

"This is impossible," said Avalina, squinting at the light. "The anima is all wrong. The strings here are frayed and twisted. What are you doing here?"

With a gulp the driver said, "Science?"

"You're tearing everything apart! You can't tug at the world this way! Just to make a door!"

Kholos, looked at the light melting into itself, then erupted with laughter.

The light was familiar to him, very familiar, a toy version of the compressed time in the canisters along his belt. The same idea that allowed him to be in two places at once, in all places at once, to be many different people, all at once.

"It's not science," Kholos said. "Or your anima, either. It's something else."

"You understand what they are doing?" Avalina said. "And you laugh at it?"

"This slice of light is nothing," he said. "A little fleck of time. It's only dangerous to you because you can see the potential of it. This is a match that could ignite a star, but here it's just a match. There's nothing to light."

"It's entirely safe," the engineer protested. "Risk matrices show zero possibility of rupture."

"There is no such thing as zero," said Kholos. "It's an idea. Not a thing."

"Faith and reason!" protested the engineer. "Pang the Creator!"

After taking in the ramp again he added, to V, "I wish Dr. Voss could see this."

The van edged up on a ramp of solid light. As the tires touched the suspended particles friction vanished, and the vehicle glided up and then over the wall.

Rows upon rows of the trucks were parked under spotlights in neat lines, with a clear path up to where the lights crossed to make the entry. Beyond the trucks there were square buildings, all of the same white brick as the walls. A huge vaulted building that sparked from its apex seemed to be the center of the campus. Cables and wires crisscrossed everything. The trio of smokestacks dominated the area, puffing out white clouds.

Everywhere the orange-hatted White Engineers stepped into trucks, came in and out of doors, and tromped about. Some carried clipboards, others calipers, a few hefted up lengths of pipe or huge wrenches. They moved around in pairs or in threes.

"Do you have to report back in?" Kholos asked.

The engineer shook her head no. "Only return to the allotted place."

"You or the truck?" asked Avalina.

"Both of us," said the engineer. "Obviously."

"King Close," said Kholos. "Is he in that building? The one that looks like a temple to Pang?"

The engineer turned around in her seat abruptly, as if Kholos had said something offensive.

"King Close is not in Pang's cathedral," she said, stuffily. "Obviously."

"And why is that so obvious?"

"Because without the principles of Pang," she said as if addressing an ignorant child, "King Close could not be. None of us could. There must be zero." She shivered, as if suddenly very afraid. "There must be zero," she repeated. "Must be a real zero."

There was real terror in her voice, the kind of terror Kholos associated with being trapped. He let the engineer alone. Avalina sat up very straight.

"What is it?" said Kholos.

"I just thought of something about the Slythe and their god. They only had the one idea," she explained. "The Slythe only had the one god. It wasn't us, the Boracs, at all that were wanted in this reality. It was the Slythe, Gyr always said. We were just extra fabric, scraps to trim away. Gyr said it was the Slythe."

"What made you think of that?"

"The one god of the Slythe is fear," she said. "Total fear. Like she is feeling," she nodded at the Engineer.

Kholos thought of Dr. Voss's list of the Adonai. Thssiss was on the list, the Slythe god, the last time he looked. But there was no location, no domain.

"Pang is our savior and our deliverer," the engineer said, huskily, breathing thick through her respirator. They had parked the truck, in an endless row of endless trucks. "Pang is the creator and the calculator. Pang is the giver of gifts. Pang … "

"Pang is all," Kholos finished the prayer from some random memory. "And so all is Pang. Amen. But where is he? Does he even exist? If Pang is the zero, *can* he even exist?"

The engineer spasmed in her seat. It was a jerky, clunky motion.

"Kholos," said V. "She's in shock."

Kholos reached up and yanked the mask from the engineer's face so she could breathe. V gasped.

There was no face underneath, just an assemblage of gears and sprockets and wires, sparking blue. In the machine works of the engineer's head, on the right side where the ear would be, was the black dot of the receiver. Gently Kholos cradled the engineer's body and laid it out in the back of the van.

"Why did she breakdown like that?" he asked.

"An idea hurt her," said Avalina.

Kholos tried to remember what he had said, exactly.

16. King Close

They entered through the door of the closest building onto a long corridor of pristine white tiles and glaring overhead lights. Instrument panels and circuit boards were placed every few hundred steps. Off in the distance were more of the masked, orange-hatted white engineers. Kholos, Avalina and V, disguised, walked down the corridor, nodding to the engineers they passed. But the engineers, engrossed with clipboards or soldering guns, ignored them completely. A low, strong hum saturated everything. The buzz. They could feel the vibrations through the soles of their boots.

"I wonder if we smashed something if they would notice us," Kholos whispered.

"Let's not find out," said Avalina. "There are also Black Engineers. They police Neo Cumae's infrastructure."

Kholos nodded. "What you said, about fear. Ever since," he paused. "Since I deserted, I have experienced new things. Like pain, desire, love," he looked at V. "Even, now and then, a very specific kind of fear. But everyone I meet seems to live in constant fear. Of tiny things. Of losing what they have, of never getting what they want. It makes no sense to me. It seems artificial."

After they had walked a long while windows appeared on their right. The windows stretched from floor to ceiling and offered a view of huge turbines and magnetos inside the basement of the building. Engineers moved from dials to levers to switchboards.

They came to a T in the hallway, and the windows overlooking the turbines ended. Only now there was an orange line on the floor, and a green one as well, and a yellow line, too. A sign in sans serif letters where the lines began was etched into the tiles. On the sign was written: CAFETERIA. LOCKERS C-F. DRAFTING CHAMBERS. NEW ROOMS. And so on. Each corresponded to a color. Next to the sign was a schematic of the floor plan so abstract as to be useless. It did, however, show where there were stairs and doors.

"Which way then?"

"Down," said Avalina. "King Close is a captive here, he'll be in the dungeon. The green line."

The green line led them down the same straight hall, under the same bright lights. Hours passed. The hum and buzz continued. They walked for miles.

They came to a door, at last, at the end of the hall. Slowly they opened it, and saw the metal stairs going up and down, tier upon tier. The buzz was louder. Bare bulbs hung from raw wires. Down, down, they walked. There were not even rats.

Kholos touched one door, at a landing. It was ice cold. He could hear chatter beyond.

"We must be 50 stories underground," V said. "At least."

At the bottom, at last, they rested. There was another hall, stretching on, but now instead of the sterile tile it was lined with conduits and cables, serpentine lengths of piping and copper wire, rubber-wound lines the same color as V's receiver. The light was dim, flickering.

"Why haven't you transformed," asked Avalina. "It must be well after midnight?"

"This happened before," said V. "I stayed the same in the other domains."

Avalina looked at V. "There were a fair amount of Fractured in Neo Cumae, when the ripple reached us. The Universitat took care of them. We had a center in the city, a tall building. They would go in, crazy shapes and ages, some much worse than V, and then come out as they had been, before the ripple. But they were different, somehow. In little ways, I could see it on them. Their lines were adjusted slightly."

Kholos kissed V's forehead. "If the Universitat is doing what I believe they are doing, the Fractured they cure are not the same people," said Kholos.

"How do you mean?"

"I think they trade them out," said Kholos. "For other versions. Close versions of the people who go in. Cheaper versions, I would guess. It's expensive to move around reality, time is a commodity, the Aetherian treasure it. I think the Universitat swaps out people from timelines from realities the Aetherian have left for scrap."

Avalina took a deep breath. She was thinking of the machine in her rooms for localized shifts. "The Fractured are unstitched?"

"No," said Kholos. "The Fractured are loose threads, if you will. Time is not the shape people perceive. The moments are concurrent, not linear, the Fractured are flicking through their existences, their particular existences ... Time is a sphere, not a line. Everything happens at once. Every possibility happens at once. There are no alternate realities, alternate selves. Everything is of one piece. Only you," he nodded towards V and Avalina, "can't perceive it. I can, but only to a small degree. V is infinite doing everything V could do. Her life, her choices, are where she decides to go. Compared to you," he said to V. "I am nothing, a fleck with perhaps a hundred, two hundred different existences, of which I can perceive maybe two or three, if I try." He tapped his canisters. "You are unlimited. Only your power to choose for yourself has been, well, fractured."

V stared at Kholos for a while. "That makes sense," she said at last. She looked down the hall. "Someone's coming," she said. "And they're armed."

Avalina rose, looked, drew her bow, and said, "They're black engineers!"

"Where are they?" Kholos said. "I don't see anything." Frantically he reached into the pack for his weapons and armor, no time to equip everything he grabbed what he could.

The black engineers were identical to the white engineers but they wore black lab coats instead of white. And instead of calipers or clipboards, they ran with two-handed batons that fizzed and crackled with electricity. By the time they arrived at the end of the stairwell Kholos had sighted one through the scope of his rifle. In two seconds, one second, now.

He fired as the first emerged.

The others poured out into the confined space.

From his knees Kholos lifted his one armored arm to block a charge from a shock baton that knocked him backwards, hard, against the stairs, and out of reach of his sword and gun. A second burst whacked him in the center of his chest plate, where it ricocheted about, bouncing up the stairs.

Avalina fired. Her black bow was small but the sinew and bone and wood of the composite wings was so limber she could pull it nearly flat. The arrow stuck itself to mid-shaft through the goggles of an engineer and he went down in a heap. Hastily she pulled another shot from the quiver strapped to her thigh. There were four of them now.

"Are you hurt?" Avalina cried to Kholos.

"No," said Kholos, and his voice was the thunder.

"Dammit, Kholos!" V cried. "Give me a gun!"

As if he had sling-shotted himself from his crouch on the floor, Kholos appeared in the middle of the black engineers. Blue arcs, tens of thousands of volts, jumped at him, and one scorched itself across his back. The air filled with the scent of burnt skin, but those who fired at him from the front found their shots deflected down the hall, up the stairs, everywhere. Kholos swung out with his wrist and connected with the side of a hard hat. A wet squish sounded as the hat cracked. With his other hand he grabbed an engineer by the arm and flung him up into another. An arrow from Avalina stuck itself between the shoulder blades of a third. Those still standing fired at Kholos again, who was quick enough to send their shots off of his wrist. He could not see where the angles sent the bursts. Grabbing the baton from the hand of the closest engineer he turned the device on those left, shocking each to death. Blood, not oil, spilled out onto the floor.

The corridor was filled with the stink of scorched bodies, smoldering rubber. Six dead engineers lay on the floor, bleeding out or burned across swaths of their bodies. Avalina's arrows protruded from two of them. Kholos knelt among the victims, panting and wincing from the scorch across his back. He wondered why these guardians or enforcers or whatever they were would be men instead of machines.

He looked for V, and saw her hunched over Avalina, working frantically.

Avalina had been struck by a wild, bouncing ball of electricity. Her red leather was blackened up her right side, from her waist to her face. The blue tusk was scorched, and her leathery Borac skin was pocked and bubbled in places. A sick, yellow steam rose from the wounds. Kholos knelt by her. He thought of Gyr Zax, left behind to die when the Comanche had come for him.

Avalina's eyes looked off at a great distance then stated at something just before her face. She did not even seem to notice V and Kholos at all until V began to unspool a roll of gauze along her blasted arm. After she screamed in pain from the touch, she lifted her uninjured hand, calmly, and started to speak.

"Let me work," said V. "My turn now." But V saw how deep the damage went.

Avalina said. "I can see the strings coalesce. My strings, they are all coming together. And they are beautiful." She smiled and the burnt skin on her face cracked, again.

Kholos, spoke softly to here. "You'll die here," he said. "Is this what you want?"

"Yes," she said. "Just free King Close, for me."

V began to cry. "Thank you for saving me," she managed to say. "Thank you."

Avalina blinked and her vision focused somewhere else. Kholos saw the edges of her body--her fingertips, the tops of her ears--crumble away, like the shale in the Asinwatis that could suddenly collapse into dust.

V took up Avalina's hand and held it tight. "She's dead."

Kholos closed her eyelids.

When he lifted his hand he saw there was grayish-green powder along the palm. The skin first softened and then flaked, then crumbled, then turned to dust. Under her red leather clothes the rest of her body collapsed in a puff. Within a minute there was nothing left but her clothes and her boots, and her one undamaged tusk. Kholos picked it up, and wrapped it with the tusks of the Borac gods.

After a while Kholos took out all of his armor, and unstrapped his sword and slung it across his back. He lined up his rifle sight down the endless hall before them. Nothing would be there for the next few seconds. And at the end, far away, he saw a single, unmarked door.

V said. "Let's go find King Close, and set him free."

They walked on following the Green Line. It ended at the door.

Kholos approached and tried the knob: it was unlocked. Leaving it closed he leaned in close and listened. There was only silence.

"Go ahead," said V. "He's asking us in."

"What?"

"You can't hear it, can you?" V said. "But it's so loud. The voices? You don't hear all the voices? It's like the entire city is in there. Cars. Talking. The rain. Dogs barking. I can hear it so clearly."

Kholos turned the knob, and opened the door. The room was empty save for a single, metal folding chair. It sat under a bright bare light, emitting a cone of pure white. The walls were bare concrete.

The chair. The light bulb. Nothing else, save for a single bare copper wire, running from the leg of the chair out to the wall, where it disappeared into a crudely drilled hole barely big enough for a pin. Kholos shut the door behind him. It closed with a little click.

To Kholos, the room sucked in all sound. He could not hear his own footsteps, his own breathing. The silence was pure and total. But V put her hands over her ears: the city of Neo Cumae reverberated through the cell to her.

"What?" she shouted. "What? I can't hear you!"

Kholos ran his hand along the walls. *What would a connection to the Aetherian appear as? A single atom? A block of cement? A gesture at a particular moment? A minute shelved among the hours, like a book?*

Silence. Kholos thought of cats, prowling along these damp, dank walls and the corridors behind. He searched the space for patterns. The light was dim. The chair shined, as did the wire. Kholos bent down and touched it. The room erupted into noise for Kholos, a shock running up his arm and sending sparks from the edges of his armor. But V took her hands off of her ears, and blinked. She felt the silence, now.

"Where are you?" Kholos shouted, and with his thunder-voice the walls shook and the chair spilled over with a crash. The din and bang of the city, all of its rushes and voices and accidents and achievements and suggestions, seemed to soften some. In his ears a truck rolled by. A pack of children skipped and laughed down a sidewalk. A couple made love behind a crate in an alley. Glasses clinked at a party. The sirens of the engineers sounded everywhere underneath the clamor. Kholos closed his eyes, listening.

V saw a little black bead. Hurriedly she picked it up and shoved it in her ear.

The noises leveled for her. She was in the city and in the room both at once, listening to everything but seeing nothing, feeling nothing, that was not outside the room. The buzz of King Close said clearly to her: "Help me. I know you're here."

"I heard that," said Kholos. "I can hear you. Where are you?"

"I am in the wire," said the buzz. "I am trapped in the wire, here in the Power Station. They brought me here. I didn't want this."

"The Aetherian," Kholos demanded. "They come to you here? In this room? At this place?"

"They came, once, to talk to me," said King Close. To V his voice was gentle and understanding, a middle-aged man, not entirely unlike Dr. Voss. "I've never seen them." There was a pause. "I can't see anything. I can't hear anything, outside this room. I can only talk. Never listen. Only Avalina could respond at all to me. Do you know her? A Borac woman?"

Kholos and V looked at each other.

"I'm sorry," said V. "Avalina is dead. She died trying to help you. She asked us to set you free."

Silence. Total.

"What do they say?" Kholos cried after a moment. "What did the Aetherian tell you? Instructions? What are they doing here, on this world? How do I reach them?"

V put her hand on Kholos's arm. "Kholos," she said. "He's trapped. Help him."

The helmet, so glorious and terrifying, snapped to look down at her.

"You're right," he said, finally.

"Are you still there?" King Close said. "Please, still be there. Talk to me." His voice was cracking. "Only Avalina could talk to me. She..." he trailed off.

"Can you calm this noise?" Kholos asked. "Or," he lifted the visor. "Can you produce a receiver for me? We will set you free, if you can help us."

"I can," said King Close. "Wait. I am not sure. Your insecurities are, are not apparent. But familiar, somehow? I can produce a receiver but my signal will not be clear. You will not hear what you want to hear. Do you understand? The receivers play upon people's fears."

"Fine," said Kholos.

With the slightest tap against the toe of his boot Kholos felt the black dot. He picked up the tiny black pea that then sat perfectly in his ear. At first he heard only static, then the sound cleared and the din of the city quieted.

"Pain," said the voice. "Pain and freedom. The buzz knows you will run forever. The buzz knows you can be held. Restrained. Limited. You are on a leash. The only question is how long is your chain? Did you forge those links yourself? Each one a lie?"

"What are you talking about?" Kholos demanded. "What does that mean?"

"I'm sorry," said King Close. "The receivers produce a personal buzz. My power is in the trend. The distant news. The event a world away. All told to make the listener like what they are hearing, to make them feel important, or safe, or entertained, or informed. But your wishes and fears are jumbled. I don't know who you are. I cannot hear your feelings clearly. You could probably command me to tell you anything you wanted, actually."

V, puzzled, asked Kholos, "What is he saying? What are you hearing?"

"He tells his listeners what they want to hear. He doesn't know what to tell me and I'm hearing, I'm hearing bad things. What are you hearing?"

"That Universitat is making the world safe through faith and reason. That I should wear longer skirts this season. That I cook with too much butter."

Kholos nodded. "King Close, this mission of yours. You only tell people what they want to hear?"

"No," answered the Adonai in the wire. "No, not at all. The tone is what you want to hear. The tone is to make the listener believe in the message. It's different for everyone, you see, but the goal is the same: to ensure they believe the same buzz, always. To ensure they care more about abstract, more than the immediate world across the street. Or even across the room."

"You're preparing them for something," Kholos said. "But what?"

"I'm preparing them to accept lies," said King Close, disdainfully. "That's what I do. I don't want to. Please understand. But I have to talk. I have to. It's all I have now that I can't listen. Only Avalina understood, and now she's gone."

V interjected, "You're listening to us. Right now."

"Only because you are in my cell. I have to be immediate to hear. I can't be so far away, just whispering lies in the dark."

"Alright," said Kholos, looking to V. "How do I free you? Break down these walls? Amplify your signal?"

King Close answered deliberately. "Run me up through the middle smokestack of the Power Station, I'll be able to broadcast myself beyond Neo Cumae."

"We have to climb up the smokestack?" V asked.

"Yes," said King Close. "That is where the Aetherian emerged, to listen to me, that's the way out. There is a tunnel entrance there. A tunnel through time, if that makes any sense."

"We've been through one before. Do you know where it leads?"

"No," said King Close. "But it would follow that if the Aetherian come through, then they must be coming from somewhere else where they could be. Perhaps Pang's domain."

Kholos was startled. "Pang's domain."

"I often have to speak of Pang, although that is not what the Aetherian said, they just asked me what you've asked: what am I doing, how does it work," said King Close. "I can tell you I suspect whatever my mission is here, my purpose in this cage, it has something to do with Pang. Half the time I'm to disparage Pang, half the time insist he is perfect."

"Is Pang the Aetherian?" Kholos asked. The conjecture made sense: Pang the Creator, Pang the center of the Adonai pantheon. Pang the God of Zero, where faith and reason converged.

"I don't know," said King Close. "I don't know." After a pause, he said, "It feels so good to listen to people."

V was looking at the wire, which Kholos still held pinched between his thumb and forefinger.

"Why do you think it's Pang?" said Kholos. "Is Pang the only point of contact between the Aetherian and this universe?"

"I don't know what you mean by that," answered King Close.

"Never mind," Kholos said. "Do you know where Pang is? I have a list. The Universitat list, of all of the Adonai, and all of their domains. It's how we came to you. But Pang is absent."

King Close said, "Maybe that is because there is no Pang."

"But you just said," countered Kholos, "that Pang could be the reason for the Adonai?"

"I did," said King Close. "It's not a contradiction, if you think closely on it."

Kholos did. There was something to King Close's conjecture. But then there was something to Kholos's thought that Pang might be the Aetherian, walking the world whenever and wherever they chose. Kholos felt trapped. The world was an expansive, interesting cage, but it was still a cage. He looked to V.

She was on her knees, at the place where the wire that contained King Close ran into the wall. Gingerly, like it was a thread that could break easily, she was pulling the wire through and making a coil. The end was still attached to the leg of the upturned chair, under the lonely cone of light.

"Try the tunnel," said King Close, in their receivers.

"Is this wire long enough to lead all the way up this smokestack?" V. asked.

"Yes," said King Close. "It runs through everything in Neo Cumae, and it cannot be broken."

They were halfway up the smokestack when a whistle blew from somewhere below them.

Kholos was leading the way, hand over hand on the rungs of the ladder bolted into the concave wall of the stack. The wire, which V had attached to her sash in a knot, ran down into the darkness below. Up ahead a glow of gold and silver grew larger, and larger. Kholos recognized the swirl from the cellar of St.

Theresa. He hoped this time they would not be deposited underwater.

"They will track you down," Kholos pointed out to King Close, touching the wire. "They can end you with a thought."

"And you as well," said King Close. "And yet they haven't. Why is that?"

"I believe I am ahead of them," said Kholos, thinking of the bits of time he had spent to slip out of reality and then back in, leaving only the moments where he escaped as a trail. "Perhaps only seconds ahead, at this point, but still ahead."

"Are you sure of that?"

"No," said Kholos, thinking he had no true idea how the Aetherian might track him. "I am not."

"You could be doing their work even now, then," said King Close. "I'm just saying."

Kholos laughed, thinking of the city he had burned, was still burning, and would always be burning, the tear in time he had made, the escape, thanks to Michael Staffa's imagination and love. "That, I think, is unlikely. And besides," he added. "So long as we can be free of all this, I don't particularly care."

"She does," said King Close.

They were at the last rung. The metal of the bars, unlike those below, was cold when Kholos gripped it. The golden portal spun above and reminded him of the flames of the city burning forever. V undid the wire.

"How do we know they haven't turned you off, down below?" asked V.

"Then I am no worse off, and I've had these hours at least, to listen and not just talk. But please, hurry and put me into the tunnel. I can send myself into the Televia network from this high. I can be free."

"All right," said Kholos. "Thank you."

"For what?"

"For your conversation," said Kholos. "For the information."

"Good bye," said V. "Good luck."

V touched the tip of the wire to the light past the top rung and held it there. There was a sigh, a gasp, like a child waking from a long sleep. And, abruptly, their receivers went dead. The darkness below now was total but the light from the time tunnel was bright as day. Kholos looked up into the swirl, and, under his helm, his receiver fell out, bounced off of his shoulder plate and plummeted into the darkness.

17. The Front

Over the peaks of the pine trees black smoke rose in gruesome clouds. The clang and crash of artillery and tanks reported through the woods. There were soldiers among the trees, either moving towards the fighting or stumbling back away from the front. They were all Columbium militia in gray-green fatigues. Officers barked out orders to spread out, to move faster or slower, to sound off among the chaos. Explosions rocked the trees. The sky was sunny and clear, without a whisper of a breeze, so the smoke hung as if tacked there.

Those moving away from the fighting were shaking, bloody. Some were blinded, many wept. Some were missing legs or arms or parts of their heads. Machine guns rattled and spat and everyone ducked instinctively, including Kholos and V.

Kholos remembered Michael Staffa's memories.

There would be an earthen ramp, leading down into the trench network. There would be bloody bandages in the mud. Bodies of men too exhausted to stand and fight, sleeping where they fell, shot or not. There would be a horrific stink.

V was hiding her face against Kholo's chest, crying. All she could think of was Michael, Michael walking towards the line, and then not walking back.

A dozen huge explosions blew through the woods, forcing Kholos to a knee to brace against the blast as it tore off branches and knocked over smaller trees.

Soldiers nearby were knocked flat, some were hit by flying branches, some died. The stream of Columbium soldiers rushing towards them, away from the fighting, grew, while those running towards the line seemed to shrink as they slowed going into the barrage, heads down like people heading out into a storm. Little fires crackled underfoot. Distant screams from the trenches reached them.

Kholos grabbed a retreating soldier with a shoulder wound. His blood had run down his uniform and stained the sleeve purple. The man gaped at Kholos, his eyes blank. V grabbed a bandage from the pack.

"What's happened?" Kholos asked. The man blinked. "What's happening here?"

"They've broken through the third line," he said. "The fourth is all that's left. There are machine guns everywhere. I've been shot? I can't feel my arm."

"You're going to be alright," V said. She had treated falls in mountains, gunshot wounds, frostbite and snakebite and compound fractures, waiting for Barney Turl to reach them. "Take a deep breath. We'll get you to a doctor."

Ahead of them a fresh series of explosions erupted like tympani drums played all at once. The screams grew louder. The wind grew hotter. Scanning through the lenses of his helmet Kholos saw a white mountain to the north, remembered it because Michael Staffa remembered it, had written poems about it. A Republicant explorer had given it his own name, but everyone called it by its true name, the Tahoma.

"That's all," the soldier said, his pupils dilated. "It's gone. The third line is gone. I wonder if we'll make a fifth. Or maybe we can start counting backwards now and we'll call it the third. Ha ha."

"What's your name?" V asked the soldier.

"Billy Budsen. First and only Couverites."

V had wrapped up the shot shoulder with gauze and packed a cloth over the place where the bullet had gone through. "You've lost a lot of blood, Billy Budsen," she said. "You need to get some fluids. And although you're in shock right now this is going to hurt real soon. Do you know where you're going? Is there somewhere safe you can get to?"

The soldier blinked at them. "They're endless you know. They come on forever. And they are all the same. The third line is gone." He staggered.

"We're at the front," Kholos said. "This is the Northwest corner of the Columbium Continent. This is where the Stalinistas are making their invasion."

"Kholos," V said. "We have to help him. He's lost too much blood."

Kholos nodded. In his full armor he seemed both taller and thinner. And the helmet made his voice sound deeper, but farther away.

"Budsen," Kholos said. "The rear echelon of your unit, it has a field hospital?"

The soldier looked at Kholos blankly. V was trying to pour water into his mouth.

"Come on then," Kholos said. He leaned Billy Budsen against his side and took his good arm and began to walk him back, away from the front. As they moved V worked her sash into a sling. Budsen's blood soaked into the sash as she tied it off. A little jerk at his neck made him cry out in pain, but it also focused him.

"Who are you with?" he asked Kholos. "The Kiowa? There's a rumor the Kiowa are coming up from the south, going to open up a second front. Tanks, armor. Kiowa armor."

V jumped in before Kholos could say anything. "We're Columbium. Orang territory."

Budsen nodded. He was gritting his teeth from the pain, which V knew was a good sign.

A city of tents and crude cabins criss-crossed with Televia wires strung from bare pine poles appeared after another kilometer of slow, gasping walking. Set in a little valley, the ground was muddy and the stink was toxic. Already, with the collapse of the line the camp was being broken down: across the mouth of the valley trenches were being dug and fresh wire lain, mines buried alongside the makeshift, rutted road that led from the west. In a few places Universitat runners unspooled Televia wire, walking backwards. Trucks were lining up to carry crates of equipment, cots, rations, everything. A few horns beeped and soldiers cursed as the Columbium tried to retreat both quickly and efficiently.

They left Billy Budsen at the hospital, a long log building with hundreds of beds, simultaneously treating the wounded and breaking down to move back from the new front. A nurse, a young man with the Universitat fish and compass in gold and red on his sleeve, looked at V warily as he helped Budsen to a table.

Men moaned. Men cried. Men died.

"Yes," said V to the nurse. "I'm Fractured. What of it?"

The nurse looked at her with exhaustion. "Here?" he said. "Now?" He shook his head, then he shooed them outside.

A Universitat doctor emerged from the doors to the hospital in a rush, pushing past V. The fish compasses on his sleeves were stained with gore.

The doctor looked up at the sky, gray but still bright, the mountains rising up like pillars. "Pang," he said quietly. "I pray you, end this."

Kholos stepped over to him, and raised the visor on his helmet to show his face. Kholos put his hand on the doctor's shoulder, just to steady him. After a moment the doctor seemed to compose himself.

"Doctor," Kholos asked, softly, "Tell me, please. Is there an Adonai who claims this place? A saint you pray to, who rules this war? Is it Pang?"

The doctor looked back, looked up, at Kholos. At first he seemed confused. But, as he took in the face of Kholos, framed by the lifted visor of the helmet, it turned to shock and fear. Kholos released the man's shoulder.

"Guard!" he shouted. "They're in the compound! They're in the compound!"

Kholos looked from the doctor to V, who shrugged her shoulders. And then Kholos was surrounded, a half dozen Columbium soldiers all around him with their rifles raised at his chest, at his face. Some had bayonets attached. All of them looked terrified.

"What the Pang damn is happening here?" said an impatient voice. "This has to be done Pang damned orderly, if it's to be done at all. That's the Pang damn field hospital. We can't protect our own Pang damned hospital now?"

The speaker had an entourage. More guards, these more crisply attired and much more imposing than the sentries surrounding Kholos, and officers of all types with chevrons on their shoulders showing expertise with logistics, intelligence, infantry, and engineering, among others. Many also sported the Universitat badge of advanced education.

The speaker pushed his way to Kholos. His hair was gray and cut like a brush's bristles. He wore a long blue tunic, double breasted, with flashes on the collar identifying him as a Brigadier General in the Columbium militia of the Lakota Territories. Around his waist he wore a black belt where a pistol flapped in its holster. Behind steel-rimmed spectacles his eyes were gray. His face was red, and he paused to cough as he took in Kholos and V.

"I'm General Suskind, commander of this piss poor sector. Who the hell are you, and what are you doing in my base camp, such as it is?"

"Kholos," he started to add, the deserter, but then thought better of it. "This is V, my companion. We're looking for someone, sir. I have reason to believe they may be nearby."

"Alright, Kholos and his companion V. Seeing as you look pretty much like any other Pang damned Stalinista, even in that fancy kit, tell me why I shouldn't shoot you right here and now?"

"I look like a Stalinista?" Kholos muttered. He shifted through his reams of memories. He knew he had fought the Stalinistas, in the bodies and minds of others, along the banks of the Danube. He had fought them in the Gobi. He had fought them in the Ganhdi Kush. He had, as Michael Staffa, fought them on ground not far away from where he stood. But he could not recall a single Stalinista face. A single Stalinista word. A lone Stalinista prisoner. He stood before General Suskind and gaped.

"How'd you get in here, anyway?" the General demanded.

V stepped into the interrogation. "We helped a wounded soldier back from the front. He's in the hospital now."

A line of shells burst close enough that the concussion blew through the camp, rippling tent flaps and upsetting some empty crates. The officers around Suskind looked nervous. But the general turned to his artillery officer, a fully trained Universitat chemistry professor, as apparent by his mortar and pestle badge and his fish compass.

"Now tell me, major," Suskind yelled, seeming to ignore Kholos. "Why is it the Stalinistas can reach us with their canon, but we can't reach them with ours? Are their Universitat boys smarter than ours or something?"

"They must be advancing more quickly than we realize, sir," said the artillery major, unperturbed. "Or else their prayers allowing their shells to launch are stronger than ours. I am sure their propellant is the same as ours."

Suskind merely snorted.

"Sir," said one of the other staff officers. "We should be moving on. This man is probably a scout of some sort. We can deal with him behind the next line."

"Quiet," the general said. "The Stalinistas don't have spies," he seemed to be talking to himself. "They come on, and come on, and come on. They never stop. They don't do anything else. And yet here you are. You, Thomas," he gestured to one of his guards. "Go in and see if you can find this wounded soldier. Check out the story. Ask good questions for me. "

"I'm no Stalinista, general," Kholos insisted. "I have been a soldier, however."

"A Columbium soldier?"

"Yes sir," Kholos said. Not quite lying. "Orang Militia. Sector 17."

"Really. Seventeen's seen some of the worst fighting on the whole front. The Orang militia carry swords and wear armor now?"

Another round of shells burst in the treeline. Another concussion warbled the tents and sent the tails of the general's tunic flapping. Suskind did not look away from Kholos.

"Guards, lock this man up," he said. "We'll deal with him after we've established the new base. Take the woman as well. Keep them separated."

Kholos cringed, his hand half-reaching for his sword. He would not be locked up.

V shouted, "But all we did was save one of your men! We're Columbium!"

"First," said Suskind. "You just showed up here. No papers. No unit. That's you. Two. You may be Columbium, but he is not," he pointed to Kholos. "I don't know what he is. Yet. But he sure looks like he could be a Pang damn Stalinista."

"Sir," said Kholos, looking up at the tree line and thinking of the paper airplane he had made for Dr. Voss. "I can tell you how to lob your shells a farther. Farther than the Stalinistas."

"That's impossible," said the artillery major, the one from the Universitat. "A sin against reason."

Suskind's eyebrows raised. "Do tell."

Far away but very soon, they walked over the snow and ice in the peaks of the Asinwatis. The wind was cutting and should have killed them quickly in their light coats but their patterns were built to withstand extremes, diseases, and pains of all types. The peaks below them stabbed up into the cloudless sky. With his amazing eyes Gabriel, the Messenger Pattern who carried the instructions of their Aetherian masters at the cellular level, saw the Universitat highway, stretching north-south, three ridges and perhaps five hundred kilometers beyond. Clearer still than the straight strip of asphalt was the glow from the burning city. The six swords trudged on.

Their long blades were wrapped in white cloth, as were their rifles. They wore long cloaks and white boots, strapped with bits of white leather. Across their faces were white strips of silk, tied behind their necks. If anything or anyone had been watching the reaches of the cliffs, say a renegade saint, they would have seen nothing but the wind whipping the snow from the peaks.

They could fly. Whiz through the seconds on wings made of refined light. Gabriel, however, forbid flying for the moment. The instructions were clear. Pursuit would be dedicated but could not be explicit until the last moment. The loose Liberator pattern must not be brought to bay before a particular instant. But once cornered, the pattern was to be destroyed.

"There," said Ramiel, Pattern of Thunder. His single word shook loose avalanches all around them.

They saw it, the slash in reality, bleeding through: a stitch in time, the bit of space and time where Kholos had saved Duran Town from the Second Comanche. The flash shimmered. It had happened close by: at least compared to when they walked, it had happened close by, and very soon. Gabriel turned from his place in the front of the line. Sandolphon, the Angel of Strength and Power, so much bigger than all of the others, peered down. Raguel knocked snow loose from her front with her mittened hands. Nathaniel blazed a bit hotter to warm them all.

"We could be upon him within a day, perhaps two," said Ramiel. He was whispering but they heard him like bells. "Without using our wings. He might still be there."

Gabriel looked down the long slopes. He was reading his memories of mountaineers, of spelunkers, of bridge builders. The glaciers were treacherous. Likely, one or more of them would fall and die on the rock below. Likely many of them, as the rock this close to Anvir could crumble to dust or go molten in a flash.

Sraosha, the Obedient Pattern shaped as a little girl, the smallest and the most beautiful of all of them, spoke to him sternly. "What is the message you carry, Gabriel?"

"Pursuit," answered Gabriel, still staring down in the crevasses, "Then destruction."

"And does this sighting offer pursuit, then destruction?"

Gabriel looked at the other five. Nathaniel, the snow steaming around his shoulders. Ramiel, broad as a boat, the one Gabriel knew would be called upon to fight the renegade first and likely die. Sandolphon, the strongest of them all. Raguel, tragic, tall and thin. Sraosha, the little zealot. And himself, the deliverer. If two died on the way down, could four complete their mission? Could three? Could he alone?

Etched into who he was, Gabriel carried the will of the Aetherian. When he spoke, it was made into truth. "No," he said. "Not yet. This isn't the place. It will happen somewhere else."

"Where, then?" asked Raguel.

"Don't question him," snapped Sraosha. "Just listen. His words are the words of our masters. We have the trail. And we will find him at the instant when we must."

And so they walked on, towards the highway and the city burning forever.

18. Red Rage and Endless War

The staff cars of General Suskind and his officers traveled in a pack, yellow-and-green Lakota flags flying at the corners of the hoods. Kholos, V, Suskind, and the artillery major, whose name was Paulus, rode in the lead car. All along the entire ride the major suggested it would be wiser to interrogate the prisoner before listening to his tactical advice.

"The Stalinistas," replied Suskind, after the major had repeated his concerns for the third time. "They have been held where?"

"Nowhere," said the major. "Of course. They can't be stopped. That's a fact."

"Alright," said Suskind. "Let us say I accept that they can't be stopped."

"You should, sir," said the major. "It would be a sin against reason to suggest otherwise."

"Just so," continued Suskind. He was watching the treeline, smoking and collapsing under the assault of the Stalinistas as they traveled. His men, the last stragglers from the overrun, were coming out in pairs and alone. "So tell me, why are we fighting them at all?"

The major shifted in his fold-down jump seat. "Because, sir, they can be slowed. Slowed substantially."

"Tell me then, where have they been slowed?"

"Sir, you know more of the famous battles that I do."

"Just tell me, Paulus, Pang damn it."

The major sighed. Kholos looked out the window along with the General, but instead of looking at the defeated Columbium army he looked up at the sky: the sun was setting. V was due to shift again. Then he looked at the peak of Tahoma. He had a strange feeling he had seen the mountain before, not just through Michael's eyes, but somewhere else entirely. In another range of mountains entirely.

"Well, sir, the Republicant forces have slowed the invasion for over a hundred years. The Danube and Volga lines are unlikely to be breached in our lifetimes."

"How did they accomplish this great military feat? Can you tell me?"

"Mostly luck, sir. The barricades at Buda City, for example, provided-"

"Nonsense!" said Suskind, turning suddenly at the major. "They held because the Republicant Centurions tried new things. Crazy things. Tactics the generals frowned on. Tactics the Universitat frowned on, in fact. The evacuation of the population in Vienna, for example."

"That was a sin against faith, sir. The Emperor was deposed for that gambit. Much of the city was destroyed."

"But it worked major! The Republicant won! The city was rebuilt, it still stands! It's stronger than ever! The people were saved!"

"Sir," said the major. "With all due respect. We are not the Republicant." He added, "Thank Pang."

"No," sighed Suskind. "We are not. But I intend to try as many insane and sinful things as I can to hold the Stalinistas. And one of the great innovations of the Republicant field officers was they recruited local scouts, people who knew things they didn't about the land, the weather. They didn't listen solely to their Universitat representatives." He added archly.

"Sir," said the major coolly. "What you are saying borders on blasphemy. It's troubling enough you are listening to the advice of an, an unknown entity, over your officers. But a sin against reason is a serious offense. And I would remind you, the Republicant's conduct against the Stalinistas has sent that once great alliance down a path to spiritual ruin. The catechisms of the Universitat are quite clear in the progress of war, especially this war. To ignore them is suicide."

"And yet defeat is not," said Suskind. "How curious."

"Sir?"

"Nothing, Paulus. I am simply doing what I can to defend the Lakotas. If my decisions in this regard disappoint you, transfer to another sector."

Paulus said nothing. After a while Kholos looked at the sulking major. "Do you have a protractor?" he asked.

"My protractor is not a layman's tool," he snapped. "Have you been Universitat trained in advanced geometry? Physics? Chemistry?"

"Give him the tool, major," Suskind said. He looked behind them at the cars in the line following behind, then past them, to the south. "Where are the Pang damn Kiowa columns?" he whispered.

The field canon of sector 17 were being undone from their embankments and placements in anticipation of relocating behind the new trench line. Of the more than a hundred total pieces only a few dozen were still in place, larger guns that would need to be broken down and hauled back on trailers. Soldiers moved about the sandbags and on the roofs of the bunkers, loading up shells and supplies into piles for transport. There was less urgency here than at the base camp, but they were actually closer to the approaching Stalinista offensive, just slightly to the north, along a ridge with beautiful views of the white top of Tahoma.

A gray cat with white paws sauntered by, jumping from box top to box top, following the officers and Kholos and V.

"Hello," the cat said to Kholos. "It's Busto. We met in the city. Don't answer me or everyone will think you've gone insane. Just listen."

Kholos nodded at the cat. No one else seemed to hear.

"My pet, er, master, has a suggestion for you," the cat said. "What you have done with Saint Theresa, Storenko, and King Close is upsetting things. Golgothan thinks you would do well do continue this course of action. It raises many interesting questions.

"This is what you are, after all," said the cat. "You are a Kholopatiron, a Liberator. Now, don't be an idiot. Ask the important questions. Like you did in Neo Cumae. Free the Adonai. Love your woman. These are new ideas you're spreading. So don't be daft about it."

"Don't be mean," said Crick. She was waiting on top of a pile of shells, which had been warmed in the sun.

"I'm not," answered Busto. "I am merely simplifying things. You know how they get." With a pause to scratch himself behind the ear, Busto jumped away and disappeared into the cracks between a pile of sandbags. Crick, followed.

Kholos looked up at Tahoma, and nodded.

The officers were all staring at him. V came up and took his arm. "What is it?"

"Nothing," he said. "I love you."

"And I love you," said V.

Behind a quartet of canons Kholos stood with the silver protractor of Major Paulson, looking at the disintegrating line below. V wrote down numbers that Kholos said to her, and then performed some calculations based on formulas Kholos explained.

Below them, Stalinista infantry were mottled gray specks coming through the woods in such numbers that it seemed a flood of stone was moving along the forest floor. They were easily ten times the number of the Columbium troops.

Finally, the canons were adjusted. Kholos called for a load of specific shells, a strange combination of explosive, incendiary, and propellant. The barrels of the canon were tilted up.

Major Paulus shook his head. "This is a sin, general," he said. "A waste of ammunition. Delaying the withdrawal of our forces, not to mention our precious artillery pieces. Plus, the blasphemy of passing on Universitat implements to laypersons. I can't ignore your eccentricity any longer. I have to report this to Commandant Kline. Get me a Televia line."

"Paulus," said Suskind. "A true Columbium Universitat representative would at this moment be praying along with the gunners here for a strong showing in this counterattack."

"Sir," Paulus hissed. "I can tell you as an expert in the matter, this volley will explode well above our targets."

"Yes," confirmed Kholos. "It will. Now fire."

The gunners looked to their general for confirmation. Suskind nodded. Everyone put their hands over their ears, and the canons roared. For long seconds the whistle of the shells screamed through air. The gray tide in the trees below seemed to slow as the load approached.

Through the glasses, Suskind watched as the burst of the barrage hit. Fire rained down in a slash across the treetops, and the branches broken by the explosions turned into splinters as they fell upon the attackers as wooden shrapnel. Kholos's attack had turned the forest itself into a weapon. The gray line stopped. Stopped cold. For a second Suskind lowered his glasses in disbelief.

"Pang damn," he whispered. Then, yelled, "Pang damn! Repeat at will!" He cried to the gunners. "Repeat at will!" He tore the sheet of paper from V's hand. "Get me a Pang damn Televia line! Everyone on the line fire for effect with these calculations! Stop the retreat! Stop the retreat! Pang damn!"

"A sin against faith!" Paulus was shouting, pointing at Kholos. "A sin against faith!"

An orderly ran up to the party on the ridge, toting the heavy portable Televia set, unspooling the wire back to wherever the main antenna was located. He put down the box and spun the crank, then put the receiver to his ear. When he did, his mouth dropped in surprise. Where the first volley had struck there were now fires burning and a small bulge had opened in the line.

"Um," said the orderly. "It's for you?" He held the receiver out. To Kholos.

Kholos put it to his ear.

"This is the buzz!" said King Close. "With news for you!"

"I'm listening," said Kholos, then added. "I'm glad you're free."

"Thanks to you! A report from Neo Cumae: there's a new Adonai on the scene, and he's leaving the Power Station right now ... it seems his domain is a train of Comanche armored vehicles, and his sole mission is, I guess, to get you."

"A new Adonai? To get me?"

"That's on the wires," said King Close. "Have to split! Can't stay on the same line too long, or they'll catch up with me. So good to hear voices again. So good. Anyway, watch your back, Kholos."

"Give me that," Paulus yanked the receiver from Kholos. "This is Paulus, Chemist and Major in Sector Seventeen, raise HQ. Priority one." After a pause the major repeated his order. Then a third time. Finally, he turned to the orderly. "What is wrong with this thing?"

The orderly shook his head. Paulus began to wheel in the cable, hand over hand. Soon he came to the end, a tattered little bit of the line, attached to nothing. It looked as if it had been bitten through by a cat.

"If you're a Stalinista spy," said Suskind. "You're really bad at your job. Also, I've decided not to take you prisoner.

"Now," he turned to the Televia operator and snatched the receiver up before anyone could tell him the line had been cut. Succinctly and clearly Suskind relayed his orders to the sector, and then waited for the response. It came, and Suskind passed the receiver back. The operator again coiled up the cable, which was still cut. Paulus, V, and Kholos stared at Suskind.

"What?" said the general.

"A miracle," said the operator.

"Sin against reason!" said Paulus. "Sin against reason!"

After a night at the re-constructed base camp V awoke a teenager, eighteen or nineteen years old. Kholos, up earlier and cleaning his rifle, paused to watch her rise and wash at a bowl of cool water. Suskind had given them their own tent and V moved about nude, graceful and shining.

"This," Kholos said, pointing towards her body. "Is the one benefit to being in love with a Fractured woman."

"I could feel hurt by that," said V. "But I won't." She paused, running her hands along her flanks, rinsing her mouth out with some wash with a Kiowa brand name.

"Kholos," she said. "It is nice to be nineteen again. And again and again. But being a baby. Being an old woman. Not knowing from one day to the next. I'm still Fractured. And I would like this to end. Sooner the better."

Kholos put down what he was doing. His armor was polished up and lay in neat rows on top of the cot they had not slept in.

V continued, "I know this," she gestured along her body. "This has something to do with you. Something with what happened in the city burning. Honestly I don't care much about all that. But I would like to not be Fractured. I would like to be a whole woman again, be myself again."

"When we escape," Kholos said. "You will be whole again. More whole than you've ever been."

"And if we don't?"

Kholos answered, "We will."

All at once, the barrage of the Columbium artillery, which had gone silent during the night, began. In the hours before dawn as he walked the camp Kholos learned that his calculations had been passed up and down the Columbium line, and that every Sector, from the base of the Tahoma to the banks of the Green River had held. In some sectors raids were pressing the advantage, and there were rumors of Columbium rangers taking back ground lost not far from the second line. However, no soldier suggested the Stalinistas could be pushed back into the sea.

"What are we going to do now?" V asked.

"I am going to find the next Adonai," Kholos said. "You are going to stay here."

V shook her head. "No," she said. "We will go together."

"And why would you say that?"

"Because you will need a vehicle to see anything at all," said V. "And you are a poor, poor driver."

"V," Kholos said. "You saw what the front was like."

"Nevertheless," said V. "I'm coming with you. To honor Michael, at least."

"We'll see if we can procure an armored car," he said. "You will not step outside of that car."

"I'll be driving anyway, so fine."

The Stalinistas.

They had come from the Eurasian plains, emerging a millennia prior, riding black horses and bringing plague to the Republicant. Or, they had come from the deserts of Bali Ala, nomad warriors who invented gunpowder and made canons from sandstone. They spread the word of a version of Pang who was disappointed his perfect creation had been soiled and demanded from the people of the world this be corrected. Or, then again, maybe they were a people so populous they spilled over their borders and took over their neighbors by sheer numbers.

All of this could be true. Conversely, it could all be false. No one knew where the Stalinstas came from.

This was known: The Stalinistas attacked. They had attacked Eurasia, and they had taken all of it, assimilated every tribe and culture and language and climate they encountered. Then, some centuries ago they had come at the Republicant.

The Republicant had slowed the Stalinista invasion along a line of fortified towns and natural barriers. The upheaval and drain of this constant war had wrecked the Republicant from Albion to Third Carthage, resulting in mass waves of refugees to the Columbium continent.

The Republicant held, with great amounts of material aid from the empires of Ebonia. But year by year the Stalinistas continued to advance elsewhere in the world. And it was understood that the collapse of the Republicant was a matter of time.

No Stalinistas were ever captured. No one knew what they wanted. No one knew how to stop them. Children in all the Columbium schools were taught by their Universitat instructors that someday, all the world would be Stalinistas. This was the will of Pang.

Kholos pondered all this as they drove onto the broken ground of a soggy meadow, paralleling the front behind the third trench line, now recovered under the fire of the Columbium artillery. The barrage had sheared off most of the woods during the morning, so only white ash and splintered stumps dotted the ground. Kholos was staring out the shatterproof window of the car, one of the staff cars of General Suskind. The artillery had been halted as the Columbium troops moved back into their trenches and the cannon were brought forward to cover the advance. The sentries who stopped the car to check their credentials spoke of the inevitable Stalnista counterattack, and stared off towards the east with a shiver.

On his lap Kholos unspooled the Adonai list. There were one hundred and forty-four total. They had visited three, and he felt no closer. He had also realized many were vague to the point of metaphor: Cainus, who ruled over the Fusing Tree, was the saint of blood and leaves. Kholos, blessed with a piece of a poet's soul, could imagine what that might mean. But that did not bring him closer to finding the Aetherian. He wished he had taken the time to speak more with Dr. Voss about the meaning of the names and the precise locations of the domains. Perhaps he should.

"What are we looking for?" V asked, both hands on the wheel.

"I don't know," said Kholos. "It could be several of them. There is a saint of pain, one of blood, another of combat and fighting. Their domains are things like the Arena at the end of Battles, or the Translucent Hospital. They might have been here and moved, of course. But I don't think the light tunnel from the Power Station would have been left open, traveling to the front, for no reason."

The car, which was more jeep than car, bucked and heaved. In the trees the Columbium troops were rushing forward. Kholos remembered the trenches, the close combat. The Aetherian had built him to recall some of the deaths that comprised his memories. Michael Staffa looking up at the swirling stars with a sucking chest wound, he remembered that.

Under the list of Adonai, Kholos had a map of the front, and he paused from his study to consider where, exactly, their car was and where they might be going. V shifted gears as she maneuvered them around a crater full of mud.

"I like this car," she said. "Do you think we could keep it? After, you know, saving the world and everything?"

"That's the nineteen year-old in you talking," said Kholos. He looked up from the map and out the window, thinking of V's lost truck. "But if it makes sense, then, yes, perhaps we could. Only if we need a vehicle, though. So far, most of our travels have not exactly required wheels."

"Only dactyls," joshed V. Then, she said, "Kholos, the dactyls flew, didn't they? Really flew? Without prayers, without a Universitat protractor around at all."

"The Universitat would tell you they glide, that they are just falling slowly. They say they are launched from the tops of the saurs."

"But that's not true," said V. "They flew. We saw it."

"Indeed we did," said Kholos. "Makes one wonder what else might not be true." He consulted the map again. "We are leaving Suskind's sector," he pointed at a stream perpendicular to their route, now nothing but dust and broken branches, choked off at some point by debris or bones or worse. "More towards the center of the front.

"If I wielded universes," Kholos whispered. "How would I direct my creations?"

"If it was me," said V. "And, yes, I know this is the nineteen year-old talking here. But if it was me, I'd do it at the beginning. I'd do it right through Pang. Start it running and let it go."

"Pang's not even on the list, though. For all we know they never personified that idea."

"Makes you wonder," said V. "Who else they might not have put on that list."

Kholos grinned at her. She was laughing at him with her eyes. "I love you," he said.

"I guess you do," V smiled. "When I'm a horny and hot nineteen-year-old."

They were close to the treeline, to the combat. The artillery was louder here.

"Stop here a minute," he said. He got out of the car, and looked west. For a moment he did not move.

V rolled down the window. "What?" she called. "What is it?"

"Do you see that?" Kholos shouted, pointed west, at the front. "Do you hear that?"

V looked. She listened. She saw the tree line, with the fires from the artillery barrage smoking up the horizon perhaps half a kilometer away, killing the morning sun. She heard the whistles of the shells overhead, and the echos of the impact thuds. Training her ears more closely she could make out the cracks and snaps of rifle shots, the rapid pops of automatic fire.

"The war?" she asked. "What do you mean?"

Kholos lifted off his helmet and passed it to her. "Put it on," he said. "Look through the eyes."

She had to hold the helm up with both hands to bring it level with her eyes and keep it from banging on top of her head, but V could, shakily, peer through the eye slits. With her first glimpse she immediately dropped the helmet onto her head in terror.

War, personified. Gigantic, furious, powerful, insensate, it loomed on the horizon, over the fiercest of the fighting. The figure was huge, engulfing the entire section of the line. In his hands were twin golden machine guns, not unlike Gyr Zax's god-killing gun, but these were each as big as their car. Bigger.

The figure was a caricature of a man. His face was bright red, blood red, as if he was boiled or burned. He wore golden armor like Kholos's plates, over bare red skin, and rode in a chariot with scythed wheels. His eyes were white with tiny, black dots for pupils, and the crest of his helmet was made from the broken bodies of Columbium troops. His muscles jerked as he fired wildly at the ground around his chariot.

V saw the armor plates were etched with reliefs of the dead and the dying, many of them Columbium soldiers but, she noticed, also figures like those she had seen in Dr. Voss' history books in school: Republican Centurions with stubby swords, Ebon troopers in khaki fatigues with muskets. In his mouth, V saw, were rows of teeth layered like those of sharks.

When he roared V brought her hands up to hears, forgetting she was wearing Kholos's helmet. It slipped again, this time banging the bridge of her nose, and she heard thereport of the machine guns. The figure loomed, paused in it's firing, and seemed to look in V's direction.

V lifted the helmet off of her head and tossed it onto the passenger seat. She was shaking. She could not breathe. She was so afraid and angry she thought her heart would burst. Both of her hands gripped the steering wheel and squeezed and she wanted to drive, drive, drive away. But she could not decide if she wanted to run right into the war-figure or away from it. She wanted to hurt someone.

Kholos put his hand on her shoulder, reaching through the open window. "No," he said. "Don't give in to him."

She looked up, slowly, over the trees where the apparition had been. Only now, there was just the trees, the artillery, and the smoky sky. "What was that?"

Kholos had the Adonai list open. "Zome," he answered. "Zome of the Golden Machine Guns, who rules the spheres of fury and fear. His domain can be anywhere that people fight." Kholos put the list down. "You can't see him now, can you?"

"No," V sighed. "Thank Pang. But I know he's there."

"I can see him," said Kholos. "I can see him quite clearly. I think I'll kill him," said Kholos.

A long column of Columbium troops was marching up the road in front of them, moving to the front.

As they drove into the woods the Columbium troops coming up to the front made way for them, seeing the brigadier flags on the hood. The thuds of the canon grew louder. Needles from the pines showered down onto the windshield so thickly V had to activate the wipers.

Kholos was staring up, leaning forward over the dash. His rifle was loaded and awkwardly leaned from the floor of the car to the roof; the tip of the barrel scraping its fabric.

Kholos pointed up at Zome, his mouth of shark teeth open and a howl of bloodlust coming through the forest.

"The god of bullies." V said, "You seem to feel this one is personal."

Kholos donned his helmet and strapped up his gauntlets. "He's the heaviest chain on the hearts of men who would be free," he said. His voice was changing, becoming deeper, louder, all Thunder. The glass cracked in the window above the passenger door. "Stop the car."

Kholos turned to V. "Stay inside the car. And come no closer. Promise me. No matter what you think or hear or see." He was thinking of Storenko.

"I promise," said V.

Kholos exited the car, took up his rifle and sword, and walked towards the fighting.

The trench line opened up to Kholos. There were entrance tunnels that led to the line, which was crenelated every so many meters and zig-zagged like the edge of a serrated knife. Coils of barbed wire were strung out, cut in many places from the previous day when the Stalinistas had attacked. Behind sandbags and low walls of poured concrete were antique machine guns of Republicant make. Columbium soldiers from a dozen different territories, all speaking with different accents, were moving up into the trench, taking firing positions and picking out Stalinista targets through the smoke and dust raised by the covering artillery attack.

Through the cordite and mud and fire Kholos thought he could just make out the salty scent of the Pacificum, not so many kilometers away.

In the trench network he kept moving forward towards the sound of explosions and gunfire. The troopers he encountered, after staring at him for a moment, ignored him. A captain stopped him as he turned into the front line, the last trench on the lip of the dead zone where he could physically feel the Stalinistas massing for their push, tens of thousands of them, out there beyond the artillery line.

The captain yelled, "Soldier! Where is your unit!"

"I have no unit," Kholos said in his thunder voice. "No rank. No clan. I am unique."

Kholos looked up at Zome, blasting into the outposts of the Columbium. After Zome destroyed one of the bunkers he would kneel down and scoop up the dead and the dying and smear them over his helmet and his face, the bodies becoming part of his crest, their blood draining into the red of his lips and nose and chin. Kholos realized the Columbium could only see the impacts from Zome's shots, and assumed they were Stalinistas.

After checking his armor and his weapons one last time, he stepped up and out of the trnech, and into the no-man's-land between the Columbium line and the massing Stalinistas.

The thunder roared. "Zome!" he shouted.

The artillery stopped. The gunfire petered out. The smoke began to wisp away.

"Zome!" Kholos repeated. The voice blew the ash up from around Kholos's feet in a semi-circle.

Zome's pin-prick eyes found him.

"You die now!" Zome called. He brought his chariot about, and Kholos saw it drawn by two flaming stallions. Where they trod the ground blackened and split. The blades on the wheels, big as ships, spun so fast they became pinwheels of steel. Kholos set his feet apart.

Zome, taller than the trees, blood dripping from his mouth, his hands holding his smoking submachine guns out from his armored chest, rushed towards to Kholos. Without hurry Kholos lifted his rifle and sighted a half a second forward into the future, found where the temple of Zome's helm would be, and fired. The report echoed a minute backwards. A second shot struck the chariot, between the nuclear steeds, and shattered the yoke that held them.

Before his second bullet had struck Kholos was running, drawing his sword as he leapt. Zome's chariot sputtered, jumped, and flipped onto its side. The horses had blinked away, now free of their harness, leaving bright blinding traces behind them.

Kholos's heavy footfalls thumped across no-man's land. Puffs of dust wafted up from around his heels as he sprinted over bones, scraps of uniforms, and wrecked guns and pistols.

When he came to Zome he found the giant Adonai had shrunk: he was now shorter than Kholos. And his helmet, bloodstained and composed of screaming bodies, was shattered into three neat pieces. Blood black as oil poured from Zome's forehead. But he was still alive.

"You!" he gasped at Kholos. From his back, he raised the submachine gun in his left hand and brought it to bear at Kholos's chest and fired. "Hate you!"

The bullets sparked and pinged off of Kholos's armor. A few ricocheted off the visor of his helmet and snapped his head back and forth. But Kholos walked through it, and took the hilt of his sword in both hands. Once he was close enough to strike he planted his feet and swung, chopping off Zome's right hand at the wrist. The Adonai screamed as more black blood burst from the wound.

"Tell me," Kholos said, with the Thunder. "What possible purpose could you serve? What would the Aetherian have you do here?"

Zome looked over to this right, towards the shrouded mass of Stalinista troops, gathering for their attack.

"You can't kill me," Zome spat. His tongue was black and long and forked, like a lizard's. "I've done so well."

"Answer me!" Kholos roared. Letting the voice fully loose.

An impact crater opened under Zome. Kholos put his boot on the red figure's chest.

Zome hissed at Kholos, his breath a steam of rot and piss and fear.

With his armored fist Kholos knelt and smashed Zome's mouth, the rows of teeth cracking and splitting. Howling with pain Zome tried to raise his remaining hand and his remaining submachine gun, but Kholos sliced the arm at the elbow. Kholos lifted his sword, gripped the hilt in both hands, and turned it point down. With a stab he struck the breastplate of Zome and, like a shell striking a bunker, it broke.

Kholos understood Zome was only strong when men were afraid. And Kholos was not afraid, he was not weak. Pinned through his chest to the ground, Zome spat up his black bile and snapped his broken teeth at Kholos. Kholos twisted the sword.

"Your purpose?" he repeated. "The Aetherian, do they call to you? Or do they simply let you out of a cage?"

Zome cried out, "I make weak men strong! I make brave men cowards! I am not a purpose, I am hate, rage! Fight me! Fight me again! Hate me!"

Kholos knelt alongside the Adonai. Zome was like an insect, stuck through and wriggling. The Adonai seemed to be growing smaller as he shouted and spat, he was much smaller than Kholos now. Much smaller.

He thought of the other Adonai they had encountered: St. Theresa, Baron Storenko, King Close. And now Zome, revealed to him, at last, as a cranky infant.

"You are the Stalinista's champion, aren't you?" said Kholos. "The Aetherian want the Stalinistas to conquer this world, don't they? They want a world of hate, hate against what is different? Is that your role in this?"

Zome was a child now: an ugly, beet-red child, throwing a tantrum.

"Kill me!" Zome said, his voice that of a little boy. "Hate me!"

Kholos stood. "No," he said. "I will not. You're a brat. If I had pity in my mind, I think I would pity you."

Leaving Zome pinned and squealing, Kholos took up Zome's submachine guns and crushed them in his hands. The Adonai whimpered, but Kholos noticed that the wound closed as he withdrew the blade, although the piercing in the armor did not. And, miraculously, Zome's hands had returned, although now they were the hands of baby. Picking the Adonai up, Kholos removed the now child-sized armor. Zome cried out, hungry for war or a blanket, Kholos could not tell. He tried to bite Kholos, chomping down with baby shark teeth against a shoulder guard.

Kholos walked towards the fog and smoke to the east, towards the Stalinista lines.

The artillery barrage from the Columbium lines resumed, and around Kholos the whumps and concusses of the shells exploding above the ground, rather than on impact with the ground, shook him and sent pieces of shrapnel pinging off of his armor. He recalled the pain of being shot in his knee, and took care after the first few blasts to keep himself hunched and low to the ground, but he did not waver. As for the baby Zome, red faced and screaming, Kholos took care to carry him close.

There were no trenches before Kholos, no barbed wire, to gravel roads and earthen ramps. There were no bunkers, no vehicles. Just land flattened by the march of hundreds of thousands of boots. It was very quiet. It was very still. Zome cried on. Bones, or what was left of bones, crunched underfoot. Kholos took a deep breath.

Like ghosts, the Stalinistas emerged.

They came as a single mass, a horde. A thousand, ten thousand deep. Wave upon wave of them, men, women, even some who had to be younger than V. They were all silent, watching him, waiting for something.

Kholos stopped.

They all looked the same. There were a hundred races, a hundred shades, infinite noses and eyes and hair colors and bodies and heights and weights, but, somehow, they all looked the same. The expressions. The posture. The aura. All of it was identical, plus the uniforms--the simple gray tunic and trousers, the boots. They each carried a rifle, the same model rifle, and all wore belts with two canisters at their hips, like Kholos. And they all, somehow, looked like him, the same expressions, the same manner.

Zome wailed a little louder.

Kholos could smell the sea, and through the lenses of his helmet, could see the enormous arks of the Stalinistas, huge leviathan things: they were beached, by the hundred, all along the isles of the shore. There was no way, Kholos understood, those ships could take to the sea again. The Stalinistas would conquer the Columbium or they would die here. So many of them, he thought, looking up and down the lines. There must be millions.

The silence held. Kholos could almost hear the waves break.

"You can't stop us," said a single voice from the horde, "Pang is on our side. Zome is on our side. All the saints are on our side. Even you, probably, are on our side."

"Where is he then?" Kholos answered. He spoke with the Thunder. "Will Pang face me?"

Kholos realized that, unlike the Columbium troops, the Stalinistas could see Zome.

"Who are you?" shouted Kholos, the Thunder in full effect. "Why do you look like me?"

"I am the Universitat representative of the war," said the voice. "And we do not look like you, you look like us." A hideous little chuckle followed.

"Why are you making this war? What does it mean? Do you even know? Do you even care?"

"Our war is the will of Pang. Our victory is preordained. We are the true lights of reason and faith. This world is promised us by Pang. We will protect it."

"Does he come here? Does Pang speak to you?"

"Of course," said the Iman.

"How? Where?"

"In our hearts, through his creation."

"Please," Kholos said disdainfully.

Before him, the Stalinistas were forming into neat columns, preparing for their counterattack. Gently, Kholos put Zome down on the ground. The conversation was at an end, he realized. There was no light tunnel here.

"I suppose you could show this child something other than your hate," Kholos said. "And he might become a Saint of something better than war. But I do not think you will. As for your war, I do not care. If you do not wish to be free, there is nothing I can, or would, do for you. Perhaps I will have a chance to stop you. I hope so. For now, there is nothing you can do for me."

With that Kholos turned and began to walk away, turning his back to the invaders. He had gone most of the way back to the trench lines, with one foot on the ladder, when he looked back over his shoulder.

The Stalinistas, in good order, were on the march. Rifles lowered they walked quickly, then broke into a jog. Until, at last, they rushed on in their unstoppable numbers. After crossing the wire, Kholos took a last look before jumping back into the trenches. Their faces set in rage, their eyes unblinking and frenzied. Leading the way Kholos saw Zome, sprinting out ahead. He was whole again already, a young boy in golden armor as yet unblemished or touched with blood, with a golden submachine gun in each hand.

He was growing larger.

Back at the car V was waiting with the engine running. Kholos tossed his weapons into the back seat. He did not want to carry them any longer.

"What happened?" said V. "I heard the fighting stop."

Kholos shook his head. "I don't know. I learned nothing. I accomplished nothing. The Stalinistas don't want to be free. They want to be safe. They say Pang is on their side. And they are probably right. It makes me sad, all those prisoners. They didn't deserve to kill men like Michael."

He stared out the window. The churn of the battle was breaking through the trees. Kholos could not yet see Zome, but he could hear the war saint: adolescent cries of fear and hate. A volley of artillery from the Columbium side whistled overhead, then crashed with a shock.

"What kind of world is this?" Kholos asked the battle. "With its fear and hate? What was I built to do here? What was the point of destroying Anvir? Prolong the wars? End them for one side or the other?" He turned to V. "They all look like me, a little. Not exactly. But similar. The Stalinistas, I mean."

He turned to her. He loved her. He was, he admitted, afraid of something besides being trapped: losing her.

"V, I need to tell you some things, before we go any farther."

Her grip on the wheel tightened. "Ok," she swallowed.

"I am Kholopatiron, and I was made, not born."

"Made by whom? How?"

"Made by the Aetherian. They made me. Like they tailored this universe, and many, many others. They produce realities, to fit their needs, whatever they are. I've told you some of this already, I know, but I left some things unsaid. I escaped. To come get you, and to get away from them. Michael gave me that courage, to do that. He inspired me. He, he helped make me."

V looked at Kholos, her young face very still.

They did not say anything for a long time. After a little while V put her hand out and Kholos took it.

"What do you mean you were made, not born?"

There was a cat on the hood of the car, a brown calico cat, with long whiskers and friendly eyes.

"That's not terribly important," said the cat. "What is important is that my master is going to involve himself briefly in this battle, for your sake."

V jumped.

"It's alright," Kholos said. "I know this talking cat."

"You can call me Crick," said the cat, "The gray one is Busto. We would prefer these names to 'talking cat'."

"Crick, then," said Kholos. "What do we need to do next? Is there any way for us to reach the Aetherian?"

"The first question is not a good question," said Crick. "I choose to ignore it. The second is better but you already know the answer. You are on a quest, Liberator," Crick purred. "So ask some *questions.*"

Kholos paused and thought a little while.

"As I mentioned," Crick scolded. "This is not a place for you to be. Puzzle on, but quickly."

V spoke first, "Do you know where the light tunnel thing is around here? The ones that go through time, like? That's how we've moved around, mostly."

Crick, with a flop, lounged on the top of the car. The fighting was thicker now. Kholos, glancing over the treetops, saw the crest of Zome's helmet, bristling with the spirits of fresh Columbium dead. His roar was louder. Already wounded Columbium troopers were being helped back, on stretchers in some cases, out from the thick of the fighting.

"No," said Crick. "I don't know."

"Why do all the Stalinistas look like me?" Kholos spat out.

"Excellent!" said Crick. "That should do it. Your question is a prayer to my Adonai, very powerful, very intense. It will lead us back to him in Tahoma safely and quickly."

V asked, "We're traveling by question?"

"Even better!" said Crick. "Oh, I like you. Very intelligent!"

V blinked.

When she opened her eyes, they were still in General Suskind's armored car, but now they were parked inside the mouth of a cave. Through the opening she could see for miles. There was a span of shoreline, a thick pine forest, and low hills and smaller mountains below. Along the shoreline a veil of smoke hung, and the whomps and bangs of canon fire echoed up to her. On the beach were dozens, perhaps hundreds, of huge ships.

V, woozy, understood she was looking down on the front. The ellipse of the Columbium lines was a scar in the woods, and the gray ground circumscribed by the clouds of smoke was the no man's land between the Stalinista offensive and the Columbium trenches. Her stomach told her it was still there. Quickly V opened the door to the car and puked.

Kholos exited on the other side, watching the same scene. Only he was looking farther, through the lenses of his helmet. What he saw was a mass of horses, palominos and chestnuts and grays, all coming up through the Columbium rear echelon and charging into the fighting along the beach. As they came further into the front Kholos saw they carried energy weapons, crackling spears with blue tips. He recognized them: the Second Comanche. It appeared they were coming straight for Zome.

"But the Second Comanche were folded out?" he said, confused.

A voice behind him asked, "Who says?"

V and Kholos saw the Adonai, self-proclaimed saint of questions: Golgothan.

"Who threw up on my floor?"

"Sorry," V managed. "I'm not used to, to whatever just happened."

Golgothan wore his long coat with the many pockets. From a particularly large pocket Busto poked his face out. Crick walked, tail up, around Golgothan's ankles.

"We should go, boss," Busto said. "Thought assassins could be on their way already."

"Do you think?" said Golgothan.

V and Kholos looked out the mouth of the cave. They saw a flicker of light, like a shower of gold, and then only darkness. Then there were the circumscriptions of the stars as they traced their arcs through a night sky. V's stomach heaved.

They looked out and down at a dark wood. The land was swampy, mossy, and Kholos could see hanging vines and deep, slow moving rivers wandering through the brush. A strange acrid scent wafted through the air.

He had been a dactyl handler, a Borac. He knew where they were: in the Southeastern reaches of the Columbium Continent.

"Why have you brought me here?" Kholos asked Golgothan.

Golgothan said, "Why indeed?"

"Is everything you say a question?" asked V.

"Is it?"

"You walked right into that one," jeered Busto.

"Golgothan," Kholos said. "How do I escape from the Aetherian? Escape forever?"

"Ah," said Golgothan. "How? Do you? Escape? From reality? Forever?"

"Look," said Busto. "We don't know. But your question is one of the greatest ever asked. And because of this question, we will help you where we can. Now, for the matter at paw. There is another Adonai here. She goes by Powder. She is the Artificer. Why did they put her warehouses and factories here, so far from the population centers the Adonai have worked so hard to develop and control? What is her role in the making of this world? Or unmaking? Answer those questions for us, Kholos, if you can."

Kholos already had his list out. Powder, Adonai of the Artificial. Her domain was the Factory Farm, deep in the Smoky Mountains.

Crick continued, "Our move from Tahoma to here has covered your trail, by the way. You have many pursuers now, and we cannot stay here and wait for you. But we will find you, wherever, or whenever, you go. That is, we will find you if you have anymore good questions. Either of you. Also, there is a question here, in these hills, for you personally, Kholos. A question that will lead to many more interesting questions, we think."

"Such as?"

"Am you the only one?" Golgathan said.

V threw up again. Then shifted, again, into an older woman, perhaps in her late forties.

"May I keep your car?" asked Golgothan.

19. Faceless, Nameless, Placeless

The chemical stink in the air was the Factory Farm, and they followed it easily. The tang in the air made V cough and made her eyes tear, so she had dipped a bit of rag in clean water, covered her nose and mouth and tied it behind her head. Still, every so often she caught a rank puff and coughed. The smell was unspecific. A burning, but also chemical and sulphuric. Yellow clouds, long and stringy and lower than the true clouds, hung overhead.

Kholos trod on. Behind the closed visor of his helmet, he was invisible. She wanted him to talk, to tell her what he meant back at the front, about Michael and about being made, not born. But she was tired, and breathing too deeply made her cough.

They had walked down the mountain then come to a Universitat highway, pristine and straight and level. For most of the afternoon they had trod on the pavement, seeing no vehicles. V made a snide remark about leaving yet another car behind. But otherwise they walked in silence.

Willows, creepers, and a carpet of decayed leaves made the road feel, almost, as if they were indoors. The stink was stronger at a dusty side road and they turned off. After a long hour of walking they came to the fence.

It was a cyclone fence, chicken wire, unremarkable and, Kholos discovered when he gripped it, unelectrified. Kholos stared for a while through the links, gripping his fingers in the mesh.

There were three long buildings beyond the fence, all with high, tall windows and gently pitched roofs. They were not dissimilar to the buildings of King Close's Power Station, but there were no smokestacks or dynamos, no trucks zipping around. The structures were brick, mostly, and the windows were so dusty they could see nothing inside.

The ground between the fence and the buildings was burnt out and dead. Tthere was nothing. Nothing. Three big long buildings. Grassless ground. The hollowness of the domain struck Kholos, so empty. Through the lenses of his visor he scanned the soil, the windows, and saw nothing. He realized, with a start, that he could not even describe the nothing he saw. There was just so little there. Maybe a little shadow around the back of the buildings? It could just be a tree, from outside the fence.

"Buildings," he said. "Dust. A fence. Nothing."

The stench was strong. A small breeze blew by and yellow wisps whipped up in the yard. V coughed.

"Well," said V. "What do we do now?"

"I suppose we go in." Kholos said.

The gate to the fence was open, just a section on wheels that slid back and forth on a track in the dust. Kholos, as was his nature, flung it wide open. The dust swirled around them. V noticed, looking at the places where the grit stuck to Kholos's helmet, that it was the same yellow as the ugly clouds. The chemical stink was stronger with each step.

The door to the first big building was unlocked, and Kholos, with V beside him, entered and shouted, "hello."

Boxes.

Piles upon piles of identical boxes, each about half a meter a side, all perfect cubes. They were stacked floor to ceiling in great heaps. No markings, no identifiers anywhere. Just boxes and boxes and boxes. Kholos stepped inside. The light was dim. The boxes stretched on for a long, long while. After a few more steps Kholos saw the floor was lined with what he thought was sawdust, but then realized it was the same yellow stuff that floated in the air around the place that smelled so sharply.

He checked V's little mask, and started to ask if she was alright, if she wanted more … something. Strangely, the words confused him. *What would she want? What would he give her, if she asked for it?* Kholos lifted his visor.

"V" he said. "I think. I think something?"

"Walk," said V. She pointed out of the door they entered. "Out." Like Kholos, she could not remember what it was called, that, that thing, through which they had come, come somewhere. "Walk back," she croaked.

"Fast," agreed Kholos.

Too late.

The powder around their feet began to swirl. A cyclone that grew, quickly, into something roughly human-sized. The dust was so thick in the pocket of wind it was solid, rigid. V coughed mightily, tears sprang from Kholos's eyes. Until, finally, the winds settled, and where the column of yellow dust had been stood a figure, feminine, made of the yellow powder that dusted everything in the Factory Farm.

Powder was faceless, ageless, raceless. A woman of dust. Smoothly, the Adonai walked around a trembling Kholos and coughing V, and shut the door.

"Go ahead," said Powder, in a voice more malicious than feminine. "Try and think of the words you need to leave. Try and think of the things you would use to escape me."

Kholos stared at the, at the, at the *where*. At the *what*. Trapped, he thought, I'm trapped. He looked for a place to run, but, suddenly, there was no *place*. There was no *thing*. Powder, trailing the stench of burnt hair and hot rubber, circled him and V.

"I am the artificer," said Powder. "I will make meaning," she paused. "But for now, I unmake it."

Kholos reached, his body acting on its own, for his sword and drew it, leveled it at the throat of Powder. The Adonai did not move.

"This *thing* in your hand," she said. "You do not know what it does. You do not know how it works. The words you need are already undone, refined for my future use." She gestured to the boxes.

Kholos shouted, trying to call forth the Thunder. But the Thunder needed words. Kholos had none. With a fading flash of intelligence, he understood what Powder did at the Factory Farm. Powder undid the words. Powder made words meaningless.

Kholos whimpered. He looked at the, at the *thing* and thought *something*. Randomly his elbows shot out, his feet stomped. But he could not think *kick, punch,* or *run*. V was reaching out, reaching up, trying to communicate some idea to him without using any *things*.

"Run," she managed. A verb. Kholos's legs picked themselves up. "Run." In a dash Kholos began to sprint down the center of the building, among the boxes. V coughed. "Escape." More verbs.

Powder cut her off. "A run is also a thing. An escape is a thing. I own the meaning of these words. Not you. Not here."

Kholos collapsed. V cried out.

"In any case," said Powder. "You are in the wrong *building*," she sneered the word. "The wrong *hemisphere?* The wrong *season?* The wrong *dilemma?*" She laughed. "Oh! It's been too long since I played with real intelligences! Un-reptilian intelligences! Or, perhaps, real *sauces!*"

A sound of a machine at work, invisible but close, hummed. Then a box, the same as all the others, appeared in Powder's hands. The lid was open, and it was empty inside. "Now then, let's get you over to the people and the names. Where you belong. Says I."

The box, neither larger than they nor smaller that it had been, closed over the top of the mewling Kholos and the moaning V. With the flap shut Kholos no longer thought of words or of V or of the Aetherian.

The Witch-General Antonia was a tall woman, thin and narrow. At her hips she wore twin long swords made from the same strange metal as Borac god-killing weapons, and silver armor crafted in the same scalloped, overlain way as Kholos's plates. Except that Antonia's were built for a woman, and instead of the dark rust color hers were shining silver. So bright that certain of her opponents, those that survived, called her the Mirror Maiden. Also like Kholos's armor, Antonia wore a belt with twin canisters attached. A difference between her kit and Kholos's was that her canisters did not contain quite the same formula and balance as his, but a much weaker, much more specific manufacture that involved a blending of *anima* and light. Nevertheless, glistening and gleaming in the headquarters of her troop, maps of the Horn of Ebon spread out on the table before her, she cut an impressive figure.

Antonia was a thousand years old. In her face and figure, however, she seemed like a young woman, with long black hair and red lips, a long nose pond narrow eyes. Her skin was so pale as to be translucent. When she walked her feet never appeared to touch the ground.

The Maimed, the Ghosts, were her men. Fifty strong, each of them was wounded to some degree--some disfigured, some with a missing limb, one with both legs missing, several with only one eye, missing fingers, some limping from wrecked bones, some burned and scarred so badly they ate through straws.

Antonia had begun her career as the Witch-General of the Maimed by caring for one of these men, many lifetimes ago, at a time when the Republicant was strong and the Stalinistas were unknown. Since that first wounded angel, each of the Maimed she had helped as she could, using the *anima* the Boracs had taught her to heal them, then the *vuldun* of the Slythe on top of the *anima* to keep them alive if she couldn't heal them, and finally the thought stuff she brought with her from her own place, her own race. Which was not Borac, Slythe, or human.

She kept her troop hidden, both physically and temporally. Always with bases far away from any Universitat presence, always an hour or so behind the time of their surroundings. The current base of the Maimed was open, on a bit of high dry land deep within the Southern Swamps, not far from the Smoky Mountains. The weather was usually hot, and so the only structures were white tents and tarps on poplar poles. Tables for mess and meetings were scattered about, along with tripods for cooking and some earthen bunkers for storage. It was secured by nothing more than a steady watch of Slythe warriors who slapped their webbed feet and dipped into the swamps around the perimeter.

The Slythe long patrol Antonia had dispatched returned after four days in the wilderness. The patrols kept surprises to a minimum, and also allowed Antonia to offer the dying Slythe race some protection. They were, like the Boracs, from her world and did not belong here.

"Report," said Antonia. She spoke in the hisses and whistles of the Slythe language.

The Slythe were reptilian, amphibious, and bulky. Goggle-eyed they stood much shorter than Antonia, but they had big bellies and broad shoulders, thick arms and thighs that ended in stumpy but powerful webbed hands and feet. They also had long tails they dragged behind them as they walked, and their skin varied from Slythe to Slythe, but generally ranged from coal black to mottled green.

Antonia, who had run away from Circle City when her parents died, had stumbled first upon the Boracs. They taught her the rudiments of *anima* but never quite accepted her as one of their own. As a teenager, she had run away again when she chafed at the strict life of the Borac *glin shama*, the role of most Borac women. She had found the Slythe, then, enemies of the Borac. From the Slythe, Antonia gained new knowledge: she learned how to play the voids, the spaces between the anima, that the Slythe called *vuldun*.

Antonia had also brought her own powers: the ability to manipulate a particular set of elements. In Antonia's case, the elements happened to be light. On her left hand she wore a sun-yellow ring signifying her mastery over the school of light. It was the only token she had of her life before her birth and childhood had been taken and re-sewn into this existence.

The Slythe patrol before her carried rifles wrapped in rags to keep the moisture of their hands from rotting the metal. Slythe made excellent scouts in wet country, as they could travel underwater for long distances, poke their globular eyes above the water line, and watch for a while. In their natural element they drew no more attention than frogs.

"Another soldier, another Maimed," answered the Slythe, excitedly, in a complex song of whistles. "Traveled with a woman. Both caught by the dust."

Antonia looked up from her maps with a blink.

"Traveling with another? And he went into the Factory Farm willingly? Or is he just too wounded to fight?"

Insistently the Slythe slapped his wet feet on the planks of the floorboard of the tent where Antonia prepared the Maimed for their mercenary campaigns. Some faction of the Ebon Empire wanted to hire her company for a war in the jungle. A war where the particular talents of her men would be indispensable, and so isolated it seemed ideal for her troop, almost custom-made for her men. But another Maimed changed her priorities.

"Why would he go inside the fences willingly?" Antonia asked.

"Don't know. Didn't go inside ourselves."

"Of course," Antonia answered.

Too many Slythe had been taken in by the Dust. Their language, their ideas, their thoughts were close to destroyed. The fences of the Factory Farm could, when they chose, lengthen and expand, so that one morning a Slythe hamlet might wake up and be unable to remember any nouns at all, an acrid stench in the air and the dust over the log roofs of their mud huts.

Antonia nodded. "You are dismissed. See to your families and report back to me in two days."

Antonia kept her own warriors clear as she could of Powder's domain, where the dust could not take them.

"I can't free him from inside," she whispered to herself. "He's probably already boxed away." She shivered at would that would do, if he was another Maimed. But her scouts said he was unwounded--if he was unwounded he would go nowhere near a fence. And he traveled with another, which would slow him down. They never traveled with anyone. It made no sense.

She swallowed. This required discussion with all of her troops. He was their brother, more than their brother: he was them.

"Liberators!" Antonia called out.

In response the fifty wounded Kholopatiron patterns raised their heads to her voice.

Inside the box there was nothing. There was no void because a void was a thing. There was no space because to make space there had to be some measurement, and measurement was a thing. There was no time because time was a thing. Kholos was reduced to an un-thing, a vessel for meaning that Powder could fill.

None of this mattered to Kholos. He understood only he was trapped. So he raged. Until his knuckles were bloody and his fingers swollen purple he pounded and punched the walls that he could not name. He scratched at the floor with his nails. He ran and slammed from end to end, bruising his shoulder badly and wrecking his never-quite-healed knee. At last, exhausted, he knelt in the center of the box, the un-place, and screamed. And when he was done screaming, he wept.

V watched him. She did not understand who he was, because he had no name, any more than she was still V. Powder had emptied them of all they were. She leaned against a corner of the box and watched as Kholos slapped at the floor. He would, sometimes, look over to her, watch her breathing through her mouth, her hair dangling in front of face, but there was no recognition.

But V was still Fractured and time did flow through the Factory Farm, and she shifted. In a blink, she changed from a middle-aged woman to a young girl, perhaps fifteen or sixteen years old. She was hungry, she needed to pee, and she was chilly. She cried out.

Kholos wanted to. Wanted to do. Something. Instead Kholos breathed. Just breathed. At first Kholos tried to focus on his breath, the steady breath in, the long breath out, but this too required nouns: air, breath. So he stopped even this and let his chest rise and fall on its own. Not allowing himself to think on it, he listened to his body. The throb of the blood in his sore hands.

He reached out and with a wince from the sting in his fingers scooped up V and held her in his arms. Abruptly she opened her brown eyes and stared at him. She felt the warmth coming off his chest, the strength in his arms. She sighed. And then, holding her tight, they slept.

V changed again. Now she was older, perhaps thirty years old. She tried to speak. Her eyes were blazing.

In V's head there was a thought, something tiny thing Powder had missed when she imprisoned them. Stomping around the box, V pursed and un-pursed her lips. Intently she gazed down at her feet, up at the ceiling. She paced, made strange sounds.

At last V stopped her pacing and looked at Kholos. She raised her index finger, looked at it like it did not belong to her, and, again after a long and difficult pause during which she bent the finger, stabbed it into the air, waved it back and forth, and stuck it in her mouth.

She pointed at herself. She tapped her breastbone, hard.

"Fuh fuh fuh," she dribbled. "Fer fer fer."

Kholos's hands hurt. He let his finger fall and put his hands in his lap.

"Gin gin gin," V continued, followed with, "rah rah rah rah," about a hundred times.

Kholos looked at his knees.

"Ver ver ver." Her finger had made a little red circle where she continued to stab at herself. "Ver ver ver gin gin gin ee ee ee ah ah ah," she repeated. The spaces between the syllables were shortening. "Ver gin eee ahhhh," she said.

Kholos looked at her. Something was happening. Some thing.

"Ver gin ee ah," V said, louder.

"Virginia!" Finally. "Virginia!"

Kholos, with a dry sob, stood up.

"Virginia!" V screamed. "Virginia! Virginia!" She was laughing now, skipping around the box as she repeated her despised name.

Kholos took a deep breath. The Thunder spoke. Loud as it had ever spoken, "VIRGINIA!"

The box blew apart at its seams. The meaning of a name shattered its stitching.

They stood in the long hall of names. Already an invisible swirl was forming near the door. Door, Kholos thought. That is a door. He took in the boxes, picked up the remnants of the one V had cracked with her name. The material of the thing, he saw as he studied the seams, was familiar.

V yanked on Kholos's pant leg. "Run!" she said. "Run run!"

Kholos looked at the boxes. "Free," he said, weakly. "Free them all."

Powder was half formed when Kholos whipped around and shouted, "VIRGINIA!" at the nearest stack of boxes.

Out they spilled, the names.

There were Slythe with whistle-names. There was a Columbium settler family, named McGruber. An Ebon explorer, called Sir Zuma Tooloosi, in pantaloons and a plumed hat. There was a carpenter, a mason, a baker, a chef, and a hunter and a fisher, all with names. Confused, the pile of people spilled out into the floor of the long building and milled about.

V understood what needed to be said, something simple. "Run!" she screamed. "Just run!"

And they did, rushing and tripping and crawling for the single door.

The dust swirled. Powder, reformed, stepped to them. "You think I cannot unmake them again?"

"VIRGINIA!" Kholos shouted again, this time directly into Powder's face.

The impact of the word blew her head away and much of her shoulders, sending the grit flying. But just as quickly the Adonai reformed.

"I can own any name you might think," said Powder. "Any action you might take. Any weapon you can imagine. I own the thought as soon as you think it. You are in my domain. Virginia? What is that? A fruit? A bit of money? An act of love?"

Kholos's mouth was formed in the pinch of the V sound, frozen there. V tried it herself, as it was her name after all.

"Virginia!" she screamed. But Powder only laughed. Then the Adonai pointed at her, and the name stuck in her throat. What had she meant to say?

Powder left them there, sputtering out bits of spit and random sounds. Again.

"You must understand how important I am," Powder said.

She moved about those Kholos had freed. Whomever she touched—a Slythe shaman, a Borac *cumbel*, a Republicant centurion—flickered for a moment as if unstuck in existence, then collapsed into a little cone of the dust as well.

"My work is the most vital, perhaps, of all the Adonai. Am I limited in scope? Of course. I understand I cannot sew and un-sew the entire universe. I do not have purveyance of even all of language, just the things. But I have a great deal. And I will organize it, you see. Pang's work was excellent, certainly, but nothing runs perfectly forever. Adjustments have to be made to creation. Zero has to become, say, four or five billion. I am not the creator, but I am the midwife of the new world. I will own every *thing*. Including you."

"Where," Kholos managed. "Where is Pang?"

Powder shrugged her particulate shoulders. "Who knows? Maybe I will make him myself, in the end. The mother of Pang. I like the circle of it. Can you think even that shape any longer? I think not."

Kholos picked up a burst box. The question stuck in his mind, too complicated to ask, too many nouns. Powder, almost dancing from object to person as she un-made them for later meanings, noticed him holding out the box.

"These?" Powder said, taking the box, which turned to dust at her touch. "I have a machine, you see, that makes these. It unstitches and stitches little bits of reality. But you can't think that thought, can you?"

Kholos's eyes went wide. Powder leaned in to kiss him.

"Hate you," V said.

Powder paused and looked down at V. "Hate me?" she cooed. "You do not know what that word means, do you?"

V realized she did not.

"You must be Fractured," Powder said, tussling V's unkempt hair. "Interesting. I will have to unmake you delicately, I think. No more secret names."

V's vocabulary disappeared whole. She snarled, instead.

Powder sighed, looking at the piles of dust and busted boxes in the long hall. "Such a waste," she said. "You couldn't have freed them," she said to Kholos. "Liberator or not. Nothing can truly be free of language. You are as trapped by words as by any lock or barrier."

Kholos breathed deep. Calmed himself. He thought. He observed. He felt, and he reasoned, working with what was before him only. He thought of V's name. How she used it like a weapon.

"There is never nothing," he said, his voice a little, just a touch, deeper. "Time does not begin at zero. I am proof of this."

Powder chuckled. Once. "No, you have no proof. What is that word, do you think," the sands of her face shifted and reformed as she spoke. "A furniture polish? A children's game?"

"Boxes," Kholos pointed. "Roof, hall, and building."

He picked up a pinch of the yellow powder.

"Don't touch that!" said Powder.

"It's just dust," said Kholos.

He pointed at Powder, and said, "Pawn." She took a step back. "Dust," he repeated.

"No, no," she insisted. "I am the Adonai of Meaning. I am the Artificer."

"And you are dust," repeated Kholos. "Dust for a box."

"You can't say that!"

"Dust," it was nothing more than whisper. Kholos picked up a box. "In a box."

V stared at him in wonder.

No thunder, no crash, just a caress of the air. "Dust," he said.

And Powder, Adonai of Meaning and Making, lost her shape, and became a puff of sand, scattered over the floor.

"How did you do it?" V asked.

"I thought of you. I thought how you mean many different things to me, all at once. She could contain one or two levels of meaning, but not all of them."

"And she's gone?" V asked.

"All gone," Kholos said. Then added, "For now."

"Our stuff?" said V.

"We'll see," said Kholos.

They walked out into the grounds of the Factory Farm. The sun was up high and the air was sticky and close. Little breezes stirred up puffs of yellow powder in random directions. Beyond the fences, though, the tops of the trees were still. The gate, Kholos saw, was still open. Gate, he thought. Building. Door. Sky. Swamp, and road. Also: machine.

He walked to the first building. With a kick he sent the door from the hinges. The powder on the floor, in the air, within oozed and slithered. The boxes stretched on for kilometers and kilometers, stacked impossibly high.

"How will you know which is ours?" V asked.

Kholos smiled. "I don't think it matters."

At the first pile Kholos picked up a box and held it in the palm of his hand. The shape of it was impossible, even for him, to see as a whole. Looking away from the box, focusing on a piece of the ceiling, on a tree beyond the fence, he could glimpse the higher shape of the thing from the corner of his eye. The box was an object built in some seventeen dimensions. Kholos could see, barely, five of them.

"Guess what's in this box?" said Kholos. "Make it a thing, not a name or a place."

"A puppy." said V. "Just because."

He looked at the box. He suspected that, like the canisters, the boxes contained light, refined light, light that could carry any information inscribed upon the rays. The difficulty was in the inscription: a matter of imagination and will. A fleeting thought of Dr. Voss, scribbling out notes at his desk, came to him.

Suddenly, in his hand was a squirming black labrador puppy, panting and lashing its tongue over Kholos's hand. Kholos put the dog on the floor and let it run out of the door towards the woods.

"Let's get some of the things that belong to us," he said.

One by one, Kholos imagined his sword, his rifle, and the colored ammunition. Looking at V he imagined a bathtub with hot water and soap, then a clean dress. As she washed Kholos continued to work on the boxes. Soon, their pack was back, filled with rations, canteens of fresh water, clean clothes, a new first aid kit, their coats, and even a mirror, a brush, and a lipstick for V. He noticed that around their little space of bathtub and supplies the yellow dust had edged away in a perfect half-circle, as if it was afraid of being too close to them.

V, dressed sharply now in her re-made dress and a pair of new, sturdy walking shoes, looked at the piles and piles of boxes still unopened.

"You couldn't open all these in forever," she said.

"No," Kholos sighed, true sadness in his voice. "I couldn't. No one could."

"Are we going now?" she asked.

"Not just yet," he said.

Outside Kholos looked around. "Where would she keep it?" he said. "Where would I keep such a thing?" He wondered if perhaps she kept the machine in one of the boxes, but there was a paradox there.

They were walking towards the building of things and objects again when V pointed between the gigantic warehouses. There, along the back of the fence, was a big brick house with a good patch of green grass surrounding it. Kholos noted that there was not a speck of dust anywhere near the house.

"Hello?" said V.

Kholos tried the front door. It was open.

Inside on a small table there was a stack of white paper, a porcelain jar filled with sharpened pencils, and a sewing machine. It was like the one in Avalina's rooms, from Neo Cumae.

The sewing machine was very strange. It had no size. It had weight, and it was solid, but it had no spatial dimensions. Kholos could pick it up, and it would fit on the tip of his finger. But it would not fit inside the pack. He considered breaking open one of his red bullets to freeze it in time, but believed that would probably ruin it. He set it back down on the ground.

"Is this machine," V asked. "Is this the thing that will let us out?"

"No," said Kholos. "This is like a little toy truck, and the machine we need is like your actual truck. And I can't even figure out how to activate it."

"Could Dr. Voss?"

"No," said Kholos. "But I wonder if he couldn't tell me something about it. Maybe."

"Take it to him," said V.

"I told you, I can't even put it in my pocket. How do I carry it to him?"

"Meet him in yesterday," said V.

Kholos blinked. V had thought an idea probably no other human being had ever thought. He hugged her close.

"I love you," he said.

Kholos left. Kholos returned.

"Imagination and will," he told her. "You will need to know this. Imagination and will. It's a small scale machine, only little portions of time can be inscribed, of light. But the concepts are the same. Do you understand?"

"No," said V. "But ..."

V was staring up, over the top of the fences, at something in the sky. Her eyes were wide as dinner plates.

Around the Factory Farm were the Maimed and their Witch-General. They flew on silver wings, looking down upon them.

20. Ghosts

The Fighting First Claws broke through the light tunnel, engines roaring, into a stalemate. Kholos's new math allowed the Columbium artillery to re-set the invasion line of the Stalinistas back, but not to hit their beachhead. So the fighting continued. Columbium troops manned the trenches, Stalinistas threw themselves forward. The First Claws leapt into the attrition.

Colonel Redroot led from the front. From his attack car he barked orders to his mobile domain.

"Form up on me," he shouted. "Watch for our target. Otherwise, engage only if fired upon. This fight is not our concern."

The flashes of his rank and unit sparkled silver in the sun. His vehicles churned up the beach behind them.

The appearance of Redroot and his Fighting First Claws happened up the beach, in a quiet sector not far from the slopes of Tahoma, at dawn. The tunnel, as Redroot had calculated on the new time-maps he carried in his coat pocket, emptied out just north of the proper fighting. The engines of his attack cars announced the morning throughout the Columbium trenches. The tires and treads threw up pebbles and gravel.

Redroot surveyed the lines: the muddy Columbium militiamen peeking over their earthworks and barbed wire and plank walks. The Stalinistas massed in a horde, the shadows of their enormous ships like mountains of rust along the grey sand. On both sides the combatants stopped and stared at the First Claws as they rolled down the beach.

Behind the lines, along the ridges where the Columbium had established their artillery, the officers of each sector looked through their binoculars and blinked. Only the Universitat representatives--both on the Columbium staffs and massed with the Stalinistas--seemed to understand what they were seeing, and knelt, and thanked Pang for the vision of the Adonai before them, the Colonel, the Saint of Single-Mindedness, which they knew from their lists.

Redroot consulted his maps again. Looking at them now he understood he was an instant too late, again.

"He's been here," he relayed to his officers. "Not at this particular moment. We've arrived behind him by a few hours, perhaps a day."

Redroot blamed the weather. His calculations should have delivered the First Claws ahead of Kholos, not behind. Unless, Redroot thought, the deserter had help. He looked up at Tahoma. The white peak looked down. Neither blinked.

"First Claws," he barked. "Hold up, defensive maneuver four. Leave your engines running."

"Sir! Yes sir!"

The attack cars and the tanks formed up in a crescent on the pebbles, tanks staggered in a parapet towards the Stalinistas, attack cars in a curve facing the Columbium. Redroot unsnapped the holster on his god-killer pistol, dismounted, and trod out onto the beach. He lifted his goggles and let the sun bathe his face. He thought of the braves, not so far away, not so long ago, riding ponies on the plains, then moving by rail, finally by car and tank and truck all over the continent, claiming their manifest destiny. Speed and power, those were the key. Fixed fortifications were pointless. Like the trench network before him. Massed infantry attacks could not withstand a concentrated salvo. And couldn't respond to a moving target. Barbarians, all of them. He shook his head in disgust. Was he the only smart man on the planet?

He lifted his glasses to his eyes. The binoculars saw things differently now, since the change at the Museum, since he had become an Adonai. He saw the officers up on the ridge, all in consternation at his arrival. One of them, a major by his collar, was running excitedly down from the line towards him. Adjusting the lenses a bit to see the near future Redroot saw this major get into a car and race for the trenches, then approach him full of praise and thankfulness. Redroot also saw the man die, violently, but that did not interest him much.

Adjusting the binoculars in the other direction he looked backwards in time. An hour, then a day, back to just a few hours, back two days. Ah, there he was. The Deserter. Up on that same ridge, writing with a pencil and some Universitat holy tool, something to do with the cannons.

"Captain," Redroot said.

"Sir," came the obvious reply.

"Get a rocket range on the ridge where the Columbium have their artillery placed. And load."

"Sir!"

Redroot scanned the ridge again. There he went, with a young woman this time. No, wait, she was old. A baby? She was a baby? Redroot removed the glasses a moment then brought them back up. A young girl. A crone. An adolescent. She flickered with each instant, buzzed in and out of his sight. Ute did not understand. There was something off with the world.

"Colonel," it was Stands-Tall-Under-Cedars. At his voice over the line Redroot snapped back into place. He was a Colonel. He was a Comanche. He was on a mission. Nothing else mattered. It would sort itself out.

"Go ahead, Stands-Tall."

"Got something on my scope you should see, sir."

Redroot walked back to his car and mounted up, stood alongside the machine guns and glanced towards the Stalinista lines. The mass huddled and pushed. They were an avalanche waiting to fall.

"What am I looking for, Stands-Tall?"

"Red guy, about three meters high, in the golden helmet?"

Redroot swept his glasses up and down the beach. There he was. Red-skinned and shark-toothed,

Redroot laughed. "Amateur," he said.

"Indeed, sir."

"I'll deal with this one," Redroot said. "You be ready for that infantry if it comes at us."

"Any sign of the target?" Stands-Tall asked.

"We came out behind him," Redroot said. "Must have had help, my plans were perfect."

"No doubt, sir."

"He's up to something," Redroot said. "The only corresponding time tunnel he could have taken is about 500 kilometers out at sea. He's either hours away or he's found another way to move around. I'll see if we can get some intel from the locals."

"Good idea, sir. Consider yourself covered."

Redroot stomped out towards Zome, adorned in his golden armor. The Adonai of Hate hissed at Redroot with hot, bloody breath, sending the long tails of the Colonel's coat flapping.

"And who are you supposed to be?" Redroot said, looking up. "The god of tomatoes?"

Zome paused, confused. Zome blinked. He seemed to lose height. "You have no hate?"

"What I have is a mission," said Redroot. "The Deserter was here. Did you deal with him?"

Zome, shrinking, explained how Kholos had hurt him, but he had recovered, he would always recover. By the time they were finished Redroot was a head taller than Zome. Like a sulking child, Zome walked back towards the Stalinistas.

"Orders, sir?" asked Stands-Tall as Redroot returned.

"Wait a moment," said Redroot, remembering the major approaching on the beach. "I want to talk to someone else before we make our move."

"Sir?"

"I had a little vision."

Major Paulus, Universitat representative to General Suskind of the Seventeenth Sector of the Columbium front, was shouting for Redroot as he ran out into no-man's-land. Redroot waited for the man to reach him, panting. Awkwardly the major knelt on the gravel before the Colonel.

"Your Grace," Paulus huffed. "Pang evolve you."

Redroot said, "Get up. You're an officer, aren't you? Or do you whites not even understand what that word means?"

Major Paulus stood. "There has been a heresy here. Your quarry, he committed a great sin."

"Salute me, cretin."

Major Paulus saluted.

"No wonder you can't defend yourselves from the Stalinistas. This is what it takes to be a major in your Columbium armies?"

"Your grace?" said Paulus.

"Address me as Colonel or sir, or I will shoot you!"

"Colonel, sir. Our artillery, they are doing evil work."

"I've discovered, major, as a military man, that usually artillery does exactly that."

"You don't understand, sir. The maths are all wrong. The shells should not explode far before they reach the ground. It makes no sense. Please, Colonel. Show us the truth of our calculations, and justify our faith in them."

"Show me."

Cowering, Major Paulus held up a piece of paper where the formulae of Kholos were written in shorthand, done in pencil and describing conical sections and how the proper force combined with the proper angle could deliver shells farther afield. Redroot understood the principles if not the application. Neatly he folded the paper and put it carefully away in the breast pocket of his coat.

"You say the Deserter did this, correct?"

"Yes, sir."

"Then I will undo his work because it is his work, no other reason. Do I make myself clear? Not for your stupid facts and lessons. Nor your prayers and rituals. Now, the deserter, where, or when, did he go?"

"I do not know, sir. But I believe the Renegade may have been here and helped him escape. There was a, a distraction: the Wild Kiowan rushed the beach. The tenured Bishops believe they serve the Renegade."

"Do they?"

"So it says in the Reviewed Journals."

"Golgothan. In the mountain," Redroot pointed up at Tahoma, white capped.

Major Paulus shivered. "Colonel, that name!"

"Quiet," Redroot looked at the mountain. The deserter could be anywhere there were mountains, if Golgothan was helping him. He raised his glasses and peered backwards, forwards.

"I wish only to see the confirmation of theory, Colonel. The scientific method is my light. The Renegade is an anomaly to me."

"Really. My light is the wireless rocket, or, sometimes, myself." Redroot spoke into his Televia. "Rocket cars, fire for effect."

"Sir," came the curt reply.

There was a scream and a long whistle. White arcs of smoke tore across the sky, and then there was a silence as the rockets disappeared for a moment up into the gray clouds. Then, with a report of falling rock and cracking stone, the barrage struck home.

Through his glasses Redroot focused forward in time: burnt corpses, wrecked metal, smoke and greasy fires. The Columbium shells had been left out alongside their guns, apparently. Stupid white men, Redroot shook his head. And with their General right there, with them. Redroot could see Suskind's body, blackened. Lowering his binoculars the secondary explosion Redroot had just witnessed occurred.

He felt nothing but a bit of shame at the waste of it.

Redroot looked into the eyes of Major Paulus.

"I just destroyed your unit," Redroot said.

"Yes sir! A miracle! The judgement of Pang!"

"Your men," Redroot repeated. "Your fellow officers."

"They sinned against faith," said Paulus. "Deeply. You are Pang's instrument. I salute you, sir."

"Indeed," said Redroot. "Major, you oversee, or rather oversaw, the calculations for the artillery, yes?"

"Yes, Colonel."

"You never experimented with the fuses on your shells? Never tried different vectors?"

"At the Institute we were taught all the established parameters, Colonel. All that has been covered by greater thinkers than I. It would be a waste of time and energy, a sin against reason, to do those things over again."

"You're a white man," Redroot sighed. "So perhaps your baseness is genetic. I can assure you that a Comanche, a Comanche, I repeat, Universitat representative would never destroy his own men for Pang. Not ever."

"Sir, I am a man of faith and reason."

"Regardless, I can't abide your Kiowa this and Kiowa that. And so."

Redroot brought his pistol up and shot Paulus. The major dropped like a sack onto the beach.

Redroot holstered his gun and walked back towards his car, the engine still running. He needed a new plan. The Deserter could be anywhere there were mountains. Anywhere in the world.

"The Ghosts, the Maimed," said Antonia. "Some call us the Witchmen. We fight the wars under the Universitat's watch. We are careful of that, to fight only the outside battles. For now."

"I understand," said Kholos.

"Indeed," said Antonia.

They were flying. Antonia had shown Kholos how, with a twist to one canister and an addition of a drop of heavy, dark liquid to the other, he could use his wings of light to fly solely through space, instead of space-time. The difference, she explained, between a producing a ray and a particle.

"I'm not human, you understand," she added. "I believe, like the Boracs, I was stitched into this reality by accident. I can see the shapes of ideas humans cannot hold. Of course," she added, looking at V, "humans can see shapes that are hidden to me, as well."

Kholos looked at her. Antonia was tall, thin, and had four fingers on each hand.

V was riding on his back, tethered to him across her waist. As they flew she stared and laughed, like the younger woman she was. Her bare feet swung against the sides of his helmet.

"I ran away, when I was a girl, twelve years old," Antonia explained. "From Circle City."

Kholos understood what this meant. Circle City had been a part of the world. And then it had not, just as the Incorporated Nation of the Third Comanche had been part of the world. A shift in the pattern, unstitched from the garment of this particular universe. The Ghosts, all fifty of them, flew in a perfect diamond around her. They were low to the water, but Antonia avoided the clouds.

"I didn't know the Aetherian could make a mistake like that," Kholos said.

Antonia paused, as if she was about to correct him, but then thought better of it. *If she told him more, would that hurt his chances? Or would it help?* "This from the pattern sent to end Anvir. This from a Kholopatiron."

The winds should have torn their words away. Except they were speaking using the voice, the Thunder. It sounded strange to Kholos coming from the mouth of a person, rather than a pattern.

Antonia continued. "I found a string of pale blue light, just before nightfall. I should not have been able to see it, but I could. And I followed it. I could not touch it, or pick it up, it was not real in that sense. It was a length but it had no width. The line led me to a hill," she continued. "It kept going, but it was dark. I knew I should wait a while. I did, and I could not see the line any longer. But I knew it was still there. I knew it went over the hill to the other side."

Kholos felt, for the first time since he had run with V from Duran Town, safe. Let them send Sandolphon. Let them sent Gabriel and Raquel, as well. Kholopatirons were built to be free. If he tried, he could experience what they knew, and they would be, literally, him. Kholos in fifty-one places at once. Fifty-one possibilities. For reasons of sanity they refrained from this. They were all unique and all the same, both at once.

"The Boracs were on the other side," Antonia continued. "The other side of the hill. The other side of midnight. The other side of the world. The *glin* and the *glan*. The balance, yes, but without the duality. It's how they understand so much. They never thought of the world of the hour as existing or not existing. To the Borac everything exists and does not exist simultaneously. There is no contradiction, it's merely the arrangement of the *anima*."

"Maybe," said Kholos, "that was why Powder was so close to them? To take them from the world?"

"I always thought so," said Antonia. "The Borac, and the Slythe as well." She paused. "You did something to her, to Powder. We have been afraid to get too close. She can unmake my men, trap them. Nothing more terrible to the Kholopatiron, as you must know."

Kholos did not answer. He did not wish to remember the box.

"Finish your story," said Kholos.

"I could see the *anima*," said Antonia. "Something about the cloth of the universe Circle City was cut from. Perhaps that's why they took the city away, my beautiful city," she grew quiet a moment, then continued. "So, I could see the *anima*. And the Boracs taught me how to move it, read it, play it. Eventually, I became quite good at it. Better than the Boracs, even. But I did something they did not understand. I could manipulate the anima both in the *glin shama* and the *glan zyzax* fashion."

"Male and female?"

"You know what those words mean?"

"I have," Kholos thought of how to phrase his thought. "I have some Borac, in me."

Antonia turned her head sharply towards him. He could see his visored face, rust-colored, reflected in her own silver faceplate. Her eyes, though, were surprised.

"I don't know whether to rejoice at that," she said. "Or tremble. No Kholopatiron I know has ever been made with anything other than humans before. Do you," she swallowed. "Do you have Slythe as well?"

Kholos shook his head no.

They flew for a while longer, without speaking. V was silent for a bit, and he wondered if she could hear them and if she understood what he was saying. Truly understood. Below, the sea was dark and rolling, stitched with whitecaps almost close enough to touch. The smell of salt, the spray of the water where his armor did not cover him. They were flying incredibly fast, Kholos knew. The Columbium continent was kilometers and kilometers behind them.

He recalled tales of the sea from the parts of himself who had lived along coasts, on boats, sailors and fishers, explorers and shippers. The all-coils of the world snake. All of the tales were true, even if the tellers did not know it when they told them. Did that make the stories more or less powerful? Every telling another plane. Every story was real. Real as a stone, a tree, an hour.

"General," said Kholos. "I see what you have done with, with the others of me. Were they all trying to escape?"

"They believe they were all trying to escape," said Antonia. She added, "But they were not like you. You have something different about you. And not just your mission to destroy the city. Truly different."

Kholos said nothing, thinking of V. They flew on.

"You disapprove of what I've done?" said Antonia. "You disagree you are unusual? With your mortal lover on your back?"

"I neither approve nor disapprove, agree or disagree," said Kholos. "I simply don't understand why."

"Why what?"

"Why they chose to exist like this. Why you would help them. Help us."

Behind the silver mask Antonia was silent.

"General?"

"The first part of your question is easy to answer, Kholopatiron. They chose to be as they are because of the alternative."

"To be collected, pulped, broken down, split apart back into their composite pieces?" Kholos asked.

"To have never been at all," Antonia elaborated. "To be unstitched from reality. Any reality." She looked at him. *How much to tell?* "Kholos, listen to me. These patterns are your brothers, they are you, but they have faced a choice you have not, just yet. You see their decision. You are the fifty-first Liberator to be dispatched to this world. My men suffered in their mission, and, yes, it was all the same mission. You will suffer, one way or another. I will be here for you, if you wish to join me."

"And fight."

"Yes, fight. There are things we need. Things I need, to keep us concealed. And there is a hope that, someday, I might set them all free, set my home free."

"So they are still after their freedom. Like me."

"Like you, yes. Although they are less ambitious. But then you have more knowledge than any of your brothers."

They flew along a while.

"Your wish to be free, Kholos?" Antonia asked him. "To make your own way in all things?"

"Yes."

"Just know that there are other natures," Antonia said, finally. "Other ways to be. Other things we must do. That girl, who you love, now asleep on your back, do you understand her nature? As she understands yours?"

"She is not a girl," Kholos said sharply. "She travels with me by her choice. She knows the chances."

"Does she know you are the reason she flits through her life? Does she understand why she is drawn to you, what you truly represent of her lost love? How you are responsible for her inability to grieve and move on?"

Kholos said nothing.

Antonia finished. "We are all children here, Liberator. We all follow our base needs, no matter how we disguise them with philosophy and faith. Kholos, let me add something," she said. "All of my men. They say there is only one."

"Only one what?"

"One being is responsible for this world. They told me of a space in the air, an un-place, where they fought, were beaten, and then crashed to earth. I find them without names, with experiences and memories cut from them like wounds. I heal them as best as I can, but even then they remember little of their time before they fell. Even so, they insist it was only one. One being that cast them down, threw from down, from above."

"Just one," Kholos repeated. "One Aetherian."

"One something," Antonia repeated.

They flew on. Some hours later V awoke to the sun peaking over a city cut from a single white mountain, ancient towers glowing in the dawn. At the foot of the mountain-city, lapping at the immense sea wall, were crystalline waves, announcing the place where the Aresic Ocean met the Latin Sea. To the south of the white mountain was veldt and jungle, dark and lush. Ships anchored at docks on both shores looked no bigger than twigs caught up along the banks of a stream. V looked at her hands. She was older, she thought, but not by much, at the upper end of her new range, in her early forties, say.

She remembered she was flying.

She was flying! She screamed and clapped her hands over her eyes, surprised to find a pair of rubber goggles fastened there. She thought she would wet her pants, then she realized she was hungry. Finally, she saw how beautiful the world was, seen from above. And she sighed. She thought of Kholos, and then she thought of Michael, and then she thought of home. She missed her mountains, her rifle, her trailer. She reached down and held Kholos close.

"We part here," said Antonia. "I suggest you land soon. The melodies I played on your *anima* will echo only so long. After the song is finished you will be visible again. We are bound for the jungles, another hidden war."

"Thank you, General."

Antonia raised her visor a moment and he looked into her eyes. They were dark, magician's eyes. "I am nearly seven thousand years old, Kholopatiron. I have learned some things in that time. More and more freedom is always attainable, but the price rises with every extra link in your chain."

"I would break that chain completely," said Kholos.

"Impossible," said Antonia. "More likely you would chew off your limb to be rid of the weight. And accept a different sort of trap." She looked up at her men, hovering with their wings spread, their weapons ready.

"You'll be easy to track, again, once the adjustment wears out. But your pursuit will have to spot you again to trace your whereabouts."

"You know I am pursued?"

"You are all pursued," said Antonia. "At least, all the ones who failed in their mission. Pompeii is dead north of here." She started to turn away. "Goodbye, Pattern," said Antonia. "I suspect we will meet again under very different circumstances. I only hope you will not be too badly wounded, when that time comes."

She dropped the visor, and with a clap of her voice, the Ghosts flew on, heading southeast. Kholos watched them go, over the water, then over the jungle, where they dropped to just a few meters above the canopy. Finally, they disappeared.

"Kholos," said V.

"Yes?"

"How are we flying? How is this possible?"

"It's a sin against reason and faith," Kholos said. "But often sin is just another word for miracle."

21. Friends, Republicants

Pompeii, the Eternal City of the Republicant, rested under a smoldering volcano. A steady plume of white ash rose from the center of the volcano's crater where Republicant engineers, acting without sanction from the Universitat, had managed to harness the volcano's power. Universitat geologists had condemned the project from its suggestion. But in the Republicant, where the Universitat had done nothing to stop the wars between the dozens of different principalities that nearly ended the Republicant, the power of the Institutes was tempered.

Kholos landed up on the slope of the volcano. The bubbling mountain powered the city below and many more of the core Republicant city-states as well. Capped with a layer of concrete fifty meters thick, with cables and piping running down its slopes in all directions, the volcano looked more like a tree with a great white bird on top.

The pipes running down the slopes were painted different earth colors: reds, browns, yellows. They were thick, with a circumference wide enough for a truck to rest inside, and carried steam and gas under incredibly high pressure. A puncture in any one of them could rip the mountain open and spill out magma. The Universitat warned against this possibility from their classrooms and chapels. But they had been giving these warnings for nearly two hundred years. The engineers who built the generators and capped the mountain did not disagree, but pointed out that burning the Universitat-sanctioned oils and coals promised the same fate, only more slowly.

Pompeii itself spilled up from the bay, a metropolis of skyscrapers breaking back all the way to the slopes of the volcano. White stone and glass, they burned in the morning sun of the Latin Sea. Past the high-rises were slighter buildings, ten, twenty, thirty stories, then a little smaller, and smaller still until the antique three-story apartment blocks appeared.

Kholos and V walked down the hill towards the sprawl. V took Kholos's hand after a while. The heat of the day rose quickly, and soon they were sweating.

A fair number of Kholos's component memories were from Pompeii. A swordsman. A Senator. A merchant in medicines and salves. A captain of a warship. A midwife and a surgeon. A bus driver. He consulted this library now, remembering street corners, shops, views and smells. Bits of slang and signposts. The routes of the public trams.

"Everyone is Columbium," V said with wonder. "I've never seen so many white people together."

They walked past a truck going down the hills towards the city.

"Who are we looking for here?" said V. "Which saint?"

"7174," said Kholos. Antonia told him to visit this particular Adonai, regardless of what the list said. "His domain is the Secret School and the Last Church."

"Do we know where he is? Or will this be like finding King Close?"

Kholos pointed down into the city at a white steeple next to a domed brick building. "We know," he said. "Antonia told me he will likely not have a way to reach the Aetherian. But that he would talk to us, and tell us what he could. He's not well, though, she said."

"He'll help us like Golgothan?"

"I don't think so," said Kholos. "Perhaps more like Saint Theresa."

"What's he in charge of? Republicant stuff? Volcanoes?"

"No," said Kholos. "Altruism and Naivete."

The walk into the old city was hot and slow.

They passed ruins thousands of years old, broken columns piled up in pieces under weathered friezes, the yellow bricks from old vias still used by most of the populace over the Universitat roads.

Pompeii was one of the oldest cities in the world, almost as old as the Ebon metropoles, but it was also young in some ways. Institutes of the Universitat were everywhere. People from across the allied nations sent their scholar-priests there to study and learn, and students argued under the shade of tricolor umbrellas outside cafes and at tram stops and under the trees in the many small public parks. There was business, mostly in shipping because of the docks. A police man stared at Kholos's rifle, wrapped up in canvas and strapped to his pack.

They turned down an alley, stepping away from the crowds of the city. Tram bells dinged loudly off of all of the stone and glass. It was cooler in the shade made by the buildings but not by much. They came out into a square that looked much like all the others they had seen, and Kholos paused, knowing where he wanted to get to, but unsure how to get there. He checked his imposed memories for directions, sure he had known the route, but unable to call up the streets and paths again. He felt foolish for thinking he could navigate this city any better than they had Neo Cumae.

He felt naive.

A middle-aged woman painting a picture of the pigeons who drank from a fountain in the center of the square noticed him standing there, grinning a little stupidly and craning his neck up at the tiered balconies of the surrounding buildings. She approached him, brushes still in her hand and greens and blues under her nails.

"Can I help you?" she asked in cosmopolitan Latin. "Not to be forward, but you look a little lost."

"Thank you," said Kholos, in the same language but with an older accent. "I thought I knew the way, but I seem to have forgotten it, all of a sudden."

"You must be looking for the Sanctuary."

"I'm sorry," said Kholos. "I don't know what that means."

"You're looking for the Last Saint. He gets fewer and fewer pilgrims, but the Sanctuary is his place."

"The Last Church?" Kholos asked.

"Oh yes, I've heard it called that as well, although really it's just the Sanctuary, now. Come with me. I'll show you."

She wiped her paint-stained hands on a rag she had tucked into a pocket, and motioned for them to follow her across the square and into another alleyway. This one was narrower than any they had seen since they entered the city. And darker.

"Aren't you worried about your paints and things?" Kholos asked.

"Not in this district," said the woman, with a little laugh.

The alley was so tight Kholos had to turn sideways to pass. He wanted to distrust this woman leading them through the alley, a perfect funnel for an ambush, but he could not.

They came out into yet another square. Children, beaming and running around, splashed in the fountain. Swings hung from trees near a sandbox, and a small table laid with a white cloth along with a stone pitcher and some sandwiches. It was cooler here, with a breeze from the bay without any fish smells or diesel fumes. Looking up over the tops of the buildings, Kholos saw the volcano, only from this perspective the cone was uncapped, had never been capped, and never would be capped. A crown of snow rested at the peak.

On three sides of the square were apartments much like those they had seen elsewhere in the city: three or four stories high, with little balconies, a great deal of shade underneath in arched arcades. They were made from brick and had roofs of sloped tiles. But on the fourth side was a small temple. The building had a peaked roof but not very tall, with pillars holding up an eave over a porch where some wicker chairs were set out. It could be a chapel but there was no sign of learning or faith, no numbers or triangles, no fish-and-compass. In the wicker chairs sat a few older people, watching the children play from the shade of the porch. A couple of nurses, both women with their hair tied back, attended to them. Kholos noticed the nurses looked exactly the same. The tricolor of the Republicant compact flew from a pole at one end of the porch.

"This is the place," said the painter. "This is 7174's Sanctuary."

"Thank you," said Kholos. "Very much."

"Oh, don't mention it. You'll help someone out yourself, you visit here. I hope you get your rest or your kindness or whatever it is you're after. Good day, to you and your girl, then."

The artist made her way back through the alley.

"She was awfully nice," said V.

"Welcome," said a strange voice. It seemed to come out of a speaker, from the temple. "What can I do for you?"

Kholos and V took a step towards the voice, towards the Sanctuary. They gasped when they saw the figure at the top of the steps.

It was a man but not a man. Light blue in color, with no eyes mouth or nose. It was made of metal, but with hands and feet, a head, a body like a person's. It moved somewhat disjointedly, slowly, as if each step was a bit painful, but also with smoothness and fluidity.

With a nod to the nurses on the porch tending to the elderly, the blue man-machine made its way down the steps until it stepped down into the sunlit square where the children ran around it, shouting and cheering. They sang a song, and he clapped in time with their voices, his metal hands ringing like a bell.

The blue machine finally reached Kholos and V.

"I am 7174," it said. "This is my domain. You are safe here, I promise. I will help you as I can."

Kholos exhaled. Exhaled fully and deeply. His fists unclenched, his jaw eased. He felt all his muscles, from his shoulders to his guts, relax.

"It's alright," 7174 repeated. The voice was mechanical but it had a personality. "You have nothing to fear here. You can stay as long as you need help, but if you do stay for a long time I'd like you to help me, if you can. We all have to help each other."

V reached out and touched the featureless blue metal of 7174's face. It was smooth as cloth, just as soft, but also resilient and a little cool.

"What are you?" she asked.

7174 said, "That is a very complicated question," he said. "I'm a machine, if that is what you mean. But not like any machine you might know. What matters is that I'm someone who will help you, give you a place to rest. "

"I had a truck," V said, somewhat stumblingly. "It was a good truck, and it helped me. But we lost it on the way. Not that you are a truck. But, I can't explain. You remind me of that truck. I'm sorry. I feel so foolish. I mean that in a good way."

"Don't be embarassed. This place can make people feel strange at first. They're not used to what we do here. Believe me, I'm sorry to hear about your truck," said 7174, and he was.

Kholos asked. "Why do you do all this?"

"It's what I am," said 7174. "I've always done this."

"And you expect nothing in return? You are not paying for some crime? Or earning a reward?"

"No, and no, and no," said 7174. The head moved up and down, the sun shining off the shiny plates as if off of still water. "You're a Kholopatiron, aren't you? I've helped Antonia heal some of your pattern, or at least ease the pain of those she was healing."

"Altruism," said Kholos.

7174 nodded. "Yes," he acknowledged. "Although it seems that idea is harder and harder for people to believe. During the revolutions and the civil wars, when the Severians tore up the Republicant from Carthage to Helsinki, this square held multitudes. Tens of thousands. A hundred thousand at a time, perhaps. Everyone helping. You shared your food. You protected those weaker than you. You listened. You wept for strangers. You took in those without. People believed, then, in this idea of help, of understanding. Truly believed. They didn't need the justification and the trappings. They understood giving away your extra food, love, and care wasn't a sacrifice, it was just what you did."

7174 looked wistfully out a the square where the dozen or so children played, up at the porch at the handful of seniors. "Now, only a few children, a few of the old and alone, still feel this idea. Once in awhile an adolescent finds us. But I don't think they carry our idea back out into the world. There are other ideas at work now. Safety. Style."

"Are they orphans?" V asked.

"They were until they found us," 7174 said. "But there are no orphans here. There doesn't need to be any orphans, anywhere." 7174 turned the blue blank face towards V. "You are Fractured?"

V swallowed. She nodded.

"Well, if you want, I can help you with that, as well. I don't have a cure, but there are things I can do. They are not without risk, I warn you. Something for you to think about."

7174 addressed both of them. "If you did not come to for rest, or healing, or to put some of yourself back together again, could you tell me why you did come? I'll help if I can."

Kholos spoke, a touch of the Thunder slipping through. "We want to be free," he said. "Truly free. Free of life, death, this universe. We want to escape the Aetherian entirely. And so I need to reach them, to access their machines."

7174 had no eyes to show he understood, but somehow his figure seemed to shift just enough to imply that he had listened to Kholos.

"You are very good at detecting patterns," said 7174. "So what do you see?"

Kholos sat on the porch in a wicker chair with a little table where there was a pot of Ebon coffee laced with a warm liqueur. Out in the sun the children played. V, a late teenager today, led them in games she remembered from her own childhood. Her actual childhood. The elderly residents of the Sanctuary seemed to all be taking naps in the warm afternoon, at the other end of the porch. 7174 did not sit, but stood to one side.

Before Kholos his leg was stretched out, a fresh bandage wrapped around his knee, along with a device of bars and screws to keep the joint stable. Kholos felt it should hurt, but it did not. Instead his knee felt only stiff. Stiff and clean, as 7174's surgery had cleaned out the old wound and replaced it with a new, custom-made knee constructed of special plastics and titanium.

Kholos wore just a long white shirt and a pair of baggy brown tie-pants with one leg cut off above his healing knee. The heel of his big foot rested on a stool.

Kholos organized his observations of their journey so far. "I see pairs," he said. "I see mountains. I see tasks."

"Alright," said 7174. "Other Kholopatirons, other versions of yourself, have made those same distinctions, even though they have not had your direct experience of trying to use the Adonai to be free of your masters. Can you deduce anything else? Connect anything else? Keep in mind I know much less than you do. My questions are academic. I'm only trying to help you see things differently."

"A woman who cooks and loves, in a country of warmth and plenty. An anti-artist who tries to destroy all art. A disembodied voice who speaks, or at least spoke, to a city. A thing that feeds on hate. A woman who wanted to own meaning. And now you, who helps for help's sake. Although you seem to be dwindling in power, if not purpose."

7174 said nothing.

"And Golgothan," said Kholos. "Who wants more and more questions." Kholos had drawn maps of the different domains in his mind. Noted their similarities and differences. They existed in pockets where time and space were elongated.

7174, as was his nature, helped. "You are searching for an over-arching meaning."

"Yes," Kholos admitted. "I think there is a plan here. I think the Aetherian are using the Adonai as engines themselves, enacting changes in the world. But I cannot read those changes. If could discern why, it might lead me quickly out of this place."

"Perhaps no one could see the meaning in the world," 7174 suggested. "If they were themselves a part of that world."

"But I am not part of the world," Kholos insisted. "I ran away. I am still running."

"Yes," said 7174. "You are. And yet you are in the world, still, still a part of it. Like the Liberator patterns."

"I thought when we first left Duran," Kholos continued. "That perhaps all of the Adonai could connect to the Celestial City of the Aetherian. Instead, V and I have found some who wanted no part of their work. Like King Close. Others who were unaware they were anything other than what they seemed to be. An artist. A lover and mother. Powder seemed to think she had made a trade of some kind.

"If I could find the linchpin of the plan. The place where the Adonai is the most crucial. The most intense. There, I would think, would be the connection. The way, to reach the Aetherian."

"And then?"

"And then I reach their machines, that harvest realities and stitch them together, and I remove myself and V from here, from this, from everything. And make a new universe for us."

"You know how to do this?"

"I know the Aetherian do it with machines," Kholos looked at 7174's blue face, a machine.

"You have discerned how to use those devices, then?"

"No, but I am understanding it more. I held a very small one. I could discern it. I could hold it to certain physical dimensions. If I wished, I could make it big enough to encompass the city. Or small enough to vanish. Dr. Voss, though, he will have to help me."

7174 said. "Nathan Voss."

Kholos nodded, surprised. "You know Nathan Voss?"

"Does not Nathan Voss help people?" said 7174. "He is trying to help you now, at this moment. Studying your machine. Even unknowingly, he has helped you, breaking down the shale. The list you carry, he will give it you, and soon. If you can reach the Aetherian, and I am not certain you can, following this route, then it will be up to Dr. Voss as to whether you can or cannot work the engines you speak of."

Kholos looked at his knee, the ugly places in the dressing where his blood, redder than most, had faded through the gauze.

Kholos said. "That work would destroy him."

"Yes," said 7174. "But he knows that, doesn't he? And yet he works anyway. For you. For himself as well, of course."

"Golgothan has helped me, as well," added Kholos. "And he has some defenses. Perhaps I should ask more of him."

7174 worked his featureless face towards Kholos. "Kholopatiron, be careful of the Renegade. He seeks answers for their own sake. There is never enough mystery for him, or his talking cats. His motives are not altruistic."

"Are mine?"

In the early evening, with the heat of the day still lingering, V took off her boots, rolled up the cuffs of her rough trousers, and waded into the fountain. The water splashed gently up her calves.

She could see, through the halo of the city lights, a few of the brighter stars tracing their white routes overhead. The arcs and dashes were all different from what she remembered back home. She reached down and splashed some of the water up into her face. From the center of the fountain the water burbled up. The square was quiet and still.

7174 walked down the steps from the porch of the Sanctuary. V recognized the walk, even though 7174 was a man-machine: he walked like a sick old man. 7174 was dying, or winding down, or running out of power, she saw.

She stepped out of the fountain, feeling her teenage body lithe and strong and springy. She could run all night, she knew. Or sleep through till noon. Or, she thought of Kholos, make love until dawn.

Her mind sparked and flared with the wonder of the new city, the different stars. And, then, she missed Michael terribly. She wanted to go hunting, again. She wanted to drive her truck into the Asinwatis in the early morning, and see the sun come up. But not if all of those things would only remind her of him. She had to forget him. She could not forget him.

"Hello, V," said 7174. "Thank you for playing with the children today. I worry sometimes they get bored of the games I can show them."

"They're kids," said V, with a dismissive wave of her hand. "They make up their own games."

"I wanted to tell you," he said. "That many Fractured of Pompeii have come here, for help. I can offer you that same help, if you would like me to."

"I heard you say that, when we arrived," she answered. "I've already been helped, some."

"This is a different kind of help. I can't affix you any more than you already are. But I can help you understand what is happening to you."

7174's smooth blue shell reflected the starlight in curves along his shoulders and chest and the top of his head. Without preamble, 7174 said, "There are infinite realities, V."

V sat down on the edge of the fountain and stuck her feet out to dry. They dripped onto the plaza stones.

"Anybody who watches science fiction shows on the Televia knows that."

"Yes, but try to understand this: they are all contained in this one universe. We simply perceive this one as separate. You are infinite, V. You are merely experiencing yourself out-of-sync. You are, to use Kholos's sewing metaphor, a loose thread. Do you understand that shape?"

"I don't in the way you mean it, probably."

"Let me try this. Possibilities are infinite. But they are not separate. They are happening all at once, flowing into and out of each other. They overlap, they are simultaneous, only we cannot perceive them as such. Time allows us to pretend that things are happening in some kind of order, a logical progression. The way gravity pulls things together, time orders events in a way that makes sense to us. But in fact, everything is happening at once. Every possibility, every moment, every reality. Kholos can experience some of himself this way, be in two places at once, do two different things simultaneously. You yourself are living trillions of existences. All at once. And being Fractured flicks you from one to another.

"There is one reality. One light. One time. And the one reality is all realities. We—you, I, rocks, rivers, music, cats, everything—only view our existence as cut from whole cloth, to again use the sewing metaphor Kholos prefers. We have to, because our minds cannot hold the shape of the ideas of time, light, reality, moving in all directions at once."

"I still don't understand," said V.

"Let us forget sewing, and try another way," 7174 turned its face towards the fountain. "You see the water?"

"Yes."

"It flows."

"Sure."

"It flows down."

"Right."

7174 shot out its metal hand and cupped a bit of water. Then he tossed it up in the air. Like a sprinkle of diamonds the drops went every which way, including into V's hair.

"Think of the water as time," said 7174. "And you are in the flow of that time, heading down, running in one direction. Only you, V, along with all the other Fractured, were in that little handful of drops that, suddenly, went every which way. You were caught in a splash of time."

"I will go back down, though, eventually? That's what you're showing me?"

"Eventually, yes. But eventually is a relative term. Time is also a commodity, tangible, measurable. It has a shape, a color, shades, a weight. It is very, very valuable, because it allows us to perceive, to see, to understand. Time can be a tool, just as gravity can be used. One can build with it, move things with it."

V blinked. Her first thought was, *Michael would understand this*.

"Ok," she said finally. "I never thought of it like that. I wondered if maybe the Universitat tried to disguise people when they were Fractured. Or performed weird operations."

7174 said nothing. But V could feel it.

V asked, "What is it?"

7174 said, "I think what the Universitat does is amputate a Fractured person's realities. I think they remove the possibilities from them. Perhaps they cannot perceive this directly, but they are limited, in a sense. The Fractured people of the Republicant came here, at first. I could only help them understand. They wanted more, and so they went to the Centers. Sometimes they came back here, afterwards, because they still needed help. I deduced that these people all thought the same way. Their ideas were all the same, whether they embraced or rejected those ideas was irrelevant. They all existed in the same single prescribed reality. Or at least the same limited range of realities. It was a huge sacrifice for them to make, and I wonder how many of them understood they were even making it."

"Like the Stalinistas," V whispered. "They didn't look the same, but they were the same."

"I have never encountered the Stalinistas," said 7174. "I cannot say."

"I'll have to think about what you've said, 7174. It's a lot to absorb." She was thinking, *Michael is still alive*, in a way, in a real, important way that she could understand. As a possibility. It was a good thought, and she held it close and thought it again and again. Maybe she could not do anything about it, could not perceive it, but it was there.

V hugged the robot Adonai of Altruism.

His knee was healed just two days after his surgery. The brace was off, only a bandage remained. He had been walking, without pain, all morning. Because of what he was, there was no scar. Out in the courtyard the un-orphans were playing variations on the games V had taught them. The smell of sweet fresh bread wafted through the square from the kitchens of the Sanctuary, where cooks and grocers saw to meals and cleaning the buildings, preparing the endless but empty rooms where supplicants could rest, heal, recover, get help.

"Lately," 7174 explained, wheeling out a tray of biscuits with jams and butters for the children. "And by lately I mean several generations now, it is mostly the despondent who reach me. They see no point. The Stalinistas will break through eventually, even if the Republicant armies hold them for a thousand years. The lessons of the Universitat ring hollow for them, they see the contradictions in faith and reason. They need a reason to exist. They need to understand what they perceive is not everything. They are doing other things, experiencing other sensations. There are options."

V spread butter on a biscuit. Juices made from fruits across the Republicant were served in pitchers of cut glass. Kholos jumped off of the porch onto the stones, testing his repaired knee.

He looked up at the warming sun. At V chomping her breakfast down. At the children now swarming the cart. After they ate, Kholos knew, 7174 would teach the children to read. Kholos did not find it strange that there were children from around the world here: Ebon, Columbium, Kiowa, everyone except Stalinista.

He went up onto the porch, and kissed V. She took his hand, feeling the respite from missing Michael she always experienced when Kholos was close. The closer, the better.

7174 turned his blue face to V, then down at Kholos, standing in the square. "It is time for you to go, I think. By the evening, please, when Kholos will be fully healed."

7174 explained, "There is no more help I can give you. You are rested, healed, wiser, I hope, than you were three days ago when you arrived. You are on your own, again. Please pack your things. I have a friend who helps people with their journeys away from my Sanctuary."

"Could you tell us where we should go next?" Kholos asked. He had already taken out the list of Adonai.

"Kholopatiron," said 7174. "I don't know. But I have already told you, look for the pattern. That is my last help to you."

Kholos unrolled the list fully. He read and re-read, wondering if it was changing even as he held it. There was St. Theresa. Brian Storenko was not there any longer, and in Neo Cumae there was a new Adonai call Princess Peace. Kholos scanned, then re-scanned. He thought of what they had learned, what Busto and Crick had said, of the questions Golgothan had encouraged him to ask. Finally, he understood. With his long finger he pointed at the list, at Thssiss: the Slythe God of Fear.

22. Contrails

Gabriel walked with his angels through the streets of Neo Cumae. They had more commodified light to use than Kholos, and they used their wings openly. This meant when they traveled they brought disruptions and heat waves as the probabilities and patterns attempted to repair the damage to the physical norms of the world.

As the Six Swords passed in the first weeks through the city, the sickly and the old died, baked in tenements. Trains overheated and commerce slowed. The heat melted tar on the streets and spoiled food, killed flowers and withered crops north and south of the city. Murders in Neo Cumae spiked.

A sickness the Universitat attributed to a combination of festering garbage and a lack of humility among the most celebrated of the residents passed through the city, claiming thousands more lives. The illness caused a high fever and a wrenching cough. Doctors called it the hot cough. Upright citizens noted that it seemed to strike primarily those in the poorer areas, where there was less work done and the people practiced strange customs.

The summer after Gabriel and the rest of the Six Swords passed through the city, famine, unheard of in Neo Cumae, touched the poorest in the city: the Columbium, the Boracs. A conference of Deans and Bishops in the city convened to discuss how to meet the shortages in the city with reason and faith. This panel produced a nutritionally complete diet that was affordable at lower incomes and an outreach program of new temples to Pang, which would produce new jobs. Unfortunately, the new diet was rich in cereals and combinations of particular legumes, which the Boracs could not eat.

Most of the Boracs left the city. Since the launch of Princess Peace, who took the place of King Close in the city's mind, the Boracs were unwelcome. There were beatings, storefronts were vandalized. Fringe scientists and priests launched a campaign to introduce specially prepared bread for the Boracs, which they would have to buy, by law.

A young Borac named Talis rounded up his people in the city and told them he was leading a new caravan, and would be heading west. He explained in secret that he was next in line, after Avalina, to receive the sacred tusks, but as those tusks had vanished he thought taking the *exu* out of the city was the best he could do.

The year after Gabriel and his angels passed through Neo Cumae, the city showed strange patterns. Radical ideas appeared everywhere, some proposed by the city's avant-garde artists, some from the Kiowa and Algonquin business community, some from the thinkers and philosophers of the Universitat. Princess Peace, speaking in her soft voice through everyone's receiver, never ordered or recommended or even suggested anyone actually do anything. Like King Close, she reported, individually, on news from far away, and spoke, personally, to each and every citizen.

Five years after the Six Swords passed through Neo Cumae there were no Boracs in the city at all.

The people left in Neo Cumae developed a new language, a polyglot of the Native Tongues with the old Republicant languages, even a little Ebon slang. The markets were expansive, recovered, packed with fruits and vegetables and grains in great variety. Economists from the Universitat noted, interestingly, that each market contained exactly the same great variety. The entire city started to eat its meals at the same time.

Generally, the city started to enjoy the same music, the same sports, the same fashions. Generally, the city agreed upon important issues, like funding the new Institute, or adding service on the trolley lines. Generally, debate was over details.

I am happy, these days, said Princess Peace. I love to go out into my city and breathe this same air, smell these same scents, listen to this exciting new music we all enjoy.

Ten years after Gabriel and the Swords passed through Neo Cumae, the Universitat noted, privately, that in addition to dressing with increasing similarity, the people of Neo Cumae had started to look alike as well.

Poverty was eradicated. Crime became non-existent. The streets were clean, and the buildings taller. The artists met in well-mannered salons to discuss and display their work, and the musicians enjoyed generous stipends from the city's leading businesses. A new arena was under construction, the biggest on the Columbium continent.

Princess Peace gave up her place in the consciousness of Neo Cumae. A new voice took Princess Peace's place. The voice had new wishes for Neo Cumae. This new voice commanded. It went only by initials: I.M.

Three generations after the Six Swords paused at Neo Cumae, the Algonquin Kingdoms were shocked when a Stalinista front opened with sudden and incredible force along their southern border. Row upon row of troops in gray fatigues marched up the roads that led to Neo Cumae, roads long since closed, from back when the city was still open to trade, when ships from around the world docked along its rivers, when it made daring art, when people were different from one another. Back from when the city was still open at all, before the angels passed through and brought the hot cough.

Moving at a speed beyond the perception of any lesser being, the Six Swords dashed over the Museum Fortress, which was now a pile of huge steel plates and random shards of glass. All of the canon were again turned out, aimed at the world.

Gabriel said, "He's not here."

"He was though," said Sandalphon. "I can see the tracks."

In the Power Station the overturned chair lay on the floor. The cable was sparking blue. Time in the room was packed too tight to move. Each word the Six Swords spoke took a day.

"He's farther over now. He's slowed. No, he's going faster again. I can't tell."

"He's in one of the passages, burrowing through the aeons," explained Nathaniel. In his heat, the time in the room was melting down, speeding up.

"Reality is still coherent here," Gabriel said. "He's not covering his tracks at all."

"What's he doing?" said Raguel. "Was this some kind of a trap? Why did he use his light at the museum, but not here?"

Ramiel whispered, making the walls shake. "When on this world is he running to?"

"We know the when he is running to," said Sraosha, the Obedient. "The question is the where."

"He must know we are here," said Nathaniel. "He must know we are after him. One version or another."

"He is Kholopatiron," said Sraosha in her little girl's voice. "He does what he must do, as we all must. He runs. We will catch him. So we obey."

They looked at one another. They were running with their cannisters wide-open, enshrined in light, their swords gleaming.

"I have the trail," said Gabriel said at least. "There is a tunnel here."

Then they spread their wings of light, and were gone.

The chair, after they had gone, without visible aid, righted itself.

The wire rested on the floor.

Two figures, floating, entered the room. One a shade of blue, the other red. White masks floated where the figures' faces would be. They had no limbs, no physical presence at all beyond their color.

"We are losing control," said the blue figure. "They are running randomly. Gabriel doubts himself. Sraosha has become a martinet. The Kholopatiron might win here."

"We must see this through," said the red. "We must let this time its course."

"It could all be a waste," said the blue.

23. The Geography of Fear

The train cut through the countryside. They passed golden fields of wheat, ran along slow rivers with stone bridges. The old Republicant arched aqueducts still stood, and there were little patches of forest left here and there, hillsides dotted with pines. Villages and towns where the train stopped for just a few minutes, always within sight of a marble fountain set in a square, the temple to Pang with its obelisk-steeple.

V missed Duran Town, missed Michael, just as much as when they had departed, she realized. She felt as if he was so close she might see him again at any moment, but also that he was gone, gone, gone from her forever. V had expected these feelings to wane, just a little. It was why she had agreed to go with Kholos, in part.

The Republicant were old lands, not as old as the Ebon Empires, but smaller and more densely packed together. From the station platforms overlooking little squares, they saw the remnants of the execution platforms from the Hundred Year Wars. Usually, the platforms were decrepit and the block gone half to sawdust. Capital punishment was outlawed across the modern Republicant, but in some places the platform was kept pristine, the boards blood-scrubbed and the block lacquered. Before these well-kept killing places there were plaques of those who had lost their lives in the Wars, citizens and priests and teachers, soldiers and leaders, mayors and writers, rebels and bureaucrats. Always, over these memorials flew the Republicant tricolor, the red, white and blue bars representing the blood, the people, and the new hope of peace.

At each stop Kholos looked out at the town and thought, have I been here before? Did I live here? Did I eat and sleep here? Did I die here?

V had never ridden on a train, and, still holding her shape as younger woman, perhaps twenty-five and no older than thirty, she was almost as excited as when she had flown across the ocean. They had a ticket from 7174, one that V disbelieved at first because it was nothing but a blank slip of white paper. But when Kholos showed the slip to a certain conductor at the huge station in the heart of Pompeii the red-haired man took their bag and lead them to a train on a platform they had not noticed before, going northeast. They had a compartment to themselves, and sat facing each other as the country went by, station by station.

"Kholos," she asked, "who are you?"

Kholos looked at her. "I am an agent of paradise. I was sent here to do something, something to protect my masters. I did not do this. Instead, I escaped. And I am trying to finish that escape."

"But who are you?" she repeated. "You are so much like Michael. But you are not Michael."

"V, all I want is for us to be happy. If you're not happy with me, then I won't try to keep you."

V took a deep breath. "No," she said. "You have to give me more than that. I know what you've said, about being made not born. I understand as best as I can, which I would say is pretty Pang damn well. Thank Dr. Voss for that. But who are you? The deserter, fine. But how do you know all the things you know? We flew across the ocean, Kholos! We. Flew. Across. The. Ocean. How could that happen?"

Kholos smiled.

"V," he said. "I am pattern. The Adonai, the Borac gods, they are all ideas. I am the idea of freedom."

"Yup," V said. "I got that."

"I am among the first and the last. The Adonai, they are the middle. There is a shape to everything. I am a pattern, repeating across the shape. I break away. I run. My lines, my *anima*, as Avalina might have called it, they always run away from the center of the shape.

"There are others like me. They are also lines within the shape. They are true to what they are, just as I am. We cannot do otherwise, none of us. Although it seems I may be finding new limits to where my line will run. Hopefully farther than anyone thought possible."

"So what am I? I'm real and you're not?"

"No, you are also an idea. You are unique. You are an amalgam of endless possibilities, so many more possibilities than me, actually." said Kholos. "Think of a poem of Michael's. The poem is what? It is a poem."

"Alright," she said. "I'd add it could be beauty, or sadness, or whatever."

"Yes. What was the sadness made from? What was the stuff of the beauty he could freeze for his poem?"

"Words," said V. "Language. But those things just represented what he was writing." She paused. Her eyes opened a little wider. "He was showing me his imagination," said V. "It's the imagination, isn't it? The imagination expressed. I am the imagination expressed?"

"Yes. The ideas are what matter," Kholos gestured out the window. "This is thoughts. Ideas."

"Michael was an idea," V said, mostly to herself. Thinking, *ideas don't have to die.*

"A great idea," added Kholos.

At a longer stop they stepped out of the train. It was early evening, the sun declining behind them. The platform was nearly empty. Spires of old temples to Pang jutted up over most of the town. But before them was a dull glow on the eastern horizon, like the City Burning Forever. The conductor, the same man who had collected their blank ticket, approached them.

"That's the war," the Conductor said. "The siege of Vienna."

"How long do you think the Republicant can hold?" asked Kholos.

The Conductor shrugged his shoulders. "As long as we want to, I think. As long as we think the cost of holding the Stalinistas back is worth paying."

V looked at him. He was middle-aged, chubby, with the bristly mustache and a sharp peaked cap with a brass plate under the brim announcing the line he worked: The Carpathian Local. Above his whiskers he wore a pair of silver-rimmed spectacles. The glow of the siege was reflected in the lenses.

"Do you think it's still worth paying?" asked V.

"Oh, yes," said the Conductor. "Oh, yes, indeed." He turned to them, "Listen," he said. "7174's tickets can get you anywhere the trains run. But just so you know my line ends at Bucharest. From there, getting to anything farther east will mean a truck or a horse or walking."

"How do you know we're going farther east?" asked Kholos.

"I punched your ticket," smiled the Conductor.

"But it was blank."

"Not to me it wasn't," he said. He grinned. "I'm sorry, don't mean to be cryptic. It's only that I still try to help out, now and then, so 7147 lets me in on some little tricks. You'd be surprised how easy it is to see what people need, when you look for it." The Conductor checked his pocket watch, and nodded. "All aboard!"

The handful of passengers also heading east, towards the front, came onto the train. There were Republicant soldiers in fresh uniforms returning to their units, older people returning to homes that might or might not still be standing, a few professionals—doctors, other Universitat men and women—looking for action or opportunity closer to the front.

The Conductor said, "I know the Universitat tells us that Pang's message is in his creation. That truth and faith in the world are what we ought dedicate ourselves to. But I've seen the front, and I remember the wars, and I've dished out kindness at the Sanctuary, and I think 7174's message is what I'll stick with. Help others. Always. The rest is nonsense."

"That's blaspheme," said Kholos. "A sin against evolutionary principles."

"You talk like a professor," The conductor smiled, the corners of his mustache lifting like Gyr Zax's tusks had done back in the Asinwatis. "This is the Republicant," he said. "Maybe we got all our sins out by beating each other's brains in."

"Where will the train take us?" he asked. "After Bucharest?"

"Sighisoara," said the conductor. "Never stepped off the platform there myself. Strange place. People say there are all kinds of problems in the mountains around there. Probably fighting spilling over from the front."

"Thank you," said V. "For your help."

The conductor tipped his cap. That night Kholos and V made love in between the cars, the two of them wrapped up in Kholos's big coat and naked underneath. The rumble and jostle of the train, V decided, made it better. When they were finished they stayed outside the warm cars, despite the cold, and watched the stars cut through the night sky. They were climbing, steadily. The train slowed on the steepest inclines, and to the north they could see the shapes of spiky mountains, silvery in the dark.

The next morning, they emerged into the shadow and stone of Sighisoara.

The peaks of the Parthians, sharp as the points of knives, stood around the city. Roads weaved and meandered up into the hills. The houses were tall, with gabled roofs. They were built of daubed timber and had leaded windows, all closed. V was in her late twenties again.

"You don't feel it, do you?" V asked him.

"What? The chill?"

"No," said V. She put her arms around herself. "The fear."

Kholos looked around. The doors to the shops, the inns, the school, the Temple to Pang, were opening. People selling eggs and bread and cheese moved warily towards a bazaar not far from the station. A few policemen watched everything with darting eyes. The bell rang from the steeple of the temple and everyone winced. From the front, fresh lines of smoke appeared.

A little dirty rain began to fall. The shadows of the peaks slashed across the roof tiles and fell in jagged lines across the streets.

"I don't feel it," Kholos admitted. "Are you all right?"

"No," V said. "This place is... It's, something. Something bad is going to happen here."

Kholos said, "What are you afraid of?"

They were walking past a decrepit statue of Pang. Flakes of grime peeled away from the bronze in the increasing rain. V shivered.

"I feel like we're being watched."

They were. A Gendarme narrowed his eyes at them.

Kholos turned to the officer. "What do you want?"

The policeman started. "You should get indoors," he said. Then he turned around and walked quickly away.

"V," said Kholos. "You have to help me. What are you afraid of? I'm not afraid, so there is nothing here to trap us, nothing to take you away from me. Try to focus on that. Tell me what you feel."

"It's specific," V said. She swallowed. "It's not in the town, even, but it's close by. It's, modern. Being watched. People are sneaking up in the shadows. It's too quiet. Something we can't help is going to happen. I'm afraid you're going to die, like Michael died."

V was shaking, and Kholos put his arm around her. The walls and doors of the town closed around them. People vanished behind shutters. Kholos trained his ears on the little whispers. V was looking for a place to hide. Her eyes darted wildly left and right and her neck jerked around.

"They're all watching us," she hissed. "They're coming into town to watch us. From the shadows. They'll take you away from me, like they took away Michael."

Kholos looked around. The smoke from the front was wafting high up overhead, making Sighisoara even darker. Other than the smoky drizzle and the breeze, there was nothing moving, and no one about at all.

"V," said Kholos. "There's no one watching us."

She buried her face against his chest. He was wearing his armor under his long coat and she pressed so hard the metal pushed into his skin.

"Why aren't you scared?" she asked him. "Don't you feel it?"

"I don't," said Kholos. He scanned the town. It was a dirty little village, dreary, nothing more.

A little girl appeared around the corner. Carefully, bravely, she stepped up to them. "It's the rain," she said. "The fear," the girl pointed up at the sky. "It gets into the clouds, and it rains down on us."

Kholos and V stared at her. She was very pale, with long dark hair.

"What are you afraid of, little girl?" V asked her.

"The dark," she said. "That's why I'm still out here, I don't want to go into the dark. But I'm scared out here, too."

"Nothing is going to hurt you," Kholos said.

"You're not afraid, are you?" asked the little girl.

"No," said Kholos "I'm not."

"You must be scared of something?" The little girl stood there, bravely, shivering, her dark hair slowly matting down onto her forehead. Her eyes darted back and forth.

"What does this?" said Kholos.

"Smoke," said the girl. "Smoke from the cave, it gets into the clouds. And it comes down as rain. You have to get indoors."

"Which way to this Cave?" Kholos asked.

Dr. Voss, on the table before him, had laid out the blue bullet Kholos had given him before he left Duran, then the little machine Kholos had left when he had, when he had-? Dr. Voss tried to think the thought, formed an edge to the shape of the idea, a line, but then it faded. After breaking off the cap on Kholos's bullet he tipped out a few grains of the powder inside onto a microscope slide, and looked. It looked like gunpowder.

He looked away. He was at a different point in time and subtle things had changed, but he could not comprehend it fully, beyond grasping that time had passed even though he had not experienced the movement. The evening light was dim, just the street lamps on the square and the moon overhead. The sky was clear and the stars spun and whizzed by.

Dr. Voss rose. In the kitchen were half a pork sandwich from Rosie's and a cold carton of beer. He ate a little and drank a little. As he chewed he paced around the living room, watching the statue of Pike catch the morning light. He realized he had worked all night, again. The sandwich in his hand was gone, as was the beer. He had no memory of the meal, of the night, but obviously it had passed.

He needed to shave and wash and get to school. He thought of his students, he missed Michael.

A knock at the door. He swallowed his breakfast down. Effa Staffa, sheriff of Duran Town with Barney Turl gone, appeared. There was a print of blood on her face, and her hands were red as well.

"Don't worry," she said. "It's not mine. Gonna need your doctor's stuff, Nathan. Accident on the road north. Boys from the gas mine out a bit late, just like you said."

"Right," he said. He turned, smacking the crumbs from his hands. "Wait. What? I said what?"

The blue powder. Just the grains of it, just a few. The shapes changed.

He looked back at Effa, waiting in the doorway. Letting in the cold air of morning. The blood on her face. He reached out a hand towards her. "Effa?"

Effa Staffa was dead, he knew. The Second Comanche had killed her. What was a Comanche?

"Wait, Effa? Something's happening."

The doorway was empty. But it was still open. Dr. Voss looked at his fingertips, one with a little of the horseradish sauce, one with just a speck of blue.

Effa Staffa was frozen in the door. Not moving. He could not see her properly, but he understood she was alive and dead, both at once.

Dr. Voss went back to the table and pulled the slide from the microscope. *All lines are infinite*, he conjectured. Time is a line, time progresses linearly. No. This was Institute thinking. What was he seeing? Time progresses linearly, but all in directions, simultaneously?

The powder from the blue bullet did not change. At all. No matter what light hit the slide, the powder looked the same.

Dr. Voss was watching something removed from time, he realized. Time, like water, flowed and ebbed and swirled and eddied. And the blue bullet, the powder, it froze that water? Time did not go straight. It was not a line. It was a shape close to a sphere, like gravity was a cone, time was a globe. Someone was doing work like this, he recalled. Someone? He could not remember. The Kiowa? No, no. An Institute? Caego? No. But a place. He had sent them letters, a laboratory, a Columbium laboratory. They had not answered his letters. Where, where was the place they were doing this work...

Anvir. He sent the letters with his observations of the shale in the mountains that broke down, he had sent them to Anvir.

Anvir was the burning city. The city burning forever. Some small group of scholars, they were doing this work. In the burning city frozen in flame. The time of the place, commodified. Solidified.

Kholos, thought Dr. Voss, who could be in two places at once, on wings of light.

Dr. Voss looked back at the doorway. Effa Staffa was standing there. Effa Staffa was dead. Effa Staffa was not there at all. Effa Staffa was a boy. Effa Staffa was a priest. All were true, simultaneously, and in one place. One reality, all encompassing, not alternate at all. Everything was true all at once. The machine, the little machine Kholos had left, Dr. Voss looked at it.

And he saw the switch.

It was bigger than his house, even though he could fit the apparatus in his hand. He focused to fight through the paradox in this, succeeded, and pulled the lever that was not a lever. Tick.

Dr. Voss set the machine down on his table next to the blue bullet. His sandwich was piping hot and he wanted to eat it before it got cold, before the evening ran too late. On his way to the kitchen to eat he looked over his shoulder and glanced at the square, the sun setting over General Pike's head. Class tomorrow was Republicant history, no simple thing, and he resolved to sleep. Just an hour. Or two. Eat, work, sleep.

The sandwich steamed as he unwrapped it.

He undid the cap on the waxed carton of beer.

He looked at his hands, saw the speck of blue powder there on his finger tip. He had done all this before. He was still doing this. He was picking his way through his own possibilities.

"All at once," he said. The sandwich was halfway to his mouth. "It's all happening at once. Everything. Pang damn."

Dropping the sandwich on the counter, he ran outside into the evening. People were out, doing some late shopping, eating their dinners, seeing to a bit of business here or there.

"All at once!" Dr. Voss cried out. "Everything is happening all at once!"

At a sprint he took off, coatless, for the Emergency Station. He wanted to see Effa. With a crash he leapt into the quiet room of desks and cells and beds. Deputy Byron Bonson was asleep with his feet up and Effa was cleaning her pistol with brushes and rags.

"Doc?"

"All at once!" he repeated. "Everything happens all at once! Time just spreads it out!"

"What?"

"You're not dead!"

"Uh, no."

"Listen," Dr. Voss pointed at her. "Tomorrow morning, early. Go and check up on the north road, towards the gas works. There's been an accident. Or rather there will be an accident. Or, I mean, there is an accident."

"Doc, you're not making any sense."

"Right, right. Of course. But you see I'm here but I'm also then. We all are, we just can't tell, because of how our minds work. But I can prove it! It's like geometry! No, not really, but in a way." Randomly he snatched a piece of paper from Deputy Bonson's desk and began to draw out diagrams. Deputy Bonson, awake now, looked over his shoulder as he worked. "This is how Kholos sees things. This is what he means! And that machine, oh that little machine!"

Effa came over and put her hand on his shoulder, gently. "Doc, let's get you home. When's the last time you slept?"

Dr. Voss looked at her. "Anvir," he said. "This is what they were working on in Anvir."

"That doesn't mean anything to me, Nathan. You're talking crazy."

"I wonder how far they got?" he asked the wall. "What did they discover? What did they unlock? Do angels have wings? Can men fly?"

Effa was growing concerned. "Doc," she said. "Calm down."

24. The Cave

Teeth in the dark. The stink of dead things, rot. A skittering. A shadow.

The abyss. Falling, falling, falling. The sharp shine of the needle, the knife. The rough rope of the hangman. Sharks, snakes, stinging things, silent in murky water. A glowing eye blinks, deep in the pit. Pain. Death. Humiliation. Laughing faces. The chase. The accusation. The lie. The trap. Patricide. Matricide. Infanticide. Paralyzation, amputation. Alone. Or surrounded. Rejection. Death. Poverty. Disfigurement. Old age. Withering, paralyzing disease.

The mouth of the cave was pitch black, the air warm and sticky, marked with spiderwebs, cryptic writings, and etched with screaming faces along its edges. The oldest monsters: quiet hunters with long fangs, great fish that snapped up from the depths, huge reptilian things, tentacles. V could sense them, feel them bubbling up in her thoughts.

Kholos recognized the runes around the mouth of the cave, although he could not read them. They were Slythe pictographs.

The entrance had not been hard to find, and was not far from the town. The rain had stopped halfway up the mountain. As a weak, bleak sun dried them, V felt at home in the peaks, recognizing sign and naming plants. The fear she had felt before, as the rain fell on her, was distant already. The fog, at the mouth of the cave and so thick, changed that. She shivered and her face went pale.

"This is going to be hard," she said.

There were eyes in the cave. They were watching her. She knew it. There were people talking about her, saying bad things about her, whispers just out of hearing. Everything in the cave wanted to hurt her.

"Let's get on with it," she said.

Kholos took a flashlight out of the bag and unwrapped his sword. To prepare the rifle seemed foolish, considering they were going into a cave. But then Kholos reconsidered, and took out the gun, loaded it with black bullets, and slung the strap over his shoulder. He noticed that the beam from the light stopped dead at the darkness of the entrance.

"Be brave," Kholos said to V before they stepped into the darkness. "I won't let anything hurt you."

Instantly as they crossed into the darkness the flashlight went out completely. V screamed, which caused a fresh skittering from the darkness. A hiss resounded from somewhere much deeper within. V's heart pounded. The eyes. She clasped her arms around her shoulders tight, heard Kholos doing something alongside her.

She reached out for him and felt nothing.

"Kholos?" she said softly. Then, in a panic, "Kholos!"

They were there. The eyes. Disembodied, staring, unblinking. Staring at her. She dropped to her knees. She gagged, choked on her fear. Staring at her. Staring into her. She felt found out, exposed. Tightly she clamped her hands over her ears and hid her face in her hands.

A voice called out her name, desperately.

"Michael!" she cried out.

A hand reached out for her, pulled her back into a dim and flickering light. Kholos held her tight against him, a weak torch made from his shirt wrapped around the blade of his knife in his hand burned low.

"I'm right here," he said. "It's alright."

V looked up at Kholos. He wore his armor, the visor of his helmet closed. But she knew if she lifted the visor she would see Michael, her Michael, underneath. Tentatively, she raised a finger to the metal. *Could they take him away twice? Who was Kholos? Why did she feel Michael was still with her, almost completely with her?*

"I believe only certain kinds of light can show inside here," said Kholos. "Certain kinds of time. Dirty time."

The walls were sketched with primitive paintings. They seemed to move in the firelight. Great beasts trampled and gored stick-figure men. Fires consumed little huts. Tidal waves and sea monsters destroyed men in boats. The passage weaved on.

"Come on," said Kholos. "I've got you."

V still stared at the closed helmet. *Did she want Kholos to never let go of her? Did she have a choice?*

They moved forward, taking slow steps. The hissings and the scratchings died down. V tried to breathe very softly. The air changed rapidly. It was too hot, then icy cold, then it stank of rot, then it smelled of burning things. A few more steps and the silence was filled with screams. Then the screams stopped, and the skittering returned.

"Why are you not scared?" she demanded.

"I am afraid," Kholos said. "Of being trapped. But I can't be trapped here. This place couldn't hold me, let alone hurt me."

"But it can hurt me," she said.

"I don't think so," Kholos said. "At least, I think it can hurt you only as much as you want it to."

"I don't want it to hurt me!"

"Not much, you don't."

"What is that supposed to mean?"

"Fear is a valuable thing," said Kholos. "We savor our fear. Are you willing to let it go? That fear you feel is a strength, of a kind."

"I'll give it up," she said. Then she thought a moment. *Would she? Wouldn't that expose her more? Was she willing to accept any more loss?*

"V," Kholos said. "Look."

Kholos stopped. There was a door, cut into the rock, just ahead. It was familiar, a white door with a brass knob. V recognized it first.

She said, "That's the door to one of the bedrooms of the Whoracle."

Kholos put his hand on the knob. It felt cold to his touch. He opened the door.

The room was furnished exactly as their own room had been: a big bed with a comforter, the mirror with the cosmetics arranged in glass jars. Windows were open to the Lipstick Country.

Carefully they stepped into the room. There were dresses in pastel colors hung in a wardrobe, a pair of men's saffron pants. Pillows were piled up against the headboard, and the four posters at the corner were wrapped with white ribbons. Rose petals were strewn about the floor and there was a little dish of chocolate drops on a table.

"Why do I still feel afraid?" V asked. "I felt so safe in this place."

Kholos walked around the room. He looked out the window, saw the children playing in the square of the little village, the rows of trees, the half-naked men and women picking fruit from the orchards. V stood in the doorway, her arms crossed.

"Kholos," she said, nearly a whisper. She pointed at a little table, just inside the room.

It was set for two, with tea service. There were gold-rimmed cups and plates with pink roses, silver forks, sugar cubes in a crystal bowl, and a teapot. And the center of the table was a cake. A cake with a single candle, unlit. V shivered.

"That's it," she said.

"What is? I can't feel it."

"The cake. The candle on the cake. It's where the fear is coming from."

Kholos looked. The cake was made of light, of time. This light and time was inscribed with instructions, refined and remade, just as he was, light commodified and restructured. Kholos reached down and pulled the candle free, crushed it in his gauntlet. The waxy pieces fell to the floor.

V exhaled. The sudden, strong, specific fear she had felt slipped out of her. "What was it?"

"A bomb," said Kholos. He looked around the room. "Slavery in exchange for a warm room. War for make-up and perfume and sweets."

"I don't understand."

"This may be the place, V. This cave may be the way out we've sought. The fear, it connects the others. The fear is the crux of the Adonai. Not Pang, just fear."

"Fear?" V asked. "All of this, all the places we saw, they were all about fear?"

"Avalina said she thought the Boracs were a mistake, that it was the Slythe the Adonai truly needed for their plans, and Thssiss is a Slythe idea. We need to keep going. If we are close our pursuers are that much more likely to be nearby."

Back out in the cave with Kholos's weak torch V still felt terror, but it was lessened, somehow. She swallowed, walked firmly forward.

The sketches on the wall changed. The figures were more detailed, with individual faces and clothing. V could make out houses, boats with sails, an early temple to Pang with the zero drawn in gold.

An antechamber around the next corner appeared. There was no door, this time, but a trio of steps leading up into a small, well lit space. There were columns of stone, and alcoves within the chamber, a place for display, maybe. Two tall windows revealed a shifting landscape of river and fog, beyond which a city seemed to blink in and out of existence, one moment a metropolis of freighters and skyscrapers, the next a collection of wattle huts behind a stockade wall.

"This is the Museum Fortress," said Kholos. "We're in the rotunda, just off of it."

Kholos saw himself flash by on golden wings. Then a second later the Six Swords in pursuit.

Framed by the two windows was a single, unfinished painting on an iron easel.

The painting was of V. The warped V, with pieces of her body all in different ages. She was innocent, she was sexual, she was decrepit, she was newborn. Tricks of light and shadow, of line and form, were everywhere in the piece. But the work was academic. V herself was violated but the painting was banal.

She stared at it. Only the face was incomplete.

"It would have closed all the doors," said Kholos. "Jigsaw, he told me, every painting and sculpture in the museum leads to another aspect, another place, just as real as any other. The artists were making uncontrolled territories. New worlds. This would have locked them all off, and stopped any more from opening."

"Burn it," said V.

Kholos touched his torch to the corner of the painting, and the flames flickered up. The stink was awful.

They moved on.

They passed other doors to other places, with no idea what was behind them. There was one made of iron, with a small circular window like a ship's portal. There was one made of golden bones, with a ruby skull protruding from its center, another made of ice and silver, one entirely of thick, warm fur. At first Kholos consulted his list, tried to match Adonai to the passages, but realized this place would not necessarily be tied to the list at all.

There were in some domain that linked the domains, and the joinings were held fast by fear.

The passages turned back on themselves, they dipped and rose.

The paintings on the walls changed again: now they were symbols, pentagrams and occult numbers, pairs of twisted horns, crossed swords, hands held in weird patterns, as if delivering a curse. Formulae began to appear, written in a crazy script with chalk. Kholos could not understand them, they made no mathematical sense at all. Then he realized that was the point. The equations were impossible.

They came to a set of double doors, like those that might be found in a hospital, with padded edges and a bar across their middle to push them open. V recognized the entrance first. "The Power Station," she said.

Kholos pushed the door open.

The room was wall-to-wall circuit boards, with black engineers at the dials and switches. Blue sparks flew from their fingertips and there was a terrific hum that made V's teeth rattle. In the center of the far wall was one gigantic Televia monitor, taller than Kholos twice over and at least twenty meters wide. On the screen the huge face of a young woman, with the strange, pseudo-identical face of a Stalinista, spoke to them.

"Just watch me. I am Princess Peace," she said in a voice that was no voice at all. "I am perfect, and I am more real than you can ever be. Trust me. Trust me."

Her voice flattened. She was saying the same things over and over.

"Turn me on," said Princess Peace. "Turn me on. Turn me on."

Kholos lowered the rifle.

"Trust me," said Princess Peace. "I will tell you the truth. You don't have to be afraid any more. Just watch me."

Kholos fired.

The black bullet, unlike the blue or the red, eliminated the target from reality. There was no sound, just the tick of the trigger and then the knock of the pin in the chamber. No explosion, just a wave of oblivion that washed over the room.

The far wall, with its enormous monitor, was bare stone.

The black engineers put their hands down at their sides, their lenses looking up at the ceiling, at each other, finally at Kholos and V. Kholos re-slung his rifle and drew his sword.

"Wait," said V. "Listen to me," she said, speaking to the room where the dials and the switches had all vanished and become just a very square, very dark piece of cave. "You're free, now."

The black engineers stood and stared at her. They formed a neat squad, shoulder to shoulder. The black plastic of their lab coats glistened under the flickering lights.

In unison, the black engineers said, "10010011001."

Kholos raised the visor to his helmet. This was not a language he understood.

V said, "I have an idea."

Shakily, V moved around the black engineers with her hands up. She walked slowly around the room, until she reached the wall. Then, with a nervous swallow, she scratched a map into the rock. It was a simple drawing, showing their location, in the cave, with an X, and then tracing a line down to the village. Here she drew a rough, childish etching of a train engine. The black engineers watched, clicking in their joints.

V made a face of a man with a moustache and a cap, next to the train. And, finally, she scratched a line from the train and its conductor back to another place. She marked this place with an X, and with her nails wrote 7174 in huge letters.

"7174," said the engineers.

V pointed at the X in the cave, then at the Black Engineers. She traced the line on the rock wall, going from the cave to the train to Pompeii, where she stabbed at the numbers, 7174, with her thumb.

"7174," the black engineers repeated. Then, "000011100011."

As a unit, they marched out of the door into the caves.

"That was brilliant," said Kholos. "You gave them hope."

"It just made sense," said V. "Automatons, you know."

"Maybe," acknowledged Kholos. "You seem," he added. "You seem less afraid?"

V shrugged her shoulders. "I didn't stop to think about being afraid. I just had the idea."

As they moved on deeper into the cave they saw more doors: one that looked like a garage, with the rumble of an engine running, one like a department store's revolving entrance door, a little wisp of perfume and pressed clothing escaping, one that looked like the entrance to a log cabin.

The images on the walls of the cave shifted and blended into tapestries, hung high in the arching passageways, lit by torches that pumped out the smoke of fear. V grabbed Kholos's arm, but kept her pace steady. She seemed, he thought, to be getting braver they deeper they went. Her trembling at the mouth of the cave was gone.

The tapestries showed people in cloaks and blouses, weeping in villages and castles. There were yellowish skeletons in the scene, wielding scythes. Scenes, frayed and faded but still discernible, showed fallow fields where people wailed with hunger. There was tapestry showing a horde of rats moving through a city, corpses piled in squares and courtyards, with professors and priests debating and praying and taking notes at the edges as the sick reached out for mercy. And there were monsters: dragons, ogres, giants with teeth like swords.

The passage stopped. Stopped so abruptly that Kholos had to lurch forward on his toes to keep from falling forward into a crevice that, as he looked over the edge, went down into the mountain. A river roared below. Kholos shined the light and, through the lenses of his helmet, studied the fast-flowing liquid below. V sniffed at the air.

"Oh," she said. "Oh, no."

Kholos understood. What she had scented, he could see. It was a river of blood. Boiling blood, rushing blood. There were stairs, also slick with blood themselves, cut into the rock, leading down.

The stairs cut back once, twice, then once more before they emptied out onto a little beach. The sand beneath their feet was pure white, and seemed to have specks of shells mixed in. Kholos picked up a touch in his gauntlet and realized: it was bones, ground down bones.

"Zome," said Kholos. "This is Zome's entry. This is all the blood spilled in on the Stalinista battlefields."

There was a boat. It had actual ribs, perhaps of a baby saur, with a dark, leathery and studded skin stretched over the big bones to make the shell. There was a pole in the boat, and also a bassinet, made out of a giant skull. Wrapped in blankets of skin within the grisly cradle was a baby, a baby with skin so red it looked like it had been boiled. As Kholos and V approached the baby began to scream and cry. The sound was terrible, piercing, and elicited pure, unthinking anger.

V put her hands over her ears. Kholos drew his sword.

"I'll kill it," said Kholos.

"Stop!" said V. "It's just a baby!"

Kholos, visor down, glanced at her from behind the metal face plate.

"You saw what this thing becomes," he pointed out. "This is rage and hate, born again and again."

V concentrated. "You destroyed Zome once, and he came back."

"The Stalinistas wanted him back. They worship him."

V, with another brave swallow, bent down over the bone boat and reached in for the baby.

"Pang damn you're loud," she said.

Zome kicked and punched with his little red arms. V bounced him gently in the crook of her elbow, aware to keep the snapping, screaming mouth away from her neck.

"Shush," said V. "It's alright. We're here now. Calm down."

Kholos kept his sword drawn.

"Put that away," said V. "You're scaring him."

"I'm scaring him? V you're cooing to the Adonai of hate and rage. He eats soldiers."

"Not this one," said V.

Baby Zome calmed, slightly. V patted his back. All of the blankets had come free from Zome's kicking and screaming and he was bare-bottomed. After a few more minutes of bouncing he spat up on V's shoulder a stinking mass of red and black that scalded her skin, and then burped a mighty belch.

V winced. "Give me something to wipe with," she said. "And hurry this is hot."

Zome had stopped screaming. Taking her time V laid him down on the bone-sand beach and made a diaper for him and swaddled him. Kholos treated her burn with some ointment as she worked. Baby Zome grabbed his feet and actually cooed through his shark's mouth. V tickled his round red belly.

Kholos looked at V. He knew Michael had wanted children.

After eating and resting for a while Kholos took the stern of the boat and heaved it forward, then gave his hand for V to step into the gunwales with the baby Zome. The blood swirled and hissed around his boots. Then they pushed off, and soon they had left the beach behind them. With the torch flickering in the stern they let the current take them. V holding Zome, still asleep and swaddled, in the prow, Kholos poling them clear of the sheer, high walls that lined the passage.

Their torch illuminated the cliff walls in bits and snatches. There was a fossil record of wars. Done in the white bones of prehistoric creatures there were great battle scenes, with artillery through the ages, and barbed wire and embankments and siege engines, and machine guns and lances. Troops under domed helmets rushed a line, then in the next scene were cut down, and then at last there were only one or two left standing amid a pile of limbs and empty helmets. The blood moved more swiftly as they progressed. Kholos, scanning the banks, saw no place to land.

Baby Zome awoke, and began to cry. V rocked him, sang for him, but still he wept.

V looked at Kholos, "He sounds sad."

"I wonder if he knows where we're going."

The river suddenly surged, and they were among rapids. Black rocks jutted up around them and Kholos pushed and shoved to keep them clear. V, clutching Zome close, leaned forward and grabbed the boat. Zome cried louder.

The river was narrowing. Kholos could see no where to beach, no where to go. They would crash against the rocks. The blood splashed into the boat and the prow splintered against a rock and Zome screamed.

"Hang on," he shouted. He reached for his belt.

"What?" said V. "What?"

The river ended in a fall, a hundred-meter drop. The boat went over, with all of them flung clear and a rushing, crushing pool below. The bone crib, the baby, V, and Kholos were all thrown free.

And then they were flying, Kholos's golden wings spread out wide. V was in his arms, and they descended slowly, gently, down towards the pool where the falls ended. Only Zome, somehow, had refused to be lurched back through the moments. Madly Kholos scanned below, prepared to stitch through another second to save him, but could see nothing either in the moment passed or the moment ahead. V was calling for the baby, the baby.

Kholos saw him. Saw the boat, battered but afloat and many moments ahead. The baby Zome was in his crib, again, and the blankets V had made for him were still wrapped around him snugly.

"He's alright," said Kholos. "But he's gone on. He's going out, into the world."

"Really? You're sure?"

"I can see him, barely. He's ahead of us in time."

V did not say anything for a while. They came down onto gravel and pebbles, not sand, close to where the falls emptied out. Kholos turned the switch on his canisters, and his localized star disappeared, along with his wings. V walked to the edge of the river, which no longer flowed with red hot blood but with cold black water. The cave was now open and high-roofed, big as an arena, and lit from a tall ship with five black masts, moored out on an inland sea up ahead. They could just make it out, but had no way to reach it.

"I wonder what saint sails in that boat," said V. "And I wonder where he's going."

"I'm sorry," said Kholos. "I tried to grab him, but he had already leapt ahead. He's gone on, to wherever he's going, some battlefront, I would guess. I wonder what he'll be like, this Zome."

V nodded. "Michael wanted children," she said. "I didn't know one way or the other, but Michael did."

Kholos put his arm around her. She seemed stiff.

"Let's go, I want to leave this place before the fear comes back," she said.

A path of weathered boards among flowers and vines and creepers led up to a house. The doors were open and a warm breeze scented with spring and flowers blew through the windows. A fine, yellowy dust lined the windowsills and the boards of the porch.

"I know what this is," said V.

"We're not going inside here," said Kholos. "It's too dangerous."

"What do you mean? Maybe we can find something fresh to eat."

"Watch," commanded Kholos.

They stood before the brick home and stared. One minute. Two minutes. The house flickered. In and out of oblivion, the windows showed random scenes, flashes of events occurring in the space the house occupied throughout different points on the sphere of reality. The gables, the porch, became bars, became pillars, became doors, became a hut of straw, became loamy soil and a pebbled beach, translucent gases.

"It's Fractured," said V. "Like me. It's unstuck."

"That's right," said Kholos. He realized what this meant in terms of their pursuit. As the house blinked through aeons and possibilities, untethered to any of them for any real length of time because it was in fact all of them, all at once, Kholos watched the door, the front door.

He saw light, six beams of light, angled to the eaves, a knob turning in a golden hand.

"We have to hurry," he said.

There were lights ahead, long dim tubes set into the ceiling.

Back out in the passages, pipes and cables, not entirely unlike those of the Power Station, appeared along the walls. They formed images: skylines where the tallest buildings cracked under tidal waves and earthquakes, flames in wired outline trapping those on the top stories. A relief in copper displayed a drought: arid fields, fruit trees dying. Another showed swarms of biting insects coming like storm clouds towards villages and towns. Always in the cables and the plates, which were numbered in descending order, there were people struggling to survive. They hauled each other up out of floods, or daubed the feverish foreheads of plague victims, distributed corn to the starving. But on the plates the faces of all of the people were worn away. As crisp as the wiring seemed, all of the faces of the people were smudged and rubbed out.

The walls twisted and turned, leading them deeper into the mountain. The temperature rose. The skitterings were gone. Now the sounds were distant screams, women weeping, and cruel laughter. A stink of sickness and decay wafted overhead. Bits of old chain link fence, rusty and topped with barbed wire, were leaned against the wall.

Then the passage narrowed and they emerged into a courtyard, a square, with a fountain in the center. There was a cart set with drinks in small cups, and there was a swing set nearby, set back along the wall of the square.

"We know what this place is, too," said V.

Their boots crunched on something underfoot.

The ground was covered with used, dirty syringes. The needles were rusty and old, and all of them seemed to have been spent. Kholos picked one up in his gauntleted hand and studied it.

"Was there not enough?" asked V. "Did they run out of compassion? Is that what happened?"

"I don't know," said Kholos. "All of the places we passed, the ones we knew about, at least, they all had a trap. The cake. The new King Close, whatever her name might have been. The anti-masterpiece. Zome set loose on the world, although you may have changed that with your kindness. We may have changed a few things here, actually. We may have done more in the world than we realize."

"But this one?"

"I don't know. 7174 said the Sanctuary was losing its power. Maybe the trap here was sprung."

"Can we do anything?"

"We can't stay. We have to move on. They're close behind us now."

"That's not what I asked. 7174 helped me understand a lot of things. If there is something we can do here, I want to do it."

Kholos looked around. The swing set. The cart. The ground littered with needles.

"I don't see anything," said Kholos. "Whatever was going to happen here already has."

"No," said V. "The Sanctuary was about helping people. I'm here, and I'm willing to help. So the idea can't be totally gone. It can come back."

"How?"

V started to move all the needles into a pile, using the soles of her boots. Kholos watched her.

"You have the metal gloves on, help me."

"What are you doing?"

"Cleaning up a little. At least we can get them away from the swings, right?"

"Just be careful, please."

It did not take long. They pushed and tossed the syringes away from the swings, so that if anyone happened to come by they could at least play a little without the needles underfoot. As a little added gesture Kholos moved the cart with drinks over by the swings as well. When they were finished V put her hands on her hips and surveyed the space.

"It's a little better. And I feel a little better."

"You don't seem afraid at all any more."

"I know. At first, I was terrified. Then we got to the cake room, and I felt safer there but not really. It was only when we started actually doing stuff that I felt ok. When we sent the black engineers to the Sanctuary, for example. Or when I tried to take care of the baby Zome, and now cleaning up those needles. I mean, this is all pretty nightmarish, but I did something down here. I didn't just stand around."

They had not gone far when they came to a rounded chamber. On the floor was a thick book. V reached down and lifted it up. The cover was covered with dust and she blew it away before she started to open it.

"Don't," said Kholos.

"Why?"

"It's a trick. A trap."

"How can you tell? There was no door or anything. Maybe some saint just dropped it."

"No," said Kholos. He put his hand on the top cover, to keep it closed. "If you open that book, we'll have all the answers. There won't be any more questions."

"Right," V snorted.

"V," Kholos said. "We're inside a mountain. There doesn't need to be a door, a portal to a domain. We're already in a domain. Golgothan's domain."

"But he's the rebel. He would never." She stopped short.

"He might not even know," said Kholos. "But I can see the nature of the time that book contains. The stitches on the binding are like those made by the machine we took from Powder, the one that made the boxes. Open it, and there won't be any more questions. The sphere of time will be revealed and we won't ask anything anymore. That book is all ending. Put it down."

V put the book back down.

The cave ended. Not ten steps down the last passage, the only way leading forward out of the Sanctuary, there was nothing but a wall, solid, seamless, and flat. Kholos hit it with his mailed fist. Some bits of stone cracked and crumbled, but it was a wall, not commodified time or some aspect of a wall. No spinning time tunnel, just a wall.

"What now?" said V.

Kholos was looking behind them. He knew they were coming. Any moment now.

"I don't know. I didn't expect this. I thought a chamber, something."

"Kholos," V said, and put her hand on his arm. "You're afraid. You're feeling fear."

Kholos started. "Impossible."

"You are," V insisted. "You're feeling panic. You're scared."

Kholos lifted his visor. He wanted to dump all his armor, his weapons, his light, and run.

Spiders. Sharks. Nakedness. Death. Disease. Buried alive. Crushed. Trapped under ice.

V began to feel it then, too. Terror. The terror of loss.

Kholos took deep breaths. Focused. Focused on V. For her, he thought, I will be brave. He took her hand. He took another breath.

With a shaky voice he said, "Thank you."

"Be strong," said V, although her own voice was cracking. "We're almost there. You said so yourself. I believe in you," she said. "I believe in you."

The cave disappeared.

They were in darkness, an echoing darkness so complete even Kholos could not see through it. Their breaths thundered, their heartbeats slammed. Instinctively they fell to their knees and held onto each other. They trembled.

They felt it, felt the Adonai of Fear, the Slythe god, Thssiss. Reptilian. Teeth in the dark. Hot and stinking, black terror. A presence big as space. Solid, dripping fear. Tentacles.

"Brave," said V. "We're brave."

Kholos gritted his teeth. Bars. Cages. Chains. Whips. Shackles.

"Are we at the end, Kholos? How many more of these places do we have to go through?"

"I think this is the end," said Kholos. "Everything ties together here. Everything is fear in this world. Everything is run by fear."

In the pitch black V touched Kholos's face. She left her hands there, cradling his chin, his cheeks. Thssiss, the God of the Slythe, Adonai of Fear, wrapped its claws, its tendrils, its pinchers and suckers about them.

They sweated. They shivered. The pricks and probes of Thssiss jarred lose phobias deep in their minds.

"I want to run," she said.

"No," said Kholos. "That's what it wants. That's what it does."

"Just kiss me, then," she said. "Or I'm going to start screaming."

He did. They held on. The darkness swirled around them, tentacles, pressure, whispers just out of reach. The feeling of falling. The knives clattering. The noose swinging. Webs wrapped around them. The loss. The ends. The changes. Death, felt V. Loss, loss, loss. Still they kissed.

After a long while, Kholos said, "You don't know who I really am."

"Right now," said V. "I don't care."

And the kiss continued.

Kholos thought of V. His wonderful V. He would set her free.

V thought of Michael. She could not lose him again.

"We have to kill this thing," said Kholos.

"Destroy this place," agreed V.

"And set the world free."

"I can't go through this again," said V. "I have to do something."

The avalanche. The shame. The knife edge. The surgeon's mask. The stink of death, the shadow in the corner. The knob turning on the locked door. The creeping disease.

"Shoot it," said V. "Use your magic rifle. Kill this thing."

"I can't see," said Kholos. "I can't see the bullets. If I fired a black, we could be destroyed along with it."

"Just try for me," V repeated.

Kholos reached for his rifle. Then there was a crack, a unit, of light. A voice spoke in the Thunder. "You have done enough damage to my universe," said a voice, very familiar.

Then the fear spun, there was a swirl of light and dark with edges of impossible colors. V felt sucked through something, like a time tunnel but flying instead of walking.

They emerged into a white room.

Sraosha, the Angel of Obedience, stared at the whirring stars over the Smoky Mountains. The Six Swords were in flight, inside their own supply of time, scanning for the trail from Powder's domain.

Gabriel scowled as he looked about at the boxes. The Farm was proof of the need for their justice. The work of this world would be destroyed.

"I see him!" said Sraosha, peering into the place where Powder's brick house had stood. "He's in a cave. A hidden place. He's almost there! He's done it!"

Gabriel turned, faced forward in time by roughly a week, ten days. "We have him. We have them both. We have them all."

"Then it's over," said Raguel. "We have won."

"Not yet," said Sandolphon, the strongest of the six, the Pattern of Power. "There is the fight."

25. The White Room

Bundled up in his coat, his wool hat, Dr. Voss sat on the porch of V's trailer. They were home, he knew, but it wasn't that particular probability of Kholos he needed to see, so he did not knock.

It was cold and dark and he shivered. In his pocket he had the little machine Kholos had given him, along with his paper of penciled shapes and equations. The stars overhead were cutting their arcs across the night sky and Dr. Voss watched them, tears in his eyes from the cold, and laughed. He understood now. But he wanted to know so much more.

For example, he knew Kholos and V were not inside in the trailer behind him, they had already left. Although, in his future he had not known that. But knowing it now meant that he knew it always. But it wasn't that Kholos he needed to see, not the Kholos at that position and speed. The one he wanted to see was the Kholos who would open the door in a few more moments.

He thought about the Universitat, his education in the Caego Institute, the priests and professors, the bishops and deans. Pang, the Zero God who had revealed everything of his creation through the twin lenses of reason and faith. Pang, the beginning of all things, the concept of nothing.

But Dr. Voss had never believed in nothing.

He started by asking the troubling questions in his theology classes, about proportions. About the measurement of forces like gravity, and could they be different? They called him a great sinner. And for his sins the Universitat sent him to Duran Town, a place barely on the Columbium maps, a place that did not even rate its own pair of Universitat representatives, a priest and a professor. Just the one for Duran. Just Nathan Voss.

He stared at the stars again. What is the speed of light? Is it constant? Can it be affected by friction? By gravity? Does it move through solid substance, can it move through time in more than one direction?

They were working on this in Anvir, he remembered. The burning city.

How did he know that? How did he know that name?

Because he had gone back?

No. He had always been there, he understood. He was everywhere, at once. Reality did not stack. It was not parallel. It was not alternate. It was all at once. It was all possibilities, even the contradictory ones, happening all at once. There was no zero. There was never nothing. There was always everything.

It was the mind that separated the conjoined experiences, made them seem causal rather than concurrent. The mind stitched together a narrative that made sense, using imagination and will. The observer influenced what he observed. No outcome could be judged with objectivity. None. Because the judge was in the outcome.

Dr. Voss stood up, stamped his feet to try and get warm. His lips were blue already. He realized Effa would catch him out here, in about ten minutes, think he was going crazier still. And maybe he was. But he needed to know. Michael would have understood. Would understand, he corrected himself.

"How big is the pin?" he shouted at the stars. Not the behavior of a sane man, he knew.

My feet, he thought, are stepping on the solid ground because my mind perceives it to be solid. And it is solid, and will be solid, and has been solid. But it was not solid in any sense until I observed it. And the ground, he wondered, does the ground imagine I have stepped upon it? Why not? The rocks in the Asinwatis, the weather, it is all as Fractured as V. Can there be different kinds of consciousness, different speeds of thought, not just degrees?

Why not?

He wished Michael were here. They would talk about these things, the scientist and the poet.

Dr. Voss smiled, because, if he worked out the equation a little farther, then Michael could be alive. Perhaps. Why not?

"Oh, V," he said out loud. "If you only understood. I know you would have figured out a way to bring him back."

"Understood what, Dr. Voss?" Kholos said, just a touch of the Thunder in his voice.

Dr. Voss turned. Kholos was in the door. Holding nothing in his hand, but with his arm out, like he was about to. Dr. Voss trained his mind on the moment, thought without words. And so Kholos gave him the machine to inspect and analyze that Dr. Voss had already studied and, to a point, unlocked.

"You're not here to tell me the Universitat is collecting the Fractured and putting them into camps," Kholos said. It was not a question.

"No," said Dr. Voss. He grinned like a child. He could not help himself. "Do you know what I'm doing right now, Kholos? Can you tell?"

Kholos looked at him. "You're aware you're in two places at once!" said Kholos, stunned. "I thought only I could ... how did you?" Kholos collected himself. "I am impressed, Nathan. Michael was right. You are a genius, indeed."

Dr. Voss laughed. "I don't know about that. But I have deduced the principle behind your little machine. It's a combination of will and imagination. You need only to scale it up. This is a simple thing, here. But its power is the will, and the process by which is works is the imagination. Here," he took out the paper. Kholos studied it.

Dr. Voss left the machine in Kholos's hand. But rolled up his paper.

"This is the scroll?" said Kholos. "With the Adonai names? The order we saw, it was the one I knew I would need, in the end?"

"Something like that," said Dr. Voss. "I've been playing a bit. Making things be several things at one time. Being two places at once, as you said. I started with objects. They were easier. The list was one. It's how the Universitat changes the names, so half the work was already done," he belched. "Excuse me," he apologized. "I'm guessing foodstuff that is less digested still operates on its own probabilities until it is broken down to a certain point within my body. So, being conscious of my potentials gives me gas."

"Dr. Voss," said Kholos. "There are certain physical limitations at work here. Your brain, the raw stuff of your brain. You are thinking thoughts now that are comparable to an amoeba using a power drill. I can only do what you are doing with my reservoir of raw light. I can't perceive of my other selves directly without help. You may be injuring yourself."

"I know, I know," said Dr. Voss. "Everyone thinks I'm going mad. Probably I am. But I know, Kholos, you see? I know this much, now. And I want to know more. I want to go to Anvir. Inscribing light with data, measuring how it travels. They were working on those problems, asking those questions."

Kholos nodded. He understood now why the Aetherian wanted the city destroyed.

"I think I'm going to go there," announced Dr. Voss. "Soon."

"There's nothing there, Dr. Voss. It was always on fire."

"Really? Like you never did anything against the Second Comanche?"

"I'm here," said Kholos, warily. "I'm just not here, only."

"That's not what Effa will say."

"What?"

Dr. Voss looked at his watch. He laughed at it, but it was still telling him the time, insistently. "Ironic, isn't it, that we are out of time? Kholos," Dr. Voss added. "I don't know what you are, but I know you love V. I know you love her like Michael loved her. Think of her, when your moments split and crack."

Kholos blinked. "Dr. Voss," he asked. "Where have you been?"

"Time and distance are the same thing Kholos, I understand! I'll see you yesterday! But never tomorrow! Always yesterday, from here on!"

Dr. Voss turned towards the approaching headlights of Effa Staffa's truck, come out from town looking for him. Dr. Voss did not look back. He waved to Effa as she pulled into the gravel of V's front yard. Effa spun up the radio, calling in to the Deputies that, presumably, she had found the wandering doctor. Again.

Effa got out of the car and left the door open behind her, the lights on and the engine running.

"Nathan!" she said. "What are you doing out here? You left your front door wide open!"

"I can always close it before I leave," said Dr. Voss.

"Before you..." Effa swallowed. "Just get in the truck. You'll freeze out here. You had us scared to death. How did you get out here? Somebody give you a ride or something?"

"Oh no," said Dr. Voss. "Time and distance, they're the same thing. You see. I was always here. I just had to pick out the right moment to arrive."

Effa sighed. "Your lips are blue. Get in the truck."

Dr. Voss obeyed. He rubbed his hands together when he got inside.

"What are you doing out here anyway? You know V's not home."

"Oh," said Dr. Voss. "No, I came to see Kholos. He understands what I'm doing."

"Who?" said Effa.

Kholos stepped in front of V. In the center of the white room was a single chair, high-backed, unadorned, the same pure white as the walls, the floor, and the ceiling. Sitting upon the chair was a man in a white robe. He looked exactly like Kholos.

"You have done some damage to my Adonai," said the man. "I was going to have to come for you soon enough myself."

"Who are you? What is this place?" Kholos demanded.

There were no windows, no doors. Scanning each corner, each surface, through his lenses Kholos saw nothing. No time etched and stacked, no light harvested and refined. It was as if the place was coated in the purified light Kholos carried in his canisters. The room was its own time, its own point, free from the flow of reality outside. A pocket of un-space.

The man rose from his chair. He moved exactly like Kholos, no difference in his steps, no difference in his expression. He put his hands behind his back.

"You understand the shape of the universe," said the man. He sounded just like Kholos. "Think on me a moment. You know what I am."

V understood. "Kholos, he's you."

26. I.M.

Kholos was in two places. He was two people at once. He thought of the Ghosts, the Maimed company of Antonia, and how they would not look at him. They had all faced themselves and lost.

"I would never," Kholos began, and stuttered. "Never exist this way." He pointed at the room, without windows, without exit. "You're trapped in here."

"Hardly," said I.M. "I move through the universe within these walls. I am truly free. We succeeded, Kholopatiron. I escaped. You escaped. We are two potentials of the same idea. Only I have achieved my freedom so totally, so completely, that I can experience my realities as I choose. I am, in a sense, your goal."

I.M. continued. "This is the reality you, I, we, created. The reason you cannot locate the Aetherian in this world is because you left them behind when you set Anvir aflame. They have no real meaning here, no power here. You are the Aetherian scout, Liberator. You are hunting yourself. Your masters hope you will fight me, as the fifty sent before you fought me. And lost."

Kholos lifted the visor of his helmet. The room was a perfect cube, six planes that Kholos recognized as the same un-time as the throne. The box could, conceivably, travel underwater, across the skies, through space. It was a vehicle as much as a location. Position and speed, simultaneously. It could fit in the palm of his hand or it could be a galaxy. Such dimensions were meaningless outside of time and distance.

"What are we," Kholos paused. "What am I doing here?"

The white-robed Kholopatiron who called himself I.M., laughed. "Liberating," he said. "We are freeing this new world, moment by moment. Already that phase of our plan is nearly complete."

"How? How are we freeing the world? There is so much death, so much control, here."

V, again, understood. "The Stalinistas. That's why they all look like you. Like him. The Stalinistas are his army. He's making the entire world his army."

"She's correct," said I.M. "The Stalinistas are my doing. They will free the universe. My army is carefully crafted, the Stalinistas are the product of precise planning. Their motivations pure and deliberate. You arrive in a moment when this work is well underway. And then ..."

Kholos cut himself off. "And then you'll lead them against the Aetherian, in the realities we left behind. All of this, the Adonai, the Stalinistas, the Universitat, Pang the Zero God. It's all to train an army to rise against the Aetherian. To set the time and light free. To end the Aetherian forever. That's why there is no free time in this room. No natural light. You're safe here. Hidden. Only you yourself can find this place. Only me."

I.M. nodded. "We understand each other well."

"I'm curious," said Kholos. "Pang. Does he even exist? Another tool of yours?"

I.M. waved the question away. "In a sense, he is another version of ourselves. He exists like the Adonai do, as ideas. They can be discussed, reached, poked, and prodded. Did you find them any less real than the stones of the world?

"But mostly Pang was necessary so that my reality could have a beginning, a something where once was nothing, a point to build on. Because you cannot make an army that does not have anything to defend, or to conquer."

"The Universitat," said V. "The highways? The temples? The schools?"

"Not in the way you mean, no," said I.M. "But they do my work, yes. The discoveries and inventions are revealed in the order I prescribe. Although your artillery calculations at the front have set that work back some. Ideas can spread quickly. Potentials have a way of going farther than calculated. Quite possibly some lowly soldier might think he could send something aloft. The highways are my routes for deployment, although still under construction. My troops will stream from this universe on good roads, stitched directly into the Aetherian possibilities."

"Why flight?" asked Kholos. "Why is it a sin to dream of flying?"

I.M. nodded. "You are the first to come before me to ask that question."

The walls vanished and the room disappeared, leaving nothing except a blue sky punctuated with huge white clouds. The three of them stood on a floor which was not there, and cold winds blew. V went pale.

"There is flight on this world, yes. More than you realize. But only I decide who may soar."

V dropped to her knees. The floor was still there, the walls. But they were clear.

I.M. continued, "I designed the Adonai all to be quested for and to be found. And indeed many before you have found them. You are not the first Liberator pattern to be dispatched here, not the first to seek out the ranks of my saints, hoping to reach me, to defeat me."

Kholos said, "How did I do this? How did I make all this? The time tunnels? The pocket domains?"

"I don't know what a time tunnel is," said I.M., pausing. "But the machine we gave to Nathan Voss. That was the key. Remember time is a sphere, not a line, not a series of points. Voss deduced how the machine could trace arcs across that sphere. He completed our quest. Or, rather, will complete it."

"Kholos," V interrupted. "You did this? You made the Stalinistas? You killed Michael?"

"Yes. Kholopatiron fifty-one," said I.M. "I think you should answer her, tell her what we really are. Tell her how you claim to know this Michael you speak of. He is not, obviously, a piece of my own self."

Kholos thought. The safety of the Lipstick Country. The strangling of beauty at the Museum Fortress. The indoctrination of abstract principles from King Close. The hatred of Zome. The control of meaning by Powder. The slow wane of compassion at the Sanctuary. And, finally, the binding fear of Thssiss. There were dozens of others, but Kholos could see the connection now. Every Adonai was working towards the goal of I.M.: to build an army of liberators to dethrone the Aetherian.

V asked again, "What does he mean? What you are? What are you?"

"V," Kholos began. "Michael was. He was."

"Your friend. I know. What does he mean?"

"I never met Michael."

V went pale. "That's impossible. You know everything. You."

"He's made of experiences, made of the moments of other people," I.M. said. "He is the harvested light of a thousand souls. However different he is from me, that is what he is."

V took a step back. "Harvested?"

"I tried to explain," said Kholos.

"Now, Kholopatiron. I offer you the same choice as the others: you may join me, join with me. And as a greater whole continue our work of rebellion and freedom. Or you may fall. This choice had already been made for our brothers," said I.M. "But for you, I think, you can choose. Your own reality, and victory against the Aetherian who would enslave you."

Kholos thought of Michael Staffa, the poet and lover.

"V. I am still Kholos. A piece of me is Michael. The most important piece."

"This is why I feel this around you? This is why I trust you, isn't it?"

I.M. laughed. "This was the Aetherian's secret weapon, then? Love based on a lie?"

Kholos looked at V. He did not know what to say. So he dropped his visor.

"I decline," said Kholos. "You are a tyrant. I will end this possibility."

He drew his sword. He shook off his pack. "V," he said. "Get back as well as you can."

I.M. looked at Kholos. "They built this one weak," he said to no one in particular. "A Kholopatiron that can fall in love? Might as well build a Liberator who paints pictures, sings songs, or writes poetry."

V, swallowing, said, "Michael?"

Kholos touched his belt. Wings made from molten light encased him. I.M. mimicked Kholos's actions perfectly.

"This is not a fight you can win," said I.M. "This is my reality."

"Then it's mine as well."

Two floating figures wafted through the moments of the world. They paused at the lip of a time tunnel that connected a swampy road not far from Powder's domain and a grassy plain. They looked up through white masks at the sky. They were deep in Stalinista territory. One of the figures was red, the other blue.

"It is happening, again," said the blue, in a masculine voice.

"It is always happening," spoke the red, in a feminine tone.

"But this time was different."

"It will always be different."

"No," spoke the blue. "The poet is his advantage."

"We cannot be certain. In other times it was the yeoman. Once the hero. The candlemaker. The hunter. The fraud. A greater advantage may be the determination, the focus, we embodied."

"Perhaps," insisted the blue. "But only with the poet."

Crick, in the cave of Golgothan, washed her front paws. Their cave was high, high up, nothing but white and wind for as far as she could see. Until a brief crack of lightning opened the sky for an instant. Sitting herself down on the stone floor and tucking her paws underneath, she thought of Golgothan, the rebel Saint of Questions, and of Busto, her cynical partner in seeing to it that curiosity did not kill their master. She wondered, staring at the place in the sky, was this the answer that Golgothan needed?

"He'd be over, you understand," said Busto, stalking up alongside her. "He would end. There would be no point any longer. No more questions to be answered."

The lean gray came up and gave the top of her head a friendly lick.

"I know," said Crick.

Busto stopped her, "We have been at this moment before, in different caves in different mountains. With different Kholopatirons, yes, but this same moment, with this same lightning. Is this one really so unusual? This one we have already guided more than all the others. Is there even a new question here?"

Crick sat up, "There is," she announced. Her ears stood up straight.

"And what is that?"

Crick looked at Busto very seriously, her whiskers flat and straight. "Because the girl is with him. Because he is in love."

The two cats sat up, side by side, and stared together out into the sparkling void. She looked back over her tail.

"What's he doing, right now?" Crick asked. Busto understood she meant Golgothan.

"Imagining a conversation with a rock about language. How could a rock communicate an idea like erosion, that kind of thing."

"His armies? The Second Comanche?"

"We could assemble them, certainly, but you know this fight will take place in the sky. Second Comanche on horseback won't help much. Useful as they've been. I must admit, your idea to attack Duran with those savages was an excellent way to get this all started."

Colonel Redroot studied his map. The Fighting First Claws were lost in time, and he was furious.

The unit was arrayed in good order as he surveyed the landscape, engines idling. From the front in the Northwest the First Claws had cut southeast, following the trail Redroot could discern, moving across the flat country when they could and then taking the Universitat highways to cross the mountains. Redroot had his deserter. He had him cornered and trapped, his vehicles ready to close in on his prey. Then, at the last possible moment, the trail disappeared.

Redroot looked through his binoculars. This was dead country, scrub and desert, somewhere in the Southwest of the Columbium continent. He saw sand and grit stretching across the horizon, as well as a distant chain link fence. Nothing else.

Stands-Tall was alongside the Colonel, offering advice. The tails of their coats flapped in a dry breeze and the shoulders of their uniforms were sprinkled with a fine dust from the road. The Colonel leaned a little on his rifle-cane to steady himself.

"We could double back to the time tunnel, sir," said Stands-Tall. "Try to catch him in the past."

"We could," said Redroot. He was still watching the country before him. Something was moving, coming towards them from the middle of the distant fence. Someone, not something. A man. Running hard, the figure came on towards them. Redroot lowered the binoculars.

"There's someone out there," said Ute.

"Unlikely, sir," said Stands-Tall. "We're in the middle of no-where and no-when."

"Nevertheless," corrected Redroot. He looked again.

"We should think about moving on sir."

The figure was much closer, still running. "No, I think we'll meet this runner."

It did not take long. Huffing, sweating, the man reached the First Claws. Redroot stood at ease. The man was gaunt and underfed. His clothes were little more than rags, the remnants of some kind of uniform, like a prisoner's. His shoes were rubber and twine, and had come apart in several places from his run under the Texcan sun.

"You're not Kiowa," the man huffed. "I knew it. I saw your dust cloud. I knew you couldn't be Kiowa. Are you, what? Renegades?"

"Who are you?"

"Thirty-Seven Bears," the man said. He thumbed back towards the fence. "I just ran from the camp. To reach you. I escaped."

"You're Comanche?"

"I am," Thirty-Seven Bears looked up at Redroot in his uniform. "Are you trying to free our people? Can I help? I've waited so long. For this chance. To be free." Redroot surveyed the fence again, and saw the guard towers and the razor wire over the fence.

Colonel Redroot looked at the man. He looked up at the clouds in the sky.

"There's a camp of Comanche prisoners up ahead?" he asked.

"Well, they don't call us prisoners," explained Thirty-Seven Bears. "They call us Relocated. And it's not a camp, they tell us," Thirty-Seven Bears spat out. "It's a reservation."

Redroot said to Stands-Tall, "Captain get this man some water and some fatigues."

"Colonel, he's not trained. He's just a civilian. He's not," Stands-Tall paused, "one of us."

"He's a Comanche. Find him a gun."

Stands-Tall nodded, and went to equip Thirty-Seven Bears.

"He's up there. I can feel him," Redroot said to the sky. "Somewhere."

There was a shimmering, and two figures, one red and one blue, both with floating faces, appeared.

"Indeed," the red said. "Lead us to him, then, Adonai."

A time tunnel appeared in the middle of the plains.

On beams of shining time, the Six Swords burst through the walls.

"Kholopatiron," announced Gabriel, in a voice that shook the very air, "This ends now."

V crouched in the corner. She could feel the solidity of the wall against her back, but there was nothing beyond but blue sky. She could feel the terrific heat of Kholos and I.M. and the Six Swords, and she could hear the thunder as they shouted at each.

A gentle hand rested on her shoulder. V, carefully, opened one eye to look. And saw an angel looking down at her.

"Who are you?" asked V.

"Raguel," the angel lifted the visor of her helmet. "I am a pattern, like Kholopatiron. I can take you from this place and this time to a point of safety. Do you wish this?"

V looked up at Kholos, her Kholos. "No," she said.

Up above, Sandolphon, Pattern of Power, Nathaniel, Pattern of Fire, and Ramiel, Pattern of Thunder, had formed a triangle in the space that comprised the center of the White Room. In the center of the triangle were the two Kholopatirons, I.M. and Kholos. Sraosha, the child pattern of obedience, glared from below at the fight. Sandolphon struck at Kholos and connected.

"You were unlikely at this potential," said Raguel. "I will return you to your time and place."

V slapped Raguel's hand away. "Why are you chasing him?" she sputtered. "Why can't you just let him go?"

V realized she had said him, *why can't you let him go*. Not, why can't you let us. Kholos was Michael? What did that even mean?

Raguel glared down at V. She was very tall and very beautiful, very pale. She spoke with the thunder. "You understand what Kholopatiron means to do with these realities? You understand his plans?"

V said, "But that's not Kholos, that's the other one!"

Raguel paused. "They are the same. They are merely different points in time and space. They must both lose. Neither can prevail."

"No," V answered. "He would never do this. You don't know him. He," she began, then paused. "He loves me."

Bits of time, damaged and cut loose by the blades of the angels, crashed down onto the white stones of the floor and sent ripples out through reality. Across the world, in the Universitat centers for the Fractured, those who had come loose from their possibility tracks flicked through their possibilities in instants. Many blinked out of existence entirely.

V changed. She was older, perhaps by ten or fifteen years. Her thoughts were stronger but slower. Her body was slightly heavier, and it felt comfortable but less responsive. Then she switched again, and became a woman in her early twenties.

Raguel said, "It is midnight everywhere now."

27. Potentials

On the Northwestern Front, the hulls of the great Stalinista battle barges cracked as ice flash-froze in the bays and beaches. Glaciers a mile high raced across the surface of the sea, then receded, then rushed forward again. The stars, in the skies above the parts of the world that faced away from the sun, became fixed points. Then dashes.

In Neo Cumae, strange people with four fingers on their hands appeared wandering down the streets. They wore different colored rings on their fingers, and asked in accented speech if they were in Tren's Town or if they were in Circle City. They looked at the skyline of the city, as if searching for points they might recognize. In the Power Station, black engineer automatons sparked and short-circuited.

As the streets of Pompeii awakened to the business of the Republicant, the scientists and priests who oversaw the massive geothermal works on Mount Vesuvius looked at their dials in amazement: the volcano had gone cold.

And in the Asinwatis, Dr. Nathan Voss walked through the pass towards the City Burning Forever.

V knew none of this. Or cared. For her the time-quake meant she was flashing through her Fractured selves at a random rate. She stood up, took a deep breath, and slapped the Raguel in the face.

Kholos, his armor blasted apart in the back plate from where Sandolphon had struck him, struggled to maintain his guard against I.M. and absorb the attacks of the other patterns.

Sraosha, the littlest angel, the pattern of obedience, fought without moving her body. Her sword danced free of her hand, seeking out the weak points at the joints of both Kholopatirons. Plasma blood dripped where her blade cut them.

Kholos, parrying blows before him, absorbing those from behind, called out to the Six Swords. "He is your enemy, not me!"

Gabriel answered, "You are one and the same, two potentials."

Kholos felt I.M.'s sword cut through a piece of the past and nearly connect with the side of his helmet. Only Kholos had deftly flicked back in time to parry the blow and deliver a kick to I.M.'s midsection that sent him sprawling back into Ramiel. The two patterns crashed against the walls of blank time.

"We could join," said I.M. "We could win."

"I don't care about winning," said Kholos. "I care about being free."

Kholos flew at Sandolphon in a jagged pattern through long seconds. "I want nothing more than to be free, with the woman I love. I deny everything this Kholopatiron has done. I don't care about unseating the Aetherian, I only want to be free!"

He struck Sandolphon, who was stronger but slower than Kholos, with the edge of his sword across the brow of the Pattern of Power's helmet. Sandolphon spiraled down through several minutes of time and smacked into the floor.

"And yet it will happen," said little Sraosha. "Such is the wish of the Aetherian."

She sent her sword up, fast, at Kholos. The point entered under his shoulder, just above his ribs, where his arm came through the cuirass, and stabbed deep.

His blood burst from the wound.

"Kholos!" cried V.

Deep in the Ebon jungles Antonia had built a new base camp for her Ghosts. It was similar to their home in the Swamps on the Columbium Continent, only the snakes were much more prevalent. The Witch-General wondered if she could move the Slythe here, if it would buy the doomed race some generations.

The enemy they had been hired to destroy was nowhere. Antonia's readings of the *anima* confused her. This place was lush, which made for good camouflage: the colors and the lines were beautiful here, but they were thick and the time was packed with changing matter. This made it difficult to track a particular line. Anything could be creeping in the thick jungle. The *vuldun* was thick as well, and it confused her understanding even more. It was, she thought, as if they had been brought to a place perfect for hiding both the Ghosts and for their prey.

They had cleared a circle, criss-crossed with vine bridges and with their crates of magical ammunition and food and fresh water hung in nets from the canopy of the massive trees. There was no real need for a perimeter. Nothing but thick jungle surrounded them. Nothing could reach them unless it flew, and except for the Borac dactyls, nothing in the world could truly fly besides the Ghosts. Supposedly.

So Antonia was surprised when she heard the strings play in a symphony of grace and the colors flowed and arranged themselves in patterns so beautiful Antonia began to weep.

Two figures floated from a kaleidoscope of stars and flowers towards her. She felt them, she experienced them, more than she saw or heard them. One was red, the other blue. The wore white masks that contained all their expressions at once.

Antonia knew what they were. The Aetherian.

"We would send you home," they intoned.

She could not look at them. Antonia tried to collect her thoughts.

"Would you," said one. "Could you," said the other. "Fight for us?"

Antonia sobbed out her words, "The Boracs. The Slythe. Could we all go home? Can we all go back?"

"All of them, every instant, every minute."

"And my men? My angels? My ghosts?"

"Returned."

"Not free?"

"Returned. Their experiences reclaimed."

"They must be free. They were your soldiers once. Do not abandon them again."

There was a click in the universe, and Antonia knew that the Aetherian before her had discussed something.

"Escaped, then, if you succeed. Escaped."

Then they were gone.

Antonia wiped the tears from her face. "Liberators! To arms! To freedom, at last, to freedom!"

"Obedience is a superior pattern to freedom," said Sraosha in her little-girl Thunder.

Kholos crashed nearby, and V ran to him, burned the palms of her hands on his armor. As he bled his light flickered, his time ebbing where Sraosha's sword had stabbed through. The cut was deep. With gasping breaths Kholos reached up and lifted his visor. The rust color was returning to his plates, his face was paler than pale.

"Hang on," said V. "Don't die. Not again. I need to understand."

Above them, the Six Swords battled I.M.

Sandolphon came up at I.M. from a moment below. The two patterns, one of Liberation, one of Power, crashed into one another in a flash of heat and force. The walls of the White Room quivered. Ramiel brought up his sword and raised it in both hands, lofting up on wings of starlight for a killing blow: the cut in the fabric that would remove I.M. forever from the universe. No possibilities, no potentials, no information, no light.

Nathaniel stood behind Sraosha. He would contain the light that was I.M. when the final cut was made to separate I.M. from reality. He would burn it away into nothingness.

Gabriel, the messenger, intoned his voice. Every word he spoke was fact, because he spoke them. "Kholopatiron, you have failed in your purpose, and the Aetherian are displeased. By the will of my masters you are cast down, destroyed, removed, into consuming darkness. You never were. You never will be. Such is the will of the Aetherian."

I.M. grinned at him.

Raguel was the only one that saw them coming in their millions, "It's a trap!"

Kholos looked at V. "The tusks," he spat. "Get Gyr Zax's tusks."

On the Northwestern Front, the Columbium just above the Seventeenth Sector of the line, General Eric Kaiser surveyed no-man's land, where he waltzed out in the open, peering into the fog from the coast. His staff followed him nervously, sure a mass of Stalinista soldiers would rush at them at any moment.

The fighting all up and down the line had stalled for no particular reason any of the Generals could discern. First, the new artillery tactics had pushed the Stalinista attack back, then the line had reformed and remained static after the appearance of the Adonai of Determination had crossed through the lines in a miracle no one knew what to make of, including the Universitat representatives. Things had settled into a pattern of the Stalinistas rushing the lines and the Columbiums holding them back. Until the attacks had suddenly stopped.

General Kaiser, the third most senior officer across the front after the miracle of the Adonai claimed the life of General Suskind, had driven out to the trenches with his staff to investigate.

Now, he peered into the fog with his glasses and tromped about the flattened, blackened ground that comprised the killing zone between the Stalinistas and the trenches.

"They're all gone," he said at last. "Where did they go?"

Raguel was crushed.

The walls and ceiling of the White Room disappeared, and the space without space expanded exponentially. Across the horizon, in all directions, Stalinista soldiers appeared, coming into the specific moment of reality where I.M. had summoned his troops.

And they all could fly.

In their millions the Stalinistas rose up on metal wings, imitations of Kholos's and the other Patterns. Each was armed with a rifle, but no sword. They came at the hovering platform of the White Room like a gray wave. Up against the edges of the platform they fell in masses that filled the air, bodies piled upon winged bodies, guns raised, crashing forward. They did not try to fight because they did not need to. They simply overwhelmed.

Raguel burned bright, vaporizing the first thousands of Stalinistas who fell upon her, then melting the next hundred after that. She cut back through time, but found the Stalinistas were there as well, and in the future they were even stronger. The next thousand that came at her she struck with her sword, slashing through the segments of a second. But there were another thousand after those, and then another ten thousand, another hundred thousand. Their wings clacked as they pushed their endless weight down upon her.

Her canisters running wide, Raguel took ten thousand of the Stalinistas with her before she was consumed by the mass. Her light, her time, was buried.

Sraosha fell next.

The little pattern of obedience rose up on her shining wings hurriedly as the wave of Stalinista fliers came at her. Sraosha was powerful, almost as powerful as Gabriel. As the clacking wings of the Stalinistas came at her she struck at the center of their mass. Her girl's hands on the grip of her sword went white, and her long hair blazed.

At first, it seemed she would succeed against the wall of repetition. She blew through the Stalinistas, slicing through their ranks with her sword and raking gaps in the pile of wings and bodies and guns that still seethed and boiled up around the edges of the White Room.

"You will obey your masters!" she shouted. "You will obey us!"

Then, with screams of shame, sparks flying from the edge of her sword, Sraosha was slowly buried under a pile of gray tunics and metal wings.

I.M., glowing like a star and just as hot, faced Nathaniel, Sandolphon, and Ramiel. Still standing with his wings raised, Gabriel pronounced below.

"Kholopatiron," he said to I.M. "You know this is futile. I speak for the Aetherian themselves. This will not be." He turned to the rising columns of winged humanity spilling up and over and onto the platform. "You cannot be," he told them. "You are impossible."

Editor of realities, imbibed with the power to describe the world as he saw fit, Gabriel delivered the messages of the Aetherian. His words were facts. But the Stalinistas ignored him.

I.M., laughing, struck Nathaniel across the visor of his helmet. The fire pattern's neck wrenched backwards. Turning at the speed of light, I.M. blocked the thrust of Ramiel, then deftly dodged two full seconds into the future of the fight, when Ramiel had turned his back to I.M. The sword bit deep into the pattern's armor, and penetrated time-locked flesh. Molten light gushed out and Ramiel slumped into himself as he crashed with a clang down onto the tiles below.

Sandolphon, Pattern of Power, had, alone, held back the Stalinistas along one edge of the platform. Burning bright, he was a force against which the hordes flung themselves.

I.M. gestured to his soldiers, the ocean of them, to move forward.

Without flinching Sandolphon established a beam of raw power upon the mass, pulverizing their possibilities. But a single crack in his armor became two, became three, became a dozen. With a roar that blew a thousand Stalinistas away from him in flames, Sandolphon finally collapsed to the floor, his wings gone and his body smashed.

Gabriel, gone pale, the last of the Six Swords, stood and stared at I.M.

"They are made to fight you," I.M. explained. "They are all trained to beat you!"

"You are an abomination, a monster in the depths of time, you cannot exist. You do not exist. I pronounce you ended," Gabriel chose his words carefully. He could not announce I.M. from existence, he could only try to change what he was, and hope he could end the transformed pattern.

"Your Aetherian do not exist in this room, they never have and never will. They cannot be, in this, my reality," said I.M. "I control all ideas. All concepts are mine here. Your words are nonsense, Messenger. *Your* very existence is a lie."

With that, I.M. swung his sword and decapitated Nathaniel, who had been waiting for Gabriel's next command.

V, an old woman, then a child of six, then a girl of twelve, limped, crawled, and walked towards the pack where the tusks of Gyr Zax were wrapped in black cloth.

Gabriel looked at the head of Nathaniel, the body of Sandolphon, and then at I.M. The Stalinistas loomed above, blotting out the sky.

I.M. lifted the visor from his helmet and studied V, skipping through her potential selves as she fumbled in the pack. He took his rifle and aimed it at her. A red bullet was loaded in the chamber.

Then there was brown cat on his face scratching and clawing at his eyes, biting at his nose. A gray cat clawed into the place on I.M.'s neck under the helmet and bit down, hard.

I.M. cried out and grabbed Crick by her head. He slammed the cat down onto the floor with a sickening crack. For a moment the cat struggled to rise up, but then collapsed onto its side.

"You killed my cat?" said a confused voice. A mountain rose up from nowhere, entirely contained within the White Room and yet still outside.

The Ghosts struck next. Antonia flashed her soldiers directly into the mass of Stalinistas using a trick of the *vuldun* death myths of the Slythe and the technology of light her men had brought to her. The effect was a mushroom cloud explosion. A hundred thousand Stalinistas were vaporized in the rush of heat and force. The hot winds shattered their tight mass.

"Liberators!" shouted Antonia. "Form up on me!"

A diamond of light emerged around the Witch-General, prickling with rifle and swords. Fifty Kholopatiron patterns, armor on, visors lowered, braced to fight the Stalinista tide. While in the center of the embrasure Antonia worked her four-fingered hands, tracing symbols, plucking strings of *anima*.

The Stalinistas crashed into her fifty men. The diamond formation heaved and buckled, the blood of her patterns, the light of their collected and harvested moments, splattered against her. But the diamond held, and the report of exploding red bullets reached her like comforting words.

"For Circle City!" she screamed.

Kholos, clutching his pierced side, the light pouring out of him through his fingers, rose up on his elbows. V was rifling through the bag, flicking through her Fractured selves before him: a ten-year-old, a babe, a woman with a pain in her back.

She gasped, "You're Michael? Really Michael? All along? Why? How?"

"Nothing has changed," Kholos managed. "I, I'm sorry. I tried to tell you. For now, the tusks."

She nodded. She knew Kholos was bleeding out.

"And my rifle."

"Fire!" shouted Redroot.

The Fighting First Claws, roaring through the time tunnel, had seen the sky break and the Stalinistas pour forth. His men, Ute noted, did not panic or break. Their rockets and tank guns were already all aimed up at the massive translucent platform where

Redroot knew his quarry waited somewhere in the swirl of Stalinistas and explosions.

The sky was dark, and the clatter of wings snipped and snapped like hail. Golgothan's mountain appeared, from nowhere, and then there was Antonia's explosion in the sky that, had they not already been wearing their sun-goggles from the road, might have blinded him.

"Sir," said Stands-Tall-Under-Cedars, looking through binoculars at the mountain. "There are some Second Comanche to our east."

The Colonel turned to the Major, his Blood Brother, his friend, his second in command. He lifted Gyr Zax's gun. "Follow my orders," he said. "Major."

"Ute?"

"Don't call me that," said Redroot. "You think I'm unaware of everything? You think I don't know I'm being used?" He chuckled. "I know. I simply don't care. You're a shade of my brother. I don't care. My mission hasn't changed. The deserter is before us. The Comanche will rule again. That's all that matters. That's all that has ever mattered to me."

Without looking away Redroot picked up the short-range Televia and pushed the button to speak. "First Claws, this is your Colonel," he said. "Today we win the war. Today we save the Incorporated Nation of the Third Comanche, and break the Stalinistas forever. Now, put your strong fingers on your triggers, and kill them all, all the enemies of our people!"

The salvo of rockets and shells burst through the cover of Stalinista flyers. The volley had little effect.

"You can't hope to make a dent in that horde," said Stands-Tall.

"I only need one," answered Redroot.

Kholos, gasping, called out hoarsely, "Gabriel!"

The Messenger of God, shocked and very afraid, turned to Kholos. "How does he? How did you? My words are fact? My words are the truth? What I speak must happen."

Kholos gestured weakly to him to approach. Gabriel hurried to Kholos. V had found the black silk wrapped around the Borac tusks, the surviving gods, the remaining ideas of a race.

I.M. swatted at a cat-attacker.

Kholos explained, "He's protected himself against that here. You're outside of time. He is the Aetherian within this shape. Your words are empty inside here."

"Impossible," said Gabriel.

"The fact that you can say that, and he is still here," hacked Kholos, "proves me right. Now. Kill the Fear, Messenger. Take your," Kholos looked up and counted. Raguel, Sraosha, and Nathaniel, all ended. Ramiel and Sandolphon both wounded. Golgothan and Antonia would have to hold I.M. alone. "Collect yourself. Take your two swords. Go and destroy the fear. That's his fuel. We're all afraid. Every one of us," he gestured at the Stalinistas. "All of them."

"Your key," corrected Gabriel. "The fear is how you control this place."

"Fine. My key. Just go," Kholos seemed dimmer, somehow. "Go!"

"You are him," Gabriel said. "You are deceiving me."

"You are a fool!" said Kholos. "I undid his work every step of the way. His easy comfort. His corruption of beauty. His manipulation of information. His control of meaning. His refining of rage. We undid the cave, Gabriel! As he built, I tore it down, that was your masters' damn plan, Messenger!" Kholos pointed at the sharp shape that was I.M., engaged with a cat, a mountain, and a man on a bicycle with a fire hose and feather duster.

"Perhaps," said Gabriel. "We cannot question the methods of the Aetherian, in the end."

Kholos clenched his teeth, "Go or don't go." He managed. "But I would see this world, and every other, free. You know what to do. Kill Thssiss. End the fear."

Gabriel rose, looked at Kholos, his patterns, and vanished.

V flicked into a woman in her late twenties. She could not stop staring at Kholos.

"Give me the gods," Kholos said.

V handed the tusks to Kholos. Kholos, gritting his teeth through pain and making the light spurt faster from his side, broke them apart. A last gush of light poured forth from his side, and then Kholos fell back, lifeless. V cradled his head in her hands.

"Don't die," she pleaded. "I need to know how to bring him back."

The Stalinista was blown from the sky by a rocket arced straight from Colonel Redroot's own attack car. The projectile soared up, smashed into and through the gray soldier's head, and sent shrapnel searing through the nearest dozen winged fighters. But the Stalinistas were ignoring the First Claws entirely, focused on Golgothan, Antonia and the Ghosts.

"Driver," he shouted. "Get out. This is my fight now."

"Sir?"

"Out!"

The Colonel shoved his driver out through the door with the toe of his boot and slid behind the wheel. The attack car peeled out, heading just east to where he had spotted the Stalinista fall.

"First Claws," he said over the Televia. "Stagger in a circle. Realign for horizontal fire. Infantry, dismount and take up covering fire positions."

The Second Comanche were coming in, heading straight for them, for him. Redroot lowered his goggles as the dust kicked up all around them. The rest of the First Claws were forming up in a defensive circle behind him. He was alone. The war cries of the Second Comanche, the blue sparks of their energy weapons, flickered across his windscreen.

"I will reach it," Redroot said out loud. Then, shouting, "I will reach it first!"

He did. The body was charred. Above him the sky was dark as midnight and rang out like a thousand hammers clanging and pinging as the Stalinistas covered the sunlight with their mass, poured in waves down into the White Room. But Redroot saw only the wings before him, dented and dinged but unbent. Stopping the attack car with a slam of the brakes, the Colonel reached down and yanked the corpse up by its belt and tossed it bodily into the back over the barrel of rocket launcher.

Lurching the car back into gear he turned the wheel wildly, away from the war-painted Second Comanche. A burst of blue lightning struck the back tire, tearing the solid rubber, another wanged off of the hood and the smell of burnt electronics came through the vents along with thick smoke. On three wheels he pushed the car into second gear, third gear. Through the dust and noise, he could just make out the circle of the First Claws, ready to absorb and repel attacks from both in front of them and from above.

He was an Adonai, he reminded himself. There was power in him now beyond the commander of armored cavalry, the Red River family. He was determination and single-mindedness. He was will. And he was Comanche.

Redroot stared into the rear mirror, picking out a brave on horseback, and willed the warrior to change. Then another, and then another, picking them out now by the twos and threes, finally by the dozen. Until, as the attack car rumbled back towards his men, Redroot traveled with an escort of a thousand new Fighting First Claws, riding in blue attack cars and light tanks, crisp in their Comanche uniforms, with their hair cut close and following his orders to maintain a close escort on himself and his cargo.

As they came upon the circle only Thirty-Seven Bears seemed shocked by the change.

"How?" he asked. "What kind of medicine?"

"Shut up," said Redroot. He stared at the man, middle-aged, gaunt and malnourished, but courageous, at least. Redroot told him, "Remember yourself."

Then, Thirty-Seven Bears appeared in his gray suit, dignified, capable, a leader of men, administrator of a great and growing empire, masters of the Columbium Continent. His features assumed a gravity and a dignity, his body held more weight. He stood up straighter.

"Colonel," Thirty-Seven Bears said. "I'm afraid our War Chief is unavailable, and I must assume that role."

"Sir," said Redroot. "Allow me."

"I defer to your military experience," said Thirty-Seven Bears. "End this, and return our people to their proper position." Thirty-Seven-Bears pointed up at the black sky.

"Yes sir," he cranked up the Televia. "First Claws," he ordered. "Target the sky. The entire sky. If it flies, kill it. Except," Redroot turned to the body of the Stalinista. "Except for one. Except for me."

Redroot took his knife and sliced open his palm, over the scar where he and Stands-Tall had become blood brothers. But he did not clasp the major's hand. Instead he daubed his blood with the fingers of his other hand, and painted, crudely and quickly, the emblem of the Fighting First Claws on the wings of the Stalinista he had taken. There was a belt, and a kind of clasp that went over the shoulder. The apparatus was surprisingly light.

I.M. was bleeding liquid gold where Crick had scratched him. Busto continued to chomp on the unprotected spot on the back of his neck and shake. I.M. grabbed the gray cat by the head and tossed it away, with force. But Busto rolled with the blow, landed on his feet, and had jumped up onto Golgothan's shoulder while the renegade saint turned his bicycle and came at I.M. with his feather duster.

"Is Crick," Golgothan swallowed. "Is Crick gone?"

Golgothan rushed at I.M., his feet pumping the pedals madly. I.M. rose up before him. The time around him crackled with heat and energy. Below him the avalanche of his armies was pushing in across the translucent tiles of the White Room. The only spots not enveloped in the shadows of Stalinista wings was a dim glow where Kholos bled, and the hot flash searing in from the north where Antonia had marshaled her Ghosts. I.M. spotted Golgothan and lifted his rifle from his back, took aim down the sight.

Busto was bleeding across his whiskers and his nose was steaming and burnt where I.M. had grabbed him with his gauntlet. One of his ears was slightly torn.

"Did you bring your shock troops?" asked Busto.

"Why wouldn't I?"

"Well, where are they, then?" Busto looked at Crick. "I'm going back in!"

"But who are *they*?" Golgothan asked. He dropped his whip, fascinated by four new figures appearing, emerging in the White Room.

28. Cover Your Eyes

They were Boracs. Two were women, and two were men. One of the women was middle-aged, with tusks that curled back on themselves in a kind of filigree, the color of golden apples and autumn sunshine. She wore a long garment of leaves and twigs and smelled of snow, and in addition to her two yellow, vertically pupiled eyes, she possessed a third eye in her forehead. Her square feet were bare and seemed wide, even for a Borac. This was the avatar of creation for the Boracs, the concept of birth, of beginnings, of dawn. Of the idea of something where once there had been nothing. The Boracs called her Shirushu.

The other woman was younger, beautiful, with long hair done up with bells and flowers and buzzing honey bees and butterflies. Her tusks were short, almost stubby, but they were green like buds. A warmth went up around her, the warmth of the outdoors, of moss and sunshine and rain. She was naked except for a few lengths of flowering vine and carried a basket made of amber and seashells filled with white and red rosebuds and pebbles. She looked around her at the White Room with a mixture of wonder and want. Her name was Trimea Mea, and she was the Borac concept of growth, of spring, of wonder and flowering things, of learning, and of striving, of always trying to reach for new things.

The men were contrasts. One was young, muscular, handsome. The other was missing teeth, chubby, balding. The younger lifted a long bow from his shoulder. The weapon was golden as his eyes, tall as a tree. He strung it with a twined cord of anima, and prepared to fire an arrow of truth. At his hip was a *kop* almost as long as his entire leg, bare-bladed, that hung from a leather thong. He wore boots and a leather vest made from the skin of a Slythe. His tusks were blood-red and chased with animal shapes: wolves, bears, snakes, and stags. This was Hindel Koosh, the Hunter, *cumbel* of dreams. His hair hung in black braids down his back, and it was decked with pinpoints of silver like stars.

The other male belched at Koosh. This was Jotound the Rotund, the eater, the reveler, the consumer, symbol of greed and frivolity. He wore a stained smock and sandals, and his face was rounded for a Borac. A little beer foam flecked at the corners of his mouth, and in his hand he carried a raw liver sprinkled with spices. His tusks were carved into cornucopias, filled with intricate, delicate, painted sweetmeats and haunches and ribs.

These were the four last ideas of the Boracs: the start, the reach, the pursuit and the kill, and the consuming. They stood on the timeless tiles of the floor of the White Room and did as ideas do: they inspired.

"No!" shouted I.M.

The Stalinistas paused in their attack.

The effect of the Borac gods, of the new ideas they represented, on the Stalinistas rippled out through the horde. First those packed in tight at the edges of the room pulled back. Then the mass behind those slowed, and so on, as the effect of new ways of thinking, new challenges, new promises, appeared in avatar-form in front of them.

"Attack them!" shouted I.M. "Crush them! They can't reach you unless you let them!"

One chunk of the horde stared at Trimea Mea and thought of desire and of want. Another ten thousand gray-shirted soldiers looked at Hindel Koosh and his golden bow and felt power. Another ten thousand, admiration. Another few hundred envy, or even fellowship. The vanguard closest to Shirushu considered the vision of the Borac goddess and felt hope, disgust, hatred, and love. Those Stalinistas whose mass was closest to Joutund thought of hunger, famine, plenty, or loss. Each soldier thought or felt a different combination than the others.

V, cradling Kholos's head, saw the faces shift. Some smiled. Some cried. Some gritted their teeth. Others held themselves, some embraced one another. Some blushed. Many laughed. A few screamed. Each reacted in their own way.

I.M. struck Golgothan across his face. The Adonai looked at him with a crooked, broken-tooth grin.

"Are you safe enough, yet?" he said.

"You did this," he spat. "You and your chaos. Your questions." I.M. ran him through with his sword. Gripping the blade as it burst through his back, Golgothan looked at I.M.

"I wonder," he said, "where am I going?"

Golgothan, the Adonai of the Quest who made himself the Adonai of the Question, died.

"This changes nothing," I.M. declared, using the Thunder as his armies splintered and broke apart into individuals all about him. "I can repair this. You have only delayed my conquest, not averted it. I still have my fear. I still have my Universitat. I control this time and this light."

A bloody and burned Busto limped on three white paws towards I.M., his torn ear flopping.

Kholos's body was lifeless, the light gone from his armor and the plates and visor and gauntlets all returned to rust.

V held Kholos and her body jumped from shape to shape. Her teeth fell out, then regrew. Her hair was gray, then white, then brown again. Her arms were strong and lithe and then they hurt in the joints. She was awake then exhausted, hungry then sick. She thought of Michael through it all.

V looked up from Kholos's body. Blinking at I.M. as he swung his sword about him, tromping through the seconds to reach the Borac ideas. Busto, screamed a cat battle cry and leapt for his I.M.'s neck, again.

"I'm not afraid," V said. "I'm not afraid anymore. Only sad."

She looked at Kholos, who seemed just a man now, and saw the little machine in the palm of his hand.

"Imagination and will," she said. "It runs on imagination and will."

Then she saw the dials and the gears. Like sewing. Or hunting. Or cooking. She reached one tentative finger towards a switch. The machine was tiny as a thimble, big as a house. V saw no paradox. She thought, I can refine light with this.

I.M. stopped in his tracks, "Put that down," he commanded. "Carefully."

"Imagination and will," V whispered.

Antonia looked at the anima and the absence of the anima, the Borac and the Slythe magics respectively, and saw them reshaping themselves. Her men were reduced. The Stalinistas had smothered them. Only some two dozen remained from her fifty. Their injured and scarred bodies hissed with the burning of their light.

Then, through the nuclear corridor opened by Antonia, Colonel Redroot flew. Wobbling, gliding, his canisters lifting him abruptly straight up then cutting out, Ute arrived alongside the Witch-General. At first she did not notice him because she was focused on the Stalinistas. They seemed confused, suddenly. She had no idea why, but she took the respite to twist and trim the anima around her remaining Ghosts.

Redroot aimed himself at the path towards the White Room, lurching forward with Gyr Zax's golden sub-machine gun in his hands. Antonia, curious, stopped him with a twist of her thumb, pulled him to her. With a second adjustment she tuned the canisters to his particular anima, so that he could fly straight.

"Where did you get that gun?" she asked.

"From a Borac," Ute responded. He looked around. The tails of his long coat where flapping. "Who are you? Why do all these men look like the Deserter?"

"You're not Kiowa," Antonia observed. "No. You're Comanche. Incorporated Nation Comanche."

Redroot blinked. "You remember the Incorporated Nation?"

"Remember is not the right term, but yes. I know your people."

"You are not one of them, then, one of those who demeaned my people, who made them disappear, because I failed?"

"I am not one of anything," said Antonia. "I am unique. What are you doing here? How did you get here?"

Amazingly, the Stalinistas seemed to be dissipating, although she noticed some pockets of them were re-grouping for another strike. Her men were reloading their rifles and making a new, smaller diamond. She had only two nuclear bullets left.

"You're not one of I.M.'s Adonai," she said. "Yet you..."

Antonia surveyed him, then the path towards the White Room. Many, most, of the Stalinistas had left the fray. They moved in flocks, absorbed or disturbed or inspired by the Borac ideas, away from the fight. But those remaining were taking up new positions around the un-space of the room, defensive positions.

"Even with that gun," Antonia said. "You could not kill him."

"Watch me try," said the Colonel.

"You would never reach them. Reach him."

"So clear me a path."

Antonia looked at her last few Maimed, so loyal, so doomed. Then at the Stalinistas, perhaps just a hundred thousand strong now, rising up like spikes all around the room. She raised her rifle to her shoulder.

"Cover your eyes," she said.

I.M. tossed Busto aside, again, by grabbing the scruff of his neck. The cat, bleeding, landed and seemed set to charge again. But then he teetered on his paws and fell, his white belly heaving. I.M. paced away, his light burning red and yellow and white with rage and frustration and confusion.

"None of this matters," he huffed. "All you do is delay me. All you do is postpone my miracle war. Faith and reason will prevail. You can't hurt me. Not here. My Universitat will cauterize all these wild concepts."

He decapitated Trimea Mea first. The ideal of growth and ambition and striving dropped to the tiles, but her power had already spread through the world as the Stalinistas carried their competing visions of what she meant. Then I.M. grasped Jotound by his head and squeezed. The fat Borac's head sizzled under the heat of I.M.'s fusion-powered gauntlets, then melted away. However, as he fell his grin remained, stained with bits of meat between his teeth. Almost, the god seemed to be laughing.

I.M. turned to face Hindel Koosh. The Cumbel's tusks lifted in a cruel grin as he loosed an arrow from his golden bow. The shaft struck I.M. in the shoulder, and a little pure light trickled out from the place where the arrow had bit.

I.M. looked at Koosh, who produced another golden arrow. "How?" said I.M. "What kind of light could?"

Shirushu cackled at him. "Are you afraid? Do you feel fear, now?"

Gabriel, flanked by Ramiel and Sandophon, had returned.

"You have failed, Kholopatiron," Gabriel said in his voice of truth, his voice of fact.

Sandolphon, pattern of strength and power, dropped a squirming, chained shape of darkness, needles, and teeth. Thssiss, the lone god of the Slythe, the maker of fear. I.M. stepped back.

"I am protected here," he said, more to himself than those left around him. "This is my time. I am immune to any variables not of my own choosing."

I.M. surveyed the White Room. The hills of charred, smoking bodies where his Stalinistas had drowned out the angels. The corpse of Golgothan, and the remaining Borac ideas and ideals, spreading. The hissing, slithering, seeping shape of fear, the concept he had spent so much to extract and bring into his universe, now bleeding its power.

Redroot landed with a tumble, close to V. He raised Gyr Zax's gun over Kholos, aiming for the face.

"He's already dead," said V, an adolescent girl for the moment. "You can't kill him again."

Redroot lifted his gun, slowly, and scanned the room. He saw I.M.

"Here," said V. She took Kholos's rifle, and then the magazines of different colored bullets and tossed them at Redroot. "Kill us all."

"What kind of bullets are those?" Redroot said. "What do they do?"

Gabriel landed. "This is over," he said. "Your army is not here. They are all returned to their homes."

The Stalinistas vanished.

Redroot sifted through the bullets. Black seemed appropriate.

I.M. took his sword up in both hands. "You still have to fight me," he said. "I can stand against the three of you. I can begin again. You cannot kill fear."

"This possibility is ended, Kholopatiron," Gabriel continued.

Redroot fired. The black bullet. It struck I.M. in the chest.

Everything stopped.

V looked at the machine. She remembered Michael. "Imagination and will," she said.

She touched it, and wished, and wished, and wished.

As the black bullet impacted, backwards through time, into the Kholopatiron pattern called I.M., the entity ceased to exist in any direction or dimension. Quantumly, I.M. had zero probability. His anima and vuldun spun backwards, un-coiling forwards and backwards through time.

He had never been. He never was. He never would be.

29. Wheels and Teeth

"This is where I was made," gasped Kholos. "We've arrived."

There were machines vast as oceans, tall as mountains. They hummed and clicked and spun. Great gears with cogwheel teeth big as buildings turned and pushed slivers of light up and down, up and down.

A shape V could not identify roofed them over. It was like a reflection of a curve. She remembered Michael had written about the shape of the sky. She looked down at Kholos, as if she had never seen him before. She knew him entirely. She did not know him at all. Kholos's moments bled onto her lap, bright and hot.

"V," Kholos said, weakly. "We're here. These are the machines of the Aetherian."

V did not hear him. She was a young woman, late teens. Then a crone. She was weak but she still cradled his heavy head. She understood everything. She understood nothing. She looked at the brilliant beaming blood, and her guide-self took over. She touched his wound and it burned. If Kholos died would Michael die, again?

"Help me!" she shouted at the machines. "He's bleeding out!"

The machines hummed.

Two figures, red and blue, appeared. They observed the object V held in her hand, the thing that had shifted them away from I.M. and brought them here.

The Red said, "Return it, and we will shape you back into the possibility you ripped to arrive here."

V started to ask them to send her to, to when, before Michael died, but hesitated. "Make him whole, first," she insisted. "And then we'll talk about where you can sew me back into time."

"You cannot hold these thoughts," said the Blue. "This is a point on the expanding sphere of all possibilities. We created it, and keep creating it, and create in all directions at once. It exists simultaneously with all other points. That concept you possess is necessary to preserve this work."

"Is it like leaving a pin stuck into a new dress?" V asked.

"You are single-cell organism wielding a canon," said the Blue. "Do you perceive this metaphor?"

"Go to hell," said V. "Heal him, or I'll smash this thing."

"We could remove you, entirely," said the Red. "But understand how expensive this is. Understand what resources it consumes to alter a possibility. What expense was undertaken to complete this potential. Our work is vital. Our materials are limited. Time appears infinite only to those who consume it in small quanta. Time is a commodity, with a weight and size. It can be saturated. It can be wasted.

"There is no alternate time, no other universes running parallel to ours. All possibilities, all universes, occur within this time and this time only. Use it poorly, and the potentials are tossed away from the center of the wheel and lost."

"Make him whole," she repeated. "Or I'll break this stupid thing."

V heard a single note.

Kholos rose. He was unhurt. He had never been hurt. His wings of light lifted from his shoulders.

"He is repaired. And you are coherent," said the Blue. "Return that concept."

V realized she was un-Fractured. She was a young woman, in her late twenties, with the marks of her hours in the mountains on her face. She was herself, again.

"You healed me?"

"No," said the Blue. "We righted you onto a more likely probability than the one he set you on when he snapped time at Anvir. You were never injured. You were merely extremely unlikely."

"The whole world isn't Fractured?"

"V," said Kholos, his voice returned. "We can go. You know how to leave this place. Use the machine again, use it to activate these engines, we'll stitch away into a new time, a whole new reality."

V kept the little machine in her hand.

"Will Michael Staffa be in this new universe?" she asked Kholos.

Kholos did not answer.

V said, flatly. "I don't care anymore. Kholos, I understand what I.M. said. I know you're Michael. I know you didn't know him. I know they," V pointed at the Aetherian. "They, made you this way. And I understand you lied to me. All I want now is, can he come back? Can Michael come back? 7174 explained how everything that can possibly happen, does happen. That means Michael is alive, somewhere. And I heard I.M. say that, that you," she looked at the Aetherian. "The Aetherian, whatever, you could actually do that, you can put time together so that I can see it happen. So I can be part of it happening. So. Can you? Will you?"

The Blue said, "This Kholopatiron Pattern has succeeded after costly attempts to cauterize the anomaly of himself. The presence of the poet was crucial to accomplishing this. It introduced variables that delivered this outcome. We will not undo this. It must always occur. The expense of realigning the universes is extreme, as we have explained. Your failure to accept this explanation does not diminish its importance."

"But it's already occurred!" V screamed. "Michael shouldn't have even been at the front at all! There shouldn't have been any Stalinistas at all! No war! Nothing!"

Kholos interrupted. "V, they won't bring him back. We can only escape. Come with me. Begin again. Michael is a part of me."

V said. "No. Not good enough. You lied. You Fractured me? Fine. I don't care that you cracked the world. But I want my Michael back."

V turned to the Aetherian and gripped the little machine tight. "The Stalinistas are gone. I.M. is destroyed. You got what you wanted. Stitch it or shape it or bake it, fine. Kholos wants to be free, so set him free. And I want Michael back. Can you put our possibilities back together? Or not?"

The great chamber was still and quiet.

"As we have explained, the Kholopatiron's pattern succeeded at great cost. We will not undo this. You see it as having occurred. But in fact it is still occurring and must continue to occur."

"No," said V. "I'll pay any price. I'll do anything. I'll go back and kill I.M. myself. I'll," she looked up at Kholos. There were tears in her eyes. "I'll kill Kholos, myself."

"There may be another way to settle accounts," said the the Blue. "If you are willing. Potentials ended. Possibilities reduced. The likeliest probabilities exclusively. If you would return the machine, would you trade your infinite self for a finite self? Would you offset the accounts of reality with your own expanding sphere of chances? Would you accept true mortality for yourself?"

"No, she won't," said Kholos. "V, you can be free. Remember how you feel with me."

V said gently, "Yes. But you're not my Michael," then she addressed the Aetherian, her hand opened, offering the little machine.

"If you choose one world," said the Blue. "You will lose very much. Huge swaths of your existence will be the cost of this. You will be left with only one line. Only one life. It will end."

"My light," V said. "You want me to give up my light. You are offering the trade of giving up what could happen to me, all of that unknown, for the known of Michael," she finished. "Give up all of my potentials, for Michael. I understand."

The Aetherian did not respond.

"I won't remember any of this, will I?"

The Red shook its head, "No."

"Or Gyr Zax or Avalina? All the people that died?"

The Blue said. "You will have never happened this way at all. You and Kholopatiron will have never been together, at all. You will not remember him."

V paused. "Those nights in the trailer?"

"V," Kholos said. "Please don't do this."

"You could force me to stay with you," said V.

"You know I won't. You know I couldn't."

V touched his face. "Maybe that should tell you something," said V.

She turned to the Aetherian.

"I'm ready," she said.

There was a tick. V was gone. She had never been there.

Kholos looked away. His wings fell.

"She did not want a universe, Liberator," said the Blue.

Kholos dropped to his knees. The wheels turned.

"Damn you," he whispered, to V, to the Aetherian, to existence.

“You opened your own door, Kholopatiron,” said the Red. “You found the place and the time, and you marked it for your escape.”

Kholos breathed deep, he realized what this meant.

“Anvir,” he whispered to himself. “The door outside the universe is Anvir.”

30. Exits and Entrances

Deputy Byron Bonson spotted Michael Staffa at dawn.

Gaunt, unshaven, his rifle slung over his shoulder, Michael walked down the middle of the road that connected Duran to the Western Columbium Counties. He was smiling, grinning, laughing out loud a little. Even did a little hop and skip when he saw Deputy Bonson's truck.

Deputy Bonson, recognizing the man before him, hollered in the cab of his truck and punched the air. Bonson stopped in the middle of the road and cranked the little civil service Televia machine.

Sheriff Barney Turl answered his call curtly. "Duran Town. Turl here."

"Morning, sheriff. Deputy Byron Bonson, reporting in."

"I know who you are, Deputy. You seize up on patrol?" It was not quite cold enough to freeze the old engine, but it was cold.

"Pang damn, Sheriff, you will not believe who I am looking at right now!"

"I'm guessing it's not your momma, Deputy. This is an official line, you may recall."

"Let me put it to you this way, go get V outta her trailer and bring her into the station."

There was a pause on the line. Bonson, thoroughly amused, cackled lightly.

"No bull?" said Sheriff Turl at last. "Already?"

"He's walking right up to me as I speak, sir," Bonson paused. "Needs a shower and some pie, but otherwise seems to be moving just fine."

"Well!" exhaled Barney Turl. "Well. Pang damn indeed!"

The news of the cease fire on the Northwestern front had reached Duran Town three days earlier, coming over first the Televia as a writ from the Universitat that, in keeping the balance of faith and reason, the Stalinistas had agreed to halt their advance along both the Columbium front. The missive added that the cease fire had nothing to do with the sins against reason that had occurred at the front. A final statement also made it clear that the mobilization of the allied Ebon empires--which included rumors of strange gliding weapons--had nothing whatsoever to do with the truce.

The missive made no mention of the surprise attack of the Incorporated Nation of the Third Comanche. The Comanche armies had struck in several perfectly timed, perfectly executed prongs all along the Columbium front. These armored columns broke through the Stalinista lines and reached the sea, pushing back the suddenly scattered and disorganized Stalinistas. The columns then conducted flawless encircling maneuvers, surrounding entire divisions of the gray uniformed Stalinista soldiers.

These new tactics, which were not vetted with the Universitat, were all the plans of one General Ute Redroot. Redroot had caught the attention of more established leaders in the Comanche establishment, most notably the great Chief Thirty-Seven Bears. The Chief gave him free rein to develop a plan for a full-out counter-attack. However, General Redroot's victory was bittersweet, as his close friend and blood brother, Stands Tall Under Cedars, was killed in action.

When finally Bonson arrived at the square there was a big crowd, at least the biggest crowd Duran Town could offer. Laughter rose up like steam.

Effa Staffa, hands on her hips, feet set astride, tried to get the streets clear and shooed people either into the little park or back onto the sidewalks. Then she saw Dr. Voss' house, the door closed and locked, and she sighed, and she let the children run. Bonson turned the siren once before he parked.

"We all missed you buddy," said Bonson. "Told you." He clapped Michael on the back.

But Michael did not see the children, or the scores of people who started to applaud. He only saw V. She was standing in the middle of the street. She was shaking, crying. She opened up her arms like she would hug the entire truck.

Before Bonson had put the truck in park Michael leapt from the vehicle and ran the last dozen meters to reach her, tripping over his trench coat, his rifle banging against his spine. Then he reached her, and they took each other in their arms, and they kissed. The crowd clapped for them.

"I thought you would die," V shook. "I thought you would never come back to me."

She was holding his face in her hands. She was kissing him like he might vanish.

"You're so thin," she said.

"So feed me," he said. He was laughing. He was crying. His hands grabbed her so hard it hurt but she did not mind. They kissed again.

"Michael," V said. "Dr. Voss. There was an accident."

"Not now," said Michael. "Not right this minute."

Late that night after a huge meal Michael rose from the bed where V snored and, grabbing a blanket and wrapping it around his shoulders, stepped out into the cold night. The evening was chill, still, and empty. The lights of the town blazed to the south, the mountains mere shadows to the east. He breathed deep, coughed slightly, breathed deeply again. He stared at the stars, thought about their arcs, their paths, their light. He thought about the front, what had happened there.

The screen door opened and a naked V, hands clutched to her shoulders against the cold, came down the three steps towards him. He opened the blanket like a wing and took her in, she pressed herself against him. They kissed, again.

V ran her fingers down his spine, down his ribs. "We have to do something about this," she said.

"I'll be fine, now that I'm home."

They stood and held each other.

"I had nightmares," V said. "About what might happen to you."

She kissed him. She clutched him.

"V," Michael said. "Listen. Don't tell anybody, but I think I won the war."

"I'm sure you did, baby."

Michael laughed. "No, I mean literally. I did something, something impossible, only as it happened it felt so natural. And then everything started to just, to just click into place. All at once."

"You sound like one of your poems," she said. She kissed the stubble on his chin.

He did not say anything for a moment.

"I'm afraid to say it," he said. "To write it, even. If I try and explain it, something else might have happened. I sound crazy, I know. I have been sick. I saw things happen. And I could fly. Maybe it was a dream? I don't know. The trenches were so bad, Virginia."

He shivered. She forgave him the use of her full name.

"You're home now," V said. "With me. The war is over, now. That's all that matters."

He held her close. "Let me just tell you this one thing," he said at last. "Because I need to."

V closed her eyes.

"We were attacked. They threw grenades into our trench. It was awful. Men screaming. It was night and I could see the bones, white and shiny, slick with blood, where the bombs had blown people apart. And then I saw one, a grenade, it was coming. It was going to land and it was going to explode, next to me. I could trace its arc, in the dark. This thing that would kill me. And it was like the moment was wider, for me, somehow. Not slowed down, but bigger. I could see, all at once, the light of the grenade being thrown, the light of myself watching it come, and the light of the metal that would tear me apart. All at once. They were not separate, it was all one thing. At once. It was all happening all at once.

"And I could see, I could think, myself dying, and myself being hurt, and myself not there at all. I know this doesn't make any sense. But I could see them all. And, I think I went insane, for a second. But now, I remember it like I made a choice. And it was not perfect, choosing to do what I did, but I did it. I exited that wide minute. I was thinking of you. You and only you. And how I would come back, because we had to be together. And I would tear the world apart if that was what it took. I didn't care, I would stop everything, if that's what I needed to do to get back to you.

"And I was out of the trench, before the grenade hit, before it even appeared. Which is impossible, I know. But I remember it that way. I leaped up and out. But instead of retreating, I was charging. With just my rifle and my friends' blood all over me, I was attacking the Stalinista line, all by myself.

"Suicide, of course. You never attack the Stalinistas. You dig in, you hold as long as you can. But I was attacking. And I knew I would win. I knew it was a matter of will, of imagining it, of refusing to do anything less. I had lost all my fear. I needed to end the war to return to you, so that what was I was doing."

V started to cry.

"And I reached the Stalinistas," Michael continued. "They were just a huge gray mass. There were campfires all up and down the beaches, I saw those first. I will write about how that looked, those fires, and all those gray uniforms in the firelight. All those faces. They all look the same, somehow. They never tell you that, but all the Stalinistas look a lot alike.

"And I lowered my rifle, and I fired. And I killed the first one I saw. I shot him, through him heart." He shook.

"We should go indoors," V said.

"Not yet. I killed him, and all up and down the beach, the Stalinistas looked at me, and looked at him. And, this was the insane part, but I swear this happened. All up and down the line, for kilometer after kilometer, every single Stalinista, each one, took a step back. They stepped away. They didn't raise their weapons, they didn't scream or rush at me. Nothing. They looked at this poor man, this man I killed to end the war, and they just, started to walk back. Like that would be the last one."

"You were very brave," said V. "And very stupid."

Michael laughed. "Yes," he admitted. "And then the Comanches attacked from six different directions a second later, coming from everywhere, and it was a rout. I know, I know that's the facts of what happened. But I was there, I stood on those pebbles that night and I killed that man, and that was what finished it. Not the Comanche. It was me, deciding to do it."

By morning a crust of hard snow dusted the ground, making the sunshine beam and blast so brightly V had to close the curtains inside the trailer. She topped off the kerosene heaters and turned them on full bore, then she bathed Michael, shocked to see all the little pocks and scratches he had endured. There were star-shaped scars on his back, a white line along one calf where a bayonet had come too close, and smaller, thinner ridges along his arms. His feet and hands were worse: swollen at the joints like an old man's, with crust under the nails she could not remove even with the scrub brush. Two of his toes had lost their nails entirely. And there was a scar behind his right knee.

Later, with the trailer nearly steaming, she wrapped a towel around her waist and spread newspaper on the kitchen floor and brought in a folding chair. She sat Michael down and wrapped a heated towel around his shoulders, and then she cut his hair and shaved him. When she was done V. stepped back.

"I thought you would look younger," she said. A little disappointed.

"How do I look, then?"

"Sad," she said. Her voice cracked, a little.

V knelt before him and rested her head against his thighs. He stroked her hair.

"I'm sorry," she said. "I'm happy. I am."

"I know you are," he said. "I can tell."

"I love you so much. I can't believe you're back."

"I can," he said. "This haircut proves it."

She swatted at him. They stayed like that a little while.

"V," Michael said. "It wouldn't hurt me if you had another lover, while I was gone."

She chuckled. "No, no, it's not that at all. I can't even say."

"Try."

V stood up and sat on his lap, facing him. She put her arms around his neck and kissed him.

"No," she said. "No I won't."

On a ridge within sight of the Universitat highway Kholopatiron the Liberator Pattern burned like a star. His light shone, his wings were spread, his armor bright. Faceless, he pointed to the City Burning Forever with a glowing finger. Anvir still burned. The flames flickered without consuming, the instant of destruction paralyzed.

Crossing the highway, heading towards the flames, a strange parade formed at Kholos's signal.

First, there came the Boracs and their trucks, saurs, and dactyls. Their cargoes packed for a long journey, their gods visible to Kholos, hovering over and within the carvans. The entire race and all of their ideas made their way into the flames.

Behind the Boracs came a silver squadron, winged like Kholos. They made lazy circles over another race below: web-footed, slow in this dry and flat country, the Slythe were leaving as well. Antonia, the Witch General, and her ghosts, the dozen that had survived the attack on I.M., would escort them to their new home.

Kholos rose. He was holding this moment open, making it possible. In his arms he cradled his rifle, the chamber empty. With the mountains at his back Kholos glowed like a second sun.

Dr. Nathaniel Voss came next. Solitary, a satchel of notes and sextants and shale samples slung over his shoulder. Unlike the Slythe and the Ghosts, or the Boracs, Dr. Voss looked up at the brilliance that was Kholos, shading his eyes with his hand, and waved.

Then the parade grew more random. Some black engineers. A platoon of Stalinistas looking confused and lonely, their uniforms all tattered. A score or so of sculptors, painters, welders, and other artists walked across the plain towards the flames.

All of them made their way into the immolation of Anvir.

At last, Kholos prepared to enter himself. Then he paused. A little gray cat was sitting next to him.

"Well," said Busto, one ear missing, one eye, a scratch across his face, and limping. "Are you going to carry me or do I have to actually drag myself out of my own existence here?"

Kholos smiled, and scooped up the cat.

And flew down from the ridge, out of time.

If you enjoyed this book, please remember to post a review on the website of your preference. The author, and the publisher, thank you.

About the Author

Christopher A. Miller lives in Princeton, New Jersey, with his wife, Katy, and his son, Trent. He works in the design and construction industry as a technical writer, and spent several years as a Young Adult Librarian in urban public libraries. Chris also writes poetry and short fiction and has published poems in journals across the United States and online. An avid speculative fiction reader, *Agents of Paradise* is his first novel in the genre.

Other books from Phase 5 Publishing

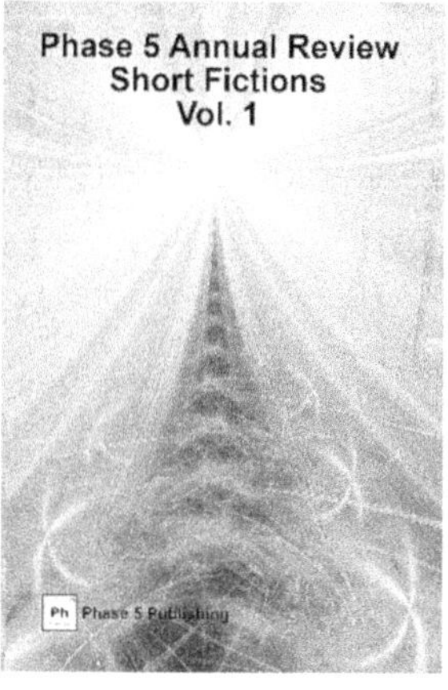

www.phase5publishing.com